Cut and Run

Cut and Run

Matt Hilton

W F HOWES LTD

This large print edition published in 2010 by
W F Howes Ltd
Unit 4, Rearsby Business Park, Gaddesby Lane,
Rearsby, Leicester LE7 4YH

1 3 5 7 9 10 8 6 4 2

First published in the United Kingdom in 2010
by Hodder & Stoughton

A CIP catalogue record for this book is available
from the British Library

ISBN 978-1-40743-534-3

Typeset by Palimpsest Book Production Limited,
Falkirk, Stirlingshire
Printed and bound in Great Britain
by MPG Books Ltd, Bodmin, Cornwall

FSC
Mixed Sources
Product group from well-managed
forests, controlled sources and
recycled wood or fiber
SA-COC-1565
www.fsc.org
© 1996 Forest Stewardship Council

This one is for my mother, Valerie

Death is not the greatest of evils; it is worse to want to die, and not be able to.

Sophocles

. . . The same is true of violence. Our violence in word and deed is but a feeble echo of the surging violence of thought in us.

Mohandas Gandhi

CHAPTER 1

His first waking thought was that his sins had caught up with him.

It was a moment of epiphany he'd never have come to without this shocking wake-up call.

Linden Case had always denied that there was anything wrong in the way he treated the whores. He paid them well, even gave them a bonus if they fully pleased him. By the nature of their trade they invited him to do to them whatever he desired. But he fully grasped his reason for being here in this basement of a building in a less than salubrious district of Tampa, Florida.

Earlier he'd been driving his Mercedes along 7th Avenue in the historic Ybor district. Although the area was famous as a tourist destination where people came to photograph the colourful buildings, it also had a darker underbelly that appealed to him. Street girls often hung out there, waiting for men like Case to offer them a ride. He was stopped by a red light – ironically under the circumstances – and checked out a woman standing on the sidewalk while waiting for the light to go green. She was Seminole: dusky-skinned with jet-black hair. On green, he decided he'd carry on. He was only interested in blondes. As he'd waited for a stocky woman to clear the crossing, his passenger door opened and a man slipped in beside him. Case was used to women being as bold, but never men.

'Hey, buddy, I'm not your type, OK?'

'You're exactly my type, Case.'

'I don't know you. How do you know my name?'

The man shoved a handgun into Case's ribs.

'Shut your mouth and drive.'

Case wasn't familiar with handguns. This one was big and black, and it was enough to know that it would kill him. He drove.

The man refused to answer Case's questions. He spoke only to direct him. They left the Ybor district, heading south over Causeway Boulevard. Case noticed a huge depot with trains parked on sidings, but he was unfamiliar with this area of the city; then the man directed him off the highway into a run-down area that was made up of derelict buildings. At a warehouse made from preformed concrete sheets, the man made Case get out the Mercedes. Case had again tried to get the man to answer his questions, but all that earned him was a smack round the head with the butt of the gun.

When Case came round he was inside the derelict warehouse. His hands and feet had been strapped to a chair using electricians' tape. Case strained against his bindings but he wasn't strong enough to break them.

2

'You're wasting your time.'

Case sat rigid in his chair. The voice had come from in front of him but he couldn't see the man who'd spoken. It was too dark for that.

'Who are you?'

'The name's Joe Hunter.'

'You're a cop?'

'No. I'm a concerned member of the public.'

'Why are you doing this to me?'

'You're a bad man. I'm here to punish you.'

The only light was a faint strip beneath a door at the far end of the room. Against the light Case saw movement as a figure moved through it.

'What do you mean? I'm not a bad man!'

'I've been watching you, Case. I've followed you. I know what you did to the women.'

'I *paid them*,' Case shouted. 'They knew what I wanted from them.'

'You hurt them.' The man's voice had dropped an octave, but the menace in his words had grown exponentially. 'Do you think cash was fair exchange for what you did to them?'

'Yes. I offered money and they agreed. Every time: it was a done deal!' Case strained at his bindings. It was pointless. The tape stretched, biting into his flesh. He heard footsteps as the man moved towards him. Case readied himself for a blow, but it didn't come. The man walked behind the chair and laid his hands on Case's shoulders.

'I want you to look at something.'

3

Before Case could reply, the man dragged him and the chair round so he was facing in the opposite direction. Case could see nothing but blackness.

The man moved away, and there was a click as he threw a switch.

A single bulb had been covered with a strip of muslin. The cloth obscured most of the light, but enough remained to see what was directly below it.

The woman strapped to the chair was barely out of her teens. She was just the kind of woman that Case usually preferred. She had blond hair and was slim. She used to be pretty. Now her eyes were swollen shut, bruises growing on both her cheeks. Her nose had been broken, split across the bridge and leaking blood. Her lips were mashed and blood-flecked drool hung in a string from her chin.

'Is this a done deal, Case?'

Case shuddered at the impotence of his situation.

The man stood alongside the woman. She moaned, but didn't have the strength to move. All she managed was a glance up at Case that spoke of shame. The look condemned Case more than the man's actions ever could.

The man balled his fist. 'Is it right that a man beats a woman?'

'Leave her alone.'

The man turned and faced Case.

4

'So it's OK for you to hurt them, but not for anyone else? Is that what you're saying, Case?' The man took out a fifty-dollar bill and laid it on the woman's thighs. Then he backhanded her across her face. Not hard, but enough so that her head was rocked on her shoulders. 'Does paying her make things right?'

'Goddamnit!' Case again fought against his bindings. He was shuddering so hard he was almost vibrating. 'Leave her alone, you bastard.'

The man took a knife from his belt. In the subdued light from the muslin-wrapped bulb, the blade looked tarnished. 'You have used your hands on women before, Case. Have you ever used one of these?'

'Nooooo . . .'

The man placed the blade against the woman's throat.

'Please,' Case cried. 'Not her. Please don't hurt my daughter.'

The man snorted. 'You didn't stop to think about the women you hurt. Why should I care?'

Then he slashed the blade across the woman's throat. Even in the dimness of the basement, Case saw the gout of blood pour down her chest. He screamed.

'The women that you hurt were other men's daughters,' the man said. 'An eye for an eye, Case.'

Case had stopped screaming now. Through his tears he watched the final seconds of his daughter's life ebb away.

The man moved towards him.

'Does what I did to your darling Jessica make me a bad man?'

'You bastard. You sick murderous bastard.'

'Yes. That answers the question.' The man lifted the blade.

'But it damns you as well, Case.'

CHAPTER 2

Don't look back or you might find the devil hot on your heels.

It's an idea I like to subscribe to. An analogy fit for one with a past full of terrible events.

The problem is, by being optimistic and only looking ahead, it can mean that you miss the devil gaining ground. Before you know it, he's right there and has rammed his toasting fork straight through your spine and is dangling you over the flames of hell.

I've made too many enemies not to cast the occasional glance over my shoulder. The practice has served me well and to date has kept me alive.

I parked my Audi A6 at an entrance to the grounds of Tampa University and got out the car while I opened up my phone and went through the motions of taking a call. Looking northwest, Kennedy Boulevard spanned the river and beside it on the eastern shore stood the cylindrical Rivergate Tower that's affectionately known to locals as the beer can. It reminded me of the leaning tower of Pisa, after Superman's evil alter ego pushed it back in line in that cheesy movie. My eyes merely skimmed over the tower – it was a familiar sight to me – and I watched the traffic approaching over the river bridge.

I was looking for a nondescript light grey sedan. It had been following me all the way across from Cypress Point Park, where I'd gone for my morning run. It was only a couple of months since Kate Piers died and I still missed her like crazy. I'd intended clearing my head with a burst of physical effort, the only thing that could shift the troubling thought that Kate died because I'd failed to keep her safe, but that wasn't to be. When I'd arrived at the park the sedan was waiting for me, and had tucked itself in behind me all the way here. Only my unscheduled stop had forced it to continue on by.

Down on the Hillsborough River, birds dove at shoals of fish and I could hear their raucous calls even over the swish of passing traffic. There was a tang of citrus and exhaust fumes on the air, and the sun was hot and still. Sunbeams bounced off the windows of the beer can, sending razors of light back at me. All these things were distractions and, like the memories of Kate Piers, I blocked them out.

The sedan returned within a minute. I leaned against my Audi, and had a full-on argument with my unheeding phone. As the car swept past I allowed my gaze to skim over it. I had all of a second to identify those within the car, but I'd trained myself to snap-shoot a scene and replay it through my mind at my leisure. The car continued on by and already its driver was looking for somewhere to stop.

I got back in my car and set off over the bridge, heading into downtown Tampa. Behind me, those in the sedan would be frantically searching for somewhere to turn. I could easily have given them the slip at that point, but I wanted to know who these people were. More than that, I wanted to know what they wanted. I drove slowly, giving them an opportunity to catch up.

Four blocks on and I saw the grey sedan in my mirror. I turned right on to Florida Avenue, then continued straight ahead until I was stopped by a red light at Whiting Street. The sedan was three cars back behind a Jeep and a Ford and I saw the passenger lean out of the window to get a better look at me. This action was amateurish or it was contrived.

While I waited for the light to change, I ran the snapshot image I'd shelved through my mind. The driver was a man in his late thirties, muscular build, short dark hair, broken nose. His front-seat passenger was a shade older, stocky build, but his hair was a tad longer and flecked with grey. Despite the heat, they wore sports jackets over formal shirts, ties knotted at their throats.

Going on green, I followed the road under the Crosstown Expressway as though I was going to head out on to Harbor Island, but at the Garrison

Channel I took a left and headed for St Pete Times Forum, a hockey stadium I'd been to a couple of times with my friend Rink. The sedan followed me on to Ice Palace Drive towards the arena with the benefit of only one car between us. I flicked on my indicators to show I was pulling over into a lay-by adjacent to the public park opposite the stadium.

There was no game today, so the parking lot across the way was almost deserted and nobody was wandering through the park next to the water. It was a good place to get myself killed if the men in the sedan were better than they looked. But I didn't think they were. When weighing up the seclusion against my own needs, it was just the spot I needed to get to the bottom of things.

The grey sedan drove past. As it did, I played at being interested in the park. From under my shirt I pulled out my SIG Sauer P226 and racked the slide. Normally I'm good to go with one in the chamber, but it wasn't a great idea to be driving round with the gun ready to discharge, particularly when my modified gun comes with no safety.

Waiting for the road to clear of traffic, I watched the sedan draw to a halt twenty feet in front of me. As soon as it did, I walked quickly up to the driver's window and slammed it with the butt of my gun. Even as glass sprayed over the driver's legs, I pressed my gun against the man's neck.

'Show me your hands.'

Both men threw their empty hands in the air, stunned by the manner of my arrival.

'OK. Both of you get out of the car now.'

They clambered out. I kept my gun close to the driver and made the other walk round towards me. He did so without lowering his hands. There was a car passing the front of the ice stadium but it was going the other way. I glanced at the nearby Marriott Hotel, but we were unobserved. I waved them in the direction of the park with a jerk of the gun barrel. Then I concealed my gun beneath my shirtfront: just in case.

They went without argument, as if perhaps they were expecting this from me. I quickly glanced about, searching for any other car I might have missed. There was nothing evident.

Winding gravel paths snaked their way round the park. We followed one until we were at the water. I made them get down on the grass, while I stood over them.

'Sit on your hands. Anyone makes a move without my say-so and he gets shot. Are we clear?' The men sat on their hands, looking back at me as though nonplussed by the situation. I had expected fear, anger and argument. It made me reappraise them. They weren't the amateurs I'd surmised: this was definitely planned. 'So what's the deal?'

The older man gave me a weary smile while the other just sat there. I nodded at the older one.

'We're not your enemies, Hunter,' he said.

'I'll decide that after you tell me why you were following me.'

'We're under orders to follow you.'

'You weren't doing a very good job.'

'We weren't hiding.' He smiled at me again. 'In fact, back there at the lights, I leaned out the car so you could see me.'

We could have gone on like that all day. It was a beautiful day, none of it to be wasted.

'Let's get to the point.'

'I'm Castle, my friend's called Soames. We're cops,' he said, as if that should explain everything. 'Homicide.'

I gave him a slow blink. Maybe that revelation was supposed to make me put my gun away. I'm not the type to be intimidated by the presence of cops, though.

'I already guessed that.'

'So why the gun and the games?'

'Not all cops have my best interests at heart.'

'Not now.' Soames looked at me with hard eyes, challenging me. I could see how he'd probably earned the broken nose.

Taking his words as a result of my treatment of them, I ignored him and asked Castle, 'What do you want from me?'

'If you'd let me get off my ass, that'd be a start.'

'Not yet.'

'Can I show you my badge so you know we're real cops?'

Studying their clothing, I said, 'That's already a given. Keep your hands where they are.'

'We don't want trouble with you, Hunter.'

'What *do* you want?'

'We need you to come in with us and answer a few questions.'

It wouldn't be the first time I'd been invited to the local precinct house on Franklin, but the manner this time was a first.

'So why didn't you just approach me instead of following me like this?'

Castle raised his eyebrows at the barrel of my SIG. 'It was either us, nice and easy like this, or it would've been a SWAT team. Knowing the way Joe Hunter is rumoured to work, our guess was there'd be less blood spilled this way.'

A worm of unease clawed its way through my guts. SWAT team?

'You're saying that I'm under arrest?'

'Prefer it if you came in under your own steam,' Castle said.

'But if you'd rather I Mirandise you and do everything by the book, that's OK by me, too.'

I put my SIG away. I'm licensed to carry, but that didn't allow me to hold police officers under threat. 'What am I supposed to have done?'

'Assaulted officers and damaged county property for a start,' Soames muttered. The man didn't like me, but he was here under orders to keep his opinions to himself. Castle seemed much easier with the situation but even he shot Soames a frown of disapproval.

'We just need to clear up a couple of things,' he said. 'You satisfy us, we'll kick you loose again in an hour.'

I'd done many things in the year I'd been living here and wondered which one of them had come back to haunt me. Nothing obvious came to mind: each and every one of them had been extremely violent – but, in my opinion, justified.

'Is there a parking ticket I've forgotten about?' I moved back, allowing the men to get up. Castle grunted as he helped himself stand with one hand propped on a thigh. Soames swarmed up and he wasn't impressed at my joke.

'You're a fucking piece of work, Hunter.'

It looked for the briefest of moments that Soames would go for his piece, but Castle grabbed at his elbow. 'I'm sure it's all a big misunderstanding. One we can clear up with Hunter's help.'

There was nothing I'd been involved in during the last couple of weeks that would attract the eye of the local police department, so I was sure that he was right.

'I'll follow you in.'

'Give me your gun,' Soames said.

Shaking my head slowly, I said, 'I'll check it in at the station.'

Soames wavered and I gave him a steady look. Castle cleared his throat, touched his partner on the elbow again. The older detective turned and walked away, but Soames felt he had something to prove.

'You might have fooled Castle, but I know *exactly* what you are.'

I didn't reply. If what he was suggesting was

true, then it would have been the Special Response Team – Florida's version of SWAT – who'd come for me, not two detectives on a peacekeeping mission.

Grunting a curse, Soames moved quickly after his partner.

And I thought that was that. I'd go along to the station and answer a few questions, put things straight and be back on the street again in an hour. It was too lovely a day to be cooped up for long. Maybe there'd still be time to have the jog round the park at Cypress Point that I'd originally planned.

I should have known better.

A volley of bullets took out both cops' brains and they crumpled to the ground.

CHAPTER 3

It went without saying that Soames and Castle were dead. Both men had lost a good portion of their skulls and there were twin fans of blood and brain matter spread across the gravel footpath next to them. My gun was up, but anyone studying the scene would notice immediately that the direction of my gun barrel and the spray of blood were at contradictory angles. Not that something so obvious would make a jot of difference. I wasn't going to stand there like a statue and wait for the police investigators to arrive at the scene.

I had to move.

Not to escape justice: I could prove that it wasn't my gun that had fired the killing shots. I had to move because whoever was out there could be adjusting their aim to put a round through my head.

As I raced off the path I was calculating the trajectory of the shots. The Marriott was a high-point to my left, but the blood from the headshots had splashed towards the hotel. We had been hidden by shrubbery and trees from anyone on the road where we'd left our cars. The shots hadn't come from a boat on Garrison Channel behind me. There was only one place left where the shooter could have been stationed.

Placing a tree bole between me and the gunman, I glanced up at the nearby ice stadium roof. St Pete Times Forum was a huge oblong building, with glass-fronted galleries on the two sides that I could see. The roof was a shallow arch, and could be negotiated by a nimble person, but it didn't appear to have a walkway or any visible service ducts where a shooter could be positioned. At each corner of the building, forming support bulwarks for the galleries, were squat square towers with flat roofs bordered by low walls. My gaze fell directly on the one nearest to me.

From the corner of this tower came a flash and almost instantaneously a chunk of the tree I was hiding behind was blasted into splinters. The crack of a high-velocity round came to my ears in the next instant. The precise moment I'd seen the flash I'd moved, and the bullet that struck bark from the tree missed me, but I wasn't sure that I'd avoid a second round. The shooter was armed with a sniper rifle, and from this distance it could put a bullet directly through a tree trunk as flimsy as this one.

Dodging to my left, I immediately reversed direction and went right, throwing myself through bushes towards the slope leading down to the channel. I heard two reports of the rifle, but thankfully no rounds ripped through my body. I

17

scrambled over the embankment, went down on my belly and placed the swell in the ground between us. He couldn't see me now, but I couldn't see him either.

My mind was racing with what had just happened. The police suspected my involvement in a crime I was innocent of, but now that the officers sent to bring me in were dead, no one would believe that. The man with the sniper rifle had seen to that. It also explained why he hadn't shot to kill. He hadn't missed me by accident but by design. I was being set up.

Someone must have heard the shots – in fact I could hear alarmed voices calling out from the nearby hotel – and the police would be coming any minute. The sensible thing to do would be to wait for the responding emergency vehicles, put down my gun and throw myself on the mercy of the justice system. But I was under no illusions; there was no way I was going to hang around, not when all they'd see was a cop killer. I'd be face down in the dirt, my hands cuffed and surrounded by armed men itching to blow me away long before I could argue my innocence.

There was only one way out of this that I could see.

I had to take down the shooter.

The shoreline was made up of stones and gravel, but gave way within a few yards to tufts of grass. If I stood up, or even crouched, I'd be an easy target. The trees and shrubbery in the park didn't offer much cover from the shooter with his high vantage either, so all I could do was belly-crawl along the shore, my knees and elbows propelling me along. I considered crawling into the channel and swimming, but decided against it. I needed my weapon dry.

Fifty yards on, I quickly raised my eyes over the embankment and saw that the shooter would have to lean out from the tower to get me now that I'd compromised his position. I didn't think he'd do that. I quickly raced up the embankment and into a small copse of trees. Crouching there, I pulled out my gun.

If I used it now, tests would show that the gun had been fired, I'd have gunshot residue on my skin and clothing: it would mean more questions if the police took me down, it would compound my guilt as a cop-killer. But I wasn't going to go against a man with a sniper rifle with only my bare hands.

Distantly I heard the first wail of sirens. The police were on their way. My window of opportunity had just been slammed in my face.

Got to move, I told myself. I have to take down this man or I'll never get the chance again.

Running as quickly as possible, I charged across the park towards the road that separated me from the stadium. When no bullets came my way I realised that the shooter had probably abandoned his position and was making his getaway. Apparently I wasn't the only one who could hear the approaching sirens.

My car and that of the dead detectives were way off on my left, but apart from them there were no other vehicles on the road. The ice stadium was a huge edifice looming over me. I was in the open, but no bullets were fired at me. Whoever was trying to set me up had many options for escape. If the stadium had been filled with Tampa Bay Lightning fans the shooter could simply melt amongst the crowds, but this was a day when the hockey team weren't playing. At most, the only people around would be a skeleton crew of staff. But that meant that the gunman could slip out unnoticed by any number of exits from the public areas or via service doors round the back.

I looked for a getaway vehicle.

There was nothing unusual among the few cars I'd noted in the car park – and anyway, it was too exposed to be the parking location of choice for a fleeing murderer. More likely the killer had left his getaway car round the back among the staff's vehicles. I started to angle that way, hoping to cut him off. I'd only got a few paces when I heard the roar of an engine. Reversing direction, I sprinted back towards the front of the building. I couldn't see anything moving on the road that ran parallel with the stadium, and there was nothing in the public car park. Coming to a standstill I listened, trying to pinpoint the noise. Beyond the stadium's official parking lot was a second open space, which I guessed was used for overspill parking on busy match days. There was still nothing moving. But then I saw a dark blue Ford erupt like a cork from a bottle from a ramp in the second lot. The ramp must have exited from a vehicle park underground, or maybe it was from a loading dock where deliveries were made to the stadium. It didn't really matter, not when the car was over a hundred yards distant and speeding away from me.

Futile as it seemed, I ran after it. It would have been a waste of ammunition to fire, so I concentrated on getting as good a look as possible at the car and its driver. The Ford sped off the lot, took a left on the service road, then a right on to Jefferson Street. Then it was gone.

Immediately I ran back the way I'd come, heading for my Audi. Converging sirens were very loud now and I had to get out of there as quickly as possible. As I ran I recited over and over again the Ford's registration number like it was a mantra. And I lodged in my mind the one glance I'd got at the shooter's face. There was something uncannily familiar about that glimpse, but I couldn't put my finger on it.

Hurling myself into my car, I started it, jammed it into gear and peeled away from the small parking bay. I headed for the ice stadium and swung into the service road towards Jefferson Street. In my mirrors I saw the flashing gumball lights of squad cars screeching to a halt where my car had just been. Then one of the cop cars revved wildly and came after me.

There was still the option of pulling over and explaining to the cops what had really happened. Anyone could see that Castle and Soames had been shot from a distance by a high-velocity rifle and that I was armed only with a nine mm handgun that hadn't been fired. But they'd only assume that I had an accomplice who'd taken the shots; I must have led the officers to this trap otherwise how would the shooter know where we were? I'd probably spend days in a cell awaiting arraignment for murder while the real killer went about his business unhindered. It didn't escape me that he was setting me up to take the fall for all his crimes and I wondered what the hell he was planning next.

Giving up wasn't an option. The way I saw it, the only way I was going to prove my innocence was to throw the gunman at their feet. Preferably alive so that he could confess, but in the present circumstances it was more likely he'd be dead. The killer was planning – or had already executed – something big. And it was down to me to stop him.

CHAPTER 4

Tampa Police Department HQ was situated at the junction of Franklin and Madison, little more than two minutes away. Luckily for me all the responding squad cars must have been out cruising round downtown when the call had gone in about the shooting in the Channelside district. The sirens sounded as though they were all responding via Franklin, the way I'd come in. I had a free run all the way up Jefferson and under the Crosstown Expressway before anyone was astute enough to set up roadblocks. Didn't mean I was free, it just gave me a wider area to move in before the cordon tightened round me.

The pursuing squad car was growing larger in my mirrors and the cop on board would be coordinating other units to block me somewhere ahead. I shot through intersection after intersection, then past the impressive George E. Edgecomb Courthouse, and another squad car idling at the corner of Zack Street while it waited for the lights to change. As I zipped by, I saw the blue lights come on and it pulled out in pursuit, falling in behind the other cruiser.

There was a major junction ahead, and I went through it laying my hand hard on the horn. Only fortune saw me through the junction safely, but all round me I saw vehicles screeching to a halt, some fishtailing in the road. The cop car behind me slammed into the back end of a pick-up truck, spinning out both vehicles.

I hoped everyone was OK: I didn't want anyone to get hurt, but neither could I go back and offer assistance. I pressed the throttle harder and kept going, taking Orange Avenue north, knowing that Interstate-4 was somewhere ahead. If I could get beyond it my options for escape would become much greater.

The cop car that had been near the courthouse took up the chase and it cut down my lead every second. Until now I hadn't been pushing the Audi for fear a pedestrian might step out in front of me, but now there was nothing for it: I tromped the gas pedal.

There was no way I could get into a duel with the pursuing cop car so I relied instead on speed, pushing the Audi under the interstate, and taking a quick left on to surface streets of a residential neighbourhood I didn't know. The cop car was still behind me, but a series of turns left him confused at the direction I'd taken. Conscious now that there could be kids playing in the streets, I slowed down to a more sensible speed and

24

continued to traverse the neighbourhoods, heading north-west through Riverside Heights and out towards the suburbs of the city.

I had a place on the Gulf Coast up near Mexico Beach but I couldn't go there. That would be the first place the cops would think to look. My best friend and the man I *officially* worked for, Jared Rington, had an office in the downtown district and a condominium in a wooded area outside Temple Terrace. Rink would help hide me, but I couldn't go to either of his registered properties because they would be points two and three on the cops' radar. At this moment it was dangerous even to make contact with Rink by the usual avenues; his phones would be checked for any calls from me and they'd try and press him for my whereabouts. Rink wouldn't tell them, and they might charge him with harbouring a felon. Something like that wouldn't help his private investigations business.

We had other ways of making contact, set up for dealing with situations just like this one.

Priority was to ditch the Audi: an APB would have gone out and police cruisers from the outlying districts would now be searching for it. Under bogus details, I'd rented a covered garage a couple miles north of here. I drove there watching for a tail, and pulled in unobserved. From a hidden safe in the floor, I took out spare ammo, fake documents and a change of clothing; exchanging my shirt and trousers for the more anonymous baseball cap, hooded sweatshirt and jeans. Finished, I pulled down the shutters and snapped a lock in place, heading out in a Taurus I'd previously parked in the garage, searching for a public telephone booth.

Back in the day, Rink and I worked for a joint task force that pulled from various UN Special Forces teams. We utilised a network of safe numbers to communicate between team members and our controllers. I used one of those numbers now to send a coded message to my friend's pager and I only had to wait a few minutes before Rink got back to me. In the meantime, our call would be shunted between satellites halfway round the world: untraceable.

'Tell me that you weren't involved, Joe.'

'Whatever you're being told; it wasn't me.'

'I knew that,' Rink said. He had wanted to hear it from my lips.

'The police have already been at the office asking about me?'

'I gave them a bum steer, but they're not idiots. They'll be back soon enough.'

'Did they give a reason why they were looking for me?'

'They wouldn't say, but I've heard word on the streets. It seems someone has fingered you for a murder in Ybor a couple days ago.' Rink held his breath for a moment. 'Someone took a punk hostage, beat the living shit outa him to teach him a lesson.'

26

'Can see how they drew the conclusion,' I admitted.

'Didn't end there, though, Joe. Whoever this guy was, he killed the guy's daughter right in front of his eyes.'

A sliver of ice wormed its way through my guts. 'And the cops think that was *me*?'

'They don't know you the way I do.' Rink was apologising for having raised the question earlier. 'Apparently the punk survived long enough to describe his attacker. He even told the cops his attacker's name.'

'My name?'

'Yup. The police don't know that you'd never harm the woman. They'll be coming for you.'

It was confirmation that the shooter had set me up, but he'd made a glaring mistake. He should have killed the man and left the woman as a witness. That would have been much more difficult to deny. Since leaving the military I've earned a name as a vigilante. I've gone up against some bad people, stopped them from hurting the innocent: but I don't make war on women.

'There are some cops who admire what you've done – not that they'd ever publicly admit it – but they ain't gonna let you go when they think you've murdered an innocent.'

Some cops. Like Castle.

But there wouldn't be a cop from Tampa PD – or from anywhere else in the country – who would be sympathetic towards me now.

I told Rink what had just happened down by Garrison Channel.

'Goddamnit! Why didn't you just put down your gun? We could've cleared this up in no time.'

'Couldn't do it, Rink. I'm being set up for something. For a start, the shooter would've known his plan was finished with. Probably he'd have just shot me dead.'

Rink cursed and ranted for a while, but he knew that I was right.

'The only way I'm going to put this right is to find him, Rink.' Giving him the registration number of the Ford, I asked him to check it out. 'It's most likely a stolen vehicle, but it's a start.'

'I'll get on to it. Y'know, I had a bad feelin' that somethin' was going down.'

'How's that?'

'Got a call from an old friend of yours, said he wanted to speak to you.'

'Who?'

'You remember Bryce Lang?'

How could I forget?

Somehow I had the feeling that things were only going to get much worse.

CHAPTER 5

'Alisha! What's keeping you?'

Rickard's wife of two years peered out from the walk-in closet with just the right amount of fear in her eyes. 'I'm making myself nice for you, Luke,' she said, teasing a blond lock behind an ear, 'just like you asked.'

'What's the problem?'

'I . . . I can't find anything to wear.'

'Step out here.'

'But I'm not ready yet.'

'I won't ask again, Alisha.'

Alisha came out of the closet with one arm crooked over her chest.

'Take your hand away,' Rickard told her. 'I didn't spend thousands of dollars for you to hide yourself from me.'

Alisha allowed her arm to slip away. Unsure of what to do with her hands she toyed with the small bow on the hip of her low-slung Agent Provocateur briefs.

'There now.' Rickard smiled up at her from the divan, his eyes lingering on her silicone-augmented breasts. 'Pretty as a picture, Alisha.'

His wife smiled at him, but it was as false as the moulded smile of a mannequin. Her eyelids fluttered with restrained fear, because she knew what was coming. Rickard patted the bed sheet beside his naked body.

'Come here.' He held out a hand.

'I thought we were going out, Luke.'

'We'll go when I say. I had a busy day today and want to relax first.'

Alisha sat on the bed, her bare back to him. Rickard stroked a finger down her spine and he felt her shudder under his touch. Her anticipation could be heard in the quickening of her breath. Rickard's breath also grew faster.

'Please, Luke . . .'

'It's OK, Alisha.' He slipped an arm round her body and cupped one of her breasts. 'We can go out afterwards.'

He pulled her down quickly, rolling on top of her, holding her down on the bed beneath his body. Snagging a hand in her briefs, he tore the flimsy material aside. He looked at the tears on her cheeks and he shuddered with an anticipation of his own. Her terror was the greatest aphrodisiac he had ever known.

'What are you afraid of?' he asked as he pushed into her.

'Nuh . . . nuh . . . nothing . . .'

Rickard knew she was lying. But that was OK: it was what he wanted. The lie only made the truth all the sweeter.

Rickard had the ability to put fear into the hearts of women. It wasn't his looks, because his wavy hair, his deep-set blue eyes, and the athletic build of his body, had often proven the opposite effect. It was only when he got close to them that they realised they were in the presence of great danger. Usually at that point they'd come up with an excuse to hurry away from him, casting nervous glances in case he chose to follow.

But Alisha couldn't run away. She was his wife.

Ordinarily a man like him would forego marriage. But he'd desired something more than any whore or mistress could ever give him. He wanted someone who would be solely his. He'd found Alisha, charmed her, promised her a lifestyle she couldn't resist. He had married her in order to exercise the very power of *ownership* over her. That way he could do to her whatever he pleased.

Alisha was right to fear him. He was responsible for the deaths of three women. Not a large number when compared to some more notorious murderers, but enough to be getting on with. It was nothing to the number of men he'd killed, so really it was the wrong sex who seemed as though they could sense his essence. He'd often wondered if he exuded some kind of putrid auric light that only women could see. Many hours he'd spent in front of mirrors, studying his reflection, looking for what they saw. He'd never seen it yet. But he didn't doubt it was there.

'Look at me, Alisha.'

Alisha fought to blink the tears off her lashes.

'Do you see it yet?'

'No, Luke.' Alisha cringed under him, knowing what was coming. 'I don't see it.'

Rickard knew there was something in him that set him apart from other men. A need, a compulsion, a thirst for blood: whatever this driving force was he could feel it coiling inside his gut like a serpent, and it had been with him since he was a small child. He could feel it worming its way through his body, seeking outlet at every turn.

'I don't believe you. You must see it.' He slapped her across the face. 'See me, Alisha!'

Alisha cried out. So did Rickard.

Then he rolled away from her.

'Get cleaned up. And put on some nice clothes. We're going out and we're going to celebrate a job well done.'

'Yes, Luke.' She got up painfully, then shuffled towards the en-suite bathroom where she closed the door behind her. Rickard lay down on his back and listened to the sobs she tried to conceal with the sound of running water.

Rickard smiled at his reflection in the mirror on the ceiling. He was happy with himself.

People argued about the psychology of men who felt the need to hurt others. How had their urge to destroy come about? Nature or nurture? *What if it was neither?* Rickard had often asked himself. What if it was both? His nature was to kill, but he'd nurtured his skills to a point where he could do so with impunity.

But he was no raging serial killer.

Any fool could kill.

His mobile phone vibrated on the cabinet next to the bed.

He smiled. Not many fools could make a living from killing and as a measure of his success, Rickard was a very wealthy man.

'Rickard,' he said into the phone.

'That was good work today,' said the voice at the other end.

'Thanks. I enjoyed it.'

'The figure we agreed is in your account.'

'Yes.' Rickard had already checked.

'OK, so Hunter can't go to the police now. We've got him on the run and I want to keep the impetus going. Are you ready for the next part of the plan?'

'When?'

'How soon can you be ready?'

Rickard cupped his hand over the phone. He called out to the closed bathroom door, 'Alisha, honey, take your time in there. Change of plans, I'm afraid. I have to go out alone tonight.'

CHAPTER 6

After yesterday, having a gun pressed to my head wasn't the best way to start my day, but it did a lot more to wake me up than the two Vente Americanos I'd already downed from the corner Starbucks. By the feel of the snub-nosed revolver touching a point just above my left ear, the man wasn't joking. I took my hands from the steering wheel of my Taurus to show I wasn't armed.

'You don't need the gun,' I told him. 'Don't forget . . . you called for this meeting.'

'I haven't stayed alive this long by taking un- necessary risks. Just do as I ask and everything will be fine.'

Slipping out of the car, I appraised the gunman. He was unremarkable: brown hair, brown eyes, medium height and medium build. He was the type of person who could blend into any crowd, your typical CIA agent. It was seven years since I'd laid eyes on Bryce Lang, but the years had been kind to him. Apart from a couple of extra lines round his eyes, he looked much the way he had when last we'd worked together.

'Am I missing something here, Bryce? I thought

we were on the same side.' I looked at him steadily and saw his eyelids droop ever so slightly.

'That's the problem, Hunter. I'm not sure whose side you're on any more.' He waved me towards a nondescript brown sedan car. 'You drive.'

'Where to?'

'I'll tell you when we're moving.'

Bryce kept the gun on me until I was seated in his car. Periodically he glanced round searching for hidden observers, but this neck of Tampa was practically deserted at this time of morning. Only the occasional harried employee ducking into the nearby Starbucks for a caffeine injection on their walk to work was in evidence. Their eyes were too sleep-muddled to make sense of the man with a gun in their midst. Happy that we'd gone un-noticed, Bryce clambered into the passenger seat. He held the gun across his thighs, the muzzle aimed at my side.

From his jacket pocket he pulled out a small contraption that he held concealed in his palm. He waved the electronic device in my direction and I heard a faint buzz in response.

'You have a mobile phone?'

'You know I do. You called me on it.' It was prepaid and unregistered, no way of linking it to me.

'Turn it off. Do it slowly. No sudden movements.'

Reaching into my shirt pocket I used two fingers to slip my Nokia out and flip it open. I depressed the red button and put the phone back in my pocket.

Bryce again swept me with the device and he seemed happy that I wasn't wired or carrying any kind of bugs or location devices on me. As he did, he relaxed his grip on the gun. If I wanted to I could have taken him out then. A quick slash of my stiffened hand into his windpipe and that would have been that. But I didn't. Like I'd told him earlier, I thought we were on the same side. Plus, the trouble I'd found myself in and the timeliness of Bryce's sudden appearance was no coincidence.

'What's going on, Bryce?'

He grimaced, but then nodded us forward. 'Drive.'

So I drove.

We headed out on Kennedy Boulevard, sitting silently. Bryce angled the wing mirror so that he could keep an eye on the road behind us. He ordered me to take a left on to a surface street, cutting through a housing scheme that appeared to be more trees than houses. Nice neighbourhood. He watched for anyone following, but the road behind us was clear. He indicated me through a couple of turns and we came out on to another boulevard, this time Henderson. I took a sharp right and we headed back towards Kennedy on the Dale Mabry Highway. At Kennedy once more, he indicated that I continue driving west out of town. I glanced across at him. His eyes were on the mirror.

'There's no one following.' I was pretty sure of

that considering I'd been checking for cops all morning. 'I came alone, like I said I would.'

'It's not anyone with you that's troubling me, Hunter.' But that was all he'd say. He again fell silent, watching behind us for a tail that I was certain wasn't there. We reached a turnpike and he gestured me through it and north on to Veterans Expressway. We were almost at Greater Northdale before Bryce finally put the gun away.

'Where am I going, Bryce?'

'Knowing Joe Hunter, you'll have a safe house somewhere. Take us there.'

'Tell me what's going on.'

'Only when I'm sure that it's safe.'

He didn't speak again until we were on US 98, heading north-west for the Gulf Coast. When he did so, it seemed like there was a touch of regret behind his words.

'I always trusted you, Hunter. You were always a good man.'

'So why the gun, Bryce? Why all the precautions?'

'It's the nature of the job, Hunter. You know that.'

'I'm not in the job any more.' I looked across at him again. 'Last I heard, neither are you. You retired, I was told.'

'People like us never retire.'

I couldn't argue with that.

I was no special agent like Bryce Lang, I was just one of the grunts sent in when the agents had done their work. Assassin isn't a term I favour, but I suppose that all depends on which end of the gun you're looking down. When you've killed for a living, it's something that you can't leave behind – however hard you try. I've tried to hide from my past, but it was a pointless exercise because the violence always seemed to find me. I'm not seen as an assassin now; these days people call me a vigilante.

I don't care for that term either.

However my ethos is simple: there's no room in this world for people prepared to make the lives of others miserable. As a soldier my enemies were sadistic, brutal and immoral people and I had no qualms about putting them down. Stripped bare, all they were was bullies and the only way I know to stop a bully is to stand up to them. If that makes me a vigilante then so be it.

'Someone from your past has come back to haunt you,' I offered.

'Someone from *our* past, Hunter.'

I looked across at him and we locked gazes. 'Colombia?'

Had to be Colombia. It was the only time we'd worked together.

Now I was the one checking my mirrors for a tail.

CHAPTER 7

Bogota, Colombia, had two faces. One was made up of modern high-rise towers, as affluent a district as boasted by any other major city in the civilised world. The second was that area that sprawled on the western edge of the city, where people lived in squalor to rival the worst ghettos anywhere. There people existed. No other term was applicable to their lives. There was no money, little food, poor sanitation and homes made from wood and sheet metal and anything else that could be scavenged. It was a city that summed up for me the very reason for battling against the corrupt people of the earth. I couldn't stand by and watch children starve to death, knowing that little more than a few miles away evil people were growing fat on their misery. The thought sullied my conscience.

I was there along with another three members of my team, plus Bryce Lang, our CIA link, and an agent from Colombia's Narcotics Task Force called Victor Montoya who was our local Departmento Administrativo de Seguridad contact. We were in the Barrio La Candelaria district of the city, surrounded by old world buildings painted in vibrant colours. This was the area that the city was originally founded upon and it retained much of its historic charm. Over the rooftops, I could make out the ornate twin spires of the cathedral in the nearby Plaza de Boliva. Beyond the spires the Andes were swathed in menacing clouds the same gunmetal blue as the SIG Sauer P226 I held in my hand.

I was in an anonymous-looking government car along with Bryce and Jack Schilling, one of the guys from my team. Montoya and my other two colleagues, Pete Hillman and Robert Muir, were set up a little distance away down the road, keeping obs on the side entrance to the house we were all watching. We had a view of the front façade of the historic house. I believed that our target would exit by the front, and it was my and Jack's responsibility to take him out. In the other car was our support team who would only engage the enemy if we were cornered, or if we failed. Six of us to take out one man. It might sound like overkill, but I hoped it would be enough.

Jesus Henao Abadia was a key player in the Colombian drug cartels. The US Treasury, Justice and State Departments had applied economic sanctions against the drug cartels under Executive Order 12978 in an effort at curtailing what they termed Specially Designated Narcotics Traffickers. Abadia was an SDNT, but he was more than that. He was a butcher. He was suspected of having personally executed rivals and government officials by way of hacking them to steaming chunks with a machete.

Not that I feared we weren't up to killing one man with a big knife. It was the protection team which travelled with Abadia that gave me cause for concern. Abadia went nowhere alone. Not even here, to the home of his long-time mistress, Jimena Antonia Grajales.

Victor's intel said that Abadia was there with the woman and only two of his protectors who would be on the ground floor of the two-storey house. Abadia was due to return to his fortress-like home near to Prado in the Colombian department – like a county or state – of Tolima this morning. This would be our best opportunity for taking out the butcher without facing down a veritable private army of retainers.

I felt uncomfortable about taking out Abadia where there was the potential for innocents to be caught in the cross-fire. It was bad enough that Jimena was here, let alone the occasional civilian who wandered along the street past the house. But I had my orders and that was that. Collateral damage was apparently acceptable if it meant stemming the flood of cocaine to the western world.

We were wearing covert earpieces, and over the scrambled channel I heard Victor announce that Abadia's white Lincoln town car had been spotted heading our way. Victor had other DAS agents – the

Colombian equivalent of secret police – in the field, watching all points of ingress.

'Two in the vehicle: driver and escort,' Victor announced in an accent redolent of his heritage. 'They should be with you in thirty seconds.'

Six to five, the odds were growing in Abadia's favour. If Jimena was a player, that meant the odds were one-on-one, but I didn't consider that too long. I didn't make war on women.

'OK, we're rolling,' Bryce said into the mike taped to his throat.

From behind our left shoulders came the white town car. We hunched down in our seats, Jack Schilling reaching for the Heckler and Koch MP5A3 sub-machine gun located under his seat. It was a variant of the usual MP5, with collapsible stock and chambered for nine mm rounds. It was favoured for close quarter battle and hostage rescue scenarios because the nine mm ammo was less likely to go through walls and hit the hostages. It also fitted nicely beneath the seat of a car and could be brought quickly into play where the longer MP5 would require more manoeuvrability. Armed with my sidearm, I'd be the man designated to hit Abadia, while it was Jack's responsibility to lay down enough rounds to keep his protectors' heads down. Bryce brought out his service pistol, a Beretta, and jacked a round into the chamber. His gun was to be used for defence only, as in effect he was our getaway driver and was no good to us if he was engaged in the fire fight.

The Lincoln rolled up outside Jimena's house on fat tyres. The house door cracked open and two men stepped outside. Neither of them was Abadia. They were tall, slim men, dark-haired, dark-skinned. They had predatory eyes as they swept the street for any sign of danger. I saw that they weren't taking any chances; they were already armed with 7.62 mm Israeli-made Galil automatic rifles.

The passenger eased out of the Lincoln and reached to open the back door. As he did so, I got out of our car and began walking slowly towards them. If I'd come in the black jumpsuit and Kevlar vest associated with my line of work, they'd have mown me down instantly. But I was dressed like anyone else in this teeming city, my skin and hair darkened with dye and my give-away blue-green eyes turned chocolate under contact lenses. I walked hunched over, feigning a slight limp. Abadia's protectors were aware of me, but they weren't concerned. One of them nodded and there in front of me stood Abadia. His two rifle-wielding guards took up position either side of him as he strode down the steps from Jimena's house towards the waiting car.

I was no more than ten yards from his position. One of the guards, the one holding open the car door, lifted the flat of his palm to me. Wait there, he commanded me in Spanish. I stopped, nodding like one used to taking orders. My finger was on the trigger of my SIG and I was a second from lifting the gun from out of my jacket pocket and placing a round in Abadia's head.

But then it happened: the uncontrollable force that has destroyed many well-laid plans throughout the ages. Normal life butted in to place a wall between me and my ability to carry out my duty.

Jimena followed Abadia to the car, demanding a final kiss. But that wasn't all. The tousle-haired boy hanging on to her waist stopped me faster than any amount of bullets that Abadia's men could have fired at me. He was maybe twelve years old, but he was much smaller and slighter of build than English boys of the same age. Something that struck me immediately: he was definitely his mother's child. But more than that, he had the same hawkish nose and deep-set eyes of his father. This boy was without a doubt the offspring of the man I'd come to kill.

My reaction to the boy must have been noticeable, much as I tried not to let it show. I saw Abadia's gaze snap my way, and his dark eyes bored directly into mine.

'Take the shot, goddamnit!' I heard Bryce whisper in my earpiece.

I couldn't. Not when the boy was there. I don't make war on women. I certainly don't against children. I could still have got Abadia clean, but that wasn't the problem. His men would lift their guns to avenge him and then the bullets would be indiscriminate.

'Abort, abort,' I whispered back, averting my gaze and hoping that the man hadn't recognised the murder in my eyes.

'Take the shot, Hunter,' Bryce snapped. 'We won't get this opportunity again.'

'Can't do it. Not with the woman and child here!'

Abadia was watching me like he'd been struck by a gorgon's stare. His face was like stone, and the only life I could detect was in the trembling of his eyelids.

In my time as a soldier, I'd often been in a position where something nebulous, some sort of super intuition or a sixth sense, was all that it took to warn me of danger. Whatever it was, it had saved my life on more than one occasion. But it seemed that I wasn't the only one who had this ability.

Abadia let out a wordless cry, and he turned to Jimena and the child, shooing them back towards the house even as his anxiety transferred to his men and they began to bring up their rifles.

In a split second everything went to shit.

I had no recourse now but to shoot or die.

The man nearest me lifted his Galil, and I swept out my SIG at the same moment. My single round took him in the throat and he went over backwards. His dying act was to pull the trigger of his rifle and bullets zipped over my head, knocking roof tiles from a nearby building.

Then everything was happening round me

like I was caught in some kind of slow-motion nightmare.

I lunged towards Abadia, even as the second Galil bore round on me, and the henchman from the Lincoln grabbed at a weapon inside his jacket. The man with the rifle was the immediate threat and I dropped low in a stress fire isosceles stance as I sent two rounds into his central body mass. Ribbons of blood flew from the man's back as he was thrown down on his side. The Galil slid harmlessly beneath the town car. Abadia had caught the boy in his arms. I couldn't shoot him now. Anyway, the man from the car was now aiming his handgun at me. I saw the gunman squint as he targeted me, and knew that his bullet would follow a fraction of a second behind the action. I dipped my body to the left, saw his gun waver as it tried to follow, then I snapped back to the upright, leaving his aim trailing and I placed a round in his forehead.

The driver was clambering out of the car. He was a danger, but my most pressing thought was where Abadia was now – or more correctly to see if I had an opportunity to drop him without placing the boy or his mother in danger.

I caught a snapshot glimpse of the situation and saw that it was hopeless. Abadia had the boy held tight to his chest with one arm, while his other hand was drawing a revolver from a snap-lock holster on his hip.

The son of a bitch. He wasn't cradling the boy

out of love. He'd recognised my reticence to shoot where the child was involved and he was now using his own son as a shield. Jimena had also come to that conclusion, and she was clawing at him to get the boy away. Her actions bought me a couple of seconds to deal with the man coming out of the car.

The driver had drawn his weapon – an H&K I immediately identified from its shape – and was bringing it over the roof of the car to shoot me. He snarled something in Spanish that I didn't catch. I was already dropping low, like an old-time gunslinger, shooting from the hip so that my bullets passed through the open car door on my side and out the open one on his. I hit him in the gut. He was sorely wounded, but not yet dead. He fired, and I'd no option but to throw myself to the ground. Now I fired under the car, blasting one of his ankles from under him. As he collapsed screaming, I again fired under the chassis and this time my bullet silenced him.

Four men dead in less than fifteen seconds, but none of them the man I'd come for.

I rolled over on to my back, bringing up my SIG.

The snapshot had changed from before.

Seeing me distracted, Abadia had released his grip on the boy, and Jimena had now taken charge of him. Abadia was taking a running step towards me, his revolver aiming at me.

So this is how I die, I thought, looking into Abadia's contorted features.

47

But then I saw Abadia shudder, and blood spattered from a wound in his chest. Another bullet tore a chunk out of his right shoulder and the revolver went spinning from his hand.

Jack Schilling, his MP5A3 rattling out death, continued to race nearer to me laying down covering fire. Behind him, I saw Bryce revving our car towards us.

I quickly came to one knee. Abadia was on the pavement not ten feet from me, face down, unmoving. Standard operating procedure dictated that I put a round in the back of his skull. But I was more concerned with the other bodies lying sprawled on the steps to the house.

They were unmoving too. Clutched in Jimena's death grip was a gun.

The operation to stem the flow of cocaine from Abadia's cartel was deemed successful – despite the unfortunate collateral damage incurred – and we all went on to further missions. All but one of us. I didn't hold Jack Schilling responsible for killing the woman. I couldn't; not when he was trying to save me. But the fact that he'd killed the boy sent an ice-cold wedge into my heart that just wouldn't thaw. We were never the same after that. Shame burned in the two of us. Jack retired from our unit before I did and I heard that he swallowed a bullet from his own gun a short time later. Maybe the killing of the boy had driven a wedge into his heart too.

CHAPTER 8

My home is on the beach overlooking the Gulf of Mexico, but we couldn't go there. The cops would have it under constant surveillance. So instead we went to another house I use, a few miles to the south. No one but Rink, Harvey Lucas, who is a friend out in Arkansas, and Walter Hayes Conrad, my old CIA controller, knew about this place. I parked Bryce's brown sedan on a turning circle above the beach. Below us was tall grass that gave way to golden sand. Beyond the beach the sea was sparkling under the early morning sun like someone had taken a handful of diamonds and scattered them across the undulating water. The view was beautiful, but I couldn't appreciate it. I was thinking ugly thoughts.

I was thinking about the boy lying dead in his mother's arms all those years ago. It was an image that occasionally came back to haunt me when sleep evaded me. Most times I'd get up and throw on some shorts and run along the beach under the scowling eye of the moon until the effort and

49

streaming perspiration shoved the image aside. Now the boy – whose name remained a mystery to me – was back, and this time there was no opportunity for a night-time run.

Bryce had become a catalyst for my nightmare. When Rink first mentioned Bryce's name yesterday, the first thing I'd thought about was that boy. The second image had been one that I hadn't witnessed, but one I could easily conjure: I saw Jack Schilling propped in a chair in some stinking apartment with his brains decorating the wall behind him. Now I actually had Bryce standing beside me and it looked like the nightmare wouldn't recede any time soon.

'We'll talk inside,' Bryce said.

'Maybe we should.' I set off for the house with Bryce following. He was alert, scanning the area for anything untoward. I didn't let it show, but all my senses were on overdrive, except nothing in the natural flow of the day warned me of hidden danger.

At the door I checked for signs that someone had been there while I was out. The faint dusting of sand I'd scattered on the doorstep was unmarked. There were no glistening marks on the locks to show anyone had finessed their way inside. Someone could have entered by the back door, but I doubted that. Everything was still and silent and felt at peace. Bryce still looked like he was expecting to die at any second.

At least Bryce had seen enough sense to put the

gun away. It was pleasing; I was growing a little tired at being threatened by someone I had deemed a friend.

We walked inside and I paused to get a feel for the house. It was as I'd left it. No eddies of air shifted to warn of stealthy movement nearby. There was no detectable odour of a nervous man waiting in concealment. I nodded Bryce inside. Bryce moved past me and if I wanted to I could have killed him easily. His fieldcraft had grown rusty, either that or the fear he was under had displaced the rules from his mind. Following him, I saw that his shoulders were rounded, as though he was already a defeated man.

I'd spent last night here, sleeping on a futon in one corner of the living room. The only other furniture was a deckchair. Bryce sat down in it uninvited.

'Tell me everything, Bryce.'

He chewed his bottom lip. He was forced to lean back in the chair to look up at me. 'First I want to apologise for holding a gun on you.'

'That'd be a start. But forget it. I knew you wouldn't use it.'

'I'm surprised you let me get close enough to pull a gun on you.'

'I was there as a friend,' I reminded him.

Bryce indicated his breast pocket. 'Not a gun this time.'

I nodded at him to go ahead and he withdrew an envelope and held it out to me. From his pinched expression, it held something nasty. The envelope disgorged a short stack of photographs.

The first photo showed a woman and a teenage boy lying dead in the street. They looked like they'd been gunned down as they were walking out the front door of their home. The second showed a woman lying in woodland. She was dead, too. Her eyes were rolled up in their sockets as though she was trying to focus on the single bullet hole in her forehead.

Sighing at the cruel nature of the world, I pushed these two photographs back in the envelope. I didn't know any of the faces.

Photograph three was different, though.

The dark-haired man had been hacked with a heavy blade. What made things worse was the fact that he was bound in a chair and had no hope of avoiding the blows. His dead face was twisted in agony. But I still recognised it: the DAS agent, Victor.

'Montoya,' Bryce confirmed. He lifted a finger and tapped the photograph. 'Also found dead in the same room were his wife and six-year-old daughter.'

Feeling my gut twist, I looked to the next photograph. Pete Hillman had been killed in an alley. There were at least five bullet wounds in his torso.

The final photograph was of Robert Muir. Muir was dead as well, and his decapitated head had been placed on a table next to his corpse. He too had been bound in a chair.

It was obvious why Bryce was feeling paranoid. We were the only two surviving members of the team sent to take out Jesus Henao Abadia.

Pulling out the first two photographs again, I said, 'These people?'

Bryce pointed at the dead woman in the woods. 'That's Robert Muir's wife. The woman and boy . . . they're Pete Hillman's wife and son. And, as you know, Victor Montoya's family were found alongside him.'

Not only were the members of the hit team being targeted, but the families of those men.

'Who's behind this, Bryce?'

'According to some people . . . you.'

That didn't deserve a response.

'It doesn't help when Linden Case was tortured in a similar manner.' Bryce, his eyes downcast, flicked a hand towards the photos in my hand. 'Just like the rest, his family was targeted as well. Case said it was you . . .'

'Someone told him my name. It doesn't make me responsible.'

'He described someone that fits your description.'

'Bryce, by the definition of our job, we're supposed to be the everyman. It wouldn't be hard to find someone my size and build, cut their hair like mine, put contact lenses in. Why'd he even kill Case? He wasn't a member of our team.'

'Case was a decoy, I suppose. To set you up as the murderer. While the cops are hunting for you it allows the real killer to carry on with his plan.'

'To kill us?'

Bryce shuddered. 'We're the only ones left.'

'That brings us back to my first question. Who's behind this?'

Bryce chewed his bottom lip. 'My best guess? Could only be Abadia.'

'Abadia's dead. You were there, Bryce. Schilling riddled him with rounds from a machine gun.'

'You know the protocol, Hunter.'

I should have made sure. I should have put a bullet in Abadia's skull as operating procedure dictated.

'He couldn't have survived,' I said. 'Not possible.'

I looked at the stack of photographs fanned in my hand. Anything's possible, I corrected myself.

It looked like Abadia was back from the dead.

CHAPTER 9

February in Maine. It sounded like the title of a song; like something that Bing Crosby or maybe Nat King Cole would have crooned over. Those old masters would have made the place sound beautiful and romantic, but Imogen Ballard didn't see things like that. It was just too damn cold and wet to get maudlin over.

Everything was grey. The trees, the sky, even the blacktop that her feet skated over. Maybe taking a run to clear her head wasn't her greatest idea. A roaring fire and scalding hot coffee would have been better. But it was too late for that now: she was two miles out from home, jogging along the coast road, overlooking the equally grey sea.

The rain was a fine mist that clung to everything. It had soaked her clothing within minutes of setting off, and now sat in heavy beads on her shoulders and on the wool cap pulled down over her short hair. Her effort kept her warm inside her clothes, but she was uncomfortable. Maybe the run wasn't so bad an idea after all: concentrating on her miserable state kept her mind off her sister. Or it did until that errant thought.

Imogen pushed harder at the road surface, exhorting herself to greater effort. The cold air bit at the back of her throat. She began to sprint, challenging the incline ahead to shake Kate loose. But she was right there, all the way up the hill, watching her – figuratively speaking – all the way to the top.

She regretted involving Kate in her problems. It was her stupidity that had killed Kate.

All her decisions had been made too rashly, she saw that now – especially her decision to move out here to Ass-end, Maine. At the time, she'd thought it was the best thing for her, being close to her parents and siblings who were buried in the family plot. She'd come here because it was the only place she felt safe. And to heal.

She'd lived through a terrible ordeal. Her lover, William Devaney, had been murdered, and so had Kate. She had heard of something called survivor guilt syndrome, and wondered if that was what she was really hiding from. Her little sister had died protecting her. Joe Hunter and a couple of his friends had gone up against some seriously dangerous men to protect her, too. Imogen had done nothing but get them all in a fix. Guilt was a burden that she had to carry, and it was extremely heavy ploughing upwards to the top of this hill.

At the crest, Imogen came to a halt. She fisted both hands on her hips, and then bent at the waist to suck in lungfuls of air. A stitch felt like a hot brand creasing her left side. Now *this* was penance, she decided.

Back in the here and now, Imogen turned to look down the hill she'd just conquered. The blacktop was a glistening ribbon, some of the greyness refracted by the equally glistening trees standing like sentries at the roadside. The run uphill had looked ugly, but now she saw the beauty that beckoned her back down the hill. Her house stood on a promontory overlooking the Atlantic. It was hidden by the trees and the folds of the land, but it was a beacon. She set off jogging again, down the decline, feeling the tug of gravity at the centre of her chest. It was as if she was being reeled in on an invisible line. She felt light and easy now.

A truck came over the hill behind her. She heard its grumbling engine and the whistle of thick tyres on the slick road surface. Without pausing in her run, she moved to the side of the road, kicking up wings of water in the puddles that gathered there. She glanced back, ensuring that the driver had seen her in the poor conditions. The truck swept past her, and cold droplets splattered off her face. She blinked against the sting and her lips pulled into a grimace.

The truck was a blocky white shape. FedEx, she saw, delivering packages. Maybe the driver was headed for points south: Lincolnville or Camden, perhaps.

The brake lights flared and the truck drew to a slow halt.

Imogen wasn't concerned. FedEx trucks were a regular feature here. Maybe this was a driver unfamiliar with the area who'd decided to stop and ask for directions.

She continued to jog towards the back of the truck. She heard the clunk of the driver's door being opened and saw a tall, muscular man in a FedEx uniform hop down from the cab. He was holding a clipboard in his hand. Yeah, she decided, he was lost.

'Hi,' the man said. 'I'm sorry to interrupt your run, ma'am.' Imogen slowed down, and then jogged in place. Her trainers made squishing sounds on the asphalt.

'I'm looking for . . .' he inspected the clipboard as though for confirmation. 'Yes, I'm looking for a Miss Imogen Ballard.'

Imogen made a living by designing websites, but she sidelined in wildlife photography for magazine publishers. It wasn't unknown to receive packages of proofs from the publishers. Her eyebrows went up, even as a hand went to her chest.

'You've found her.'

'Wow,' said the man. 'That was very fortuitous.'

Too fortuitous to be real, Imogen was slow to realise. Who used words like *fortuitous* these days? She squinted at the man, and his lips pulled into a sneer. Something about the coldness of his eyes warned her that his accidental luck was her misfortune.

From under the clipboard he pulled out a gun.

It had a long broad barrel that glistened under the same refracted light that made the road seem ethereal. There was nothing beautiful about it.

'Oh!' Imogen said. It was all her mind could come up with while it was feverishly computing the information her senses fed it. She was thinking: Joe Hunter had killed all of my enemies, so what's this about? She should have been thinking how to get out of this alive. Then there was no more time for thinking, or for anything.

The man lifted the gun and shot her once in the chest.

CHAPTER 10

There is a belief among soldiers that a highly tuned warrior exists in a state of readiness that transcends the norm. On high alert, all the senses thrum and, combined, they supersede anything that any of the individual senses can assimilate. This super-sense is what warns the soldier of ambush, of a silent assassin's approach, of impending death. Such is the belief that studies have been conducted and scientists have designated this state Rapid Intuitive Experience. Fancifully it has been deemed some kind of ESP. I've experienced RIE on too many occasions to dismiss it out of hand, but I don't consider myself psychic or even any more intuitive than anyone else. Never had I given credibility to anything like premonitions or crisis apparitions.

Until now, that was.

Not only was I in danger, but so were members of my family. My brother John was hidden deep in a witness protection programme, out of harm's way, but my parents and my ex-wife, Diane, were over in England, not necessarily out of reach of those trying to hurt me. Despite us divorcing, in my own way I still loved Diane, and to think of anything like that happening to her was enough to make me feel sick. I had to get a warning to her, set up some protection for her and my parents, but there was a more pressing matter.

Lately I'd shared a couple of telephone calls with Imogen Ballard, the sister of a woman I'd been intimate with. Kate Piers had died when I failed to keep her safe, but her sister didn't blame me. We'd talked, sharing our grief, and I'd even been up to Maine on a weekend visit. I had the feeling that Imogen wanted more from me, but I still missed Kate too much for that. We were only friends, but that wouldn't mean a thing. Whoever was setting me up could have gained the wrong impression and perhaps set out to hurt Imogen, the way they'd done to the families of the other members of our team.

I had a flash image of Imogen's face. She was lying on her back in some desolate place, glassy-eyed, mouth open . . . dead.

The photographs that Bryce showed me had a lot to do with that picture, but I had to squeeze my eyes tight to clear it from my mind.

Pulling out my phone, I switched the power on and stabbed out Imogen's number.

'Who are you calling?' Bryce sat up in the chair as if he was going to snatch the phone from my hand.

'Shut up, will you?' I snapped, and listened for the ringtone. Bryce watched me intently.

The phone rang and rang, and I expected it to go to a messaging service. But then there was a metallic ping as someone picked up the handset. I heard breathing.

My first thought was that the police had made the connection between us and that I was being listened to by a roomful of detectives or FBI agents. They'd try to trace my call, and in my hurry to warn Imogen I hadn't taken any precautions. But, somehow I knew that wasn't the case. If the police were there, they'd have given Imogen instructions to act natural and to engage me in conversation. Listening to each other breathe into the mouthpiece was not natural.

'Imogen?'

There was a grunt: too masculine a sound to have come from Imogen. Fleetingly I wondered if she had found herself a new friend since last we'd spoken, but that thought was a non-starter.

'Where's Imogen?'

The man holding the phone wasn't ready to answer me yet. The chance of me phoning like this might possibly have shaken him. Or maybe he'd been sitting by the telephone waiting exactly for that.

'If you've harmed her—'

The man cut me off curtly, 'It's enough that you fear that I might.'

'I'm going to kill you.'

'No, *Joe Hunter*. I will kill you, but first I will kill all that you hold dear.'

'Imogen means nothing to me.'

'I'm expected to believe that? If that was true, why would she be the first person you thought to call?'

'Don't hurt her.' I wasn't begging. It was one thing that I was being targeted – in some respects I could expect some people to hate me enough to want to hurt me – but now that that had spilled over to include innocent people, it added new urgency to my need to stop this man.

'I don't fear you, Hunter. Your threats mean nothing to me.'

'So face me. Leave Imogen alone and meet me.'

'You would like that, wouldn't you?'

'Yes.'

'It wouldn't change a thing. I would kill you.'

'You're so sure, let's do it then.'

'I could have killed you yesterday. I could have killed you a dozen times while I've followed you unobserved. I could have killed you when I shot those two idiotic policemen.'

'But instead you ran away. Like a coward.'

'No. I allowed you to live so that I could make you *suffer*. We will meet, Hunter, but only when you're begging to be released from your torment.'

'Whoever is behind this, I will kill him too.'

The man didn't respond to that, which meant I'd hit a raw nerve.

'Tell him that *this time* I won't hesitate to put a bullet through his skull.'

'Hunter,' the man said, 'you think you know what this is all about? You know nothing.'

He hung up.

Bryce stirred from where he was sitting. He approached me slowly. He had grown pale. It probably had as much to do with the look on my face as what he already feared. 'Was it him?'

Him? He was talking about Jesus Henao Abadia. A dead man.

Yes, it was a dead man. If I had my way I'd make certain of that. But it wasn't Abadia. This man's voice was North American.

Bryce's face couldn't have grown any paler if I'd put a slug through his heart. His eyes watered and I could see him shuddering.

'Get a grip, Bryce,' I told him. 'You're no good to anyone in this state.'

Harsh words perhaps, but they were aimed as much at me as they were at him. I'd failed to keep Kate safe, and now it looked like I'd failed her sister as well.

The man had expected me to call Imogen, and had waited for my call. His intention was to throw me off-kilter, make me fear what would happen next. Instead, he'd got me thinking.

Putting away my phone, I stared at Bryce. He hadn't stumbled on this case all by himself. He was retired from the Agency. Someone had fed him the details of the murders, someone had supplied him the photographs. Whoever had done so, they were not the same as the people threatening us. They wouldn't have given him fair warning, they would have simply taken him and he would have been strapped in a chair and tortured like all the rest.

'You know more than you're saying, Bryce. I want it all.'

'I was going to tell you everything, Hunter. I just wanted to be sure that we were on the same side first.'

'God damn you, Bryce. If you'd told me everything when you first contacted me, I could have stopped *this* from happening.'

'I'm sorry.'

'Yes, Bryce. So am I. But at least you know now whose fucking side I'm on.'

Stalking away from him, I went through into the kitchen to pull out a strongbox I'd concealed behind a panel in one of the kitchen cupboards. Inside I found spare magazines of nine mm ammunition, also a Ka-Bar knife. Out of necessity I didn't want to have to replace my weapons every time I jumped on an airplane, so I had fake documents that showed I was licensed to carry concealed weapons. My docs would pass the scrutiny of Homeland Security if it ever came to that. There was a wad of cash and a number of credit cards. Killing men is cheap, but never an inexpensive vocation.

Secreting my kit round my body I went back into the living room and found Bryce leaning against a wall cradling his head between his hands.

'I never believed you were responsible, Hunter. I was worried about contacting you for another reason: I was afraid that I'd lead the bastards to you, but it looks like you were already under surveillance.'

'Looks that way, doesn't it?' The man on the phone had already implied as much. He'd found Imogen so he could use her as leverage against me. But someone must have pointed him my way first.

Since leaving the Special Forces I've been working under the radar. Only select people – namely my close circle of friends – know where to find me: Rink, Harvey Lucas, Imogen Ballard and Walter Hayes Conrad.

That took me to only one person. Rink and Harvey would die before they gave me up; Imogen was out of the equation. So that left Walter.

Walter and Bryce had connections, too.

When I was with the unit, I worked under a team of commanders based at Arrowsake in the UK, but I had a specific handler in each respective country. My stateside handler was Walter Hayes Conrad IV. Walter was also Bryce Lang's CIA boss. Ultimately it was Walter who'd organised the hit on Abadia.

'Walter gave you the tip-off,' I said.

Bryce nodded.

Walter was first and foremost a CIA Sub-Division Controller, a director of black ops, but he was also my friend and mentor. Why the hell hadn't he warned me?

I took out my phone again.

'You're wasting your time,' Bryce said. 'I've been unable to contact him.'

And he was right. I couldn't raise Walter by any of the normal routes.

Whoever was behind this, they were tied to what had happened in Bogota and they'd gained information pertaining to the hit on Abadia. That would mean that they knew about everyone involved, all the way up to Walter Conrad. The fact that Walter was now incapable of answering my call could mean that they'd got to him too. Or, following his tip-off, he'd gone deliberately incommunicado until the issue was resolved one way or another. Without Walter sanctioning my actions, it would mean I was once again acting outside the law, but I didn't care. These people had chosen to declare war on me: so be it.

I hung up and said to Bryce, 'We're out of here.'

'Where are we going?'

'Maine. Where else?'

'Jesus, Hunter. How did things come to this?'

I don't remember Bryce as being so indecisive. This time I noticed he was plucking at his clothing and shifting from one foot to the other.

'It's just the way it is. Now, if you want to live to see an end to this, we have to get moving.'

Bryce ran a hand over his face. Then he surreptitiously wiped his palm on the leg of his trousers, leaving a dark smear. He was frightened. So was I, to be honest, but I wasn't going to give in to the fear. I was going to use it, the way I always did.

CHAPTER 11

'See me.'

An opportunity to test his theory should never be wasted, Luke Rickard thought.

'See me,' he said again.

Following his telephone conversation with Joe Hunter, he'd sat on the foot of the bed staring into the vanity mirror. Phasing his vision in and out proved ineffective as he peered into the reflective surface, trying to delve beyond his blurred image to what lay beneath. He could feel the serpent coiling in his innards, but he caught no sign of the slithering thing. Only women had the ability to look upon his true essence.

He finally stood up and looked down on the woman lying on the bed. The drug he'd shot into her had ensured that she remained unconscious while he'd bundled her into the FedEx truck and brought her back to her house. Slumped in his arms, he'd carried her here to her bedroom and laid her out on top of the comforter. That was more than two hours ago; by now the drug should have worn off.

'See me, Imogen,' he said.

The day was overcast, precipitation threatening again, so the room was in shadow. Imogen's face was a pale oval beneath her cap of dark hair, her chin tilted on her left shoulder. He could hear her breathing, slow and long exhalations. To all intents and purposes she looked like she was sleeping, but he knew otherwise. Her eyelids were too taut, as though she was holding them closed, and there was no movement beneath them as there would be if she was lost in dreamland.

He leaned in close to her, blowing on her ear. Imogen didn't stir as a sleeping person would have.

'I know you are awake. Open your eyes and look at me.'

Imogen didn't respond, except for the faintest flutter of her lashes.

'I said *open your eyes*.'

Rickard grasped Imogen's chin in one hand, pinching hard. White blotches surrounded his fingertips but still Imogen didn't respond. Rickard grunted out a laugh.

Releasing her jaw, he trailed his hand down her chest and stomach. She was still in the sweats that she'd worn for her run; damp from the rain. He dipped his hand under the hem of her top and ran his fingers over the warmth of her abdomen. He felt her shudder involuntarily, but to her credit she still feigned unconsciousness. He finger-crawled higher, touching the swell of one breast. She was wearing a plain sports bra, unlike the lace and ribbons and bows that he preferred, but her breasts felt full and firm the way he liked them. Not as full and firm as Alisha's, but in her defence this woman was fifteen years older and silicone-free. He pawed her, then took a breast in his hand and squeezed. He'd have liked to have felt her respond but there was no hardening of the nub beneath his palm.

Maybe the bitch was still under the influence of the tranquilliser.

He slipped his hand from beneath her top, worming his fingers into the waistband of her trousers.

Fucking cotton panties.

He cupped the mound of her pubis. Pushed with his fingers, trying to insert a finger under the elastic.

Imogen came awake like an alley cat.

Shrieking and clawing, she tore at his hand, tore at his face.

Rickard reared away from her, his laughter ringing loud.

'I knew you were awake,' he said.

Imogen tried to bolt from the bed. Rickard grabbed her by an ankle, and she went down chest first on the floor. She kicked and squirmed, and he dragged her back on to the bed, threw her down, her face pushing into the pillows to smother her screams.

Rickard rolled her over, avoiding her nails as they raked at his eyes. He slapped her arms away, then lashed her across the face with his palm. Then he climbed on top of her, bracing his knees either side of her ribs, holding a wrist in each of his hands and forcing them above her head.

'Are you like this when you're with Hunter?'

'Get off me. Get off! Get off!'

'I can see why he likes you, Imogen. Quite the spirited little thing, aren't you?'

Imogen screamed again, words lost in her terror.

Rickard smiled, liking her response. 'I even made myself look like him for you. Though, I must say, I'm more handsome. Don't you agree?'

She screamed again.

Rickard leaned in very close. Imogen thrashed and their foreheads bumped. He forced his head against hers so that she was pressed down against the mattress. They were eye to eye.

'Do you look into his eyes when you're together?' Rickard asked. 'Do you search his soul?'

Imogen screwed her eyes tight.

'Open your eyes, Imogen. Open them, or I'll cut off your eyelids so you have no option but look at me.

Imogen cried.

'Now!'

Her lids flickered open. He was so close he could see her pupils dilate.

'Do you see it?'

She mewled like a cat.

'You do? You see it? Tell me what you see.'

'You're a *monster!*' Imogen howled.

'Yes . . .' Finally, Rickard thought, proof that he was right all along. 'Tell me more, Imogen. Describe *it* to me.'

'Get away from me, you bastard.'

'Tell me what you see.'

Moaning loudly Imogen tried to fight free. Rickard forced himself against her, bearing down with all his weight. It was no contest. He forced her wrists together, grasping both in one of his hands. His other fingers he twined in her hair, twisting it tight.

'Tell me, you goddamn bitch.'

'Touch me and you will die!'

'No one can help you,' Rickard said. 'I can do to you anything I wish.'

'Joe Hunter will kill you. He'll come for you and you'll die.'

'I didn't go to all this trouble for nothing. I want him to come. But he'll be too late to help you.' Imogen struggled again, Rickard laughing at her ineffectiveness. 'I'll kill him as easily as I'll kill you.'

Imogen screamed.

Surf crashed below the house on its clifftop promontory and gulls wheeled in the iron-grey sky. Her scream was lost amid the tumult of nature beyond the walls.

He let go of her hair, sliding his knees out behind him and forcing a leg between hers. 'Joe Hunter will suffer before he dies, Imogen. He will know that I've had his woman, and the shame will make him burn.'

He ripped her trousers from her, tore at her panties while she fought hard against him. She yanked loose her wrists and pulled at his hair, but he was beyond caring. He pulled down his trousers and he was harder than any time he could ever remember with Alisha.

But his ardour only lasted as long as it took to realise that the pounding on the door meant big trouble.

'God damn it.'

Pulling away from Imogen, he held out a hand, halting her from following. He pulled up his trousers, quickly reached to a dresser where he'd placed his gun.

'Say a word and I'll shoot you in the face.'

He moved across the bedroom to the window, standing alongside the drapes to peer outside. His angle meant he couldn't see who was at the front door, but he could see the two police cruisers parked on the hard stand next to the house. An overweight cop was standing at the open door of his vehicle, one hand on his radio and one on the butt of his holstered gun. The cop glanced his way, but Rickard pulled back.

Joe Hunter, you sneaky son of a . . .

A fist banged firmly on the front door.

'Mrs Ballard. State police. Open up, please.'

Imogen struggled into her clothes, throwing her feet over the edge of the bed. Rickard raced across to her, catching her elbow and jamming his gun under her chin. 'Do not make a sound.'

But Imogen was defiant. She struggled away from the gun, yelling at the top of her voice.

Rickard backhanded her across the jaw, knocking her against a wall so that a photograph of a surly-looking man in Desert Storm fatigues was twisted askew. Rickard glanced at the face and thought that the man was scowling at him.

'Fuck you, too,' he snapped.

He grabbed Imogen by the nape of her neck, pushing her towards the door and out on to a landing that overlooked the entrance hall. A shadow moved beyond the glass pane in the front door.

The state trooper shouted an announcement again, trying the door handle. The door swung open and the uniformed man followed inside. His service revolver was out, but it was aimed along the vestibule.

'Look out,' Imogen yelled.

The trooper's eyes went wide, his head coming up, but the gun was a fraction slower.

Rickard fired and blood blossomed on the trooper's shirt.

The trooper went down on his backside, then spun on the floor, gripping at his gut. Screaming in agony.

Instantly, Rickard forced Imogen down the stairs. There was another cop outside, the fat one. Have to get by him, Rickard knew, before reinforcements can arrive. The last thing he wanted was to be stuck inside the house with a cordon of armed cops all round. He'd been in worse predicaments, but he could do without the inconvenience.

The gut-shot cop wasn't a concern. He wasn't going to die immediately, but that was a good thing. His screams of agony would help confuse and dismay his buddy outside and would ultimately slow down any pursuit as any further troopers responding to the scene would see their fallen comrade as their first priority.

Rickard snatched the cop's revolver off the floor and jammed it into his belt. Then, looping an arm round Imogen's throat, he moved into the doorway.

The second trooper had retreated to the far side of his cruiser and was leaning over the bonnet, his gun trained on them.

'Police,' he yelled. 'Put down the gun.'

Rickard ignored the challenge and pushed Imogen forwards, down the steps and across the yard. The cop could shoot, but he'd hit Imogen first.

'Drop your weapon!' The cop's words were a loud screech.

Crash through their defences, cut them down. Rickard came on, forcing the trooper to stand up and back away.

Staring into the man's eyes, Rickard saw that he was jammed firmly between running for his life and doing his duty. While he was stuck there, he wasn't doing either. Rickard shot him in his huge belly. Twice for good measure.

The cop went down, and his screams matched those of his fallen companion. Imogen joined in, and now it was the surf and the seagulls that had to take a back seat.

Dispassionately, Rickard pulled Imogen away from the sorely wounded man and marched her across to where he'd left the FedEx truck. It was good for carrying an unconscious woman, but too distinctive to avoid detection for long.

'Give me your keys.'

Imogen's Suburban was parked next to the house.

When she wasn't forthcoming, Rickard smacked the butt of his gun on the nape of her neck and she sprawled at his feet.

Leaving her where she lay, he went back inside the house, stepping over the trooper in the vestibule to get to a stand where Imogen had left her purse. A bunch of keys were disgorged from the bag and he swept them into his palm.

He was inside no more than ten seconds, but the scene in the yard had changed. Imogen had crawled a small distance away, and was now on her hands and knees, shaking her head like a dog with a flea in its ear. But more importantly, the overweight cop had managed to claw himself inside his cruiser. White-faced and oozing perspiration, he was shouting into the radio mike.

Rickard glanced between the two of them, then

stalked towards the police car. He lifted his gun, aiming it through the window.

'You should have just kept screaming until I was gone,' Rickard said. 'Maybe you would have lived.'

He fired twice, shattering the window and the man. This time there was no screaming.

Rickard leaned in the car, groping for the dead cop's utility belt. He drew the man's handcuffs from their holder.

Imogen was now on her feet and was taking her first confused steps away from him. Rickard raced after her, caught hold of her neck again and hustled her towards the Suburban.

'We have unfinished business, bitch.'

CHAPTER 12

'Maybe that wasn't such a good idea,' Bryce Lang said to me from the other side of the sedan. He was driving now, while I scrunched down in my seat with a baseball cap on my head and dark sunglasses hiding my eyes. The weight of the law enforcement community was hunting me. The train stations, airports and harbours round Tampa were all closed down tight, and with roadblocks set up at all intersections in and out of the city they thought it was only a matter of time before they hauled me in. Little did they know we were already beyond the noose, but we weren't in the clear yet. Bryce followed a winding route via roads that took us through the swamps. 'They realise who phoned them, they'll try to trace your phone.'

'I can always replace it if needs be.'

Bryce's lips made a tight slash.

'By implicating me in a double murder, and then making it look like I'm a cop-killer, the people we're up against think they're shutting down the places I can go for help.'

'They're probably right,' Bryce said.

78

'They are, but there was nothing else I could do to help Imogen. I had to call the cops. I only hope they got there in time to save her.'

'You still want to go all the way to Maine?'

'Yes. That's where the killer is.'

'But if we're too late . . .'

'We *are* going to be too late. But we might be able to pick up his trail.'

'We should be concentrating on finding Abadia.'

'Abadia's dead, Bryce. He was cremated, remember?'

'Someone was cremated, that was for sure. But we weren't in a position to check inside the coffin.'

Glancing across at him, I wondered what he was getting at. An ex-CIA agent-cum-conspiracy theorist; that wasn't something you came across every day. 'Bryce, this is someone else.'

'You've seen the photographs, Hunter. Who else would target the team sent to kill him? He's also making sure that our families die because his girlfriend and child were killed during the hit. The murders were committed in Abadia's style.'

It was strong evidence, but I was there when Abadia was shot. I was certain that he was dead.

But I should've followed protocol and made damn sure.

'Do you have a wife and family?' I asked.

He didn't reply but his silence said it all.

'Maybe you don't, Bryce, but I do. There's nothing more I want than to go to them now, but I've chosen to stay here. I've contacted a friend over in the UK who's going to look after them. For me, the best way I can protect them is to find whoever it is and stop him for good.'

'OK, OK, I get you,' Bryce said. 'But we've got a problem.'

We had a lot more than one in my estimation.

'What are you getting at?'

'If we drive it'll take days. We can't fly or jump on a train. There'll be people checking, and we won't avoid scrutiny. Not if you intend taking your weapons with you.'

'I'm going to need them. Don't worry, Bryce, I've already made our travel arrangements. All I need is for Rink to give the slip to the cops tailing him.'

'You think he's up to it?'

'There's no one better.'

'So where do we meet him.'

'Just keep heading south. I'll give you directions when we get close.'

Key Largo is at the southernmost point of Florida, the most northerly of the Florida Keys. It is an island but is connected to the mainland by US Highway I and is a Mecca for scuba divers visiting the nearby coral reefs. I'd been there before: not to dive but on a whim to see what it was like, having caught the old Bogart – Bacall movie on a cable channel. It would take us hours to get there, but it would be worth the effort.

On the drive down I tried to nap for a short time while Bryce continued south, taking roads that didn't show on many maps. My sleep was troubled: I kept replaying the death of Jimena and her child through my mind. It was vivid, their deaths Technicolor-gory and as pointless as ever they had been in real life. Instead, I spelled Bryce for a while as we went through the Everglades, then handed over the driving duties when we were back in the built-up areas of Miami Dade County. Finally, approaching Key Largo, I directed Bryce to take the Card Sound Bridge on to the island.

'There's a toll booth there. They might have been given your description,' Bryce said.

'Doubt it,' I said. But we had to be careful.

The toll road was barrier-controlled. A single booth gave access into Monroe County, but we'd arrived at a time of day when there was a queue of traffic edging forwards and they were being nudged through the barrier perfunctorily. We crept along, flanked by signs warning us to beware of crossing crocodiles. Bryce opened his window, handed over the correct change, and then we were through without even raising an eyebrow of the elderly man working the controls.

We crossed the bridge, the water scintillating below us, and on to the island. Mangroves clung to the shoreline and the heady aroma of rotting vegetation invaded the sedan. The island was a prehistoric coral reef, exposed millennia ago and eroded by subsequent ice ages. At its highest point it stood little more than fifteen feet above sea level, but you wouldn't know it because we were surrounded by trees all the way down to the town of North Key Largo.

'Don't stop until we find signs for Pelican Key,' I said. Without comment Bryce followed the lazy flow of traffic south. He found the spur of land jutting out into the sea, but I nodded him on. 'OK, there should be a place a little ahead of us. Rock Harbor.'

'Got it,' he said, nodding at overhead signs.

I pointed out a road on our right and we pulled into it, approaching an exclusive resort. There was a hotel surrounded by palm trees, and a wharf that jutted out over the beach and into the sea. Boats were moored alongside the wharf, and vehicles were parked near to them on a concrete lot.

'You can pull in here, Bryce.'

Bryce parked adjacent to a Porsche Boxster that was so black it glistened in the sun and reflected the boats lined up across the way. I looked across at the driver of the Porsche and smiled in greeting at my best friend, Rink.

We got out of our cars, Bryce stretching after the long journey. I shook hands with Rink, appraising his appearance.

'Is this what you mean by discreet?'

He was wearing a gaudy Hawaiian shirt, bright blue with reds and yellows all over it, parrots and palm trees if you looked closely; but I tried not to. He had on wraparound shades that reflected my gaze and concealed his hooded eyes, and his normally straight black hair had been slicked back.

His ensemble was completed by cargo pants with big pockets on the thighs, and walking boots. Not for the first time, Rink reminded me of a character out of *Magnum PI*. He was tall like Tom Selleck, but he was twice as solid with muscle.

Rink flashed a grin at me, his teeth very white against his tawny skin, a match for the pale scar on his jaw. His grin told me that he was nervous, something about the way it fixed as he looked over my shoulder at Bryce.

'That the spook?'

'Bryce Lang,' I said, 'meet Jared Rington.'

'Call me Rink.'

I was glad that Rink offered his nickname: it meant that we were all going to get along. The two shook hands, and Rink flipped his shades back on his head. His size and his Arkansas drawl often surprise people when they notice his eyes; he has the epicanthic fold common to eastern races that comes courtesy of his Japanese mother. Bryce didn't do a double start – partly because I'd told him that Rink was Asian-American, partly because he was already familiar with Rink's file – but I saw Rink reading the man's reaction and judging him by it. Rink seemed happy and his grin became less fixed.

'Great to meet you, Rink. We never had the opportunity to work together before, but I've heard good things about you.' Bryce gave me a quick glance, and I guessed that he was wishing Rink had been in Bogota that fateful day. Maybe he thought Rink would have pulled the trigger where I hadn't. He didn't know Rink the way I did.

Rink leaned back into his Porsche and pulled out a canvas bag. 'Supplies.'

Dropping my hands down my body, I indicated that I'd everything I needed right there. Rink shook his head, a smile twitching the corner of his mouth. 'There's a guy I've paid to take my car outa here. No sense in leavin' it here an' giving the cops a heads up.'

Rink led us along the wharf to a cabin cruiser and stepped on to the boat. Bryce went next while I checked behind us. There was no sign of any surveillance, but that didn't mean they weren't there. I'd missed the shooter when he was tailing me in Tampa. That time I'd been distracted by Castle and Soames, and I wasn't about to make the same mistake again.

A young black guy in baggy shorts was at the controls. An older man unhitched the ropes from the wharf and used a kick of his foot to push us clear. He clambered past us towards the cabin, talking quickly to the young man. I didn't catch a word they said to each other.

Watching Bryce's expression, I said, 'No. We don't intend sailing all the way to Maine.'

The motor stuttered then roared and the cabin cruiser angled out into the gently undulating water. The older black guy was doing a lot of gesticulating while the younger one ignored him stoically. Father and son, I assumed.

'Used these guys before?' I asked Rink.

'No. But they're being paid to keep their lips zipped. You don't have to worry about them.'

'Where are we going?' Bryce had sat on a bench and was watching Rock Harbor recede away from us.

'Out in the Keys,' Rink said. But that was all.

Back during Fidel Castro's takeover of Cuba, many people fleeing oppression and poverty had sought a new life in the States. As it was less than one hundred miles between Cuba and Key West, 'boat people' often used the islands as stepping stones to the mainland. Now, all these years later, illegal immigrants still chose this route into the USA. People with the necessary cash could purchase entry via any number of men willing to smuggle them ashore. Ordinarily I'd balk at using men who profit from the suffering of others, but in the circumstances I just had to keep my opinion to myself. Desperate times, as they say.

'We're taking a chance out here,' Bryce said. 'There was no other way you could think of?'

Because of the problem of illegal immigrants, the US Border Patrol was very active in this area, watching for suspicious boats or sea planes. We were running the risk of being hailed by a patrol boat. But that wasn't what Bryce was getting at.

'There are many agents based here,' he offered in a whisper. The Keys were also a staging post for people entering Communist-controlled Cuba. 'People who might recognise me.'

'Just keep your head down, Bryce.'

'Want my shades?' Rink asked.

We were on the boat for over an hour, and during that time, I brought Rink up to speed with everything that had happened. He checked out the photographs that Bryce had brought along. Rink had worked with Schilling, Hillman and Muir on a few missions and I could see the sadness in his eyes as he studied the photos. The sadness was replaced by anger when looking at the innocent dead: the women and children. His shoulders tightened and I knew that my friend was thinking bad thoughts about the people responsible.

'And now they have Imogen.'

'I'm trying not to think about that,' I said.

The Florida Keys are an archipelago of more than seventeen hundred islands, many of them inhabited, but others merely nameless limestone mounds on the surface of the sea. Depending on the hurricanes that roar through the area, some of these islets disappear and reappear like Brigadoon of the fables. A large number of islands have been colonised by plant life but have no natural fresh water and in general people avoid these as dwelling places. We were headed for one such island now.

The old guy set up a new fluster of gesticulations that his son accepted without argument. The cabin cruiser swung in and approached an island that rose from the surface of the sea with dramatic limestone cliffs crowned by bushes and the occasional palm tree. On closer inspection the cliffs weren't as tall as they first looked, little higher than twenty feet, but they still appeared to be a natural bulwark against the sea. We followed a spur of the cliff and turned into a natural cove, where men with automatic rifles waited for us.

Bryce inhaled sharply, but a quick glance at Rink's nonchalance made him relax. Rink raised a hand in greeting and the men lowered their guns and waved back.

Rink bunged the old guy a roll of dollars as we disembarked on to a short jetty made from weathered wood. Then the cabin cruiser backed out and took off for Rock Harbor.

Twenty minutes later, the three of us were on a plane headed north on the first of three hops to Maine. In a few short hours we'd go from tropical sunshine to icy rain and just the thought made me shudder. But it wasn't the prospect of the impending cold that made me shake: it was what I might find when we arrived there.

CHAPTER 13

In a woodland glade near to the Narraquaquas River in Washington County, Rickard shot Imogen Ballard.

It was easier transporting her if she couldn't put up a fight.

Depending on her outlook when she finally woke up, she'd probably prefer it that he'd used the gun with which he'd shot the state troopers instead of the same tranquilliser gun he'd used on her the first time.

He propped her in the passenger seat of his newly appropriated vehicle, a blanket tucked round her and a pillow behind her head as though she was taking a well-earned nap. He slipped a hand under the blanket, caressing her thigh while he made an overdue telephone call to his wife.

'Hi, honey, it's me.'

In their loft apartment in Miami, Alisha held her breath for a second too long.

'Aren't you happy to hear from me?' Rickard asked.

'Of course I am, Luke.'

'Me too, babe. I'm missing you. Are you missing me?'

'Yes.'

'Doesn't sound like it.'

'I am, Luke, I'm missing you like crazy. I wish you were home . . .'

Rickard smiled to himself, and allowed his hand to slip between Imogen's legs.

'There's nothing more that I want, but you know how things are: if you want all these fine things, I have to work all the hours I can. You're not growing ungrateful, I hope . . .'

'I don't care about anything else, Luke. I'd be as happy with nothing.'

'As long as you're with me, right?'

'That's what I meant, Luke. I only want you.'

'I want you, too.' Rickard closed his eyes and sucked in a deep breath, shuddered it out again. His fingers were working with more urgency. As deep as she was in slumber, Imogen squirmed in an effort to get away from him.

'When will you be home?' Alisha's voice came out barely above a whisper. Rickard withdrew his hand and made a fist on the steering wheel.

'I don't know for sure. A day, maybe two. Why do you ask?'

'Because I . . . uh . . . I miss you.'

'If it was possible I'd be there now,' he said. 'But it isn't. But just think how great things will be when I get back.'

'That's what keeps me going, babe.'

'Tell me, honey. Tell me what you're going to do to me when I get home.'

Alisha told him, and his fist unfurled. After a few seconds it crept back under the blanket. But all he did this time was straighten Imogen's clothing.

Rickard hung up.

He could feel the serpent coiling inside him and he glanced at the rear-view mirror in hope of catching it out. All that looked back at him were his own deep-set eyes. They were creased with anger and it was an effort to make them smooth out.

Alisha, the little whore, was in need of reminding about the correct etiquette for answering his calls. She'd said the right words, but her tone had done nothing to reassure him. The fear was there, and that was good. But the desultory, almost robotic pitch of her voice was as faked as those phone-sex hookers he occasionally called. He was beginning to think that the ungrateful bitch didn't fear him enough.

Beside him, Imogen was as still as a mannequin. Her face was pale and waxen. After the troubled moans she'd made minutes ago, she was silent; even her breath was barely audible. He wished now that he hadn't doped her so deeply; he would do to her what he planned to do to Alisha on his return. Imogen, he knew, would show him the correct amount of terror.

Among his tools he had brought an antidote to the tranquilliser and he was seconds away from administering it. But he decided no. There would be time for Imogen later. He had other things to do first.

He punched numbers into his phone.

'I have the woman,' he said.

'Is she dead?'

'Not yet.'

'Is there a problem?'

'Slight hiccup, but nothing I can't handle.'

'You were told to kill her, Rickard.'

'And that's what I will do. But it's better this way. You wanted Joe Hunter punished. This way I get to make things much, much worse for him.'

'Maybe our plan to make him run worked too well. Hunter has dropped off the map.'

'We expected him to. Not to worry, though, he'll come to me when I'm ready.'

'You're sure that you are his equal?'

'No.'

'No, Rickard?'

'I'm better than him.'

'I hope so.'

This time it was the other person who hung up first. Rickard stared at the phone, his left hand curling into a fist again.

'You hope so?' He spoke into the unresponsive phone. '*You fucking hope so?*'

Twice he'd been disrespected in as many minutes.

Rickard punched the steering wheel. When it didn't break, he punched it again and again in a frenzy that didn't halt until his blood slicked the wheel.

CHAPTER 14

Imogen's house was situated on the bluffs above Little Kennebec Bay, the nearest town being the tiny harbour of Machiasport. To get there we had to put down at a private airstrip outside the small town of Holden, because there was no way we'd get through security at Bangor International, then we drove up the rugged coastline in a 4x4 supplied by Rink's contact at the airstrip.

Icy rain thundered on the cab. The heater was cranked high, blowing hot, dry gusts against my face, but outside it *looked* cold. Wearing my Florida get-up, I might succumb to hypothermia in an hour. Rink's flamboyant shirt would be no protection at all.

'We need to stop and get kitted out,' I said.

Bryce was perhaps the best equipped for the cold, but even he nodded. We needed coats and hats that were designed for keeping the heat in rather than the sun out.

There were plenty of places on the way up to Little Kennebec Bay, and taking twenty minutes out of our journey, we restocked at a fishing tackle store. We bought fleece-lined coats and hats with ear-flaps, and we rigged Bryce out with a new pair of boots. Rink and I lived in our boots, so we were OK in that department. We paid with a credit card with a faked name. It sounds bad, but there was actually money I'd deposited into the account, so it was a genuine transaction: it would just never be traced back to me.

Behind the counter a radio was playing. A newscaster regaled his audience with the latest news. The top story centred on a gunfight where one cop had died and another was critically injured. It came as no surprise that my name was thrown into the pot, but I walked out of the store pretty thankful. There was no mention of a woman having been found mutilated.

Because mobile telephones are deceptively easy to trace, I turned off the one I'd used in Tampa, removing the battery for good measure, and purchased another with prepaid credit at a service station a little further along our route. I tried Walter Hayes Conrad again, but with similar results.

'You don't think Walter's involved, do you?' Rink asked when we were back in the 4x4 and on the road again. His tone told me that he didn't give his words much credence.

'Stuff like that only happens in the movies,' I said. But I did wonder where he'd gone to. My greatest fear was that he'd already been targeted by the people we were up against, but it was highly unlikely. Walter rarely travelled anywhere without an entourage of bodyguards. I preferred to think that he was simply too busy with his own investigation to reply to my calls. Then a thought struck me. I stared directly at Bryce.

'When we first met, you said you wanted to check whose side I was on. Again, back at the safe house, you also mentioned that "according to some people" I was the one responsible for killing our team. Was Walter one of these people?'

'No. Walter argued that it wasn't you. It was why he contacted me and sent me to find you instead.'

'He knew where to find me,' I pointed out.

'News had just come in about the murder of Jessica and Linden Case and how Case mentioned your name before he died. Walter couldn't contact you directly for fear of being implicated in that crime. He was worried that his communications were being monitored.'

'But he felt safe contacting you?'

'We keep in touch on an informal basis: face to face. We occasionally meet up to have a beer and reminisce over the good old days.'

Bryce was obfuscating the way that Walter was also famous for. If a hit on a black ops team was under investigation, the CIA would have been on to Bryce much earlier than they'd been on to me. I noticed that Rink had picked up on the lie by the way he jutted out his chin. I let it go.

But then I laughed.

'You know what this is, don't you?'

Bryce frowned. Rink's chin relaxed and a smile curled his lips.

'Walter – in his own inimitable style – has reactivated us to clear up his shit. He sent you to put me on the right track, Bryce, knowing full well that I'd be like a dog after a bone. He knew that Rink would step up to help me.'

'Figures,' Rink said.

'This is another embarrassment to the intelligence community. He wants it buried, so he's chosen us to do his dirty work for him again.'

'Just like Tubal Cain,' Rink said. He unconsciously thumbed the white scar on his chin – a reminder of said psychopath.

Bryce wasn't party to what had happened with Tubal Cain. Cain was actually Martin Maxwell, a former member of the secret service, better known as a bone-harvesting serial killer. When my brother John was kidnapped by Cain it was inevitable that I hunted the man down, but it served Walter that I bury him without a trace. On that occasion Walter had given me unofficial sanction to kill the maniac; it looked like I was being offered the same terms again.

'I'm right, Bryce?'

'I was supposed to show you the photos and then put you on Abadia's trail,' Bryce said. 'Walter didn't anticipate that you would be a fugitive from the law.'

'If he'd come directly to me those cops wouldn't have died, Imogen would be safe, and I wouldn't be being hunted like a rabid dog.'

'An' we wouldn't have to freeze our asses in

Maine.' Rink said. To add validity to his words, he flicked on the windscreen wipers to bat away sleet. 'There *is* a good reason why I live in Florida.'

'Won't be here long,' I promised him.

'I think we're wasting our time coming here,' Bryce said. 'The woman's already dead.'

'We don't know that. Until we know for sure, we assume she's still alive.'

'You've seen the photos, Hunter. You know what happens to the victims.'

'That's exactly why we're here: I'm not going to let that happen to her.'

'We should concentrate on finding Abadia.'

'No, Bryce. We concentrate on finding Imogen first.'

The woman was in danger through no fault of her own. She'd been snatched as a way of hurting me. Kate and I had been together – if only briefly – before she was murdered, and I thought now that if Kate was still alive I'd be looking at Imogen as an extended member of my family. And no one fucks with my family.

My problem was where to start.

Imogen's house was the obvious place, but for the time being it would be cordoned off behind crime scene tape and a horde of investigators. Going there would solve nothing and most likely see us behind bars.

'Does Walter have any idea who's behind this?'

'Abadia.'

'OK. Let's play make-believe for a minute,' I

said. 'Let's just suppose that Abadia survived three point-blank rounds in the chest and he's now looking for revenge: where would he start?'

'He starts by identifying the men sent to kill him.'

'Exactly. But those files were buried. So how does he get to them?'

'He needs someone on the inside,' Bryce said. It was like he'd just confessed a sin and he jerked upright in his seat. 'Hey, now hold on! I hope you don't think I had anything to do with this?'

'Calm yourself, Bryce. If I thought you were involved, I'd have already broken your neck. I'm thinking someone else.'

'There is no one else.'

'There are plenty. There were officers from the Drug Action Service along for the ride. Any one of them could've been forced into feeding him the information he'd need.'

Bryce looked pensive. 'Victor Montoya was the first to die. It's possible that someone led Abadia to Victor and then the other names were extracted from him. Remember he was tortured. Maybe it was because he wouldn't speak that his family were murdered in front of him.'

It sounded feasible.

'Next question: who does Abadia use to get his revenge? All of us are highly trained; he doesn't send someone incapable of getting the job done.'

'Has to be ex-military,' Rink said.

'A mercenary,' Bryce offered.

97

'Probably Special Forces,' I said. 'Someone just like us.'

'That doesn't narrow things down very much,' Bryce said. 'There have got to be thousands of ex-Special Ops out there looking to make a buck.'

'Most of them are men of honour. They wouldn't make war on women and children.' Rink stared directly ahead into the growing storm. 'Most of them.'

'Why would they have to be Special Forces?' Bryce asked.

'Could be something else,' I concurred. 'Whoever it is, he's highly trained and highly efficient. He has experience with sniper rifles. It's possible that he's a freelance assassin or a cop or maybe even a run-of-the-mill soldier. But I'm still running with the Special Forces angle.'

'Why are you so sure?'

'The guy I spoke to on the phone sounded Caucasian. I think that Abadia – or whoever – met the killer while he was on active duty in Colombia. British and American Special Ops guys have been in and out of Colombia for years, training and equipping the anti-narcotics cops down there. The SAS were there back in the nineties, more recently it's been the US Army Rangers.'

Beside me Rink grunted. Rink was a Ranger before he joined my unit.

'Next time we stop,' he said, 'I'll get Harvey on to it.'

Harvey Lucas was also a Ranger in his past life.

He still had connections: maybe he could draw information from someone that would send us in the right direction. If not, Harvey was still a good man to have at our backs.

'If he's a Ranger, we're in for one helluva fight,' Rink said. He squirmed a little, as though his loyalty to his old troop meant he had to give the killer a modicum of respect. It was an abrasive notion.

'We're surmising an awful lot,' Bryce said.

'Yeah.'

Maybe I was way off base in my thinking. But as usual I was going to prepare for the worst-case scenario. Anything less would be a welcome bonus.

CHAPTER 15

Culver in Hancock County, Maine is somewhere that you would normally struggle
to find on a map, but the small town was
where Rickard headed. Following the assassina-
tion of the two cops in Tampa, he'd travelled to
Bangor on a scheduled flight, but from Bangor
had jumped to the coastline on a small seaplane.
From Trenton, he'd then used a speedboat to cross
the bay to Culver, where he'd collected the FedEx
truck that was necessary to his ploy. His boat was
moored in a disused boathouse ready for the
return trip across the water. At Trenton, the plane
was waiting for his return, but there wasn't room
in the cabin for the pilot and him, plus an unconscious woman. But that was OK, he never
intended for Imogen Ballard to leave Maine alive.

The car he'd appropriated after dumping Imogen's
Suburban would have to be torched to eliminate
any trace evidence, but that was a task he'd see
to prior to firing up the outboard motor on his
boat.

'First we deal with you, Imogen,' he said. 'Let's
see if we can raise a little fire in you, shall we?'

Imogen was incapable of replying. But that would be rectified within a minute or so.

The boathouse, once used to house a fishing boat, was not one of those fancy type buildings you see in rich men's playgrounds but a wholly utilitarian affair of sun-bleached planks and wind-scoured shingles. It was like a small hangar, open to the bay at one end with a normal door on the side and another two doors where a truck with a winch could drag a boat out of the water on the landward side. Wooden walkways ran the length of both inner walls, while a beaten earth ramp down the centre gave way to the cold North Atlantic. Rickard's boat was moored on the right-hand side; the other walkway was clear.

Upright beams held the shell of the building together and supported the sagging roof. To one of the beams on the walkway opposite the boat, Rickard cuffed Imogen. He fed the cuffs behind the beam, then snapped her wrists into them. A cross-beam held the cuffs from slipping down, forcing the unconscious woman to stand upright. If she awoke her position would be torturous.

Rickard dumped his kit in the boat, the dart gun stripped down now and the delivery driver's uniform finished with. Both would be sunk to the bottom of the bay when he travelled to Trenton. His sidearm was holstered in his shoulder rig because he wouldn't need it for what he now planned. From a holder on his belt, he pulled out a small ceramic object with a switch on the side.

101

He slid the switch, baring three inches of razor-sharp ceramic blade. When security measures would detect a gun or other metal weapon, Rickard counted on the undetectable ceramic knife to keep him armed.

'It's not a machete, but it will do,' he said to the unresponsive woman.

When mutilating the others, he'd employed various tools on them: guns, knives, a machete, even a meat cleaver to decapitate one of his victims, but the intimacy that the small ceramic knife brought gave him the most satisfaction. He'd last used the knife on Jessica Case and her father. If he checked he was pretty sure that he would find traces of their blood caught in the mechanism.

He jabbed a hypodermic syringe in Imogen's arm and depressed the plunger. Then he held the knife ready because her return to wakefulness would be almost instantaneous.

He watched her eyelids flicker, then her head snapped up and she was staring directly at the blade of the knife. A siren song began to rise in her throat. Prepared for this, Rickard jammed a wadded rag into her mouth.

'Spit it out and I'll have to gag you in a different way. I'll cut out your tongue.'

She shuddered, pulling against the cuffs. Her right shoulder was twisted painfully towards him. It wasn't for her comfort that he reached out and stood her upright again. He wanted a good view of her. Taking hold of the neckline of her top, he sliced down with the knife. The ceramic blade was sharper than any steel and it parted the material like he was slicing a sheet of paper.

'Nice-looking body,' he noted. 'You keep yourself fit and toned. That's good.'

Behind the gag, Imogen yelled something, but her words were just a garbled shriek.

'That was supposed to be a compliment,' Rickard said.

He slid the knife under the front of her bra, snicked through the elastic band and exposed her breasts. Imogen yelled again and kicked out at him with both feet, one at a time like she was climbing a steep flight of stairs. One foot caught him sharply on his shin, but the other missed entirely as he skipped out of the way. Imogen twisted her head to follow him and he could see the veins thrumming in her throat like harp strings.

Rickard laughed at her. Wiggling the knife at her, he swayed along with it, as though caught in a slow dance. 'I thought it might take a little more to get a rise out of you.'

Imogen gnawed on the rag as if it was a tough piece of meat. She pushed it free with her tongue, spitting and retching. 'Who are you? What do you want from me?'

Rickard allowed his earlier threat to drop. He would get more out of her if she could talk. 'I want you to see me.'

'I see you. You're a maniac; that's what I see!'

'I need you to look deeper than that, Imogen.'

She wrenched at the cuffs again, the metal crossbar digging into flesh and wood with equal ferocity. The support beam creaked ominously and dust and old shingles sifted down, pitter-pattering in the water. Rickard pounced, grabbing her chin in his left hand and guiding the blade very close to her eyes with the other. 'Stop that. Stop struggling or I'll blind you.'

Imogen went very still, but there was something in her posture that made Rickard step back. Imogen nodded at the knife. 'You do that, you pig. But how will I *see you* then?'

Rickard stared at her. His breath came heavy, in time with the lapping tide. He allowed the blade to drop by his side. He took another step back, his heels very close to the edge of the walkway.

'Tell me, Imogen. Tell me and maybe I'll let you live.'

She shook her head. 'You're going to kill me whatever I say.'

He folded the blade away and slipped the holder into the pouch on his belt. He showed her his empty hands. 'You have my word.'

'That *maybe* I'll live?'

'I can't offer more. Satisfy my curiosity, Imogen. Tell me the truth and I will consider what happens next.'

Rickard watched her. He saw the machinations of hope and denial and mistrust make war in her mind. Hope seemed the stronger emotion.

'What am I supposed to see in you?'

'My true essence,' Rickard said.

Tears welled in the corners of her eyes and she shook her head slowly. 'I don't know what you mean.'

'The *serpent*,' Rickard said.

Imogen nodded slowly, peering into his eyes. The tears rolled down her cheeks and she blinked quickly to clear her vision. 'Yes. I see it.'

Rickard smiled.

'I see it in you. A great big snake. Its forked tongue flicking in and out.'

Rickard's smile froze. Then melted away.

'Liar.'

'No. I'm not lying!' Imogen pushed herself upright against the beam, worming her shoulders round so she was less constricted. 'I can see it like a superimposed shadow towering over you.'

'Liar!' Rickard lunged forwards and grasped her throat in one hand, his other fist poised to strike. 'You don't see *that*. The serpent is nothing like you describe. Now, do it: look into my eyes and tell me what you really see.'

Imogen could barely breathe. She twisted against the beam and there was a crack of shifting wood. She pressed down with her chin, trying in vain to push away his hand.

Rickard slapped her across the face and the shock sent a wave of blackness through her skull.

'Tell me, goddamn you . . .'

'Go to hell!'

Imogen kicked out blindly, but her foot found a viable target in the juncture of Rickard's thighs. Caught unprepared, Rickard's eyes bugged and a red flush crept up his face. He let out a groan. Imogen didn't stop; she kicked out with both legs as though pedalling a cycle, thrusting at his legs and stomach. Rickard hopped backwards and his heels skidded on the edge of the walkway. He grabbed at her to halt his slide, but Imogen snatched herself back from him and his groping fingers found only empty space. One foot went off the walkway and then he plummeted down, suspended on the platform by the strength in only one bent knee. Imogen kicked again.

Rickard let out a wordless cry and toppled over, going down on his back in the water. Foamy bubbles rushed over him for a moment, then he erupted out again and roared in anger. Water streamed through his dark hair and from his clothing.

'You filthy, stinking whore! I'm going to skin you alive for that.'

Imogen shrieked in denial, throwing her weight against the upright beam. She felt it shift, heard the agonised squeal of nails pulling loose. Rickard squinted up at her, then dashed salty water from his mouth with the back of one hand as he reached for his ceramic knife with the other. Imogen became frantic. She stamped at the boards, throwing her shoulders against the beam, bumping it and bumping it with all her might. The beam split, triggering a small cloud of rotted particles. Rickard snorted at her attempt at escape, then waded forward and placed a palm flat on the walkway to aid him in stepping up. Imogen kicked at him again but Rickard easily avoided the blow. Suspended by only the cuffs, Imogen skidded and fell, twisting awkwardly. She screamed in pain as her wrists were lacerated by the tight metal hoops. There was a low rumble from above and more dust and slivers of wood rained down.

Rickard surged forwards once more, a wave pushing ahead of him, his attention alternating between Imogen and the suddenly dipping roof. Leaning over, he reached to grab at Imogen's ankles, but she swung sideways, avoiding his grip, and again threw her entire body weight into her escape. This time she didn't work against the beam but away from it. The effort almost dislocated her shoulders but the beam pulled away from the roof and fell, showering her with shards of broken planks. The roof sagged, but, held firmly by the remaining upright beams, it didn't collapse on them. Immediately she got her feet under her and yanked free from the broken end of the beam. Then she scrambled away from Rickard, who changed direction and waded quickly towards the earth ramp.

Imogen slipped on to one knee. But in the next instant she was up again, barely avoiding the swipe of Rickard's knife as he slashed at her. Rickard came on wordlessly, Imogen trying her hardest to avoid his gaze as if by doing so it would ensure her escape: as pointless as an ostrich burying its head in sand.

Running was difficult with her arms cuffed behind her, but adrenalin gave an extra lift to her heels and she raced along the walkway towards the double doors. When Rickard had brought her inside, he hadn't locked them – a padlock was useless when the wood supporting it was so rotten. She skidded up to the doors, banged against them with her shoulder and they burst open. Imogen charged outside into the cold and softly falling rain. She felt neither of them on her hot skin.

'What in God's name is going on?'

Imogen barely made sense of the words, but the figures looming up in front of her made her collapse to her backside and she rolled on the floor at the feet of the two men standing over her. From her ignominious position in the dirt she stared up at a burly old man and a slighter built teenage boy. Both were shocked to find a semi-naked, handcuffed woman lying at their feet and the rifles in their hands drooped ineffectually.

'Help me,' she screamed. 'He's trying to kill me!'

Rickard appeared in the open doorway, dripping wet and vibrating with anger.

The younger man saw him, made sense of the knife clutched in Rickard's hand and let out a croak as he slapped at his father's arm. The older man, made of sterner stuff, brought up his rifle.

'Hold it right there, mister,' he barked.

'Shoot him,' Imogen yelled. 'He's a murderer. Shoot him, for Christ's sake!'

The older man tensed his finger on the trigger, but he wasn't ready to fire yet. His mind was in too much turmoil to shoot a man without all the facts at hand. To the teenager, he said, 'Best you ring nine-one-one, boy.'

The younger man back-pedalled, then raced up the trail towards a nearby house.

Rickard stood stock-still. He still held the knife in his hand, but he was staring directly into the eyes of the older man.

'This is no business of yours,' he said.

'It became my business when you moored in my boathouse,' said the man. 'I thought you were only trespassing, mister, and I've been waiting for you to come back to put you straight. Now I see that what you're up to is *much* worse.'

Rickard shook his head. 'Get out of the way and you won't get hurt.'

'There's only one man going to get hurt round here. Take another step and I'll drop you.'

Imogen crawled round behind the man, placing him between her and Rickard. She came to her knees. 'Shoot him.'

The old man ignored her, steadying his aim on Rickard's chest.

'I'm warning you, mister, I did two tours in 'Nam. It was a long time ago, but I still remember how to fire a gun. Now drop the knife and step out here where I can see you.'

Rickard only sneered at the man. Then his gaze shifted to Imogen.

'We're not finished, bitch. You think you've got a protector, but no one will stop me. Not him. Not Joe Hunter. I'll see you again.'

Then he turned quickly and disappeared back inside the boathouse.

The old man grunted, started after him, but Imogen's warning cry brought him to a halt. 'He has a gun in there.'

The man retreated, took hold of Imogen's arm and heaved her up. Holding her, he moved backwards with his rifle braced against his shoulder, watching the doorway in case Rickard reappeared.

They made it part-way up the trail when the roar of an engine sounded from within the boathouse.

'Damn it, he's going to get away,' the man muttered. 'Where's that fool boy got to with the police?'

Beside him Imogen didn't seem to care. She was sobbing and trembling in relief. Or maybe it was fear, because Rickard's warning had been served with a certainty that was chilling.

CHAPTER 16

We heard the news about Imogen's miraculous escape on the car radio and a tsunami of relief crashed through my senses and left me dizzy. I'm not a praying man, but I said my silent thanks to God.

We'd bypassed Culver by then, but Rink immediately spun the car in the road and headed for the small town. It was taking a big risk because the area would be swarming with cops, but I needed to satisfy myself that Imogen wasn't merely safe but unharmed. I also wanted to speak with her. It was possible that she could tell me who my enemy was.

We were still a couple of miles from Culver when Rink's phone chimed. He put it on speaker so we could all hear. Harvey Lucas was already doing his magic with his computer.

'Law enforcement's trying to track a plane that took off from Trenton without filing a flight plan. They think our boy's on board 'cause the pilot's doing his damndest to avoid radar.'

'Direction?' I asked.

'South.'

'Back towards Florida,' Bryce Lang assumed. 'We came here for nothing, just like I said.'

'Not for nothing,' I told him. 'I came here for Imogen Ballard and I'm not leaving until I'm sure she's out of harm's way. I owe her that: she shouldn't have to suffer for our crimes, Bryce.'

'Everything we did was lawfully sanctioned, Hunter.'

'Lawfully sanctioned, my arse! Even if it was an approved hit, does that make what happened to Jimena and the boy OK with you?'

'That's the way of war. Collateral damage is—'

'The death of innocents,' I finished for him. 'Whichever way the CIA looks at it. And I'm not prepared to let that happen to Imogen.'

'It hasn't happened to Imogen,' Bryce argued. 'She's safe now. We should go after the killer instead of wasting any more time.'

I stared at him until he closed his eyes in defeat. The silence was rather strained. Harvey coughed, maybe to remind us he was still at the other end of the phone. 'What's the latest from Tampa, Harve?' I asked.

'Mixed messages at best. Ballistics have shown that the weapon used to kill the two cops was an M40 sniper rifle. They know now that you couldn't've been the shooter, but your guess that they'd assume you had an accomplice is still the main theory.'

'So they're still looking for me?'

'Big style,' Harvey said. 'Rink, too, seeing as he's

harbouring a felon. And because he has marksman training.'

Rink grunted, sounding amused.

It stood to reason that we'd be on the Most Wanted list, but right then I didn't care. If we stopped the real killer everything would be put right. I was thinking about the rifle that the shooter had used to kill Castle and Soames. The M40A1 is a specialist rifle developed for and handmade for Marine Corps snipers by craftsmen at Quantico, Virginia. Based on the Remington 700, it was a heavy barrelled rifle, bolt action and fed by an internal magazine of five 7.62 mm rounds. Not the kind of gun that was readily available on the open market. It made me think again that the shooter came from a military background. Maybe he'd even trained at the Marine Corps Training Unit in Quantico.

I told Harvey my theory.

'I'll look into it and cross-reference names against anyone who has served in Colombia.'

'Thanks, Harvey,' I said. 'Keep us updated with anything on the plane's whereabouts, OK?'

'Will do. What's your plan now? You heading back home?'

'Not yet. I have to see Imogen first.'

'Right,' he said. 'Give her my best, huh? I'll see y'all back in Florida.'

'You're flying over?'

'I am. I'm more use to you there than I am in Little Rock.'

113

We said our goodbyes while Rink aimed the 4x4 along the last quarter-mile of road to Culver. The town was very small, with the number of cops on scene boosting the population tenfold. Really it was just a collection of houses strung out along the road that hugged the coastline. Most of the police cruisers were parked near to a timber-framed house that looked like the one Norman Bates called home. A narrow track was cordoned off with crime scene tape, leading no doubt to the boathouse where Imogen had made her break for freedom.

'She'll be gone from here by now,' Rink said.

'Nearest hospital?'

'More likely she's been taken to a police station,' Bryce said. 'They'll want to interview her as soon as possible.'

The parked police cars bore the livery of the Hancock County Sheriff Department and also some from the local police. Often the sheriff and police departments shared offices to keep down running costs, so it was no stretch of the imagination to think Imogen had been taken to Ellsworth, the nearest large town.

Rink was cautious passing the throng of police and we barely registered with them as we went past. Then he stomped the throttle and we headed for Ellsworth. On the way I came to a decision.

'No way can I con my way into a police station. Neither could you, Rink. By now our faces will be on every bulletin board in the USA.'

114

Bryce peered across at me. 'You want *me* to do it?'

He didn't appear too happy at the idea.

'No, Bryce. I have to do this myself. I have to see Imogen face to face.'

'They'll arrest you.'

'Probably,' I said. But I'd been taken prisoner by worse jailers than the HCSD before now, and no one had managed to hold me long. The only difference here was that on those other occasions I'd hurt people – killed others – and that was unthinkable this time. 'I'm not worried. I can prove I had nothing to do with the shooting of the cops.'

'There's always Jessica and her father. They still think you were responsible for that,' Bryce said.

'That was before the real killer targeted Imogen. Her testimony can clear things up.'

Rink stirred. 'Not necessarily, Hunter. Before he died, Linden Case named you as his attacker and his daughter's murderer. Even if they don't arrest you they'll have to talk to you about it. They'll want to know every detail about how the two cops died in Tampa. Whether you're behind bars or not, you won't see the outside of a police station any time soon.'

His words made sense, but I wanted to reassure myself of Imogen's safety more than I was concerned about my liberty. Also, I was growing tired of running from something I was innocent of and the few hours it would take to clear my name would be time well spent. I'd rather be chasing this man without having to keep one eye over my shoulder in case a well-meaning cop put a bullet in my spine.

'If I'm still inside when Harvey gets back to you, it'll be down to you guys to take the asshole out.'

Rink grunted assent, but Bryce looked fearful at the notion.

Arriving at Ellsworth, we took a spin past City Hall and the adjoining HCSD office building.

'We don't know for sure if she's even in there,' Bryce said.

'If not, I'll find out where they took her. If I'm under arrest. I'll demand my phone call and let you know.'

Rink found a motel where they'd wait for my return. I unloaded my SIGs and my Ka-Bar and all the fake documents I had on my person: no reason to give the cops another reason for holding me. I took off the heavy coat and hat as well. No sense in walking into a police station and giving the impression that I'd come packing an arsenal under my clothes. Take everything very easy and reasonable and the cops should reciprocate. Though I'm not a great believer in words like should or could; in my experience things never seem to go that way.

It was a short walk to the sheriff's office. I side-tracked to a Seven/Eleven and picked up a super-large coffee. The caffeine injection helped clear the fog of all the travelling I'd done lately, but it also made my stomach growl – or maybe that was the nerves kicking in. Despite what I'd said to Bryce about clearing my name, I could very well be booking myself a cell in a high-security prison.

When I walked in the door and presented myself at the enquiry desk the front office was deserted. Not surprisingly: everyone was out at Culver or searching Trenton for where the killer had left his getaway boat. Typical, I thought, America's most wanted man wants to hand himself in and staff shortages makes things impossible.

I pressed a buzzer and waited.

No one was in a rush to answer, so I pressed it again and kept the button depressed. I could hear the annoying buzzer sounding in the room next door. Finally a door opened and a fresh-faced young woman, dark hair pulled back in a pony-tail, walked into the front office. She smiled: a fixed response.

'Hello,' she said. There was no hint of recognition in her face. She was carrying a ring folder and bent down to place it on a shelf under the counter separating us. When she stood up again, I read her name badge. Caroline Lehrer, a civilian support worker. 'How may I help you, sir?'

'I think a friend of mine might have been brought here.'

I saw her eyes widen slightly, but it wasn't in alarm. Sometimes I got the same reaction when people heard my accent. Usually they ask if I'm from England. But Caroline Lehrer was more professional than that and allowed her curiosity to slide. 'If your friend was arrested they'd be over at our State Street offices.'

'Witness,' I corrected. 'She's the victim of the kidnapping earlier today.'

Caroline's shoulders tightened at my words and she studied me more intently. She was weighing and balancing my description against that of the suspect. Colour crept into her throat. She gave me a look that said she expected me to throw myself against the perspex shield that separated us. Her hand crept surreptitiously towards an emergency button under the shelf.

'I only want to speak to Imogen Ballard. I understand that that may not be possible under the circumstances, but if you get me the sheriff maybe something can be arranged.'

Caroline lifted a finger – at least it wasn't heading for the panic alarm any more. Not that she didn't intend rounding up the troops. 'The sheriff is unavailable. If you just give me a moment, sir, I'll find someone that you can speak to.'

'That's all I want.'

Caroline backed out through the door and fastened it securely behind her. I heard a dull electronic thud and guessed that from somewhere inside a switch had been thrown and the exit door was now also secure. No way could I escape while she rounded up some burly officers to come and take me down. There was a row of chairs bolted to the floor. I sat in one of them and kept my hands open, palms up on my thighs, while I listened to the low buzz of activity beyond the door. There was a CCTV camera aiming directly at me and I could picture a group of deputies staring at the corresponding screen trying to decide exactly who I was. And how dangerous I might be.

A few minutes later the door opened, and I was surprised at the number of people coming to get me. There was only Caroline Lehrer. She had the fixed smile on her face again.

'Would you like to come this way, sir?'

She opened a door at the end of the desk as I stood up. She held it open for me while I went through and behind the counter. She waved me towards the door to the back office while she again locked up. I pulled open the door, and got my second surprise.

Part of me had expected a group of uniformed deputies standing waiting to arrest me, but instead I found two men in sharp suits. One of them was a gaunt, almost skeletal man whom I did not know. The other was my friend and mentor, Walter Hayes Conrad IV.

'Hunter,' Walter said frowning. 'You took your time getting here.'

Then he came and clapped a hand on my shoulder, giving me a reassuring squeeze.

'What the hell's going on, Walter?'

'As direct to the point as ever, eh?'

'Things would've been much more direct if you'd answered my calls,' I told him.

He shrugged. 'I've been busy.'

'So have I.'

He gave me a grimace, then waved at the skeletal man who was watching me with eyes like dark pinpricks. 'This is Don Hubbard. He's the Special Agent in Charge from the Bangor FBI field office.'

Hubbard didn't extend a hand so I didn't offer him mine. There was nothing ambivalent in his nod of greeting and I guessed that whatever Walter had told him hadn't fully allayed his suspicion of me.

'We need to speak,' Walter went on. 'All three of us.'

'I want to see Imogen first.'

'The woman's fine. She's over at the hospital having her wounds treated.'

'Wounds?'

'Superficial only.'

'She'd better have a guard, Walter. The killer might try for her again.'

'I have agents with her,' Hubbard said in a gravelly voice. 'We still need to conduct a thorough debrief with her.'

'I want to talk to her.'

Hubbard shook his head.

'I insist,' I said.

'You're not in a position to insist on a thing. In fact you're very lucky that we talked Sheriff Hughes out of locking you in a cell. You're a wanted felon, remember? A suspected copkiller.' His last words came out with enough venom to kill an elephant. 'A *murderer*.'

Somehow I suspected that SAC Hubbard and I weren't going to get along.

'But we know that is wrong,' Walter interjected. Walter is a short, rotund man, bald and pallid, but he has the presence of a giant and the weight of presidents behind him. Hubbard didn't argue, just continued to look at me with his small raisin-like eyes. Finally he glanced away. Caroline Lehrer was standing nearby, wavering in indecision.

'Ahem,' she said, 'would you like me to take you back through to the office?'

Walter smiled at her. 'We can find our own way, thanks.'

He waved me before him to a door at the end of the room. I passed desks holding ongoing criminal files and flickering computer screens, wondering where the office's usual occupants were. I found them outside in a short hallway. Most of them were civilian clerks, but there were two deputies and they gave me a look like I was something they'd trodden in and tracked all over the carpet. I ignored them and walked along the hall with Walter and Hubbard bringing up the rear. Now that we were out of the way the displaced office staff filed back into the room. Passing an open door, I glanced inside and saw a solid, silver-haired man sitting behind a desk. His stare was laser-guided as it met my eyes. The sheriff: pissed off that he'd been relegated to house arrest in his own office while the G-men ran all the shots. Walter flicked him a salute as he passed and I heard him grumble in response.

We entered an office at the end of the hall, a utilitarian area with work desks and PCs and laser printers. There were chairs at the desks but nobody sat.

'So what's the deal?'

Walter chuckled to himself. 'There's a lot to go over, Hunter, but first things first. I've got a deal for you.'

'Spit it out, then.'

Hubbard crossed his arms on his chest, not fully at ease with what Walter was about to offer but with no recourse but to go along with the black-ops controller's plan.

'You've been a loose cannon since your arrival in the US. It's time to change that.'

I looked at Walter. 'I'm not standing down. Someone's trying to hurt me and people round me: I'm going to stop them.'

Walter nodded at my words.

'We don't want you to step down.'

Hubbard muttered something under his breath, but I paid him no heed. My attention was fully on Walter.

He smiled. 'I want you to step up. I want you to come back and work for me, Hunter. As a fully sanctioned asset.'

I just knew it.

CHAPTER 17

It was time to check in with a progress report.
It wouldn't be good.

His plan to sate his need for dominance over Imogen Ballard had been ruined by the untimely arrival of that damned old man and his idiot grandson. Plus, he'd had to leave behind incriminating evidence: there'd be fingerprints in Imogen's car which he'd intended destroying by setting the car ablaze. Worse than that, her survival meant that Imogen could describe him and there was no way now that he could continue with the plan to implicate Joe Hunter in his crimes. The surgery he'd undergone – and the time spent recuperating – had been a complete waste of time.

But he wasn't bothered by that.

He was one for more direct action, anyway: crash through their defences, cut them down. He didn't care for this charade where Hunter was set up. He should have just shot the man when he had him in the sights of his rifle, not fooled around playing Hunter the way his employer asked. He could have put a 7.62 mm round through the base of Hunter's spine. Made a paraplegic of him, consigned him to a wheelchair for the rest of his days: supreme torture to a man of constant action. His employer should know that, it had been quoted often enough when the plan was outlined: 'Death is not the greatest of evils; it is worse to want to die, and not be able to.'

He pressed buttons on his phone and it was answered immediately.

'It's Rickard.'

'What happened?'

'You've heard the news, then?'

'The wonders of modern technology . . .'

'A series of unforeseen circumstances,' Rickard said.

'I expect more from people working for me. You should have made contingencies.'

'I'm alive. Joe Hunter's on the run. What's the problem?'

'A trail that could lead back to me?'

'It won't lead back to you.'

'The woman can identify you. So can the forensics.'

Rickard laughed. 'All the forensics will do is lead them to a dead end. As for the woman, she can only tell them what I look like now. It's a simple matter to change my appearance. It isn't as if I haven't done so before, is it?'

There was a pause on the line.

'Where are you, Rickard?'

'Back in Miami. We had a bumpy and roundabout route, but your pilot was good. I'm confident that we made it here undetected. It was a shame I had to silence him.'

'And Joe Hunter?'

'Don't know.'

'Find out.'

Easier said than done: now Hunter was a fugitive and had gone underground. Rickard had always known that part of the plan would cause problems later. Still, he was confident he could draw him out into the open whenever he chose.

'Hunter will be looking for me,' he said. 'All I need to do is wait for him to show up.'

'Kill him. I see now that I should've let you have your way from the outset. It seems like the woman was an inconsequential part of the plan. We made an error in including her; Hunter was involved with her sister, not Imogen as we first thought.'

'Knowing how Hunter thinks, it wouldn't make any difference.'

'You're right.' Rickard was surprised by his employer's candour; before, mistakes had always been laid at other people's feet. Something about this turn of events was troubling. 'Why didn't you simply kill her when you had the opportunity?'

'You wanted her tortured first, remember? Someone – I suspect it was Hunter – tipped off the police and they arrived before I could get it done.'

'And the boathouse?'

'It wasn't as deserted as your people thought. I was disturbed by the owners and had to get out before the police arrived.'

'You couldn't just kill her before you left?'

Rickard wasn't about to say that Imogen had caught him off-guard and knocked him into the water before tearing free from the rotted beam he'd cuffed her to. In hindsight, both had been supreme errors of judgement. Slips like that would plant more than a seed of doubt into his employer's mind about his ability to finish the job. And that simply wouldn't do.

'Circumstances overtook me,' was all he'd say in reply.

'Then let us ensure that circumstances always bend our way in future.'

The dial tone cut in.

Hung up on again? Rickard jammed his phone into his pocket. He fucking hated that. And he fucking hated his employer. If it wasn't for the huge sum of money he was being paid he would forfeit the work in exchange for putting a bullet in the unctuous bastard's face, after he'd introduced the serpent by way of its ceramic-bladed fangs.

He was in the private parking lot under the tower where he lived with Alisha. Thirteen floors above him, in the converted loft, his beautiful young wife would be waiting for him. She wouldn't be expecting him back yet. Nice surprise coming, Alisha honey.

He locked his Lexus, the tools of his trade secure in a hidden compartment under the back seat, and walked through the silence and faint exhaust fumes of the underground lot. Other cars were parked in their allotted spaces, but it was a work day and many of the tower's residents were out, so much of the lot was empty. His heels tapped the concrete, the echo a faint drum roll in his ears. It was like the build-up to a shocking turn of events.

He wondered again about his employer's words. Where are you?

He stopped and listened.

Checked the shadows.

Nothing.

Don't get paranoid, he told himself.

He called the elevator, taking out his keys that would allow him private access to the uppermost floor. While the elevator descended with a mechanical roar, he placed his back to the doors and spied back into the parking lot. There was no movement, no subtle sounds of a man in hiding. He exhaled. Turned as the doors swept open and he took a step inside.

The man standing in the elevator held something in his right hand. He was in the process of lifting it.

Rickard jerked, and so did the man.

But then the man came forwards with a sheepish grin on his face.

'Jeez! Don't you just hate it when that happens?' he said.

'Gave me the fright of my life,' Rickard laughed.

The man weaved round Rickard, continuing to

bring his mobile phone to his ear. Over his shoulder, he said, 'Have a nice day, buddy.'

'You too,' Rickard said, as he pushed his key into the override control and flicked it to the extreme right and jabbed fourteen. Rickard's fingers were trembling as he watched the man walk away to his Mercedes.

His shivering wasn't fear. It was a release of the violence that jolted through his system at the man's appearance. The man had been a split second from having his windpipe collapsed before Rickard had checked himself. He didn't recognise the man as a tenant of the building, but he'd never socialised with any of them before so he could very well be. What he had recognised was that the object in his hand was nothing more dangerous than a mobile phone.

The doors closed with a hiss and started the steady climb to his loft. The enclosed space was full of the man's cologne. His back to the wall, he counted each floor as he passed, steadying himself. At twelve he let out a ragged breath as he felt the elevator slow on pneumatic brakes. Unlucky thirteen was never a factor in any hotel, and it wasn't here either. The doors opened on to floor fourteen. He pulled out his key and moved out into the short corridor leading to his apartment. He could hear the soft strains of music wafting along the corridor. Amy Winehouse feeling sorry for herself for being no good. Interesting choice of music, he thought.

He inserted his key in his door, pushed it open silently and stepped inside. He couldn't see Alisha anywhere in the open space of the living room. The music volume was high. Depressing song, but uplifting in its force. He closed the door and stood while the music throbbed round him. He inhaled. He could smell her. And something else. Cologne. It was as musky as it had been in the elevator.

He exhaled.

He wouldn't jump to conclusions. Maybe the scent had been carried in on his own clothes.

That was the plan, but he stalked quickly across the room and threw open the door that led to his bedroom. Alisha wasn't there either. He checked the spare bedroom and the gymnasium, went back into his bedroom and checked the en-suite bath. Empty. Steam and heat still permeated the air. Someone had showered recently. He checked the toilet. Then he backed out of the room and went through into the living room again. The cologne had dissipated, but its memory was still there. He noticed that the door to the roof was unlatched.

A short flight of stairs led up to the roof. He didn't have time for gardening, but in her spare time he knew that Alisha liked to go up there and sit among the palms and fronds she'd imported. She had a deckchair and a little table beside it where she'd rest those damn paperbacks she was so fond of reading. Often she'd have a margarita while devouring her latest book.

She wasn't in her customary position.

Alisha was standing with her arms resting on the rail at the side of the building. She was looking down. Probably watching as the Mercedes was driven away. Her blond hair was loose and hung halfway down her back, damp from a recent shower. She was wearing a sheer gown over equally sheer underwear. Her tanned legs looked just great. One ankle was bent as she rolled her toes in her sandals. He thought about touching that ankle. Snaking his fingers round it. Good leverage for flipping her over the guard rail.

CHAPTER 18

'He thinks that there's a serpent inside him.'

'Another loon,' Rink said. 'What's with all these fruitcakes anyway?'

'I must attract them.'

'It seems like Imogen has the knack, as well.'

'She's lucky to have survived,' I said.

Imogen was shaken but other than a few scrapes and bumps she was going to be all right. The doctors were still trying to identify the drug used to sedate her, and until they were confident that her system was clear of the residue they wouldn't sign her out. The feebie, SAC Hubbard, wanted to conduct a thorough debrief with her once she was released from the hospital and he promised that afterwards he would put a guard on her until this was all finished with. Now that he'd heard from Imogen, Walter and Bryce Lang, he'd come to the same conclusion as I had, that the killer had disguised himself as me, dropped my name to Linden Case, because he'd been trying to set me up for his crimes. Hubbard wasn't so sour, and his raisin eyes held a more genuine twinkle

131

now. Maybe my first opinion of him had been a little misguided: he proved a decent enough sort. Officially, he pulled off the hunt for me, but asked that no one inform the media just yet. Let my enemies think I was still hindered by the law enforcement community and they'd be over-confident and wouldn't be as difficult to find.

I'd been given five minutes with Imogen and it was nowhere near enough. For most of it she'd cried in my arms. Her ordeal had brought every-thing flooding back and she cried for her dead sister; to be frank, so did I. Then she'd told me all about her latest nightmare and I toughened up again. The man who'd taken her had intended murdering her in order to punish me, but first he wanted to sate another desire. He was the worst kind of monster imaginable.

When my time was up, she wouldn't let go of me. I gently extricated myself from her arms. Then I leaned in to kiss her on the forehead, just as she lifted her head to look at me. Our lips brushed. She'd blinked in astonishment, but then had watched me all the way to the door. Something in her gaze made me regret the intimacy, but that was overwhelmed by the sense that it was the right thing to do.

Now we were in Walter's private jet heading south. There was me, Rink, Bryce and Walter, plus two who were the CIA man's bodyguards. They sat behind us, iPod wires trailing from their ears.

'Whoever or whatever he is, he's just the man

doing the dirty work,' Walter said. 'Someone is behind him, and it's important we find out who that is.'

'I'm still going with Abadia,' Bryce said.

'Abadia died.' Walter was sitting in a plush leather chair, one of six in the Lear's cabin. The plane was strictly non-smoking but he had a cigar between his teeth. The cigar wasn't alight. He pulled it out and studied the tip. 'He was cremated.'

Walter's words came back to me from when I'd stopped Tubal Cain: *we don't bury the living*. My seat was directly opposite his and I could stare into his eyes. He returned my look, and the skin at the corner of his mouth tweaked. He aimed the cigar at me. 'You were there, Hunter. Nice and close. Did Abadia look dead to you?'

Schilling's rounds had torn cavities in his chest. Then I thought about Jimena and the small boy and I had to shake loose the image.

'He was dead, no doubt about it.'

'So we forget about him and start looking for who's really responsible,' Walter said. It was a command, and Bryce dipped his head in acquiescence.

Back in the sheriff's office, Walter had offered me a deal. The deal also extended to Rink. Come back to work for him. He'd offered immunity from prosecution, sanction to use deadly force and a reward package for a job well done. Neither of us had given him our answer yet, but it looked like

133

our old controller had taken it as a given. I was prepared to go along with that misconception while his resources would help us find and kill those responsible for murdering my team.

'When we find this lunatic, we'll make him tell us who's responsible.'

'Yeah.' Rink was as loquacious as usual.

I told Walter about our suspicions and how Harvey was cross-referencing spec-ops who had been on active duty in Colombia and who had also trained at Quantico. 'I'm hopeful that it will point us in the right direction.'

Walter didn't question how a retired soldier still had the wherewithal to enter the necessary databases, and I didn't enlighten him. But maybe in future I should negotiate the same deal for Harvey that Walter had offered us.

'We should widen the search,' Walter pointed out. 'Primarily it has been US and British specialists who have trained the Jungla. But other allies have been involved. I'll get our analysts on to it.'

The Jungla are a crack team set up by the Colombian government whose express mission is to eradicate the problem of cocaine production in the country. They're highly trained specialists, on a par with many military special forces, but they're not military, they're police. Where DAS are akin to the secret police, the Jungla are the storm troopers.

One of the bodyguards stood up and leaned over to whisper in Walter's ear. Walter nodded slowly.

As the bodyguard sat down again, Walter said, 'They obviously have a network inside the country. The man who kidnapped Imogen couldn't have been working on his own. A boat, a delivery truck and a plane were all necessary to his plans and he needed others to set that up. We have been looking at this angle. We've found the plane.'

'Great,' I said.

Before I could ask, Walter went on, 'It's at a private airstrip outside of Miami. But the pilot isn't speaking.'

'Give me a couple minutes with him,' Rink said.

'Still won't speak,' Walter said. 'He's dead. A single round to the back of the head. His body was found jammed into a dumpster.'

'So the killer's covering his tracks, eliminating anyone who can identify him?' It didn't bode well for Imogen.

Walter read my meaning. 'I'll contact Hubbard and have her guard doubled. But I wouldn't worry.'

Easier said than done, but I knew what he was getting at. The killer had moved on to the next part of his plan.

'You have people on this already,' I said. 'Where has their investigation led?'

'Initially they were looking at you.'

'But you knew there was no truth in that.' I nodded at Bryce, who'd already confirmed that. 'They must have been looking at others.'

'We have a team on it in Colombia, another at

135

this end. Up until now they've come up empty-handed. We're working with the FBI on this, so they have people on it as well.'

'I don't want any of them getting in our way.'

'It's every man for himself, Hunter. The CIA is on board because of the international implications of this one, but it's the FBI who have jurisdiction because of the federal nature of the crimes.'

'All these G-men running round but still you've come to us.' Rink's words more or less echoed my own thoughts.

'It serves a purpose, Rink.'

'As usual,' Rink said.

'As usual. These people are threatening us all. I'm as valid a target as Hunter or Bryce. It's in all our interests if we put a stop to them. No trials, no chance of them getting away, no retribution.'

'Sounds like we don't have official sanction after all,' I said.

Walter jammed his cigar between his teeth, speaking round it like one of those gangsters in old black and white movies. 'You have *my* sanction. The paperwork can be sorted later.'

Basically what he was saying was that we were going to be his personal assassins. Ordinarily I'd have told him to stick his sanction, except this time I was happy with the arrangement. While the killer was still out there, Imogen and others were still in great danger. It would remain that way until the killer, and whoever was guiding him, was stopped for good.

CHAPTER 19

Alisha screamed all the way down, hit the pavement and then was silent. Her corpse was sprawled like a stringless marionette, surrounded by a growing pool of blood.

At least in Rickard's mind, that was the way things happened.

In reality he eased up to her and wrapped his arms round her waist, pulled her tightly to him and nuzzled her neck. 'Hi, babe.'

Alisha stiffened for the briefest of moments, but then, having realised who had caught her in a hug – or more likely because it was what was expected of her – she melted back against him, purring as he kissed her all the way down to her shoulder. Rickard released her, turned her round slowly and looked down at her upturned face. He kissed her gently on the tip of her nose.

'I wasn't expecting you,' Alisha said.

'Couldn't stay away any longer,' Rickard said. 'Did you miss me?'

'Like crazy.' Alisha searched for his lips. Rickard held back, teasing her, making her go up on her toes before returning the kiss. She smelled of soap and shampoo. No trace of cologne.

Got to get a hold of myself, he thought. The man in the lift had been nowhere near his apartment. Nowhere near *his* Alisha. She was too afraid of him to bring other men to their bed. She did not know what he did for a living, but she suspected what was in his mind and what he was capable of.

He'd taught her well what would happen if ever she betrayed him.

Paranoia is an ugly, debilitating thing. It was that damned phone call he'd made that had planted the seed of doubt in his mind. *Where are you, Rickard?* His failure to see through his plan to rape and then dismember Imogen Ballard had been unforeseen by both his employer and him. *I expect more from people working for me.* Yes, he thought, and so do I. I also expect more from the people round me.

'What are you doing out here, babe?' Rickard peered over Alisha's shoulder at the Miami nightscape. It was still warm, and he could smell exhaust fumes and garbage on the trembling breeze.

'Oh, nothing. Just thinking.'

'About me?'

Alisha stirred and looked up at him with her big blue eyes. 'Who else?'

He didn't reply, but strong cologne was in his olfactory memory. He wound his fingers in her hair. 'I've been thinking about you as well.'

Without releasing his grip, he led her back inside and down the short flight of stairs. Amy Winehouse had moved on to croon over someone called Mr Jones. Rickard pictured the guy as a man in a suit, with short greying hair and a mobile phone in his hand. He turned off the CD as he passed then steered Alisha towards the bedroom.

When he came back out of the bedroom he was on his own. Alisha was taking her second shower of the evening and tending to the welts on her arms. When he'd entered her he'd been thinking of Imogen Ballard and he wasn't gentle then, either. Behind the bathroom door she was sobbing and that pleased him.

Naked, he stood in the centre of his apartment, surveying it with a perfectionist's eye for detail. Alisha had kept the room almost as spick and span as he demanded. The pile on the carpet was crushed down in places and there was a copy of a Stieg Larsson novel open on the table next to the settee. He'd make sure that she tidied up once she was done making herself pretty again.

He was very hungry. He went to the refrigerator and scanned the contents. Settled on drinking milk direct from the carton, then grabbed a handful of roast chicken from scraps on a plate. He wolfed the food down. Voracious. But, then, he thought whimsically, he was eating for two. He cleaned the grease from his fingers on a kitchen towel, then shoved it into the wash basket.

He was padding back across to check on Alisha's

progress when he heard something out of place on this private floor of the building. It was the faint crunch of a heel on grit. Most people would have gone to the front door to peer out through the peephole, but Rickard didn't act the way others did. He knew without checking that someone with no right to be there was in his hall. He ducked into the bedroom, pulled on his trousers and unsnapped the ceramic knife from its holder. No time for shoes or shirt. He moved to the en-suite bath. Alisha had her back to him and the scratches on her back were livid. He unsnagged her gown from where she'd hung it and threw it to her. 'Put that on. Lock the door and don't come out until I tell you. Whatever you hear.'

Alisha's face elongated, but before she could say anything, he pulled the door closed. He heard her throwing the bolt: another alien sound to this apartment.

Then he moved back across the room. He cursed the fact that his gun was locked inside his car, but shoved the thought aside. His knife would be enough until he could arm himself otherwise.

On his way into the apartment he'd been distracted. He had not armed the intruder alarms. He hadn't thrown the locks on the doors. OK, so there'd be less damage when they came in; maybe that wasn't so bad after all.

They.

He was sure that there'd be more than one.

Only a series of unforeseen events had caused the messup in Maine, but his employer knew how good he was. More than one man would have been sent to dispatch him; to close down the trail that might lead back to its source.

He avoided the urge to peer out the peephole. He'd heard of assassins waiting until the peephole became shadowed, when they would press a gun to the lens and fire a round through the orbital socket and into the brain. Maybe that was just in the movies, but Rickard wouldn't fall for it. He moved instead for the door leading to the flight of stairs to the roof. He'd been remiss in locking that door too, and the one on to the roof.

Although he owned the uppermost floor, building regulations meant that there had to be ample escape routes in the event of an emergency. He could lock the elevator by way of his key, but access could be gained via two fire escapes: one was inside the building and one outside. The internal one had already been breached and so too, he guessed, had the metal stairwell on the side of the building. Against fire regulations he'd installed a gate that he kept padlocked, but anyone with a pair of bolt croppers could be through that in seconds.

Rickard moved quickly up the stairs.

He paused at the door to the roof, listening. He couldn't hear anything but that didn't mean they weren't there. He placed the knife between his teeth, and dropping low so he was supported on

141

his fingers and toes, he crawled out. Alisha's imported plants were both a blessing and a curse. They gave him cover as he made his way over to a service conduit, but they also blocked his view of anyone coming on to the roof via the fire escape.

In the shadows of the conduit, he crouched, feeding the knife from lips to hand. He didn't have to wait long. Beyond Alisha's palms he caught movement. Big man in dark clothing, beanie hat pulled low. The man was holding a handgun. Judging by the length of the barrel it wasn't silenced, which Rickard found odd. Impulse was to attack the man immediately, stick him in the throat and open his carotid artery, but Rickard waited.

A second figure came over the balustrade and on to the roof. He too was dressed in dark clothing and packing a gun.

So, at least three of them. Rickard weighed the equation in his mind. Three men, possibly more, with guns. Him with a knife. No problem.

The men made their way across the roof warily, eyes scanning. They paused to whisper to each other, then one of them lifted something and pressed a button. To his credit he didn't talk into the radio, just depressed the button in a prearranged sequence. Giving the all clear to the others downstairs.

The men paused at the open door, but then one of them shrugged and used the barrel of his gun to tease it wider. Bad form, Rickard noted: you never compromise your weapon like that. Then one of them went down the stairs. A few seconds later – a final check over his shoulder – and the second man followed into the stairwell.

Rickard moved after them.

Dressed only in trousers, chest bared, he felt primal, like an unstoppable force of nature.

At the entrance to his apartment both men had halted. One of them nudged open the door and took a quick look into the room. The one with the radio quickly keyed the send button. Almost immediately, there was the sound of the front door crashing back on the jamb as someone powered their way inside. From the bathroom, Alisha shrieked loudly.

Good girl, Rickard thought. Her screech attracted the attention of both men in the stairwell. One of them moved forwards, his friend's hand on his shoulder.

Rickard came down the stairs silently.

His knife whispered across the throat of the man at the back. The ceramic blade was sharper than any made of steel and opened him up from ear to ear. The man dropped as though pole-axed. Rickard stood on him as he fell, used him as a springboard and went after the leading man. At the same time, he was looking for and assessing the others in the room. There was only one more.

Goddamnit! I knew it!

Coming in through the front door was the man from the elevator. He'd changed his suit for a windcheater and jeans, and the mobile for a radio and a handgun.

So he wasn't Alisha's secret fling, but an assassin scoping the terrain before making his assault. His reaction when surprised by Rickard's appearance as the elevator doors opened now held more sense.

It took Rickard all of a split second to analyse the facts and to act on them. The elevator man was surprised by his sudden unexpected arrival and he was a second too slow in lifting his gun. His shot missed and put a hole in the wall a foot behind Rickard's moving form. Rickard caught up with the big guy in the beanie hat just as the man was turning round. He jabbed his knife under the man's jaw, the blade cutting through the tissue and piercing his tongue. Not an immediately fatal stab but one designed to cause debilitation of the senses and a lot of blood. Without stopping, Rickard ducked under the man's arms and came up behind him. Elevator Man had no clear shot. Rickard jammed his blade into his human shield just below his floating rib, not deep enough to reach the liver, but enough to induce shocking pain. He released the handle and grabbed the gun out of the man's lifeless grip. Considerately the big man had already racked the slide, putting a bullet in the firing chamber.

Realising the inevitability of the next few seconds, Elevator Man was already turning, hoping to make it back out the door where he could at least use the cover of the door jamb to return fire.

Should have just gone for it, Rickard thought. Then he shot the man between his shoulder blades as Alisha screamed a second time. The dead man made it to the doorway, but he was face down, his arms outstretched.

In the same moment Rickard disengaged from the big guy, plucked free his knife then shot the man in the side of the head. The guy went over sideways and landed on the carpet, his blood fanning out on the usually pristine flooring. Rickard grimaced at the mess because he was fastidious about those kinds of things. But not now. The apartment was no longer his; he was moving out immediately.

CHAPTER 20

'Tell me what I want to know or I'm going to put you out of business. Permanently.'

'You're gonna shoot me, Hunter? Do it. See how much information that gets you.'

'I'm not going to shoot you. Not yet.' With my left hand I grabbed Kenneth Wetherby by his throat, sinking my fingers tightly each side of his oesophagus, and hauled him backwards over his own desk. A laser printer and a stack of papers were knocked flying and scattered over the floor. Then I dumped Wetherby on his back on the threadbare carpet. I slipped my SIG back into my waistband and bunched my right fist. 'First I'm going to beat the living shit out of you.'

I'd only been in Miami a little over twelve hours and already I'd made a few new enemies and re-acquainted myself with another. Rink had also earned himself some anger, but the man he'd knocked cold wasn't voicing an opinion just yet. Rink stood threatening another two men with his fists while I roughed up their boss.

I loosened my grip on Wetherby's throat enough

that he could answer my questions. 'Tell me who it is.'

'Are you fucking insane? Coming here like this, you've just earned yourself a bullet with your name on it.'

'I've already got someone trying to kill me,' I snarled. 'And you know who it is. Tell me, you fuckin' arsehole.'

'I don't know, goddamnit! Whoever it is, he's not on my books.'

I grabbed him off the floor. But only for as long as it took to slam him against his office wall. Wetherby slid back down to the ground, his arms covering his head. I kicked him in the pit of his stomach: should have gone for his balls, but I was more interested in intimidating him than putting him fully out of commission.

Wetherby's pinched gaze went to his two friends. 'You gonna help me here? What the fuck am I payin' you idiots for?'

The two men glanced at their fallen companion. They'd just witnessed Rink putting the biggest of them out with a single back fist strike to his jaw. Maybe they thought it was a lucky punch – maybe they had a little sense of duty – because they launched themselves at Rink. Bad mistake.

Rink ducked the first man's cumbersome over-hand punch, came up and blasted the point of his elbow into the man's face. I heard his nose break all the way from the other side of the room. Even as he was falling, Rink caught the second man's right arm, pivoted so that the elbow was hyper-extended and pulled the man forwards and off balance. In the next instant Rink reversed direction, folding the man's wrist back on itself. In an aikido dojo, the recipient of such a move would flip out of the joint lock and avoid injury – but this thug was no aikido specialist. He went the wrong way and his wrist and elbow snapped as loudly as had his friend's nose. Rink released the man's arm. It was useless now as a point of control. The man went to his knees cradling his busted arm. He was screaming. Rink whipped a shin kick into the man's head to put him out of his misery.

Rink turned and fed his thumbs into his belt. He grinned at Wetherby. 'What are you payin' those idiots for?'

I caught Wetherby by his collar and pulled him up. He was out of wind from the kick to his guts and I wasn't going to give him an opportunity to catch his breath. I spun him round and threw him backwards so that he landed in his office chair. The chair skidded a couple of feet before he banged against the office window overlooking MacArthur Causeway. We were only nine floors up the fifty-storey building but the road still looked a long way down from here. I followed him and caught him by the chin, twisting his head so he got a skewed look out over Biscayne Bay. 'Unless you want a one-way trip down there, you'd better start talking, Wetherby.'

'This has got nothing to do with me. I don't even know why you'd think that.'

There were reasons. Harvey Lucas had come up with a couple of names from his search of ex-military with sniper training. They were on Wetherby's books. Then there was the fact that Wetherby had once tried to recruit me, except the kind of people he supplied muscle to were the type I usually banged heads with. I'd told Wetherby to stick his job where the sun didn't shine and as a parting shot Wetherby had told me I'd made a big mistake crossing him and his outfit. There had to be a reckoning. Sooner or later I'd have been calling on Wetherby again, so this visit had turned out to be quite fortunate, just a little sooner than anticipated.

'We know that your business is just a front,' I said. 'You can masquerade as a security consultancy, but the truth is that you supply mercenaries to those willing to pay your fees. It's well known that you're indiscreet about the kind of people you serve.'

'Listen to me, Hunter. Doesn't matter what you think . . . *this has nothing to do with me.*'

'Stop screaming like a bitch,' I snapped. 'Now, we have two names: Jean Shrier and Ben Le Duke. Where are they now?'

'I'm not telling you that. I have a duty of care to those who work for me. You can't expect me to divulge classified information?'

'You will unless you fancy takin' a dive through that window,' Rink said.

I grabbed hold of his chair and dragged it back to his desk. The computer had avoided the crashing fall to the floor that had cleared the rest of his work space. 'Bring up their files, Wetherby.'

'Don't need to. Neither of them are who you're looking for.'

'Where are they?'

Wetherby sighed. His eyes went to the loose pile of unconscious men littering his office. 'You didn't get this from me, OK?'

'Just get on with it,' I said.

'Shrier's got a gig protecting a Hong Kong businessman. Le Duke, he's over in Nigeria protecting an oil field. I told you . . . they're not involved.'

I pulled out a photograph supplied to me by Walter.

'Him?'

'Don't know the guy.'

'Look again,' I ordered. 'He was a pilot. Miguel Suarez. Did he work for you?'

Wetherby picked up on the past tense.

'He's dead?'

'A bullet in the skull kinda has that effect on most folks,' Rink said. His words were loaded and Wetherby picked up on that too.

Wetherby shook his head. 'Still don't know him.'

'You don't seem to know very much,' I said. 'For such a top guy as you think you are.'

He shrugged and I could see he was beginning to gather a little composure. 'I told you that all along.'

'You're still a prick.'

He gave me a sickly smile. 'You're wrong about me. In every way.'

'Just hope that I never find out otherwise, Wetherby. If I have to come back again, things will be much worse next time.'

I punched him directly in his face, aiming to cause pain rather than unconsciousness. Let him dwell on that for a while.

We left Wetherby tending his bleeding face. Back outside the office building we stood side by side and looked out across the water towards Miami Beach. It was early in the morning in late February, and here in the subtropics it was unseasonably warm, but I felt very cold.

'Dead end,' I said to Rink.

'It was always a long shot. At least you taught Wetherby not to fuck with you again.'

'Maybe.' I clapped him on the shoulder. 'Except if they're going to be frightened of anyone, I guess that it'll be you. Those were some good moves back there.'

'It don't take much to slap down a few pussies like them,' he said, playing it cool.

'I'm surprised you broke that guy's arm. You're not usually as brutal as that.'

'You didn't see the switchblade he pulled outa his pocket?'

'Too busy with Wetherby,' I admitted.

'Here,' he said, handing me a black-handled flick knife – old type, like something out of *Rebel without a Cause*. 'Memento for you.'

I slipped the knife into my jeans pocket. My mobile was ringing and I pulled it out.

It was Harvey.

'How'd things go with Wetherby?'

'Waste of time,' I said. 'We're going to keep looking, though. Couple other names in Miami I want to look up.'

'You might want to get yourselves back here first.'

'Problem?'

'No. A possible lead.'

'Who?'

'Not who: what. Walter's liaising with the local PD on what looks like a hit that went wrong. The mark turned the tables this time.'

'He's dead?' Part of me wished that was true, but another part was full of regret. After what he'd done to Imogen I still wanted my day with the killer.

'That's the thing, Hunter. It looks like the man you're after was the mark this time. He killed three men as quick as you like.'

It was just an expression, but in reality I would have said quite the opposite. I didn't like this turn of events one bit.

CHAPTER 21

'Dry your eyes, Alisha. People are starting to notice you.'

Sitting looking at his wife, Luke Rickard wondered what to do with her. Right now she was baggage that he could do without. Ordinarily he fed off the fear in her, but now it was too damn inconvenient. Her snivelling had grown so annoying that he considered doing her right there and then in front of the breakfast crowd in the diner.

She used a napkin to dab her eyes, lifting her sunglasses one lens at a time. 'I . . . I'm sorry, Luke. I just can't get those men's faces out of my mind.'

Rickard took her wrists in his hands. 'Don't speak about that here.'

'When can we speak about it? You haven't answered any of my questions.'

Rickard took a less-than-surreptitious look round. At a nearby table an elderly man was eyeing him back over the top of his coffee mug. Rickard stared directly at the man until the guy got the message and returned his attention to his eggs and ham. Rickard turned back to Alisha. 'We can talk about it later.'

'You've been saying that for hours.'

Rickard lowered his voice. 'They wanted to kill me, Alisha. Would you rather it was me lying dead back there?'

Her face went rigid. 'No. Of course not. But . . . well . . . maybe they weren't coming to kill you.'

He expelled a breath. 'Why else would men with guns sneak into our apartment?'

Alisha turned her face away. It was only a momentary dipping of her chin, but Rickard caught it. It was a sign of deception. He recalled the smell of the lead assassin's cologne and how he was sure that it had lingered in his apartment on his return home. Maybe he'd been scoping the terrain a little closer than was expected.

'You knew him, didn't you, Alisha? The one with the grey hair?'

Alisha shook her head with just a little more exaggeration than was necessary.

'He was in my home,' Rickard said. 'You must have let him in.'

'I didn't . . .' Her voice was a child's whimper.

'What lies did he tell you?'

'He didn't . . . I mean . . . he wasn't there.'

Rickard was still holding her wrists. Not in a supportive manner now.

'Luke,' Alisha said. 'You're hurting me.'

He squeezed harder. 'He came to my apartment, Alisha. He spoke to you. What did he say?'

'N . . . othing.' Alisha tried to pull her wrists free, but Rickard wouldn't let her go. 'I haven't ever seen him before, Luke. I promise.'

Staring at her, Rickard thought back. There were a few details about the entire episode that he did not like. Below his private floor, he didn't have sole right to the elevator, so it wasn't unusual to find another person on board, but the manner in which the man had reacted when the doors opened and he found Rickard standing there was a little over the top. He hadn't expected Rickard to return home so soon. He'd been mid-conversation on his mobile phone: someone warning him that Rickard was back in town. *Where are you, Rickard?* Had the man been talking with his employer, or was he having a final conversation with someone much closer to home?

Then there was the fact that the man had gained access to his private floor without causing damage. Rickard had first thought that he had entered via the fire escape door, which made sense as he'd need a key to manage the elevator. The trouble was, although the fire escape gave easy access from the hall outside his apartment, to gain egress he would need to have punched in a code that only he and Alisha knew. There were ways round electronic locks, but Rickard had checked the dead man and found no devices.

Then there was the door to his apartment. As the man had entered on cue with those coming from the roof, the door had been thrown open and had crashed against the wall. But Rickard had an eye for details, and thinking back, he couldn't remember any sign that the latch had been broken loose. He hadn't thrown the locks, but a key was still needed from the outside. That or a lock-pick, but that had been conspicuous by its absence as well.

One more point was troubling him, but that was something to be considered later.

'I believe you, honey,' he said. He slowly released her wrists, transferred his fingers to her hands and patted them gently. Beneath her sunglasses she was blinking very fast. He caught flashes of her blue eyes like strobes going off.

'You do?'

'Of course, babe. I love you, don't I?'

'I love you too. It's just that . . . well . . .'

'What is it?'

'The way you killed those men . . .'

'I was lucky.' He smiled at her. 'No. That isn't true. There was something very precious to me that I just had to protect. You, babe. I didn't think about my own life. I just didn't want them hurting you. Given that kind of motivation, no one could have stood in my way.'

Up until now she'd been as pale as death, but colour pinpricked her cheeks. But she wasn't flattered. She had picked up on his lies. And by the way she withdrew her hands from under his fingers, she knew that he knew it too.

'Now, babe, I've been thinking. We can't go to

156

the police over this. I don't trust them to find the people responsible for sending those men. Others might come. We have to get out of here first. Go somewhere safe.'

Alisha nodded at him, even though by the trembling of her jaw she was buying none of it.

'What I want you to do is go to the restroom back there. You need to freshen yourself up. Fix your hair and make-up. You're so pretty other people can't help looking at you, but I don't want them to see your tears.'

He made a play of searching his pockets. His hands came out empty. 'I must have left my phone in the car. Here,' he said, reaching for her purse, 'give me yours. I need to make a couple of calls, find us somewhere safe until we can figure this thing out.'

He took out her phone and passed the purse back to her. Alisha stared at the phone like it was a lifeline.

'Go on now.' Rickard nodded towards the back corner of the building. 'Go make yourself pretty again.'

Alisha got up, looking unsteady on her feet. Those expensive Prada shoes weren't the best in which to make a run for it, but they matched the rest of her designer ensemble. Training shoes would have attracted undue attention. Rickard had told her to wear them. Now he wasn't so sure it had been his best idea. They made her legs look as long as a boring week. Two or three men in the diner watched her progress towards the restrooms, including the old guy from earlier. She was so beautiful that she was distinctive. She'd be recalled, and so would the man who was with her.

'Can't let that stop me.'

She's baggage. That's all. He should have left her in the gutter where he'd found her, instead of wooing her and making her his wife. He'd allowed his desire to totally control a woman to overwhelm his best senses. In hindsight she'd always been a liability, and one that could ultimately have led to his downfall.

As soon as she was through the restroom door, he opened up her phone and checked her incoming calls. Withheld numbers. He checked her outgoings. Withheld numbers again, but one of them coincided with his arrival back at the parking lot at his apartment. He closed the phone and placed it in his pocket alongside his own phone. He flicked some dollars on the table to pay for the food they hadn't touched. Took out his ceramic knife and cupped it in his palm.

He stood up and walked towards the restrooms.

Just baggage, he thought again.

CHAPTER 22

We didn't get access to the crime scene but it didn't really matter. I'd seen enough death in my time to know what it would be like. The blood and the stench; the frailty of flesh versus bullets and blades; the surety that, somewhere down the line, I could be found in similar circumstances.

I waited in our car with Rink and Harvey while Walter and Bryce spoke to the detectives on site. The Miami PD had turned out, but so had the FBI. There were CSI techs and people from the coroner's office. And there were a large number of reporters from the press and TV. The latter were our greatest inconvenience. Once we attracted an inquisitive look from a reporter who wandered off and came back carrying a BlackBerry. He was searching the screen then peering back our way.

'Better move,' I said to Harvey, who was our driver. Last thing any of us wanted was for the reporter to start yelling that there was a cop-killer in their midst. The police on scene might act first and ask questions later.

Harvey started up the Chrysler and pulled out

past the cordon of yellow tape. I averted my face as we passed the reporter but in my peripheral vision I could see him doing a double take between me and whatever was on his screen. But then we were gone and the moment had passed.

Harvey took us to a nearby strip mall where there was a choice of eateries. We entered the nearest diner and ordered coffee. I got the largest, most potent mix I could find on the menu then asked for an extra shot of espresso. Over the last few days what little sleep I'd had was in snatches of a couple hours here and there and I was in need of the caffeine kick-start. We sat in a booth where we could watch the entrance – old habit – but where we were out of earshot of any of the other customers. I called Bryce and told him where we were.

'So what do you think all of this means?' Harvey was referring to the identities of the men found dead in the apartment.

'The cops are looking at it as a hit gone wrong, but I don't think that's the case,' I said.

'Me neither,' Rink said. 'I know Del Chisholm. He's been in the PI game for years, and he's always played things straight up. Can't see him heading a hit team. No way.'

'There's no denying that he went to that apartment expecting trouble,' Harvey pointed out. 'All three of them were armed.'

'Two of them only had Saturday Night Specials.' Rink was referring to the .38 revolvers the men were packing. 'Not the weapon of choice of most assassins.'

I gulped coffee. 'That's what's troubling me the most. If you'd been hired to take out a pro-shooter, you'd take something along that was sure to put him down.'

'There were three of them, don't forget, one of 'em had an automatic. Maybe they thought they could take him out between them.' Harvey sat back and ran a hand over his bald head. He didn't believe that any more than we did, and was only adding conjecture to the pot to get the thought processes bubbling. He took a sip of his coffee, then said, 'Unless they'd no idea who they were going up against. Sorry – rephrase that – *what* they were going up against.'

'Stands to reason.' Habit made me glance round the diner. People had their heads down spooning food into their mouths, or were reading the morning papers or texting on mobile phones. No one was looking our way. My eyes lingered for a moment on a man and woman sitting at a table near the exit door. The woman was a beauty. The man was ten or more years older than her. Nothing unusual about that. I turned my attention back to my friends. 'My guess is that there was some other reason for them being there. They had no idea who this man was or what he was up to. What does that leave?'

'They were after someone else,' Harvey offered.

'Or they went there at someone else's bidding,' said Rink.

'How well did you know Chisholm?'

Rink see-sawed his head. 'Well enough to nod in passing. I knew him more by reputation than from sharing a beer, if that's what you mean.'

'What did he specialise in?'

Rink was a PI and so was Harvey, but even they had different slants on what that entailed. There were different niches in the market that PI outfits concentrated on. 'Far as I know he was happy with low-end cases. You've seen *Cheaters* on TV, right? That's Chisholm's usual type of gig.'

'So it'd be a big step up for him to go to something like this?'

'Yup.'

'You think he was after this guy 'cause he was playing away from home?' Harvey laughed under his breath at the irony of it.

'Maybe that's all they thought Rickard was up to.' I'd already learned the killer's name. And that of his wife. 'I don't think that Alisha knew what he was involved in. Maybe she didn't trust him, thought he was up to no good, put two and two together and got five. She called in Chisholm to put some meat on her suspicions.'

'Makes sense,' Rink said. 'But that doesn't explain why Chisholm takes two heavies along and breaks into the apartment.'

It didn't.

'Sounds like an extraction,' Harvey said.

We nodded along with him.

'Alisha wanted out and asked Chisholm to help.

162

They thought that by waving a gun under his nose, maybe intimidating him by way of the two heavies, Rickard would be a good little boy and back down.'

'Big mistake,' I said.

'The worst kind,' Rink added.

I looked again at the couple by the door. The woman got up and walked in our direction, heading for the restrooms on our left. She was a fine-looking woman. She was wearing a wedding band, and I looked away. Her man had stood up and turned our way too. He started forwards, digging in a pocket. Then he diverted to the cashier's desk and paid their bill. He rested an elbow on the counter and talked with the young female teller. From where I sat, he was flirting with the girl. A job in the making for the likes of Del Chisholm, I thought. The woman came back out of the restroom and joined the man. They shared a joke with the girl at the till, then the woman gave the man a playful thump on the shoulder and they walked out the diner together.

As they went out the door someone caught my eye on the pavement outside. We were expecting Walter and Bryce, but it wasn't either of them. It was the bloody reporter who'd been watching us outside Rickard's apartment building.

'Trouble, guys.'

The exit door had swung shut, but now it was opening again.

'Move.'

The way we scattered might seem an overreaction

to a reporter finding us, but there was more to it than that. The man wasn't carrying a BlackBerry this time and he wasn't alone. He stepped into the diner lifting a compact Uzi sub-machine gun. His three friends following him in were as heavily armed.

I went one way while Rink and Harvey went the other. It suited me: these men were after me, not my friends, and I preferred that their attention focused only on me.

'Get down,' I yelled at the barista at the espresso machine.

I went over the serving counter in a dive, knocking the young man to the floor just as the bogus reporter let loose a hail of bullets at us. The machine was cut to shreds and scalding hot coffee splashed all round our bodies. The young man tried to claw his way from under me, but I pressed him down, even as with my other hand I went for my SIG. More Uzi chatter filled the room, joined by the screams and shouts of the customers trying to flee the chaos. Glass shattered and tinkled. Someone yelped in pain. Then I heard the crack of a handgun; either Rink or Harvey firing back.

I scrambled away, using the serving counter as cover. I made it all the way to the cashier's till and found the young girl crouching under the counter. A minimum wage she would put up with, but not this. She looked at me, the gun in my hand, and screamed in terror.

I bobbed up. Got a snapshot image of the place and didn't like it one bit.

There were people clambering over tables in an attempt to escape, while three of the attackers laid down an indiscriminate barrage of bullets. One old man caught a cross-stitch pattern of bullets across his lower back and went down. A woman was huddled over, cradling her bleeding face in her hands. I could see neither of my friends. Then there was no more time for looking.

The fake reporter spun my way.

He pulled on the trigger of his sub-machine gun, letting out a wordless roar. The rounds blasted chunks from the counter and I rolled away. Suddenly the cashier went silent.

Bastard, I thought. That was all, but it was all the galvanising I needed. I bobbed up again and fired a single shot.

The round hit the 'reporter' in his open mouth. Must have severed his spine the way he dropped like a stone. It was too clean a death for the murderous son of a bitch.

Had there been time I would have checked on the girl, but there wasn't. I was pretty sure the Uzi had cut through the counter and also through her. Terrible, but there was nothing I could do about that now except avenge her. There were still three killers in the diner and they would murder other innocent people if I didn't do something about it.

I came over the counter supported on one hand,

already shooting with the other. I hit one man in his shoulder and he dropped his machine gun. He turned towards me and I shot him again, this time in his chest. Two down, two to go.

The remaining killers were mid-way down the diner. Most of the uninjured customers had managed to get out the way, but there were those who'd already been shot who either lay crying or were very silent. I saw one of the killers shoot a young man who was trying to hide under a table. There was no reason for it. The other killer was blasting a circular table that had been tipped on its end. It looked like a waste of bullets, because, other than pocking the heavy Formica they weren't getting through. I caught a glimpse of movement behind the table, a dark hand holding a Glock. Then I saw Harvey lean all the way out and fire off a close-knit grouping of shots at the killer. Two of the bullets struck the man, once in the gut, once in his right thigh. It didn't kill him outright, but it was enough to stop him shooting for a moment. Rink jumped up from the other side of the table and he fired and this time the man did go down. Half his brain now decorated the ceiling.

While all this was happening I wasn't standing idle. I was already running at the final man – the one who'd killed the man under the table in cold blood. I should've just shot the bastard, but I preferred that he hurt before he died. Plus, I wanted answers.

Who were these bastards, and why had they

come after me? What connection had they to Rickard and the person guiding him? Had they been sent by Wetherby?

Rink and Harvey held their fire. The man probably heard me coming, because he turned my way, bringing round the Uzi.

I kicked the gun away and smacked the butt of my SIG directly in the centre of his chest. The man was slightly shorter than me, lighter in build, and I was able to force him backwards with the pressure of my gun against his sternum. He checked against a partition that was smeared by someone else's blood and the first thing he did was drop the Uzi and swing his bunched fist at my head. He was a player, for certain.

Blocking his fist with my gun hand, I used the angle to bounce my next blow to the side of his face. My SIG furrowed skin from his cheek, but he was already moving. He brought his knee up at my groin and I barely avoided it, but then he snapped a kick into my shin. Hurt like hell, but it would take more than that to stop me. His elbow sought my chin and I ducked. Then I kicked him in his shin. He rode the blow, looped his foot round the back of my knee even as he thrust at my chest with the palm of one hand. I should have been tripped, but he hadn't caught me off guard; I stamped down with my trapped leg, centring myself, marrying my balance to gravity. Palming his arm away, I slashed my right elbow into his ribs, swung up outside his arms and back-fisted him across the nape of his neck in a classic move from Kenpo karate.

The man staggered away from me and the added weight of the gun in my hand made my next blow telling. I cracked him in the centre of his forehead and he went to his knees.

Grabbing a fistful of his hair, I jerked his head back, bending it painfully on his neck while I jammed the SIG in his left eye socket. 'Who sent you?'

'Fuck you!'

'You want to die?'

'Fuck you, man . . .'

'Tell me who sent you, goddamnit! Was it Wetherby?'

'Who the fuck is Wetherby?'

'Who was it then?'

'I ain't saying nothing. Shoot me. It's better than what I'll get if I talk.'

I almost did pull the trigger. I thought of his cold-blooded murder of the man under the table and I would've been justified if I had shown him as little regard. But I didn't. I just whacked him across the temple with the barrel of my gun and left him unconscious on the floor.

'Maybe Walter's boys can make him talk,' I said as my friends came up.

The howl of approaching police sirens sounded like a pack of banshees was descending on us.

CHAPTER 23

'Alisha. Honey? Are you about done in there?'

Rickard used the tip of his knife to push open the door into the ladies' restroom. He recalled his admonishment of the man on his apartment roof doing something similar with his gun, but this time it was different. Alisha was no threat to him, not in a physical sense.

He was in a short passage that led from the dining area, three doors all on the right-hand side. The first was the men's room, the second the ladies'. The final door had proved to be a janitors' closet. No exit. The air smelled of bleach and there was a sickly underlying aroma of urine and perfumed tissue paper.

Peering into the alien territory of a ladies' room, he checked out the porcelain sinks, pot-pourri in little bowls on a shelf, two stalls with the doors closed tight. He walked further into the room, his shoes squeaking on terracotta tiles. 'Alisha?'

No answer came. But this wasn't uncommon. Often Alisha would play at being coy.

He crouched to scan the floor under each stall.

One of them was definitely empty, and when he touched the knife to the door it swung inward silently. Next he tried the second door and it resisted him. He crouched again. 'Alisha, honey . . .'

He straightened up.

He considered kicking open the door, but realised there was no need for that. Instead he went into the vacant stall and stepped up on to the toilet bowl. He looked over the dividing wall into an equally vacant space. No, not true: Alisha's stiletto-heeled shoes were standing where she'd left them. Rickard grunted, looked at the narrow window where she must have crawled out. It had a security feature, a bar that allowed the window to open only partially. The gap was little more than ten inches wide. No way that a fully grown man could have squeezed through, but a slip like Alisha wouldn't have had much difficulty.

He should have been enraged, but Rickard felt cool about it, mildly amused even. Alisha had actually pleased him by showing this resourceful side, although it meant she had escaped him. Her betrayal had already harmed him; running off didn't make that much difference. He thought maybe this was even better. He had planned on murdering her right there in that stall, but that could have proved an inconvenience. It would be difficult getting out of the diner unnoticed if he was covered in her blood. Better then that he caught up with and killed her somewhere less public.

He stood down from the bowl, exited the stall and headed for the door. When he pulled it open he came face to face with the old man who'd taken too much interest in him earlier. The old man squinted at him, then at the sign on the door.

'You know that's for the girls, don't you,' he said.

By way of answer, Rickard dropped his left hand and gripped his own genitals. 'Yeah, and so is this.'

The other wasn't impressed by his lewdness. 'I've been watching you, boy. I just knew you were a strange one.'

Rickard merely smiled.

The old man tried to peer past him inside the room. 'That lady of yours, where's she at?'

'What's it to you?'

'You upset her, you did. I want to check she's OK.'

Rickard moved aside, swung his left thumb over his shoulder. 'Go on then. Check all you want.'

The old man frowned at him, placed a hand on Rickard's chest to press him further out of the way. 'Your posturing don't frighten me none, boy. Now get outa my way.'

He rapped on the door as he peeked inside. From this angle the toes of Alisha's shoes could be seen under the gap in the door. 'Lady? You OK in there, lady?'

'You think I'm strange?'

The old man turned and found Rickard standing directly behind him. Rickard had invaded his personal space and he took a half-step back.

Rickard said, 'What I find strange is how the girls get sweet-smelling pot-pourri while us guys get nothing. Do they think they're better than us?'

The man shook his head at the absurdity of Rickard's comment. He glanced again at the closed door. 'Lady?'

'Something else that's strange,' Rickard said, 'is how some senile old fool thinks he has the right to stick his nose into other people's business.'

'It became my business when I saw you hurting that lady. You're a bully, but you don't frighten me.'

'Is that so?'

'No, boy, you don't. Not one bit.' The old guy shoved at him, moving nearer the closed door. 'Hey, lady? No need to be afraid of this one!'

'You don't happen to have a son by the name of Joe Hunter, do you?' Rickard asked. 'He's a self-righteous prick just like you.'

Rickard grabbed the old man, spun him round and ran him at the sinks. The man's hip jammed up against one of the porcelain bowls, but Rickard continued to force him backwards, his left hand clamped over his mouth, stifling his yell. Rickard's right hand pistoned in and out, jamming his blade repeatedly in the man's stomach and ribs. He hissed through his clamped teeth as he watched the light go out of the old man's eyes. It wasn't a quick death for him; more punishment.

The man slumped to the floor. Rickard reached into one of the bowls of pot-pourri and scattered some of the perfume-laden petals on the man's dead body. It didn't cover the rank smells of blood or the man's voided bowel.

That done with Rickard finally peered at his reflection in the mirror above the sinks. For the most minuscule of moments he thought he saw a nimbus of light round him, but then it was gone. He leaned over the dead man so he could get closer to the mirror. Briefly he stared into his reflection, one eye at a time. The mirror was smeared by a hand print, the greasy stain giving the illusion of colour that wasn't really there.

He looked down at his jacket. It was liberally splashed by the dead man's blood. So much for not getting messy. Rickard shrugged out of the jacket, took it over to a sanitary wear disposal bin and shoved it through the flip lid. He wiped his blade and his hands on a perfumed tissue which he flushed down a toilet. He walked out of the room nonchalantly, making his way towards the exit. Behind him a woman got up and headed for the restroom. In seconds the screaming would start.

He tossed dollars on the table as he passed, didn't want a cashier chasing him into the street. Then he was out the door and walking quickly away from the diner.

He heard a wail, not from someone discovering the dead guy, but the distant sound of emergency sirens. Across town something major was happening. Good, he thought, a diversion while he got away from here and took up the chase for Alisha.

He found his car and clambered inside, started the engine. About to pull into the street, he had to wait while a squad car rocketed by with its lights flashing, the cop lying heavily on the siren to clear a way through the traffic.

It looked like all available response vehicles were heading downtown.

On a whim, he followed.

His apartment was in the same vicinity that all the police cars were converging on. Alisha could wait for now; he wanted to know what was happening.

He wasn't fully sure how he felt when he arrived at the scene.

It was still a couple blocks short of where his apartment was, but if his instincts had been correct this latest emergency was tied to him, only in a way that he couldn't quite fathom at first.

Parking outside the cordon of police cars he watched in fascination as the officers jostled for covering positions behind their cars, circling the front of a diner similar to the one he'd just left. It was obvious that a gunfight had recently taken place, judging by the pockmarks in the front window of the diner, and the people scrambling outside and collapsing on the street in shock and dismay.

The glare of the morning sun made seeing through the diner's windows impossible. The sounds of the gun battle had stopped and now only the faint cries of the injured could be heard.

Distantly he caught the strident calls of other responding police cruisers. Or maybe they were ambulances for the injured. Should get out of here, he thought. But curiosity held him in place.

His decision to wait and see what transpired rewarded him within seconds. Three men walked outside, showing empty hands. Between them they dragged a fourth man who was unconscious or dead, whom they threw down at the feet of the police.

They were an unusual-looking trio: a giant Asian-American, a tall African-American and – in Rickard's opinion – a walking dead man.

CHAPTER 24

There was no avoiding a trip to the local police precinct house this time. We'd been involved in a shoot-out where three hitmen and three members of the public had died. There were four others seriously wounded and a couple with minor injuries from flying glass. And there was one unconscious killer.

We chose to take our Fifth Amendment right until Walter arrived. The cops weren't happy, but Walter had us kicked loose under rules governing the arrest and incarceration of active CIA agents. We made nobody any the wiser. As soon as we were off the record, I told the homicide detectives what I knew about our attackers. It wasn't much. I didn't mention a possible connection to Wetherby because I wasn't sure that there was one. Then we went and collected our weapons from where they'd been stored after they were seized as evidence. That raised the anger level tenfold, but there was nothing the cops could say or do at the time.

I seriously pissed off the lead investigator, Lieutenant Jonah Hawke, a big, red-faced detective

176

with twenty years under his belt, when I asked to look at the file concerning the murders at Luke Rickard's apartment. I actually thought that he was going to swing for me and we had an awkward moment before Walter stepped in and made the request official.

'I only want a look at the suspect's face,' I told the cop.

'Can't help you. He's not on record. He wasn't the type to keep snapshots either; there were no photographs of him lifted from his apartment.' Hawke was more than a little smug in the way he announced this. 'We've checked his prints. They've come up in connection with a few unsolved crimes, but that's it. The name Luke Rickard's bogus. As of now he's designated as an Unknown Subject. The guy's a goddamn ghost.'

He will be if I get my way, I thought.

'What about his physical description? You must have canvassed the other tenants in the building by now.'

Hawke held my gaze steadily. 'Physical description, huh? I'm looking at it.'

The cop's words struck me deeply. I was already aware that Rickard had disguised himself in order to set me up, but now I wondered just how far he'd gone in stealing my face. It wasn't a nice thought considering that there was someone out there who was the total antithesis of me, but who was my identical double. I walked away from Hawke before he noted the shaking of my hands.

Our Chrysler had been abandoned back at the diner when we'd been taken in. We had to grab a taxi to go and collect it, and none of us spoke about what happened on the journey over. Then we went to a hotel room to hook back up with Walter and Bryce. Neither of the CIA men – active or retired – was there yet so we made ourselves busy gathering our own information. Harvey was as good at digging up data as any other person involved.

Up in Maine, the police there were a little ahead of the game. Probably it was because SAC Hubbard was pushing them for answers. Harvey brought up a couple of digital photo-fits formed from descriptions given by Imogen and by the boathouse owner who'd disturbed Rickard. There were subtle differences between both images, but they were enough alike to be the same man. Lieutenant Jonah Hawke was right: Rickard did have a resemblance to me. Slightly darker in the hair and definitely darker in the eye, but there were more similarities than there were disparities. For the purpose of incriminating me, Rickard had gone to a lot of trouble, maybe as far as having cosmetic surgery. It was an uncanny feeling looking at my evil twin.

Rickard was a fucking abomination.

I had been hoping to recognise the man's face, but not in this way. Part of me had even wondered if Jesus Henao Abadia had risen from the grave and was tormenting me like a vengeful spectre from my past. I'd even wondered about Jack Schilling; I heard he'd killed himself, but I never saw the body. It sounds like a stretch, but Martin Maxwell had faked his own death before going on a rampage as the serial killer Tubal Cain, so I was ready to investigate any angle. But this man was neither Abadia nor Schilling. I'd never seen him before in my life – except for in a mirror.

Harvey pressed buttons on his laptop. He brought up more pictures and then tapped the screen. 'These two are Jean Shrier and Ben Le Duke. It looks like Wetherby was telling the truth about them. They're deployed to Hong Kong and Nigeria respectively.'

A simple glance at the men's mugshots told me that neither of them was the killer calling himself Luke Rickard. To all intents and purposes we were back to square one. Except for one thing.

'What about his wife?'

I'd no sooner asked the question than Walter and Bryce came in the room. Walter's bodyguards waited outside in the hall. Maybe they should have followed him in because Walter looked like he'd need their help to aid him in standing, he was so washed out.

He sat down on the edge of one of the twin beds and let out a ragged breath. He glanced over at Bryce, who didn't look that much better. 'You don't know how well off you are. I wish I could spend my days sitting beside a river watching the salmon avoiding my hook.'

'Retirement's not all it's cracked up to be,' Bryce grunted. He sat down on the other bed.

'I take it that things weren't easy with the cops this time?' I said.

Walter grunted. 'There are complaints running all up and down the spout. The chief's threatening to take this all the way to the governor, to Congress if needs be. Do you think there's a chance you can keep things a little lower key in future?' He looked at me, Rink and Harvey in turn.

I spoke for the three of us. 'Not a chance, Walt.'

He shook his head, laughing softly. It had been a pointless request anyway. I wasn't the only one who had the feeling that things could get much worse. 'I can't blame you guys, I suppose. It wasn't you who went in and shot up that place with machine pistols. It took a lot of convincing the chief, though. He said they wouldn't have shot the damn place to pieces if you guys hadn't been in there in the first place.'

'He has a point,' I said.

'You probably saved a lot of people in there.'

'Doesn't make me feel any better.' People had died: a terrified guy under a table; the young girl hiding behind the cashier's desk, among others. Their deaths weighed heavily on my soul, regardless of how many others I might have saved. Seemed my life was destined to be filled with *collateral damage*; something that would never sit well with me.

Walter waved me down, then searched his

pockets for his cigar. He thumbed the cigar into his mouth and sat staring into space.

'Haven't you anything else for us?' I asked.

'Only something very strange.'

I shared a glance with Rink.

Walter shook himself. 'There was another murder across town from where your gunfight took place. Someone was butchered with a knife.'

We were in a huge city with its fair share of crime. Knife crime wasn't so unfamiliar in Miami – just like anywhere else – but Walter was right: it was too much of a coincidence to be unrelated. Once again I wondered about what had become of Alisha Rickard.

'Elderly male,' Walter began, allaying my first fears. But his next words put me right back in the same place again. 'Knifed to death in the ladies' restroom. Rickard's fingerprints were at the scene.'

'What about his wife?'

'No sign. Only her shoes were found. It looks like she might've crawled out of a window.'

'She's running from him?' So, it seemed that Chisholm and his team had been involved in an extraction when Rickard had killed them. They'd come for the woman and found something much worse than they – and maybe even his wife – had ever anticipated.

'Looks that way. I've got someone over at Chisholm's office going through his records to see what we can find out.'

'Who's looking for the woman?'

'The police are. But at the moment they've more on their plate to worry about.'

I took out my SIG and ejected the depleted magazine. Fed in a full one and racked the slide.

'I'm going out.'

Walter looked at me. 'We have work to do here, Hunter.'

I was never that great a detective. Every man in the room was a far better investigator than me. Let them find out who Rickard really was, then point me in the right direction. That's where my special skills lay. I was more concerned with finding Alisha before her husband did.

'I'm going out,' I repeated.

CHAPTER 25

This corner of Liberty City wasn't a safe place to hide for someone like Alisha Rickard. It was ironic that Rickard had originally found her in this neighbourhood, but since she'd been with him she'd undergone a major transformation. Now she simply did not fit. For one, her clothing and salon-perfect hairdo picked her out as someone no longer from these parts. Her designer purse, and the probable weight of cash or credit cards she carried within it, marked her as an easy target for any of a number of people willing to take it off her. Then there were the men who watched her with the eyes of pit bull terriers. They thought only two things about her: flesh for the taking or an obvious police set-up. Neither boded well for the young woman.

Except Rickard would not allow anyone to harm her.

She was his alone to hurt.

He'd ditched his car after retrieving his weapons, replaced it with an unremarkable Ford Taurus he'd hotwired, and taken up the hunt for his wayward wife. It was a decision that had come easy to his mind, even if it meant giving up his opportunity to finish Joe Hunter once and for all. When he'd seen Hunter at the diner he'd been momentarily confused: judging by the commotion, Hunter and his two friends had been involved in the gun battle that had torn the place apart. Yet – confused or not – he'd also seen his chance to blast Hunter to death. The only thing that had stopped him was his desire to finish things with Alisha first. The hit on Hunter was professional, about the money, but Alisha's betrayal had stung him where it really hurt: his ego. Hunter had been taken into custody by the cops arriving at the scene, but not in the manner befitting a suspected cop-killer. So had the big plan been a waste of time as he'd suspected? Rickard was optimistic enough to think that Hunter would be free within hours and another opening would present itself to take him out. So, straightening things with Alisha came first.

A quick check of the area behind the strip mall showed that Alisha had only one feasible escape route. He found the window where she'd crawled out of the restroom in a service alley that was blocked at one end by a large steel fence, beyond which construction of another building was taking place. The fence hadn't been breached. Even if there had been a way through, the land beyond was full of trenches and semi-erected foundations from which jutted steel wires: unwelcoming terrain for a barefoot young woman. She had to have left the alleyway the same way in which he'd entered.

He backtracked, searched for dusty footprints on the pavement and saw a couple of fresh scuffs next to a public telephone kiosk. A quick glance inside the booth showed a prominently displayed notice advertising a local taxicab company. Rickard dropped quarters into the slot, hit the redial button and asked for a cab.

A few minutes later his driver arrived. Rickard made enquiries with the driver, money changed hands and Rickard knew where Alisha had headed to. He thanked the driver, then shot him in the nape of the neck. After taking back the cash he'd handed over, he quickly left the area, found the Taurus and took up the chase.

And now here he was in Liberty City, a suburb of Miami, watching from a distance as Alisha limped towards a house on a street where gangstas stood brazenly on a wooden porch watching for police spies. Alisha passed them with her head down, ignoring the remarks made by the men who added colour to their comments by way of actions. She knocked on the front door.

From his hiding place Rickard watched two men in baggy jeans, training shoes and white vests push in either side of her. Both men were fit and lithe and their muscular arms were covered in gang tattoos. One of them had a handgun jammed down the front of his jeans. The other held a pistol in his hand and he pushed it into Alisha's stomach. Rickard wasn't worried that the man was going to shoot; it was all just part of the macho bullshit these idiots enjoyed. He saw Alisha's chin come up and she must have said something harsh, because the gunman stepped away, raising his arms. The second man stopped pawing her at much the same instant. Rickard nodded to himself.

Rickard knew now why she'd come here. The return of the prodigal girlfriend.

Although he did not like to think that other men had been with her before him, he'd once made her tell him about her past boyfriends. She had resisted, but only until he'd twisted her hair and demanded to know the truth. She'd listed a couple of high-school boys who he had no interest in, then a guy who'd been more into computer games than he was into her. She'd mentioned in passing a man who'd picked her up in a bar who she dumped very quickly when it turned out he was a local cocaine supplier. Rickard had watched her as she'd talked about the young thug and she couldn't disguise the lie. Then she'd moved on to more recent men, one night stands who were up for having a hot girl on their arm but not for a meaningful relationship. The one that had stuck in his head was the only other person who could be described in the same bad-boy mould as he: the cocaine dealer from Liberty City. Rickard had considered paying this man a visit – putting him out of Alisha's thoughts for good – but hadn't got round to it yet.

Now it looked like he was going to get his chance.

The front door of the house opened and a tall, slim man appraised Alisha with a nonplussed expression. He studied her clothing, the body beneath it, and then an eyebrow lifted as he saw her bare and dusty feet. He nodded, then jerked his head, directing her inside. As Alisha moved past him, the man stepped forwards on to the porch and said something to the two guards. All three of them took a long look round. Rickard hunkered down in the seat of his car. The tall man then went inside.

Rickard started the car and drove away.

He took a couple of left turns, and drove down the next parallel street. The houses here were similar to the one where Alisha had sought sanctuary: single-level homes made from wooden beams and planks, peaked roofs, kids' toys or abandoned vehicles left to rot in the front yards. Occasionally the houses looked like their occupants were attempting to stave off the destitution of the neighbourhood by planting shrubs and flowers to brighten their gardens. But these were the exception to the norm.

Rickard drove by the house back-to-back with the drug dealer's place. Guards were placed there as well. He suspected that other spotters further afield would be watching for unmarked police cars. He continued on to the end of the street and this time took a right. Up along on the left he noticed the burnt-out shell of a house. He turned the Taurus into the garden, manoeuvred round a

187

pile of shattered and scorched furniture piled on the sun-bleached lawn, and parked under a tree. A rope hung from one of the branches, frayed at the end. In some neighbourhoods this would have been a child's swing, but here he guessed that a large dog would once have been tethered. He checked his weapons, gun and knife, then climbed out of the car.

As soon as he walked out from under the tree he saw trouble. A teenage black kid on a cycle was wheeling circles in the road. The boy watched him with baleful animosity. The kid had made him: not necessarily as a cop, but as someone who had no business being here. Rickard walked towards him, feet crunching through brittle grass. The boy immediately rode away, watching Rickard over his shoulder. He stopped fifty yards away. Standing with his legs splayed either side of the cycle he watched Rickard turn and head off away from him. When Rickard next checked, the kid was gone. Rickard picked up his pace. There were no guarantees but the kid could simply be a local child with the inherited distrust of strangers. Or maybe he was a spotter for another dealer. Place like this there would be more than one outfit peddling narcotics, he thought. It was still a good idea to get to the target house before the alarm was sounded.

When he rounded the bend on to the street running parallel to the one he wanted, two men were waiting for him. They were the guards stationed in the garden of the house behind the one Alisha hid in. Rickard saw that one of them was holding a mobile phone to his ear – probably getting an update from the kid on the bike. They were scrawny men, like rejects from the *Jerry Springer Show*, but they were packing guns so they were still dangerous. Going for Rickard was the fact that they thought he was a cop. They could intimidate and run him off without fear of immediate retribution.

Rickard would have smiled, but that would maybe warn them that he wasn't what he seemed. He walked directly towards them, pulled out his handgun and shot them once each in the chest. Both men fell in the street and he barely gave them any further notice. As he approached them he snatched up the mobile phone from where it had fallen in the gutter.

'You should've kept your mouth shut, boy! If I see you again, you're dead.'

Rickard dropped the phone and stamped it to ruin. Then he scooped up the men's handguns and slipped them into his belt. He had a feeling he was going to need the firepower. From a distance he heard shouting. Likely it was the kid on the bike hollering the alarm to all who would listen.

Rickard knew that to be successful he had to move quickly and decisively. Crash through their defences, cut them down. His greatest weapon was that punks like these prepared to defend themselves against a dawn raid by the cops, or drive-by shootings by rival gangs. They would never have seen anything like him before.

He ran into the garden where these men had been standing moments before, and round the side of the house. The shooting must have alerted those inside the house with Alisha, but he had a feeling that their reaction wouldn't be to mount a defence against someone coming to kill them; they'd be too busy flushing the evidence of their illegal pursuits for that.

Whenever the Miami Dade Special Response Team conducted a raid on one of these crack houses, they came in force. An armoured truck nicknamed a Bear Cat would spearhead the raid, men in flak jackets clinging to the sides, before rushing forwards behind a shield wall to smash down the doors. Non-lethal flash-bang grenades or tear gas would be launched inside the building, and then the armoured officers would go in sweeping and clearing each room in turn. The occupants would be arrested while evidence was secured. It was conducted with military precision. In situations like that, the dealers had their own routines. Usually they laid down their weapons, got down on their bellies with their hands on their heads and waited for the inevitable. Rickard was hoping that their ingrained reaction would play out this time. But – if it didn't – well, so be it. He'd plenty of guns.

Gun in hand, he swept the rear garden for any

other guards, but there were none. A high wire fence separated this property from the dealer's house, but there was a gate in one corner where the guards could come and go. The gate was locked, but it was no taller than Rickard. He sprang up, caught the top with his left hand then swung over it. He landed on both feet facing the back wall of Alisha's hiding place. Junk lay all over the yard, some of it so old it was partially embedded in the earth. There was an engine block from some ancient vehicle, an oil drum on its side, a stack of building blocks from an abandoned project. There was also a dog. It was a Rottweiler-mix, a huge, bulky monstrosity that launched itself at him with slavering ferocity. Before it reached him the dog came to a sudden halt, checked by the heavy chain round its neck. It strained at the length of its tether, jaws snapping as it barked with a madness close to insanity. Rickard shot the dog in the head.

Then he was moving again.

One of the tattooed thugs who had first met Alisha came round the side of the house. He was bouncing on the balls of his feet, undecided whether to run or to fight. He was expecting a cop, and Rickard's appearance threw him long enough for Rickard to snap his gun up and shoot at the man. His round struck high in the man's right shoulder and knocked him down. The man screamed curses: he knew now that Rickard was no cop. Rickard leaned over him, and with his ceramic knife slit his throat, shutting him up.

The most obvious play would be to take out the remaining guard, but Rickard could not see him. Maybe he'd fled inside at the first sound of gunfire. Maybe he'd high-tailed it to avoid arrest. Whatever, he wasn't apparent. Rickard turned his attention to getting inside the house. This, without doubt, would be the most difficult and dangerous part of his attack plan. He could hear alarmed voices sounding from within the house, three distinct ones.

He spied at the door on this side of the house. It was a heavy timber door with the original glass boarded over, surrounded by a porch with a flat roof. Knowing how these places were protected, there could possibly be an inner door of steel or wire mesh to thwart easy access by the police. Next he checked the windows. They were boarded over as well. He'd need a crowbar to pry his way inside. So he didn't bother with either. He stuffed his weapons in his belt, then jumped and grabbed at the roofline, swinging up and on to the porch. From there it was an easy jump up to the actual roof of the house, and he clambered up the eave so that he was on the roof's apex. From there he had a panoramic view of the surrounding streets. They were as deserted as a ghost town as people with better sense hid themselves from harm.

Ordinarily, houses that proved impregnable at the ground level were never as heavily fortified against an attack from above and Rickard was counting on this being true here. He readied himself, gripping tightly as he prepared to swing down and kick his way through the small attic window he'd noticed earlier.

He took a deep breath, as though about to dive into deep water. Then, in the next instant, he let it out again. He straightened up, staring in disbelief at the car roaring along the street towards him.

CHAPTER 26

When the urge to get moving takes me I've no option but obey. It didn't matter that I had no firm plan of action in mind, just that there was yet another woman out there fleeing for her life from a maniac. I had to do something. I was sick of running away, or playing catch-up, and it was about time I put Rickard on the back foot for a change.

'I need some air. I'm coming with you.'

I didn't argue with Rink. We come from the same school of thought and I knew that he felt exactly the same way as I did.

Harvey stayed behind. He was as good as any analyst that Walter had access to, and would be able to help the CIA men coordinate the search for Rickard from the hotel room. 'If anything comes up, I'll call,' he promised.

We took the Chrysler and went back to the office block from where Ken Wetherby ran his operation. Wetherby wasn't pleased to see us. His face had swollen where I'd given him the parting shot, but hadn't begun to bruise yet. Maybe he thought

I was going to give him a matching lump on the other side.

'OK, take it easy, Wetherby. I'm not here for trouble this time.'

The two men that Rink had beaten up were conspicuous by their absence. Probably down at A & E, I assumed. Only the third man, the first to feel a clubbing right from Rink, was there, and he looked no easier than Wetherby did about us showing up again. His hand crept towards a gun in a holster on his hip. Rink gave him a slow shake of his head and the man's fingers drifted from his gun and dug awkwardly in his trouser pocket.

'Can we have a little privacy?' My question was more to spare the young mercenary any further discomfort, and offered him a way out without him losing any more face.

'You OK with that, sir?'

Wetherby scowled at the young man, then waved him out of the room. When the man was gone, Wetherby grunted. 'Not as if he was going to be much help anyway.'

'Like I said, we're not here for trouble this time.'

Wetherby slumped in the chair behind his desk. I noticed that his papers and laser printer had been returned to their rightful place, but it didn't look like much work had been done since our last visit.

'What *are* you here for, Hunter?'

Propping myself on the corner of his desk, I folded my arms over my chest and looked down at him from a position of dominance. 'I want your help.'

There was nothing of a request in my voice. Wetherby could refuse my order, but I didn't think he would.

'I told you that none of the people on my books were involved. What more do you want from me?'

'Tell me about Luke Rickard.'

A strobe of emotions flickered across Wetherby's face. The one that took root was fear. He looked down at his desk, focusing on the untidy pile of documents.

'Don't deny that you know him,' I said. 'You'd be wasting all our time.'

'I don't know him.' His voice was barely above a whisper. He looked up at me and then across the room to where Rink lounged against a wall. 'But I know of him.'

'You tried to recruit him?'

'I don't approach people. They come to me.'

'You came to me,' I reminded him. It was why I'd come back to clear things up with him. Most of the people on his books were all above board, applicants who were recruited via his website: usually they were soldiers returning from war with no hope of going back to a humdrum civilian lifestyle. After Wetherby put them through a rigorous selection process he sent them off to a training camp that he ran in the Everglades. Those that passed the course were shipped off to be close protection bodyguards to business people or minders to celebrities. But then there were other contracts that Wetherby negotiated – for these he sought and recruited *specialists*. Basically he was pimping murderers. It was this arm of his business that I'd taken umbrage with.

'Contrary to what you think, I don't deal with criminals,' Wetherby said. 'When I found out about Rickard, I immediately severed all communication.'

'He's that bad?'

'And then some.'

I shared a glance with Rink. Returning my attention to Wetherby, I asked, 'So how is it that no one seems to have heard of him?'

'He's that good at what he does.'

Imogen Ballard had thwarted him twice, and now so had his wife. 'So why's he making all these mistakes all of a sudden?'

'I can't begin to imagine why,' Wetherby said.

'Tell me about him.'

Wetherby didn't have to rack his brains very much and I wondered if he'd been considering Rickard as the shooter the first time we were here. If he'd said so then maybe a couple of his men wouldn't have needed a few days off to recuperate.

'First off, he's not really called Luke Rickard. That's an assumed identity.'

I'd already come to that conclusion. 'So who is he?'

He shrugged his shoulders. 'No idea.'

'How did you hear about him?'

'Some of the other men were talking about him. They'd heard stories from out in the field. It seems that Rickard is a freelance assassin who works for those willing to pay the highest fee.'

I thought about a man I'd killed last year. Dantalion: a freak who went by the name of a fallen angel. He had been a freelance assassin too. He didn't work through the usual channels either.

'What's his background?'

'I'd guess that he was military.'

'His prints aren't on record, so that rules that out.'

'Assuming that he's an American, you mean?'

He had a point. Both the FBI and CIA had been concentrating on their own databases. I made a mental note to have Harvey cast the net further afield. 'From what you were able to dig up on him, who are the people he's worked for in the past?'

'You know how difficult something like that is to substantiate. I can only tell you about the rumours . . .'

'So tell me.'

'Paramilitary groups mostly. He's been in Sierra Leone, Darfur, Bosnia, Lebanon and Gaza.'

'What about closer to home?'

'Yes, there are rumours that he's done select work here before.'

'OK. Next question, Wetherby, and I want the truth. You tried to recruit him. Who was it for?'

'I can't disclose any details about my clients. You can't expect me to do that.'

Rink picks and chooses his time to speak, but when he does his words mean something. 'Unless you want us to have another falling out, we do.'

Wetherby threw his hands in the air. 'You realise what my name will mean if this gets out?'

'Shit?' Rink asked.

'Exactly.' Wetherby ran his hands over his face. He probed the spot where I'd punched him earlier and it was a catalyst for his anger. 'Why the hell should I tell you anything? I don't owe you a goddamn thing.'

'No one will get anything from us,' I said. 'You have my word.'

He made a noise in his throat like he was being strangled. The anger went out of him like he was a deflating balloon. With resigned deliberation he leaned down and slid open a drawer in his desk. It was a good place to conceal a gun, but I was at an angle where I could see that wasn't the case. He pulled out a folder and opened it on his desk.

'I don't have a name, just a number. Maybe you have better resources than I do and can trace it.'

That was a given fact but I made him none the wiser. I borrowed a pen and jotted the number on a slip of paper that I pocketed. 'So what were your feelings?'

'About what?'

'About the people who wanted Rickard to work for them?'

Wetherby rolled his head on his shoulders. 'Like I told you: I don't use criminals.'

'But you were happy to make the introductions between the two parties?'

Wetherby's pause told me that I'd struck a nerve. 'It will please you to know that I got nothing from the deal. Yes, I put Rickard in touch with them, but that was it. I wouldn't have it any other way.'

'Did you know why they wanted him?'

Wetherby sat there straight-faced. 'No.'

Standing up I looked down at him with a face equally flat. 'We'll leave things at that, then.'

'You didn't get that from me, right?' Wetherby nodded at my pocket where I'd slipped the note. I patted him on the shoulder. 'As long as we're good now.'

'We're good,' he said.

Rink came up and dug a twenty-dollar bill from his pocket which he placed on the desk. 'Buy your guys a beer when they get back from hospital, Wetherby. Forget all about us. Everything will feel so much better afterwards.'

We left him staring at the tip and made our way outside.

'He's lying, Rink.'

'Of course he is. But he's also a self-serving asshole. I think the phone number's genuine, though. Why'd you think he gave us it?'

'My guess? He's greedy. Like he said, he didn't get anything from the deal. Maybe this is his way of getting something he wants.'

We'd just made it back to the Chrysler when my mobile phone rang.

Without preamble Harvey gave me an address over in Liberty City. 'Cops are already on the way there now, so you'd better hurry if you want to get Rickard first.'

Rink drove so I could get the rest of the details.

'It's him for sure?' Over the roar of the engine, I had to shout and Harvey sounded a little breathless in his need to tell me the facts.

'Without a doubt. Someone murdered a cab driver from the same company that picked up Alisha Rickard from behind the mall. Just before he died the cabbie radioed and asked his co-worker where he'd taken his fare and then that was it. It looks like Rickard has gone after his wife.'

I felt a jolt of adrenalin.

'OK, Harvey. We're on our way.'

Rink's normal mode of transport is his Porsche, and he drives it like a pro. He made no exception behind the wheel of the Chrysler. We blasted across town, hoping to beat the cops heading to the same location. Going for us was the fact that we were good to go while the police would be planning their approach. Directions would be shooting back and forth over the radio as the chain of command was organised. Their orders would be for a covert approach, the area surveilled and then a plan of action drawn up. The Miami Dade Special Response Team would be mobilised, negotiators brought in, the FBI on standby. All of that would take time. In comparison our plan was simple: get there quick and kill Rickard even quicker.

CHAPTER 27

Standing on the peak of the roof, silhouetted against the skyline, Rickard should have felt exposed, but he didn't. He felt invincible. Like he was a god towering over the mortals below him. He watched the car speed along the street and then come to a skidding halt. His first thought was that this was an unmarked police cruiser responding to the shots fired, but the two men leaping out the car weren't cops. They were tough guys with guns, but no one of any consequence to him. They were just a couple more of the drug dealer's gang called in as reinforcements. They would die as easily as every other man that got between him and Alisha.

The two newcomers took cover behind the car, and he could hear them swearing in that clipped manner of gangbangers. From further along the street came another curse and Rickard realised where the other guard had gone. He was hunkering down behind some trash cans. Unless they were full of building bricks, the cans were no cover for the man. Rickard braced his feet each side of the roof, while with both hands he drew a gun from his belt and flicked off the safety catches.

He fired seconds before the men below him did. His intention wasn't necessarily to kill, only to keep them down and unable to get a clear shot at him. His guns rolled a double volley, one at the car and one at the trash cans. The men's return fire was disjointed and badly aimed, but even so he was too obvious a target where he stood. His thoughts of giants and invincibility could only last as long as was pragmatic. A bullet drilled the roofline next to his right foot and he felt the sting of splinters in his shin. He crouched now, and depleted both guns at his twin targets. A yelp came from the man behind the trash cans but it sounded more a shout of alarm than that of someone taking a mortal wound.

Rickard dropped both empty guns; they clattered down the roof and thumped to the ground. Rickard heard none of that because he was already reaching for the third gun: his own. He fired repeatedly, swinging his aim from one target to the other. Then, in a practised move, he dipped his hand into a pocket and came out with a full magazine. He ejected the empty one from his gun, pushed the other in and racked the slide. Fired one round. All in the space of two seconds.

In the next two seconds he grabbed the roof at its apex and swung down and kicked through the window. To the men below ducking for cover it would have been like he'd done a disappearing act. He forgot all about them for now. Unless they intended climbing the roof they were stuck outside and no immediate threat, so he went after those who were inside. The room he found himself in was a cramped and jumbled space, little more than a peaked crawl space filled with junk and old furniture. There was no bulb in the ceiling fixture, but enough ambient light was coming through the shattered window for him to negotiate the junk and make for the exit door. He didn't observe niceties, just booted open the flimsy door and leaned out and fired his gun in a short volley of three rounds. The man he'd expected to find waiting on him didn't disappoint: he took two of the bullets in his chest and went down screaming. An illegal machine pistol clattered on the floor beside him. Rickard quickly stooped and grabbed the gun in his left hand. Distractedly he noted that the gun was a Czechoslovakian Scorpion – the old type that still used .32 ACP rounds. It was a popular machine pistol throughout the world; he only hoped that there weren't any more in the house.

Earlier he'd counted three male voices from inside – the mathematics were subjective: maybe there were others who were more disciplined and could keep their mouths shut, so he had no idea how many he was going up against. He didn't care because the Scorpion kind of levelled the playing field in his favour.

He was in a short hallway with a flight of steps

leading down to the living space: a bottleneck if he didn't move. He went down the stairs at a run and ducked into the nearest doorway he could find, the machine pistol extended in his left hand. Without looking he unloaded a burst of fire into the room, sweeping low where people would naturally crouch. The bullets churned the furniture, and struck flesh. Rickard barely flicked a glance at the man lying dead behind a grimy settee. He turned and looked back out into the hallway. Whispering voices filtered to him from rooms nearer the back of the house. He quickly scanned over his shoulder and saw that the main entrance was indeed barricaded by a steel door with a single slot cut in it through which money would be exchanged for drugs. The reinforcements couldn't come on him that way. Immediately he went along the hall. On his right was a kitchen area. Of course this house wasn't where the drug dealer lived – he'd have a fancy-assed pad somewhere – so the kitchen wasn't used in its conventional sense. He saw counters with weighing scales and stacks of polythene bags and there were traces of white dust on many of the surfaces. No way any of these guys were going to call for police assistance, not with that amount of evidence lying round.

There was also a guard.

He was a big man with a network of scars all over his face. He looked like he'd been in a fire once over and had suffered greatly. That's what comes of cooking your own crack, Rickard thought, as he fired at the man. The guy threw himself down behind a counter and returned fire with an old-fashioned Colt revolver. His shots were blind, and Rickard dodged away from the line of fire even as he rushed towards the man. He leaned over the counter and drilled the man full of bullets, watching the man's eyelids flicker as each round punched holes in his upper body. Then there was no more reaction and the man slumped down.

Rickard left him there and went back out into the hall.

That made three dead inside the house; which meant there had to be more than he'd originally reckoned. None of the men he'd killed looked like anyone that could have snared Alisha's attention.

The next room he checked was a bedroom. The only thing that told him so was the presence of a stained mattress propped up against a wall. The rest of the room was devoid of home comforts and it seemed to have become a repository for old newspapers and girlie magazines.

On his left a closet door stood open. He glanced inside to ensure nobody lurked in the dark space and found it empty. Moving on, he found the door that let outside where he'd clambered up on to the porch. The door wasn't as heavily fortified as the front door, having only a beam nestled in brackets to hold it firm. He paid it little attention, choosing instead to move immediately to the remaining room. Whoever was inside had fallen silent now, but he guessed that was where he'd find Alisha and her ex-boyfriend.

He wanted a personal reckoning with Alisha. He'd teach her what it meant to betray him, but first he wanted to show her the true value of her ex-lover. He wanted to kill him personally too, although not at the expense of walking into a trap. He shoved his gun into his waistband and transferred the Scorpion to his right hand. He braced his wrist against his hip, then let loose the full fury of the gun, firing through walls and door alike. The bullets cut through the flimsy barricade and into the room beyond. Then he dropped the gun and burst open the door and followed inside. As he did he pulled out his ceramic blade and thumbed it open.

He was surprised by what he found: a lone man sitting with his back to a wall. No sign of Alisha. The man was dressed a little snappier than the guards he'd already killed, and he was young and handsome with a full head of wavy hair. He was the tall man who had met Alisha at the door. He was lightly tanned, but some of the colour had drained out of his features, making him look slick and pasty. Rickard glanced at the bullet wound in the man's gut. The man had one hand clamped over it to staunch the flow of blood, while his other hand still gripped the stock of a Glock 18. The man rolled his head up to stare at Rickard and though he was in agony he still mustered enough hatred to make his eyes flash.

Rickard lunged in quickly and jammed a heel down on the man's gun hand.

'Where is my wife?'

The young man twisted, trying to free his gun, but Rickard only pushed down harder with his heel.

'I asked you a question!'

'Fuck you!'

'Once more: where is my wife?'

'Gone, asshole. You're too late.'

Rickard heard movement behind him and recognised it as someone removing the beam from the brackets on the side door. Alisha making a break for it. He scolded himself for not checking behind the damn mattress in the bedroom he'd passed, but it was too late for recriminations now. Alisha wouldn't get far before he could catch her again. He had time to make this man sorry for sticking his nose in his business.

'Then that means you're no use to me any more,' he said. He slashed with the knife and opened up the man's throat. It was a calculated cut that sliced his trachea wide but missed the major blood vessels. The man would die, but it would take minutes and he had no hope of screaming for help.

Rickard leaned down and took the Glock from the man's fingers. He stepped slowly off the pinioned hand and watched as the man grasped at his throat. The gut shot was forgotten as he tried to stem his life from ebbing away.

Rickard turned away, left the man to die in silent torment and went back into the hall. Glancing into the bedroom he saw that the mattress was now lying on the floor – so Alisha had been hiding there – and the door to the outside was wide open. Again he felt a trickle of admiration that Alisha was proving more worthy than he'd ever have thought, but it was only fleeting. It wouldn't stop him from making her scream in agony. He went outside, switching the Glock to automatic fire.

CHAPTER 28

'There are reports of shots fired,' Harvey said. 'You'd better haul ass, guys. Cops are responding to nine-one-one calls, so they'll be going in hard.'

'Not far now,' I said. I put away my phone and checked my gun.

Rink drove the Chrysler like a crazy man, laying his hand heavily on the horn to clear a passage through traffic that seemed to have been sent by Rickard's guardian angel to thwart us. We lost a mirror and gained a few stripes of gleaming metal in the paintwork, and more than a couple people screamed obscenities at us as we squeezed by. But we were still ahead of the blue lights and sirens heading in the same direction.

We got on to surface streets that gave us a cleaner run into Liberty City, and Rink now lay heavily on the throttle. We shot through at high speed and I was only happy that it was a school day and there weren't children out playing in the road. Keeping one eye on the way ahead, I counted off the blocks on my right.

'Two blocks,' I indicated and Rink nodded in acknowledgement.

Approaching our turn Rink decelerated rapidly, engine compression slowing the vehicle, then took a turn that had the tyres stuttering on the paved road. Then he gave the vehicle everything and we shot like a bullet towards the next intersection.

'Next left.' Rink already knew the way but I felt like I had to say something. Again he took us through a ninety-degree turn at speed, and then it was a straight run along a street that could never be described as a tourist destination. The houses looked different, but I could have been in the council scheme where I'd grown up. Rickard had brought further trouble to a neighbourhood with enough of its own.

Rink braked.

Ahead of us was a scene like a Western gunfight, only here the cowboys had automatic handguns and machine pistols instead of six-guns. I took in the scene in an instant.

One man in a vest and tattoos had his arm propped over the top of a wooden fence. He fired but his shots were ill-timed and most of them got nowhere near where he was aiming.

Two others were crouching behind a car, firing randomly towards the front of a wooden house.

Lying on the road behind the two gunmen was a young woman. She had her arms folded over her head and was screaming in terror.

My attention snapped from the woman to the man walking out as bold as a man of steel from the side of the house. He was holding what looked to me like a Glock 18 and he fired off short bursts of bullets directly through the body of the car the two gunmen were behind. The vehicle was no protection and I saw one of the men spin away, shrieking as he clutched at his side. The other man took flight, throwing himself backwards and trying to scuttle away across the road. The man with the Glock continued advancing, but he angled his aim at the man behind the fence. The gun stuttered and a stitch-pattern of rounds cut through the fence, a right-to-left oblique angle that almost cut the tattooed man in half.

I had no memory of jumping out the Chrysler and running. Somewhere along the way I'd racked my SIG. I shouted wordlessly and saw the young woman's face come up. She stared at me, and something in her face made me wonder why I caused her to jerk in fear. Maybe it was the gun in my hand, or more likely it was because I looked so much like the man stalking towards her on the other side of the vehicle. I looked across at him and got a good look at Rickard for the first time.

The word doppelgänger went through my mind. Viewing the photo-fit of the man who'd snatched Imogen Ballard, I'd whimsically thought of him as my evil twin. Now there was no whimsy in it. Luke Rickard did look very much like me. It was enough of a likeness that I'd thought of him as an abomination that I couldn't suffer to live. If anything the feeling was even stronger in me now and if I could I'd have concentrated on that there and then.

But my first priority was the safety of the young woman.

Rickard looked at me and his eyes went to slits. He smiled coldly, but then he continued his march towards the vehicle. The remaining gunman had made it all the way across the street and it looked like the fight had gone out of him. He went down on his backside, throwing down his gun. His hands came up in a pleading gesture but there wasn't an ounce of compassion in Rickard. He unloaded a spray of bullets at the man and I saw tatters of his body sifting in the breeze.

I was still running. Behind me I could hear the crunch of Rink's boots as he shadowed me. At a run I fired, but all my bullets went high and wide. I was too busy looking at Alisha to care. I shouted at her to come to me and finally it was as if she realised that I wasn't her husband and she came first to her knees, then to a crouch and began running towards me.

Rickard swivelled.

'No!' I yelled.

He aimed the Glock 18 at his wife, tracking her movement with a slow, lazy smile on his lips. Pulled the trigger. The machine pistol rattled and there was a corresponding jig from Alisha as if she was dancing to its beat.

I shouted in denial, then lunged to catch the woman in my arms. I pressed her to the ground, covering her with my body, even though it was probably a pointless act. She was deathly still beneath me and the coppery smell of blood was strong in my senses.

Beside me Rink skidded to a halt. His gun came up and the sound was like a roaring cannon.

'Frog-giggin' son of a bitch!'

I heard his snarl and knew that he'd missed Rickard. Lifting my head, I searched for the killer, but caught only a hint of shadow as he raced back round the side of the house.

'We can't let him get away . . .'

Even as I said the words, I knew that he was making a run for it and I jammed a knee under me ready to take up the chase. Alisha shuddered beneath me and mewled out a cry of agony. Then I forgot all about chasing Rickard as I rolled the woman towards me and cradled her body to mine. Coming to my feet, I held her in my arms, jogging with her back to our car. Rink covered our retreat as I took the woman out of the line of fire. There was no guarantee that Rickard had fled the scene and he might burst out of hiding at any second.

Laying her on the road, I pulled off my jacket and bunched it under her head. Then I checked her for wounds. She'd been hit in three places: two of the wounds weren't going to kill her yet but they could be serious enough to require amputation of her left leg to save her life. The final wound was the most pressing. It was in her lower back, but the angle of the bullet could mean that the round had torn through her liver and without immediate assistance she was going to die. I pressed my hand down hard on the wound, trying to stop the flow of blood. I looked up at Rink and my face was probably a picture of desperation judging by what I saw reflected there.

'Why . . . ?'

Alisha's voice was as brittle as cracked ice. It was only one simple word but it would take more than I could offer to answer her.

'Hush,' I said. 'Don't talk. Try to be as still as you can be.'

'Am I . . . going to . . . die?'

'No.' I tilted away from her so that she couldn't see the lie in my face.

When I looked back at her she was watching my face, but there was little recognition in her eyes. The pupils were as small as pinpricks. 'Why did you do this to me, Luke?'

Whether her question was rhetorical or she was swimming through delirium, I felt her words like a vice closing on my throat. I wasn't like him: physically maybe, but not in my heart.

'Shush, now. Help's coming, Alisha.'

Rink nodded his head over us, and I became aware of the sound of sirens and vehicles braking to a halt. Seconds later there followed shouted orders and the clatter of running feet.

Somewhere along the line I'd put my gun back

in my belt, and I noted now that Rink had put his away. My friend lifted his open hands to the cops shouting at him and then waved them over.

'This woman needs help *now*.' I stared up at the cop who had his sidearm pointed at my face. 'Get a goddamn medic.'

Other cops pounded by us, some doing a nervous dance as they approached the vehicle surrounded by dead men; others moved towards the house. I didn't give any of it much more than fleeting notice as I was too busy trying to keep Alisha alive. Next moment hands were pulling me away, and the people bending over Alisha wore different uniforms. I relinquished my hold on her, handing her over to the paramedics.

I looked down at her blood on my hands. Please . . . not another innocent, I prayed.

Next thing I was aware of was moving ahead with Rink, passing cops who tried to grab at us; we brushed them aside. Then we had passed the side of the house. My senses had pinholed during the last few minutes, but now they were returning as we took up the chase. The smell of gunpowder hung heavily in the air, and there was also the familiar tang of death. The house held no interest for us and we raced into the backyard. A man was dead on the floor and a little distance away a dog lay oozing its brains out of a hole in its skull. I barely glanced at them, heading for the open gate through which Rickard must have fled.

We went through another garden and on to a

parallel street where we found another two dead men. People from the neighbouring houses were beginning to come out to see the show. It was a bad sign. It meant that Rickard was gone.

The appearance of me and Rink sent a few of them fleeing back to the relative safety of their homes, but there were others who were a little bolder. They thought we were cops and they felt they had a right to harangue us for not being there to serve and protect when they needed us most.

A fat man, his large belly protruding beneath the line of his T-shirt like a cow's udder, came at me and he was just about frothing at the mouth. 'You don't care about us. You don't care!'

Right then and there he was right: I stiff-armed him out of my way and he went down on his backside. There was a collective shout of anger. Someone shouted something about police brutality. People began to wheel round us and for a moment I thought they were going to attack us like a pack of hyenas.

'Where the fuck did he go?' Rink roared at the top of his lungs.

The pack was shredded by his anger, some of them actually taking off at a run as though Rink was about to blast them to death with the gun he waved.

'The man who killed these people . . .' I waved at the two on the ground. 'Where did he go? Someone must have seen something?'

From beyond the group of neighbours I heard

a high-pitched whistle. Looking over their heads I saw a young black boy on a cycle. He was pointing his finger in stabbing motions to a junction further along. I knocked Rink's elbow and we shoved through the crowd towards the boy.

The boy wheeled ahead of us, all the way to the corner where he skidded to a halt using his feet as brakes.

'Up there,' he said. 'See the burned-down house? He ran in there.'

I nodded thanks at him.

'You see him, shoot him,' the boy ordered. 'He shouldn't have shot that poor dog.'

Under any other circumstances I'd have found the boy's statement absurd, but not this time. He had no love for the men Rickard had shot; in fact plenty of people would be secretly pleased that someone had done away with those blighting their neighbourhood with narcotics.

Rink was slightly ahead of me, but as he approached the burned-down house he came to a halt and covered as I moved forwards. I went by him, took up a covering position and then Rink moved ahead again. It was a one-two manoeuvre we sometimes called pepper-potting back in our military days, and the technique hadn't left us.

We had to approach with caution. We knew that Rickard was armed and extremely dangerous, but more than that he held a superior position. If we both entered the grounds at the same time he could take us down with one burst of gunfire. This way, one of us would still get a chance to kill him if he got the other.

In the next instant that consideration was taken away.

I heard an engine burst to life and a car came hurtling out of the yard in reverse. I had to dive clear and went down on my chest. Twisting round, I saw the bulk of the vehicle spin past me as Rickard hit a skid that angled it away from us. I fired into the body of the vehicle, but I must have missed him, because Rickard hit the gas and the wheels spun furiously before biting into the road surface and launching the car away from me.

Rink held his gun with both hands as he fired repeatedly. The back windscreen of what I now recognised as an older model Ford Taurus imploded, and as I rose up I caught only a fleeting glimpse of the top of Rickard's head where he hunkered low in the driving seat.

I took a few running steps after the accelerating vehicle. Came to a halt. Centred myself and fired. The front windscreen exploded but Rickard continued on. At the far end of the block, he spun the wheel and the Taurus was gone.

Shoulder to shoulder, we stood there in silent contemplation.

It's never a nice feeling when you realise you've failed, but at least we had one thing going for us. We were still alive and could take up the chase again. Too many others in Liberty City weren't so fortunate.

CHAPTER 29

Escaping from the police cordon was his first priority. Everything else could come later. Rickard dumped the Ford Taurus at an underpass beneath Route 95, then walked out and into an industrial estate struggling to remain viable in the current market but falling into decay. He left behind all but his own gun and knife. During the gun battle he'd used up all the ammunition for the Glock 18: he'd have liked to hold on to it for a little longer, but in the circumstances it was simply dead weight. At the very most his own gun held four rounds and he knew he'd have to rectify that soon.

At a mail forwarding depot, he ducked inside the nearest door and found a woman sitting behind a desk. She was surprised by his sudden appearance and had to put away the gossip magazine she was reading. Evidently she didn't get too many visitors in a day. She definitely wasn't the public face of the company, dressed as she was in a dull grey sweatshirt and matching pants, her brown hair scraped back into a ponytail held in place with a rubber band. The polish on her nails was chipped and stained by the cigarette wedged between her pinched lips.

She squinted up at him. 'Sorry. We don't allow personal pick-ups from the office.'

'I'm not here to pick anything up,' Rickard grunted. He looked round the office, his eyes drifting over the faded posters to the open door into a small warehouse. There appeared to be nobody else there.

'You want to send something, you have to do it via a carrier.' She took the cigarette out of her mouth, flicked ash into a ringed coffee mug. Then she stuck the cigarette back between her lips and sat staring up at him through the smoke.

Rickard ignored her and reached over her desk. He grabbed hold of her handbag and dragged it towards him. The woman lunged for the bag, digging her nails into his hands. She let out a shout of outrage but still managed to hold on to the cigarette like it was fused to her lip. Rickard wrenched loose, scowling at the scratches in his flesh. He'd just fought a gun battle, killed six or so people without a scratch, and now this?

'You shouldn't have done that.'

The woman clawed at her bag again but Rickard snatched it out of her way. He dug inside it. Came out empty. He upended the contents on her desk.

'Where are the keys to your car?'

'You're not having them. Get out now before I call the police.' The woman made to drag her personal belongings across the desk. Among the dross was a mobile phone. As she did, Rickard grabbed her by her hair, using the tail at the back to twist her head sharply on one side.

'Where are your keys, bitch?' From his belt he drew the ceramic knife and thumbed it open. He placed the point as close to her right eye as possible without blinding her. Then he nudged it a little more. The woman shrieked, all her toughness gone. She flailed at Rickard's hands trying to get away from the blade but he just gripped her all the tighter.

'If you want to keep your other eye, you'll tell me where they are.'

Between howling in terror and trying to wrench away, she dug a hand into her sweatshirt pocket and pulled out a bundle of keys. The ring was overloaded with small stuffed animals and Disney character fobs. Rickard released her and she bent over, holding her damaged eye with both hands as she sobbed. He looked at the frippery then tore loose the accumulated keepsakes and scattered them across the desk. He held up the key for the Ford Focus parked outside in the depot lot.

'Look at me,' he commanded.

The woman moaned.

'Look at me.'

'I'm blind!'

'You still have one good eye. Tell me what you see.'

When she didn't raise her head, he shrugged. He grabbed her hair to yank her up and quickly slashed her throat. His hand was guided by frustration but it was still a clean cut that opened her up almost all the way to the spine. The woman died instantly. There wasn't even a shudder – with the vagus nerves severed, there was no route between the brain and viscera to send any residual commands to her system. Killing the woman had formed no part of his original plan. He'd intended stealing her car, before dumping it nearby and transferring to another stolen less obviously than this. He had wanted the woman alive in order to raise the alarm about her stolen car so that while the cops were busy searching for the Focus he'd have a clear run out of town.

'You should have looked at me, goddamn you,' he said, as though her death was her own doing.

He walked out of the office and approached the Focus. He glanced all round, then, pretty certain that no one was observing him, he unlocked it and climbed in, then drove out of the lot. The car stank of cigarette smoke and was flecked with ash. Even the windscreen was discoloured with nicotine. He opened the windows to let some fresh air inside, feeling the draught ruffle his hair. He drove off the industrial estate and back under the highway, noting distractedly that the Taurus remained undiscovered, before taking a ramp to join the northbound traffic.

He decided to keep the Focus for the time being. The woman looked like she'd spent most of her days alone, smoking herself into oblivion, so it wasn't likely that her murder would be discovered any time soon. If there were roadblocks ahead, he'd take the chance that the identification he carried would get him by without question, so it was more important to put distance behind him now than lay false trails. He only required a couple of hours and then he'd be out of the country and free of pursuit.

Since arriving home at his apartment yesterday, his mind had been working in a mode commandeered by a strange sense of disassociation. He was driven by a self-righteous wind that pushed at him insisting on immediate and positive action for all the betrayal he'd suffered. Alisha – and the man whose arms she'd run to – demanded punishment. So too did the one that had sent men to kill him at his apartment. This was what he must concentrate on.

Now that his pulse had calmed somewhat and the breeze was helping to clear the smell of smoke from the car and the cobwebs from his mind, he was beginning to think a little sharper. Draft plans were beginning to take shape.

After a couple of miles of following frustratingly slow traffic, he took the Focus off the highway on to surface streets of a housing scheme not dissimilar to Liberty City. He followed the streets until he found what he was looking for. A convenience store was like a candle to moths, drawing people to its doors with the promise of bargains. Rickard parked the Focus in a row of similarly non-intrusive vehicles, blending himself among the clientele going in and out of the store. Unlike the others who parked nose in to the kerb, he reversed into the parking space in order that he'd have a quick getaway if the cops turned up. He angled his mirrors so he could discreetly check anyone coming towards him from the direction of the store and then swept the roadway with his gaze. Happy that he wasn't attracting any unto-ward attention, he pulled out his mobile phone and tapped a hot key.

The phone rang a half dozen times.

The buzzing in his ear told him what he'd already taken for granted. Any other time his client had picked up almost immediately but this time there was reticence in answering. Probably wasn't expecting a call from a dead man, he thought. Except enough time had passed since the attempt on his life back at his apartment for the news to have filtered back that he'd escaped unscathed. However, the last thing expected of him would be for him to call in now.

'Rickard?'

At the sound of the voice he blinked slowly.

'You were perhaps expecting someone else?'

His retort was ignored. 'Why didn't you call in sooner?'

'I've been rather busy.'

'So I've seen. Things are getting out of hand up there. I lost some good people.'

'They weren't *that* good,' Rickard said.

'Obviously not. Joe Hunter took them out easily . . . he's more dangerous than I thought.'

Rickard felt a dull thud in his gut. Something squirmed there, reaching for his heart. The serpent stirring.

Hunter took them out.

Rickard had no sense of speaking the words aloud and was surprised to hear an answer. 'I sent a team to offer you assistance. They spotted Hunter and rashly believed that they were his equal. All but one of them was killed.'

Rickard struggled to comprehend what he was being told. Finally he understood. The diner. The shoot-out. Those were the people his client was talking about. Of course there was no way that he'd get a confession about the three who'd come to his apartment.

'You shouldn't have sent anyone.' His words were loaded.

'I thought it best.' No argument. 'Hunter has proven himself to be the most dangerous of your targets. The situation with Imogen Ballard told me that the job would require more than one man to complete.'

Rickard grunted. 'I told you, circumstances overtook me in Maine. It does not mean I'm incapable of finishing the job. Alone.'

There was a long pause. The ticking of the cooling engine, a distant bark of an excited dog, was all that filled the seconds.

'I have reconsidered our arrangement.'

'In what way?' Rickard asked.

'You were employed to set Hunter up. I wanted him to suffer greatly. I wanted him to lose people he cared for in the knowledge that he could do nothing to stop their deaths. He was to have no one to turn to, no place to hide. But it seems all of that was ridiculously grandiose of me. I should have simply had you take him out at the first opportunity, allowed you to kill him.' Rickard couldn't argue with that: it was what he'd thought all along. So he just listened. 'The plan has backfired. It has caused problems I could do without. I said I did not want a trail leading back to me.'

I am a trail to you, Rickard realised.

But that was not what was said. 'Hunter killed three of those I sent to help you. One of them is still alive and in the hands of law enforcement. I can't risk having him mention my name.'

'You want me to kill him?'

'No, I have other people who will do that for me.'

'I'll do it.'

'No, Rickard. I want you to disappear for a while. The police are looking for you now. So is Joe Hunter. I will pay you for your services to date and will also see that you receive a weighty bonus. However, that is it. You must have no more involvement in this case.'

'That's not the way I work.'

'I understand your disappointment, Rickard. But that's the way it must be.'

'You don't understand what I'm saying . . .'

'I do. You took the job on the understanding that you would ultimately kill Hunter. Professionally you want to see that task through. I know that you wish to finish things but it's better this way.'

'Better?'

'You delivered exactly what was asked of you, it just did not have the result I was hoping for. From here on in I wish to play things differently.'

'You're saying that you're severing our contract?'

'For the time being. However I may use you again in the future.'

'Use me?'

'You're disappointed. I understand. I will compensate you well: believe me, you will be happy with the bonus I mentioned.'

'I am more than disappointed,' Rickard said, his voice low. He had begun to shake, vibrating like a tuning fork.

'Rickard, you *are* going to drop out of sight for a while. My own people will deal with this from now on. Should I need your services again, I will contact you.'

The line went dead.

As though his strength of will could summon the voice again, he pressed the phone to his ear, listening to the soft whoosh of blood through his skull. He sat like that for some time, vision glazed over as he stared into middle space. But the voice didn't come back. All that happened was that the

228

trembling inside him intensified. He was like a pot coming to the boil, about to spurt scalding liquid everywhere. And now his effort of will was aimed at bringing that under control.

First he closed his phone and slipped it into his pocket. No way would he hit that hot key again. The phone would go unanswered, adding further insult to what he'd already suffered.

He started the car and nosed out into the roadway, blinking his blurred vision away as he swung north. He drove a shade below the speed limit. Careful and considerate: it was a struggle because his rage demanded speed and reckless manoeuvres and perhaps a little mayhem and destruction along the way.

I may use you again.

It was those words that angered him most.

He inhaled deeply and then shuddered out a long breath.

No one uses me, he thought. He laughed at the absurdity of it. But the laughter would fool no one, let alone him. So he stopped laughing and chewed at his bottom lip.

He was a professional killer of men, a craftsman, and a master of his art. No one *used* him. His services came with an unconditional guarantee of excellence. It was a contractual partnership, one that he would never shirk once the deal was made, and a binding promise that his client could not step away from either. Once you were in you were in for the journey. Of course, the manner of his trade meant that a broken contract could not be pursued in the same way as other businesses. The client's offer of a 'weighty bonus' just did not cut it. Compensation wasn't the issue. His standing as one at the top of his tree was. No one used Luke Rickard then threw him away like he was a senseless thug scrabbling in the dirt for a handful of scattered coins.

His plan to get out of the country now took on a far more pointed purpose than avoiding a manhunt.

CHAPTER 30

'Man, this takes me back, guys.' Rink was nipping the tip of his tongue between his teeth, enjoying every minute of the experience.

'I'd forgotten how uncomfortable it was,' I grumbled over the high-pitched rush of air snapping at my jumpsuit and trappings.

'Can't wait,' Rink went on. 'The rush, man, haven't you missed it?'

I just grunted, said, 'Just make sure you don't land on your head.'

Rink laughed at me. Harvey leaned forward, looking past Rink, and shot me a grin of his own. 'Worse will be if he lands on our heads.'

We were in a MC-130H Combat Talon II, the Lockheed variant of the Hercules transport airplanes used during military operations. The last time I'd been in one was on a drop behind enemy lines during Operation Desert Storm. On that occasion I'd been one of fifty-two paratroopers stacked side by side in the troop carrier, but this time there was only me and my friends preparing to jump.

We were only minutes away from our designated drop and I felt the familiar trickle of adrenalin I got when preparing for contact. Rink always became excitable, a nervous energy making him grin like a crazy man. On the other hand the surge of chemicals through my system had the adverse effect of sending me into a state that some – even my best friend – took as a resolute calmness. Rink would comment on my ability to stay calm like it was something admirable, but really there was nothing admirable about it. I was as nervous as everyone else: I just didn't let it show.

Embrace fear and make it your friend. That had been the philosophy of my instructors at Arrowsake, the secret base where I'd undergone intense military training. It was an ethos I've carried with me ever since. Fear keeps you wary and in a high state of alert. It can keep you alive.

I wished that I feared Luke Rickard, but I didn't. I just loathed everything about him.

Even if he wasn't a stone-cold killer who had earned himself a substantial amount of wealth from murder, I'd still want to put the bastard down. From Imogen Ballard I'd learned that he was a sick-minded beast who had used the threat of rape to torture her, but from Alisha – his wife – I found that he'd gone way beyond threats. At first he'd been the archetypal gentleman, a loving and caring man who'd saved her from a life on the streets. He'd whisked her away, married her on a beach in the Bahamas, set her up in a penthouse suite in Miami, given her everything. But then things changed. The mask had slipped and for two years he'd subjected her to vicious and agonising sexual abuse in an attempt at dominating her every thought. I was surprised that she'd waited as long as that before asking Del Chisholm to get her away from the monster. I only wished that she'd come to us instead.

Rickard's bullets had shattered the femur in her left leg and had nicked an artery. Immediate fears that she would lose the leg were negated by the superb team of surgeons who worked on her through the evening and into the small hours. They saved the limb, but she'd never walk again without a limp. She also had to forgo her spleen and a portion of her liver to save her life. She spent the remainder of the night deeply anaesthetised and it wasn't until the next day that she had related her story in a whisper that told more of continued terror than it did of the pain she was suffering.

If Rickard was allowed to live, Alisha would never shed that terror. Imogen too would live in fear of his promised return. For both their sakes I was determined to put the son of a bitch in a deep dark hole. But my reason for hunting down the killer went way beyond that. He'd murdered people I'd once called friends, viciously torturing them and their loved ones in an insane attempt at punishing me. He'd murdered other innocent people too, and the list was long. I was his intended victim; he should have just come for me and had done. He'd fouled up and I hoped I was now going to get the opportunity to redress that.

It was the reason I'd accepted Walter's 'official sanction' and promise of amnesty from prosecution – not the incentive of a hefty pay cheque for getting the job done. Good friends that they were, Rink and Harvey had snapped his hand off too.

One of the aircraft's seven-man crew signalled that we were approaching our drop point. We'd been very specific about checking our gear but it didn't hurt to check again. We went through the routine, then helped to check each other. We'd joked about landing on heads, but it was the last thing we wanted.

A light in the bulkhead went to red and we moved towards the open hatch at the rear of the plane. The crew man counted down and the light turned green. Harvey jumped out and it was like a giant hand had snatched him away. Rink followed and he too was gone in a blink. Then it was my turn. One step. No turning back now.

It was like the airplane shot up and away from me at the same instant and I was falling towards blackness devoid of all light. There was no real sense of falling, but I plummeted like a stone, head down and my arms by my sides to streamline my body and cut down on wind resistance. From this altitude the surface could have been the fathomless depths of an ocean, but I was streaking towards a different kind of sea. The undulating blackness was the uppermost canopy of trees clinging to the slopes of the Cordillera mountain range, a spur of the Andes.

I'd made many HALO jumps in the past but all of them at least five years ago. The high-altitude, low-opening technique was second nature, though. Rink was right: it was a rush.

I bowed out, spreading my arms and legs, taking up the classic freefall position, checking instinctively the altimeter on my wrist. We'd jumped from just below ten thousand feet, without oxygen, but with obligatory helmet and goggles. Condensation spread across the lenses and I wiped at them with a sleeve. When next I looked at my altimeter it told me that the jungle was rushing up to meet me like an old friend. Off on my left, as if in a synchronised dance, I saw the opening of both my friends' canopies. I made the double salute position with my arms, signalling deployment, then pulled at my ripcord. The chute unfurled and I felt the tugging of my harness as I caught air under the canopy. I checked everything was in order with my rig, double-checked, then searched for the landing point.

A flare suddenly burned bright, casting dancing shadows on the trees surrounding a clearing cut out of the forest. I manipulated the guide lines, angling towards the clearing, noting Rink and Harvey already swooping that way. We went into land in an oblique stack, Harvey alighting first with an ease as though he'd simply stepped off a box. Rink needed a couple of running steps before he had full control of his landing, but it was still good for someone who hadn't jumped in all those years. I also showed my experience, coming down surefooted as I used the resistance and angle of my chute to bring me to a feather-soft contact with the ground.

Walter had been busy in the day or so since Luke Rickard escaped us. The telephone number supplied to me by Ken Wetherby had turned up trumps, leading back to a similar broker of mercenaries in Bogota. Men sent by Walter had eased the name of the broker's client out of him. When I say eased, that's as much of a euphemism as Walter would hint at: I was guessing that the broker had done a sudden and inexplicable disappearing act after their visit. Then it was a matter for my CIA friend to set us up with contacts here in Colombia and arrange our secret arrival in the country.

Across our chests we had Heckler and Koch MP5A5 submachine guns and before we saw to our canopies we saw to our weapons. The flare had been lit to guide us in, but it didn't mean that it had been set by the people we expected. We took up a defensive position while two Jungla troopers came and identified themselves.

The two men were young and fit, typically military in their bearing. One of them was much darker of skin than the other, and I wondered if the paler of the two was actually Colombian. They'd forgone the black jumpsuit and helmet they'd wear while on active duty, dressing in civilian clothes instead. I noted the bulges under their jackets where they concealed firearms. We shook hands, both sides showing a wary respect. Both men spoke with American accents, which didn't surprise me. The Jungla are an elite police force whose task it is to curtail the production and supply of cocaine. Ninety-nine per cent of those involved are good, righteous men, but where there are drugs and huge amounts of money at stake you can never guarantee the complete eradication of corruption. The two men who met us were CIA plants, there to ensure that the inevitable one per cent did not flourish. So Walter said.

Once our parachutes and jumpsuits were stowed, we clambered into a Grand Cherokee jeep that was sufficiently scuffed on the outside that it didn't look like a government vehicle. Under the hood, it was a different story. The tinted windows were also bulletproof. We were, I understood, in the heart of bandit territory. We kept our machine guns ready, and I had my SIG to hand.

For the drop site we had only been given co-ordinates, but we were in dense forest on the eastern slopes of the Cordillera Central range, somewhere above the city of Ibagué. There were highways south of us leading through the passes between the cities of Bogota and Armenia, but here the roads were little more than tracks. Juan Charles, whose father I discovered was an

American and explained his fair complexion and blond hair, drove the big 4x4 along the rutted trail like a pro. His darker companion, Hector Nunez, brought us up to speed with the latest communication from Walter.

'The man responsible for hiring Luke Rickard has been identified as Jorge Gutierrez. This may surprise you: he is not a key player in any of the well-known cartels and hasn't featured in any recent intelligence reports.'

'Maybe he's good at concealing his involvement,' I said.

Nunez, who appeared to be the more talkative of the two, nodded. 'There is that. But we,' he indicated his blond friend at the wheel 'have been thinking this through. We think that Gutierrez is yet another front concealing the real person.'

That made a great deal of sense. 'What is his background?'

'DAS.' Nunez almost spat out the acronym.

'He's a police officer?'

'Not like us.'

The way he said it told me that despite being an agent of the American government he was also very proud to be a member of the elite Junglas. By the intensity in his gaze he bore no love for the Department of Administrative Security. Not surprisingly, really. There had been scandals where directors of the Colombian secret police were accused of feeding information to right-wing paramilitary death squads, giving them the names of rebel sympathisers who opposed the president. One director had been imprisoned, such was the strength of the accusations. The DAS had gone down a long way in the seven years since I'd worked alongside Victor Montoya.

It put a whole new slant on who Rickard could be working for. Bryce Lang had been convinced that the murders were tied to the hit we'd carried out on Jesus Henao Abadia and I realised now that I'd been going along with him for want of another motive. Now I wondered if we'd been on the wrong track all along.

Rink and Harvey held their peace but I could feel the heat radiating from them as they made sense of this new information. I leaned forwards, resting a forearm on the back of Nunez's seat. 'You're leading us to do a hit on a member of the security services?'

'Gutierrez is a traitor to his country,' Nunez said.

'You said that he did not feature in any recent intelligence reports, but now you're saying he's a traitor . . . that's some jump.'

Nunez nodded. He flicked a glance over at the driver. Charles looked at the rear-view mirror and met my gaze staring back at him.

'He is obviously working for one of the death squads who blight this country,' Charles stated. 'The same people who are trying to kill you, Hunter, and the people already responsible for murdering the members of your team. What do you believe that makes him?'

Sitting back in my seat, I grunted in assent. But I wasn't happy. Not for the first time, I had the feeling that those who were supposed to be my allies were using me to meet their own ends. From the stillness of my two friends they were thinking the same thoughts.

'Any sign of Luke Rickard yet?' When all was said and done, that was why I was there, and for whatever reason this situation had come about it really made no difference. Forget the politics: Rickard was my enemy whoever had engaged him to murder my team.

Both Nunez and Charles shook their heads. But then Nunez said, 'He's probably going to the same place as we are.'

And that was good enough for me.

CHAPTER 31

Rickard didn't have the resources of his Colombian employer to fall back on now but it mattered not. He'd been in the business of killing men for long enough that he'd set up his own network of contacts and had various drops where he stored sufficient weapons, cash and documentation to get a job done. Plus there was his man in Miami, who he could still rely on to arrange the things he couldn't.

Flying direct to Colombia was a no-no, as the likelihood that he'd be spotted was too great a possibility. Instead he arrived in neighbouring Ecuador, having transferred commercial airlines three times. Then he had organised a flight across the border and up towards the district of Tolima, paying hard cash to a one-eyed pilot. Rickard wasn't choosy about the man's lack of vision: he bragged about having been half-blinded by shrapnel when his plane was forced down by DEA agents while doing a narcotics delivery to the US mainland. The pilot had evaded capture, had his wounds tended, then had got right back in the saddle. Rickard admired his tenacity, but not the stench of body odour wafting from him. The man didn't offer a name beyond Romeo and Rickard didn't ask.

The plane put down in a field cleared by local farmers, ready for sowing the next crop of erythroxylaceae, a plant with great significance to the Andean culture and also the basis of the drug cocaine. From there he hitched a ride on the back of a flatbed pick-up truck to a small village that had an unusual profusion of shacks covered in black plastic sheeting.

In what amounted to the village square, he clambered down off the flat-bed and slung his bag of equipment over his shoulder. The pick-up immediately drove away, leaving him standing in the cool breeze washing off the hills round him. There he was met by mistrust and a number of guns levelled at his chest. Rickard looked each of the four men surrounding him in the face. He showed them as much disdain as they directed at him.

Since looking like Joe Hunter was no longer an issue, he'd cut and dyed his hair a sleek black, tinted his skin and added dark contact lenses to his new image. He looked passable as a local, but no one here was fooled. It didn't matter as they knew exactly who he was anyway; if not by name then by reputation.

'Silva didn't see fit to come meet me himself?'

The four men sneered at him now.

'Didn't expect he would,' Rickard shrugged. 'But I didn't think he'd send the Marx Brothers either. Which one of you is Groucho?'

'That would be Guarapo,' said one of the men, slapping the back of a hand to his chest. He was a tall, sloping-shouldered man whose round face looked like he'd done a few rounds in the boxing ring. There were ridges of scar tissue along his eyebrows and his nose had been flattened along the bridge. He indicated that Rickard follow him, while the others made a loose skirmish line behind him. Rickard smiled at the man's naivety as he walked.

Parked under a lean-to was a much newer pick-up than the one Rickard had travelled here on. It had a tarpaulin canopy on the back and bench seats. He didn't expect to ride up front, so Rickard tossed his bag inside and then clambered up, taking a seat at a back corner. Guarapo and a curly-haired man climbed in the front while the others kept Rickard company. They held their assault rifles across their thighs and he thought that if he wished he could take out both of them with his knife before they got off a shot. But to do that would disenfranchise him with the local warlord, Alvaro Silva, and for the time being Rickard needed him.

In recent years Colombia had been in internal strife. Senators and congressmen and even high-ranking members of the secret police had been arrested and tried at the Supreme Court for various crimes including corruption, extortion, funding paramilitary groups and even ordering murder. The president himself hadn't escaped suspicion and neither had his alleged ties to the

United Self-Defence Forces of Colombia, known locally as the AUC. For some time now the AUC had been in peace negotiations with the government, but there still remained breakaway groups headed by men like Alvaro Silva. People talked about the cartels when in fact more of the cocaine making its way to the Western world was trafficked by these paramilitary groups. Silva had no love for Rickard's previous employer and would gladly help him wipe out a major rival.

Guarapo drove the pick-up like he owned the roads, honking the horn and demanding right of way whenever he came across another vehicle. There was an excessive amount of braking and swerving and driving with two wheels along verges. Rickard had a feeling that some of the driver's aggressive actions were to unsettle him in the back. Rickard didn't let his discomfort show; he simply sat with his ankles crossed and his hands folded in his lap, smiling wistfully. His armed guards didn't fare so well. They rocked and bounced with each lurch of the vehicle.

The journey took them north through land that alternated between arable pastures and untamed forest. On one occasion Guarapo slowed down as a convoy of vehicles sped by in the other direction. The convoy was made up of buses full of workers destined for coca plantations. They were travelling under guard of Jungla troopers to rip the plants out of the ground. Rickard heard Guarapo swearing savagely from the front. In situations like this, he guessed, Guarapo and his men would follow the workers and try to pick them off from sniper positions on the hillsides. Stuck with transporting him, they had no option but to trust the landmines they'd sown among the coca leaves to derail the effort.

An hour later the truck plodded its way up a winding track overlooking a river valley. Everything here was green and dripping wet. Rickard still kept his cool even when his guards began to sweat and squirm uncomfortably. Both men had stopped watching him some time back and had started a low conversation, muttering and cursing in their native tongue. A few of their comments were aimed surreptitiously his way. But now he noticed that both men had fallen silent. They were approaching their destination and the men were once again preparing themselves to take him under their weapons to their vaunted leader.

Guarapo halted the truck at a checkpoint. He exchanged pleasantries with the two men armed with assault rifles who pulled the temporary sawhorse blockade aside and waved them through. As the truck again picked up speed, Rickard watched the guardsmen muscle the barricade back in place. He couldn't help but think that – for the hidden base of a feared death squad – security was woefully inadequate. If he chose to invade this place he could slip inside, kill Silva and be gone again without anyone noticing.

Guarapo drove the truck over a hill and down

into a valley. Trees clung to the slopes, their canopies almost, but not quite, concealing the camp below from aerial observation. Buildings had been erected under the trees, all except for a large white hacienda-type structure standing in its own field. As they drove past, Rickard studied the number of men and vehicles mingling among the trees. Maybe getting in undetected wouldn't be as easy as he'd first assumed.

With a crunch of gravel under the tyres, Guarapo brought the truck to a halt. He banged his hand on the cab wall, shouting in his native language. His voice was garbled but emphatic: out now.

Rickard climbed down, hitching his bag on his shoulder, then walked towards the large ranch house. His guards rushed to surround him.

'Easy, gang,' Rickard said. 'We're all friends here.'

It seemed that Guarapo was the only one of the four who could speak English. Rickard could have conversed with them all in Spanish, but he didn't care to.

'You must give up your weapons before you meet with Señor Silva.'

Rickard shook his head. 'I'm afraid not, Sugar.'

Guarapo was the name of a local drink laced with sugar, a delicacy that was sickly sweet to some palates. It didn't much fit the man's demeanour.

He squinted at Rickard from below his lumpy eyebrows. Not so much at his refusal to hand over his weapons but at the use of the nickname that Rickard chose. 'You know of me?'

'I've heard your name mentioned, yes.' Rickard didn't expound. He simply continued to walk.

'Then you will know I am not a man to be ignored, *marricon*.'

Rickard grunted at the man's choice of words. He was anything but a faggot. He chose instead to respond to the man's insult by ignoring him.

Guarapo grasped hold of Rickard's elbow, tugging him to a stop. '*No me jodas!* You are making a mistake if you think I'm someone to be disregarded like this.'

Rickard unhooked his elbow from the man's grasp. He turned to stare into Guarapo's blunt features. 'I want to meet with your boss, Sugar. When I've done that if you want to renew this conversation then let's do it. However, for now *vete al infierno!* I've more important matters than to butt heads with someone who smells like a donkey's ass.'

Guarapo blinked slowly. Then a smile grew, showing discoloured teeth. Guarapo lifted his assault rifle so that it was braced across his chest: a reminder of his power. 'You are either insane or you are a very brave man.'

'Maybe I'm both.' Rickard gave a subtle dip of his head, inviting Guarapo to follow his gaze. The tip of Rickard's ceramic knife was a mere hair's breadth from the self-styled soldier's groin. 'Do you still want to contest which of us has the biggest *cojones*, Sugar?'

'*Coño!*' Guarapo swore. Then his self-satisfied grin wavered and he edged slowly away.

'I didn't think so.' Rickard turned away from him and continued walking. Behind him he could hear the muttered curses of all four men. Then Guarapo swore savagely – something about shitting in Rickard's milk – and all four of them hurried to surround him again. This time they all moved off, and Guarapo attempted to regain some of his composure in front of his men by edging ahead so it looked like he was leading. Rickard allowed him the illusion.

There had been no real threat of violence during their exchange; Rickard knew that he had been undergoing a test. One that he'd passed. If he had backed down it was probable that Alvaro Silva had ordered Guarapo and his men to gun him down where he stood. Test number two would come soon.

On the approach to the ranch house, some care had been taken to mow the lawn and a path of white gravel had been laid all the way to the front door. It was an attempt at giving the place an illusion of respectability, but it was purely masculine; no hint of a woman's touch could be discerned in the sterile flower beds or the hangings in the windows. It did not look like Alvaro Silva had lived here very long and Rickard guessed that the warlord had taken ownership following a bribe from an official or having extorted it from its previous owner. Maybe said owner was in one of those flower beds he'd passed.

The door opened and they were met by a tall, muscular man wearing khaki fatigues. His blond hair had been recently cut into a flat-top, as angular as his Teutonic features. Rickard took the man to be of northern European stock even before he invited them inside in a gruff German accent. A mercenary – not unlike Rickard – he'd been drafted as extra muscle for Silva's campaign to capitalise on the collapse of the AUC. One of many, Rickard assumed, judging by the other pale faces he'd noted out in the woods.

The German led Rickard inside. Of the original group only Guarapo followed. The others went off, pulling out packs of cigarettes and searching for matches.

As he walked, Rickard judged the man walking ahead of him. The German had that straight-backed stance of someone indoctrinated by military training, but he also walked with the free and easy grace of the most dangerous of killers. A man cut from the same ream as Rickard and Joe Hunter. Special Forces undoubtedly; maybe even from GSG 9 – *Grenzschutzgruppe* 9 – the famed counter-terrorism unit of the German Federal Police or from KSK – *Kommando Spezialkräfte* – the army equivalent. With men of the German's ilk already on Silva's books, he wondered if the warlord was as eager to engage Rickard's services as he'd made out when they talked on the phone. Maybe he should kill the German now and ensure there was a vacancy open for him.

He let the thought go in the next instant. He was waved into a large room that once had been a family living room. Now it was purely utilitarian, a work space. A desk was situated centrally, a leather office chair behind it. Other chairs, wooden with straight backs, were ranged round the wall. In each and every one of those chairs sat men who regarded Rickard with mean eyes. They all wore clothing reminiscent of paramilitary groups the world over: green or khaki fatigues, berets pushed into their shoulder epaulettes. Sidearms strapped to their hips. The man sitting in the leather chair was distinguished by his maroon belt and the tassels drooping from his shoulders.

Alvaro Silva stood up. He was a man of medium height and build, a slightly protruding belly pushing at the fabric of his dress shirt. He looked mildly amused as he extended his hand across his desk to welcome Rickard to his war counsel. He looked like a genial old man playing at soldiers; however Rickard knew that Silva was anything but.

Silva had a good grasp of the English language and spoke with barely a trace of accent. 'I am pleased that you could join us, Mr Rickard. I trust that your journey here went without incident?' His eyes flicked past Rickard and came to rest on Guarapo, who had stationed himself beside the doorway.

'Your men were pleasant company on the ride over. They made me very welcome.' Rickard didn't bother looking at Guarapo, but knew he probably hadn't earned himself any less enmity from the rough-faced man.

'Good. Good.' Silva indicated a chair that one

of his men placed alongside the desk. 'Please be seated, Mr Rickard. We have much to plan and much to do. But first! There *was* something you promised me . . . ?'

The second test. Rickard placed down his bag of equipment. He sat, placing his forearms on his thighs and peered across at the men ranged round the room. 'Yes, Señor Silva, there was. So . . . which of these men is the DAS commander?'

Directly opposite him, a moustachioed man jerked at his words. He looked at Rickard and then swung his disbelieving gaze on to Alvaro Silva. The man's face began to elongate in realisation of his fate, a mix of hurt and resolution.

From the front of his jacket Rickard pulled out a Glock 17 and fired a single round between the eyes of Jorge Gutierrez.

There was a stunned silence. It was broken moments later by Alvaro Silva's slow handclap, which was joined by the others in the room, growing in volume and enthusiasm with each beat.

Rickard slipped the Glock 17 back inside his jacket as the man who had acted as intermediary between him and his original employer slumped down in his chair.

'I think that amply proves whose side I'm on now.'

Silva smiled in his genial old man way. 'Gutierrez has been playing both sides, going between me and my competitor, Cesar Calle, taking money from the two of us. It's right that you killed the traitor for me. I'm only sorry that you didn't make it last a little longer.'

'It's like you said earlier, Señor Silva, we have much to plan and much to do. Wasting time on that two-faced dog would be counterproductive.'

Silva indicated Guarapo. 'Take him out of here before he stinks up the place. Make sure that he disappears, Guarapo. He is DAS after all and will be missed.'

Rickard had loaded his Glock with hollow-points. The bullet had punched through the policeman's forehead and fragmented inside, pulping his brain, but there was no exit hole. A slow trickle of blood leaked down his face, following the contours of his large nose and pooling along the edge of his moustache. There wasn't much threat of a mess from the wound, but the man had voided his bowel and a rank stench drifted from him.

Guarapo – obviously deeming the unsavoury task below him – called for help from some of his men outside. Two of those who had sneaked off for a smoke came in looking sheepish under the stares of their leaders, took Gutierrez by his elbows and knees and carted him away. Guarapo gave them explicit orders for his disposal, which earned a lazy smile from Silva.

When they were gone, Guarapo closed the door. He leaned against the door frame, watching Rickard with the same undisguised hatred as earlier. The big German took his post at the other side, but he merely looked aloof at the proceedings. Rickard ignored them both.

He twisted in his seat so that he could stare directly into the eyes of Silva. 'I can give you Cesar Calle, but my terms remain the same as we discussed.'

Silva waved a hand at the circle of men. 'They are all in agreement with me. Lead them to Calle and when he is dead you are welcome to take your prize.'

'Calle is well protected, but I see you have massed your troops. I think they will be enough to keep his army busy while I see to him.'

'I want him to die in pain, Señor Rickard. I want Calle to know what it is to think he can take what belongs to me.'

'You will hear the screaming all the way from here.'

Rickard stood up and lifted his bag to his shoulder. To the assembled group of soldiers, he said, 'Are you ready, gentlemen?'

Rickard didn't care about Cesar Calle. Like Jorge Gutierrez, he was simply a go-between for the one that had hired him to slay Joe Hunter and his team. He would kill Calle, but it wasn't his priority. He wanted his prize: time with the one who thought that Rickard could be discarded like a soiled rag.

CHAPTER 32

'Is there anything else you need?'

I shook my head at Hector Nunez, and touched the SIG where I'd stowed it in a quick-draw holster on my hip. 'Got everything I need right here.'

He smiled tight-lipped, then nodded me over to the Cherokee. Rink and Harvey were already in the back and Charles in the driver's post. The engine grumbled and a wisp of smoke rose slowly from the exhaust pipe. I climbed in, giving my friends a wink. We were about to get moving again after hours of inactivity I could have done without.

We had arrived at a staging base the evening before – an abandoned shack on the slope of a wooded hill. There we went through our plans for taking down Jorge Gutierrez and forcing the name of my real enemy from him. Normally I'm not one for intricate plans, but in the circumstances we had to be wary. Gutierrez was moving in dangerous circles. We were in a hurry to get started but there were things to do first. Top of the list came showering the sweat from my body. I'd acclimatised somewhat to the heat of Florida, so the temperature wasn't an issue. But here in these high jungles the moisture in the air was so thick it was like a damp rag had been wrapped round my limbs. The shower turned out to be a stream trickling down the face of the hillside, but it did the job nicely. Lack of personal hygiene could kill a soldier as quickly as disease or infected wounds. More than once in my career I'd picked out a hidden ambush by the stench wafting off those waiting nervously in hiding.

Food and water were next on the agenda. I accepted both from Hector Nunez, but turned down the offer of a cigarette. It was a long time since I'd taken a hit of nicotine, and things were going to stay that way. The smell of smoke could give me away as easily as body odour. Nunez dragged on his hand-rolled cigarette, though, and I allowed him the comfort. There was a high probability that some – or all – of us would not be coming back from the raid we planned: a condemned man's last wish shouldn't be turned down.

But now we were in the jeep there'd be no more.

Charles took us back down the hill and on to a single-lane back road where he swung to the south. Somewhere ahead of us lay the house where Gutierrez was reportedly visiting regularly enough to cause suspicion with the CIA agents. Immediate intel said he wasn't there now, but he was due a visit. Our plan was to infiltrate the surrounding countryside and wait for him. It sounds simple in the saying but can be quite different in the execution. Going for us was that we had Rink along for the ride. Rink has the ability to penetrate enemy lines with an ease verging on the supernatural.

Lower down the foothills we passed farmers toiling in fields, and we went through a few small villages where the signs were all in Spanish except for the obligatory Coca-Cola advertisements above café doors. I didn't see a McDonald's but if we looked hard enough I was pretty sure we'd find one.

Charles had studied maps the previous evening, so was ready for when a track edged up a hillside and disappeared though a canyon. He took the right turn and within minutes we were back in the wilderness. A river wound its way through the valley beyond, twisting and turning with the contours of the land. We abandoned the Cherokee where the trail ended and set off on foot, carrying our H&K MP5A5's ready. Rink took point and I brought up the rear, with Harvey and the two Jungla troopers spread out between us.

The going was slow, the trees hemming us in, the rumble of the river making it difficult to hear anyone approaching. Everything was green and wet. Beneath the green the glistening darkness could have hidden an entire squadron of soldiers. It was some years since I'd engaged in jungle warfare, but the lessons had stayed with me. The trick is to look beyond the darkness, use your peripheral vision which is better at picking up movement than looking directly. And remember to check above regularly.

We walked for hours.

The terrain was constant, high valleys and trees, the river a grumbling companion. It was easy to be lulled into a sense of security by the tranquillity of the forest or by the river's hypnotic music. But we were all on high alert. Without exception we were thrumming with anticipation. We were now within hailing distance of our enemies.

Hector Nunez called a halt and we huddled in a ring, each watching over our opposite's shoulder for anyone moving in on us.

Nunez pointed to the cliffs on our left. 'Beyond that ridge, we will find a trail that leads down into a valley. The house is directly below it.' He spread a diagram swathed in clear plastic on his thighs. Pointing to hand-sketched symbols, he indicated the house and outlying buildings. There was a clear space beyond them and the broken lines of a road coming from the opposite end of the valley. 'Sentries will be posted here,' he said, placing his finger on the map at the far end of the road, 'and here on the cliffs surrounding the buildings.' This time his finger danced over four different locations. One of them was directly above us.

'Do we dare take out the ones up there?' Rink nodded up at the towering ridge. The boulders looked ragged and had been invaded by growths of vines and trees that prickled with sharp thorns. Rink looked like he was upset that he wasn't going to get the chance to scale the cliff. 'If they're in regular contact with the others, we risk giving ourselves away.'

'We need to set up from other vantage points,' I said. 'Near enough to the sentries that we can take them out when the time comes.'

'No problem.' Rink nodded satisfaction. That was his kind of work.

On his map Nunez pointed out the cliffs on each side of the valley. At the base of both was a line of cross-hatching. 'The valley was cleared of shrubbery recently. There are mounds of logs piled all along the valley floor. They would make good observation posts.'

'Below the sentries on the cliffs?' Harvey looked incredulous.

'The sentries are watching the trails into the valley. If we got by them, we wouldn't be noticed hiding in the lea of the cliffs.' Nunez looked to his friend for support.

'We have done it before,' Charles confirmed as he batted an insect away from his face. 'They are more concerned with watching for anyone coming from the road and they are there to lay down covering fire from a high vantage. If we're careful they'll be unaware of us.'

'We don't want them above us.' Harvey was in agreement with me. 'Things will be different this time. When you've been here before it was only to gather intelligence. Sneak in, sneak out again. This time there's going to be shooting. I don't want to be pinned down by men on the ridges while reinforcements are brought in.'

'Then we must take them out,' Nunez concurred.

Rink withdrew his Ka-Bar and looked at its razor edge. 'I'll do the ones on the cliff above us, then move on to the others on the far ridge. We only need someone to do the guys on this side. Don't think we have much to worry about with the men at the far end. By the time they realise something's going down, we can be in and out again.'

I stabbed a finger at the cross-hatching nearest the houses. 'I'll take that point. I want to be the one that goes inside. Harvey? You happy taking the sentries on this side of the valley?'

'Sure,' he said.

Nunez and Charles looked at each other.

'I want you guys with me,' I said. 'Rink and Harvey can cover from up on the cliffs, but I'm going to need someone covering the house so I'm not disturbed while I'm inside. When I get Gutierrez I want to know I can fall back without having to run a gauntlet.'

'What about Cesar Calle?' Nunez asked.

'If he's the person responsible for sending Luke Rickard, I'll kill him.'

The best known of the Colombian drug-trafficking groups are the Cali, Medellin and Norte del Valle cartels. They're the most high-profile, but there are others. There are the North-Coast, Bogota and Santander de Quilichao cartels as well. Add the demobilised factions of the AUC, ELN, FARC and Águilas Negras paramilitary organisations to the seething pot, and you'd think there was no room left for another enterprising group. But there were plenty.

Cesar Calle headed his own group, and though the meanderings of the trail twisted back and forth over the intervening seven years, Calle did have connections to Jesus Henao Abadia. Therein lay a motive for Calle ordering a hit on the team that brought down his old friend, but it was pretty weak. I still believed there was more to it than that.

Last night Juan Charles had mentioned the crimes that Calle was suspected of. They included torturing a pair of French students whose backpacking adventure had brought them unexpectedly to one of his cocaine production bases. The students – little more than children – had been found in a shallow grave, semi-decomposed, but their injuries were still very evident. Calle was never brought to book: a few well-placed bribes in the correct hands saw to that.

Even if he wasn't the person responsible for sending Rickard, I'd have no regrets about killing him. In fact, his card was already marked.

We did a controlled starburst, Rink and Harvey heading off on their tasks while I now led the Jungla troopers further along the forest trail. A cleft through the cliff marked on the map was about a hundred yards ahead, but it meant a climb to get to it. On our right the river twisted away in a tight curve, bottlenecking between massive algae-slick boulders. The noise from the gushing flume beyond was the same as the blood in my inner ears.

Reaching a small cliff-face that blocked our path, I slung my sub-machine gun over my shoulder and hauled myself up on to a ledge. I could see old boot prints in the mud that had gathered in a shallow indentation: proof that Nunez and Charles had been here before. It was bad form to leave such obvious evidence, but I chose not to comment. If anyone had noticed and was watching the trail we'd have been cut down long before this. I nodded to the troopers, then scurried up the cliff, using vines and protruding rocks to pull myself up. About twenty feet up I found the cleft and it was like a huge knife slash through the hillside. Taking my H&K in my hands I edged forwards as Nunez clambered up behind me. I indicated that he should keep an eye on the steep cliffs above us: until Rink was in place I didn't want one of Calle's sentries to spot us. I moved on, stepping carefully among loose rocks, while Charles made the climb.

I could see daylight at the far end of the cleft, but it was only a narrow chink through which I could make out nothing of the land ahead, just pale blue sky dotted by clouds of moisture rising from the jungle on far slopes. It was idyllic in its own way, and there was nothing about it to suggest what horrors lay ahead of us.

The first hint I got was the crack of gunfire followed by a man's agonised scream.

CHAPTER 33

Rickard watched the big German, Burkhard Metzger, stand up in the bed of the jeep and shoot both guards at the front gate. And that was it. The assault of Cesar Calle's stronghold was on.

One of the guards didn't die immediately and reached to hit an alarm in a metal box fixed to a post. Metzger hopped down from the jeep, cleaving the man's hand from his wrist with a large-bladed knife direct from a Rambo movie, halting the warning. He then backhanded the blade across the man's face, chopping loose his jaw and the man's cry of agony, before throwing open the barrier and waving the convoy of Silva's soldiers through. In the German language, Metzger translates as *butcher*. He was living up to the name.

Scrambling back up on to the leading jeep, he steadied himself by bracing his legs. He glanced sideways at Rickard.

'Good job, Metzger.'

The German set his jaw at Rickard's feigned exuberance.

262

Rickard shrugged his shoulders. He was impressed by Metzger's cold-blooded manner, but wasn't about to admit it. To do so meant undermining his own considerable abilities. Better that he just got down to business and showed exactly which of them was the better man-killer. He lifted his rifle and fired three quick rounds at a group of men charging out of a hut at the edge of the road. All three went down like tin ducks in a shooting gallery. Beside him, Rickard heard Metzger's grunt of admiration. *Stick around*, he wanted to say, *and you'll learn a thing or two*. But he left the boast unsaid, choosing instead to allow his actions to prove the point.

Trees encroached on each side of the road, left to thrive by Calle's people in order to conceal the view of the land beyond, but once the convoy of five vehicles was through the forest the valley opened up to fields cleared of cover, surrounded on all sides by tall cliffs. Timber barricades like giant caltrops ensured that a free approach to the buildings at the far end was impossible. The wide swathe of grass was a typical killing ground where an enemy could be cut down while traversing the open space.

But that was all supposing that Cesar Calle's troops were prepared for such a full-frontal assault. The brashness of the attack had caught them napping, and resistance was slow to follow. It was a good half minute before guns began rattling from up on the clifftops and already

Rickard and his team were mid-way through the valley. Second in line in the group was a truck with a M240 belt-fed machine gun mounted on the roof. With a cyclical rate of up to seven hundred and fifty rounds a minute and Guarapo at the trigger, the M240 laid down a torrent of fire that kept the sentries on the cliffs from getting a clear shot. Over the roar of the machine gun Rickard could hear Guarapo swearing viciously. Not the sweet man his name suggested.

The convoy sped through the twisting route between the barricades, the fearless attack taking them beyond the defensive lines and towards the buildings. The house wasn't dissimilar to the one back at Silva's compound. If anything, it was larger and more luxurious. On either side were outbuildings, quarters for Calle's people or perhaps visiting dignitaries judging by the apparent lushness of the gardens the structures were set in.

Up on the cliff at the back of the house, rifles cracked and bullets struck sparks from the cab of the jeep a few inches from Rickard's head. He ducked, cursing when he noticed that Metzger stood his ground and returned fire. Who does he think he is, Rickard wondered, the goddamn Terminator?

As the jeep lurched to a halt, Rickard vaulted over the side and sprinted quickly to the corner of one of the outbuildings. Glancing back, he saw that the German had also leapt from the stalled vehicle and was running towards cover on the far side. Bullet holes starred the windscreen of the jeep and there was a distinct lack of movement from their driver. Didn't matter to Rickard; the driver had served his purpose in getting him close enough to assault the house.

Leaving Metzger and Guarapo and their goons to engage any resistance from Calle's troops, Rickard rushed through a garden of flowers in full bloom. He hurdled over a fence and found himself on a path, white pebbles underfoot. Machine guns crackled all round him, a din sounding like New Year in Chinatown. Men shouted and others screamed. Rickard blocked it all out, fixating on a window at the side of the main house. As he ran, he raised his rifle and fired a short burst. Glass shattered and the curtains inside danced as the bullets tugged at them. In the next instant Rickard dived bodily through the broken window, thumping down on the top of a dresser and scattering trinkets on the floor. Continuing his roll, he came off the dresser and on to the floor. Without looking, he knew a man was rushing into the room to investigate the commotion, and he lifted his gun and fired. True to form, he heard the agonised yelp of a person mortally wounded.

Coming to his knees, he searched for other targets, but there was only one man squirming on the floor a few feet away. Rickard steadied the rifle and put a bullet into the man's skull. Next he stood and headed for the doorway, heedless of the blood streaming from his forehead where glass had sliced him.

He'd never been inside this house before, but instinct told him the way he must go. The sharp stink of medication helped guide him too. He followed the pungent aroma along a short passageway and to a flight of stairs sloping down. The house had been erected following the contours of the cliffs, and unbeknown to any observer approaching the front, a passage led into the rock face and to a chamber surrounded by solid rock. Maybe Calle expected a nuclear strike and this was his idea of a panic room. Before entering the passage, he checked behind him. Metzger, Guarapo and the others were engaging the enemy outside the house – just as had been agreed. Gunfire and shouts made an ungodly cacophony.

Rickard checked the rooms nearest the front of the house. In one he found two men in quasi-military costumes, using an expensive leather settee as a barricade from which they returned fire through the shattered windows. They were exposed to his bullets and he riddled them each with a short burst of his assault rifle. They died without ever having realised that the house had been breached. Rickard believed there'd be other defenders in the house, but those who were an immediate threat were no more.

Quickly he retraced his steps to the flight of stairs and went down. He got another waft of medicated air, as though he'd just walked into a hospital's accident and emergency room. Time, he decided, wasn't always the healer it was cracked up to be.

Releasing the depleted magazine from his assault rifle, he jammed a full one in place, pulled the bolt to charge the firing mechanism. Not that he wanted to rely on the rifle – his ceramic blade was his weapon of choice this time – but there could be heavy resistance from whoever was in the hidden chamber and he was happy to use the rifle on them.

At the base of the stairs he paused. The door to another passage lay open. He could hear voices from within a room at the far end. Two or more men were waiting for him there and if he approached along the passage they'd cut him down instantly. Problem being: there was no other way inside.

Turning back to the stairs, Rickard loosed a barrage of bullets into the empty space at the top. He shouted, then fired a couple of single rounds. He followed that by another burst, shooting at the stairs this time. The volume of gunfire was horrendous, but in the hidden chamber it would echo even louder, serving to confuse those within. Immediately, he spun on his heel and pounded along the passageway. As he ran he was shouting full voice in fluent Spanish. 'Señor Calle! Señor Calle! You must get away. Silva is here. He's in the house!'

His bullets and his frantic shout did the trick:

they confused the men into thinking that he was one of their own defenders. It was a charade that would last only as long as it took for them to cast their gaze on him, but that was enough for him. He made it along the passage and into the room without being cut down, whereupon he immediately lifted his rifle.

Staring back at him in incredulity were three people. Two of them were armed with handguns and he indicated that they drop them. Cesar Calle and a henchman both allowed their guns to fall to the floor and they raised their hands in surrender. Rickard eyed them in disdain, then he shot them both as though they were paper targets beneath his contempt.

Calle dead was a promise fulfilled to Alvaro Silva. Maybe Rickard hadn't made him scream but he didn't care. What he was here for was his prize. Rickard smiled at the figure propped in the hospital bed.

'I bet you weren't expecting me?'

CHAPTER 34

'So much for plans,' I muttered over my shoulder.

Nunez didn't look happy at the sounds of gunfire ringing in our ears but he was pragmatic enough to shrug and then follow me. Charles, bringing up the rear, swore quietly under his breath, but he moved after us. Neither man had bought into a full-on war, thinking they had nothing better to do than play chaperone to the ones who were really going to pick up all the shit. But they were there and experience told them that they would most likely have to kill men if they were going to get out of this alive.

Both Jungla troopers were good men. I knew that the first time I looked at them. They would be top notch warriors – no one who wasn't made it into the Junglas, even men placed there by the CIA – but they were still cops and they were governed by a different rule book than me and my friends. I only wished that it was Rink and Harvey watching my six, except they were up on the cliffs. I trusted them to make the correct decisions based on what was happening in the valley

269

below us: they wouldn't be hiding and watching for Gutierrez to arrive now.

At the end of the cleft was a jumble of boulders that had fallen from the cliffs across the years. The jungle had got its hooks in and bushes and vines made a tangled maze between the boulders, but Nunez pointed out a trail under the foliage that he'd used last time he was here. I had to go down on my belly to slither through, but then I could stand with the rocks obscuring me from anyone down below. As my Jungla friends joined me, I peered around the rocks and tried to take in the chaos below.

Five vehicles had made it all the way across the valley and had parked in a scattered formation before Cesar Calle's house. Men in paramilitary uniforms used the jeeps and trucks to shield them from the bullets of other men defending the buildings. Those with the vehicles had the edge on firepower, but Calle's people held the advantage of position. From up on the clifftops the sentries were firing at the exposed backs of the attackers, forcing them to fight a battle on different fronts. Suddenly, above me, the guns of the sentries went silent and I guessed that Rink had decided to take them out of the equation.

Nunez nudged my elbow.

'That man there.' He indicated a soldier on the back of a jeep, a round-faced man with black wiry hair, who was manning a M240 machine gun with devastating effect. 'That is Manuel Cervantes.

Known as Guarapo. He is an officer of *Organización Halcón de Roja*, one of Alvaro Silva's top killers.'

The Red Hawks I'd heard of, but Alvaro Silva's name meant nothing to me. 'I take it they're enemies of Calle?'

'Not that I was aware of. But who knows? Since the break-up of the AUC many factions have been jostling for power and for control of the narcotics industry. It looks like Silva's decided to bring the fight directly to his nearest competitor.'

'Just because they're Calle's enemies, it doesn't make them our friends.' No, it was probable that every man down there would lift guns against us. Some of them – Guarapo for one – appeared to be competent fighters. A tall, fair-haired man looked like an anomaly, but when I started to look further he wasn't the only Caucasian. Mercenaries, I realised, had been drafted in by Silva to help him wipe out the opposition.

I'd come here to find Jorge Gutierrez, the man playing go-between with Luke Rickard and his employer, and to force that name from him. But if Silva's army managed to kill everyone then that route would be closed to me. No information had come in to say that Gutierrez was at the Calle house, but he could have been missed for all we knew. The prospects of having to intercede in this war between opposing military factions was beginning to look like a real probability.

The Junglas were probably wondering how the

271

hell they were going to explain their reason for being here, but that was for them to worry about. Still, I offered them a way out. 'The plan's changed. Stay here. I'm going in alone.'

'We can cover you,' Nunez offered.

'You can do that from here. If I'm killed, get away. No one needs to know that you were ever helping me.'

Before they could argue, I slipped round the side of the boulders and negotiated the slope at a jog. Below me to my left was an outbuilding. A pile of logs was stacked beneath a lean-to and I headed for them. At the woodpile I crouched, using the timber as cover while I spied along the side of the building. I'd just gained that position when I heard gunfire very close by and a window on the side of Calle's house shattered. A dark-haired man dressed in fatigues, heavily armed, followed the volley through the window a moment later.

Despite myself, I blinked in surprise.

To say I was confused was an understatement. The way I'd seen it, Luke Rickard had been working under the guidance of someone associated with Gutierrez – my bet going on Cesar Calle – and yet here he was, in all his glory, leading the attack on behalf of Calle's enemy. The dark hair and the tint of his skin didn't fool me. The man had walked directly towards me, cold-bloodedly shooting his own wife, and I'd burned that image into my memory. He could have had green hair and a clown's painted face and I'd still have recognised him.

What the hell was he doing?

From within the house came the rattle of a machine gun. The noise snapped me out of my confusion.

And I knew.

Luke Rickard was not only a murderer. He was a rapist, and misogynist. He was also a control freak beyond any I'd ever come across before. Rickard, I believed, had come here to exact retribution for some perceived slight against his twisted ego. Maybe Calle had dispensed with his services following his failed attempt at ruining me, and this was Rickard's way of showing his dissatisfaction at the betrayal.

Didn't matter.

Whatever his reason for turning up at Calle's place, he was here now. My hunt for him had just been offered a great boost I'd never expected. And regardless of the fact that he was embroiled at the centre of a power war, I had a chance at nailing him. It was time to get down to killing the bastard.

After that thought followed immediate action. I stood up, ready to follow Rickard through the broken window, then had to duck as tracer rounds zipped by my head. Bullets knocked chips of wood from the pile and I screwed my eyes tight to avoid being blinded by flying splinters. The smell of sap competed with the stinging burn of heated wood to overwhelm my senses.

Retreat wasn't in my plan but I'd no option. I ran at a crouch away from the woodpile towards the far corner of the building then ducked round the side. The rear end of one of the vehicles could be seen, but there was no sign of any of the attackers. Whoever had been shooting at me must have been further away. Making it to the front corner of the house, I searched for targets. Men bobbed up and down behind the shielding trucks and jeeps, but none of them was paying me any attention. The shots fired my way had to have been random. I backtracked to the woodpile.

Glancing back up to the cleft, I could see Juan Charles leaning out from the rocks, his face a pale blob against the deep-green shrubbery. He'd moved further across from where I'd left him and Nunez, and was now in a position to offer covering fire. He gave me a thumb-up signal, before leaning into the stock of his assault rifle. I nodded and then ran full pelt for the shattered window. Now the tracer rounds zipping over my head were heading in the other direction.

A small fence was no obstacle. I went over it without breaking stride and pounded through a flower bed. At the house I turned, pressing my left shoulder to the wall, and brought up my H&K. Smoke drifted in my vision from all the gunfire and I caught the same smell that follows a firework display. But I had no target. Charles continued to lay down covering fire and I could hear the metallic ting of his bullets striking the vehicles. Quickly I stood, taking a glance in the window and sweeping the room with my gun. It

274

appeared clear. Grabbing at the sill, I clambered inside, over a dresser and into the room beyond. A man lay ten feet away. He was dead. Unfortunately it wasn't Rickard.

Moving through the room, I heard the rattle of a gunfight somewhere in the house, someone screaming in Spanish. At the door I peeked out into a hallway. Cordite hung in the air. I walked slowly, checking and clearing rooms as I progressed. One room I came across held the bodies of two men who looked to have been cut down from behind. Almost opposite that room were a door and a short flight of steps leading down. I thought I heard voices.

Just as I turned to investigate, bullets cut through the house, knocking pictures out of frames and plaster from the walls. In reaction I ducked. At the other end of the hallway a man ran into view. He was a second or so in recognising I was a stranger – and therefore an enemy – and in that time I brought up my gun and gave him a measured burst. The bullets knocked him sprawling, his gun flying out of his hands.

The walls of the house shook to a detonation. Not the boom of a Hollywood explosion but a dull thud. Someone was throwing hand grenades. Following the noise there was a moment of utter silence, but it didn't last long. Somewhere a man began to scream. Guns began rattling again, and I turned my attention back to the short flight of stairs. I went down them stealthily, holding my

H&K ready for anything that might present itself. Periodically I checked over my shoulder for anyone following but it seemed I had the stairs to myself. The short passage in front of me was also empty.

When caught up in battle your senses can compress so that you are operating in a narrow sphere of consciousness: the vision can become tunnelled, the hearing a dull whoosh in the ears, touch and taste and smell can be relegated to some hidden corner of the mind. Other times quite the opposite can be true. I felt like a plucked guitar, I was buzzing so much. It was as though electricity played over my skin, prickling me like a static charge. Partly it was due to the endorphins flooding my system, but more than that it was because I felt that an end to everything that had happened the last few days was in the chamber at the end of the passageway.

Rickard was there – I felt it.

But so was whoever had hired him to destroy me.

Gritting my teeth, I moved forwards.

The antiseptic smell hit me, but I paid it no mind. I continued along the passage, listening for my enemies and gauging their positions. Surprisingly they spoke with lowered voices, as though in gentle conversation. I could make nothing of their words. But the tone and timbre of one voice gave me momentary pause.

I shook my head.

Couldn't be.

But then I lunged into the room and found my worst fear come true.

It wasn't for the fact that two men lay dead, their bodies riddled with bullets, or that Luke Rickard stood with a knife in his hand poised to strike his victim. The hospital-style bed, complete with medical accoutrements and electronic gauges, didn't halt me in my tracks. It was because of *who* was in the bed.

The person Rickard had been getting his orders from, on whose behalf he'd murdered my old team-mates and their families, and for whom he'd tried to kill Imogen Ballard, was the last person I expected.

Not Jesus Henao Abadia.

The person that Rickard stood poised to gut with his knife was Abadia's mistress: Jimena Antonia Grajales.

CHAPTER 35

Rickard studied the woman lying in the hospital bed. She in turn stared back at him, and there was barely a trace of confusion at his appearance. Her taut mouth spoke only of anger and one eyelid trembled in an effort to hold it in.

'I guess that you weren't expecting me?'

'No,' said the woman. 'I wasn't.'

Seven years ago Jack Schilling riddled Jimena Grajales with over half a dozen bullets. Three of those rounds had caused superficial injuries, but the remainder had torn through major organs and had nicked her spinal column. By all rights she should have been dead just like her lover, Jesus Abadia, and their child. Yet the woman had survived. And despite having lost the complete use of her body from a point just below her diaphragm – meaning she must suffer regular renal dialysis, a colostomy bag and a permanent catheter – she had clawed her way back to a position of power in Abadia's organisation.

Cesar Calle might be the name at the head of the cartel, but Jimena was the iron hand that commanded it from this hidden chamber. It was Jimena who had sought Rickard's services, when after seven years the rage tearing at her had become all-consuming. The need to avenge her child's death was such that it twisted all reason. She ordered all of the team responsible, and their loved ones, murdered in the most vicious fashion. Joe Hunter, she commanded, should be left for last. Of all the men involved, Jimena held him most responsible. If Hunter had shot Abadia, she would not be this bed-bound freak. Her child would still be alive. Hunter was supposed to suffer as much as she had.

'Why *are* you here, Rickard?' Her voice was stronger than expected coming from such a frail body and sounded exactly as it had when passing instructions to him via his phone. It held little trace of an accent, and even less of the shock of having watched her latest lover cut down by Rickard's bullets.

'I told you to disappear for a while.'

Rickard grunted. 'Told me?'

'Yes. You were being paid a lot of money to do as you were told.'

'That was never the way I saw our arrangement. You *told* me nothing. You asked and I delivered.'

'That is not quite true.'

'I did everything I was asked.' Rickard dabbed at a trickle of blood on his forehead.

'You failed to kill *his* woman.'

'Ballard wasn't his woman.'

'That's beside the point. Your instructions were to pose as Joe Hunter. I accept that you did that quite well. You framed him for murder, but that was supposed to force him into running for his life. Hunter did not run, though; he came after you. And instead of concentrating on your prime directive, you chose to go off on a private vendetta against your wife.'

'My wife betrayed me. She led *your* people to me.' Rickard laughed at that. 'She needed punishing.'

Jimena's breath sounded like a whistle in the back of her throat. She looked confused at his words. She stirred, attempting to sit straight in her bed. 'I didn't send anyone after you.'

'Three men died in my apartment,' Rickard crowed.

'Explain that.'

'I can't. All I know is that your actions attracted the notice of the very people you were supposed to kill, but you didn't do that.'

'I haven't finished yet.'

Jimena shook her head as though at a recalcitrant child. 'You were attracting too much attention. That is why you were told to disappear. I *did* send a team to kill Joe Hunter because I lost confidence in you.'

'The ones at the diner? They didn't do a very good job.'

She shrugged. 'They paid for their failure. The one who survived? He won't survive the night . . . I have already arranged that.'

280

'You have a low opinion of those working for you.'

'Only when they displease me. You didn't find Bryce Lang and ultimately you failed to kill Hunter.'

'Like I said: I haven't finished yet.'

'Oh, but you have.' She lifted a hand from under the sheets and waved it at Cesar Calle and his henchman lying on the floor. 'This severs our contract, Rickard. You have led Alvaro Silva's men to my home, and you have murdered the man who was financing you . . . it is over.'

'It doesn't work that way. Only I say when it's over.' Rickard put down his assault rifle and pulled his blade from his belt. 'Not an ugly whore like you.'

A bullet had stroked her face, blinding her in one eye, and cutting a furrow up her forehead to her hairline. She was permanently disfigured, but only when viewed from one angle: from her untouched side she was still incredibly beautiful. Not that he saw her that way. Jimena's beauty might hold power over the likes of Cesar Calle, forcing the man to do her bidding like her personal lapdog, but to him she was just a hopeless bitch in need of putting in her place.

Deep in his gut he felt the stirring of the serpent. It was not a supernatural creature that infested him, but the expression of the rage and fury he held for all women. It was the culmination of the seed planted there when as a child his mother had abandoned him and left him in the hands of his brutal and sexually deviant stepfather. He had suffered terribly and for that he hated all females. And he had a desire to show that he was not someone a woman could disregard like he was garbage to be thrown in the gutter.

The serpent coiled and demanded release.

He lifted the blade.

Jimena laughed at him.

Rickard paused. 'I'm going to kill you and you laugh at me?'

'Do it, Rickard. You will be doing me a huge favour.' Jimena allowed her hand to flutter across her body and down to her paralysed legs. Then she reached up and touched the horrendous scar on her face.

Death is not the greatest of evils; it is worse to want to die, and not be able to. Rickard remembered the words that Jimena had once quoted to him. He believed they were the words of the philosopher Sophocles. 'What is this, bitch? Reverse psychology. You think that if you invite death I'll spare you?'

'You will kill me or one of Silva's men will do it. I don't care. I will be with my child again.' She glanced again at the wreckage of her body, then calmly at Rickard. 'I will be whole again.'

'That's debatable,' Rickard said. 'Considering that I'm going to cut you to pieces.'

Jimena peered up at him with her one good eye. In its dark depths there was resolution. 'Just make sure that you do it right this time. I've suffered enough: don't leave me the way you left your wife.'

'My wife's dead.'

A smile tugged at Jimena's lips. Again it was as if she was patronising an obstinate boy.

Rickard's eyes puckered. 'I shot her.'

Jimena coughed out a laugh. 'I was shot, too, and much worse than Alisha was. You failed to kill her the way you failed everything else.'

'You're lying.'

'Why would I?'

'Because you're a deceitful bitch, just like every other woman I ever—' Rickard noted the subtle movement of Jimena's other hand beneath the sheets. 'What have you got there?'

He leaned down, readying the knife.

And that was when he heard the clipped command from behind him.

'Drop the knife, Rickard.'

The metamorphosis that came over Jimena's features was shocking. She went from calm resolution to insane hatred in a heartbeat. Without looking, Rickard knew who had just entered the room. Jimena twisted, surprisingly fast for one who'd appeared so feeble all this time, and the gun that she had concealed under the sheet switched from aiming directly at his gut to the man in the doorway behind him. Jimena shrieked and fired at the same time.

Bullets punched through the sheets, making a series of small black holes in the material. Then

283

they sped at supersonic speed past Rickard. He was already reacting, spinning away, but he wasn't quick enough and felt like he'd been kicked in the ribs. His feet caught under the bent knee of Cesar Calle and he stumbled, falling over the dead man to sprawl on the floor. Rickard immediately rolled over, going for his own gun, as he stared incredulously back at the woman.

Jimena was still screeching like a wildcat. She tore her hand from under the sheet, lifting out a Smith and Wesson Sigma, and reared up to get a cleaner shot at her target. Instinctively Rickard knew that the gun had a capacity for seventeen rounds; enough were left that Jimena was a real threat to his ongoing existence.

But so was Joe Hunter.

Rickard looked for the man, but couldn't immediately see him. Maybe Jimena had killed him and he was on the ground, or he'd fled back out the door. He turned back to Jimena, just as she brought her Sigma round towards him.

It would have been more fulfilling to use the ceramic blade, but he was no sentimental fool. He fired. One-two-three bullets in a close group. Every one of them struck the target: Jimena's chest. She was flung back against the pillows and her mouth opened with a rush of air and blood forced from her lungs. Then her head dipped and she didn't move again. The Sigma fell from her limp fingers, bounced once on the mattress then clattered to the floor on the far side of the bed.

In the brief moment that he paid her any notice, Jimena looked at peace. Bitch!

Rickard came to his feet.

He looked to the door. Beyond it he could hear the rattle of a machine gun. The fight now sounded like it was in the house. That, of course, was the least of his concerns. Joe Hunter was much closer by. He just couldn't see . . .

Hunter came up over the top of the bed, a SIG Sauer in hand. He looked unharmed and wholly intent on killing.

But Rickard wasn't one to stand round and wait for death.

They both fired at the same time.

CHAPTER 36

Jimena Grajales hated me with every atom of her being.

The instant she saw me in the doorway the switch on her sanity flicked over and hit meltdown.

It kind of blew my chances of saving her life.

Sounds crazy, I guess, but even as I realised the true identity of my enemy I couldn't dredge up the minutest grain of enmity towards her. She'd been terribly wounded, had lost her child, and it was all because I hadn't had it in me to shoot when I had the chance. As misguided as that was, it wasn't so surprising that she hated me so much. She'd ordered the other members of the hit team killed, had extended that order to include their families: I should have hated her equally. But I didn't. All I saw was a horrifically injured woman grieving the loss of her baby boy. In that moment I'd have given up my life to save hers.

Then she began shooting at me.

I saw the tug of the gun barrel on the sheet and I dropped low. Her bullets punched the wall above my head, scattering particles of plaster on my shoulders. She was struggling with the gun and I went to my knees, under her line of fire, dumping the machine gun which had become an encumbrance and pulling out my SIG. I still didn't want to shoot her, but that choice was taken from me in the next instant. I heard three almost simultaneous cracks of a gun and Jimena went silent. Her Sigma clattered on the floor next to me.

Snatching a glance under the bed, I could see movement directly opposite me. Rickard had gone down, tripping over a corpse, but he was already coming back to his feet. I was only a beat behind him. I stood up, my gun extended, and fired.

Rickard fired too.

I felt the tug of his bullet as it struck my SIG. Damn well near tore my hand off as it ripped the gun out of my grip. That was either the best or the luckiest shot I'd ever witnessed. My bet was on the latter.

My bullet hit Rickard high in his left trapezius muscle and he twisted with the impact, so that his second shot went over my head, struck the light fixture in the ceiling and plunged us into half-light.

I looked for my gun. Couldn't see it. Maybe it was damaged beyond repair. The Sigma was a few feet away. So was my assault rifle where I'd dropped it. There was no time for any of them; I vaulted up on to Jimena's deathbed, then through the air at Rickard.

He was already bringing his gun round to shoot

me again, but his angle was wrong. I landed on my feet directly in front of him, even as I swept my forearm against his gun, knocking his next shot astray. Then my momentum took me chest to chest with him and we both crashed into a wall. I punched Rickard in the face. It took everything not to scream; an agonising flame leaped from my hand all the way to my brain. Something felt like it had broken in my hand when my SIG had been wrenched away.

Yet I couldn't let that stop me. If I gave him even the briefest of moments to rally, he would shoot me point-blank and that would be the end of it. So, my damaged hand became a bludgeon as I drove it four times in quick succession into his body.

Yelling directly into his face, I grappled with his gun. He yelled back. Nothing either of us said made any sense; it was just the bestial roaring of two wild animals engaged in a life or death battle.

Rickard was no slouch. He gave me a couple punches of his own. One of them got me in my right ear, the other dangerously close to the eye socket. I head-butted him, and he gave me one right back. He kneed at my groin, but I jammed his leg between mine and forced him against the wall. We were too close for clean strikes now and we both clawed. I got my fingers in his nostrils and forced his head back. Rickard stuck his thumb in my already stinging eye. Finally I managed to bang his gun against the wall and he released it. But that gave him two functioning hands as weapons. He punched me in the ribs. Air left my lungs, but I wasn't about to back away now. If I did that he might draw that blade he'd been holding earlier and then I'd be in real trouble. Instead, I sank my teeth into his shoulder at the exact point where my bullet had nicked him moments before. Rickard howled, and I echoed his scream through my clamped teeth.

We were both in frenzy, unmindful of the form standing in the open door behind us. We were too intent on ripping lumps from each other. But even in that primal state something impinged upon my senses. The blocking shadow in the doorway suddenly fled, allowing light to spill inside from the passageway. On the beam of light I saw the tumbling cylindrical object arch towards us as if it was moving in super-slow motion.

I experienced one of those snapshot moments.

L2A2.

My subconscious mind identified the object. It took another split second for it to push the military term to its hiding place in the back of my head and come up with the layman's name. Hand grenade.

Dear God!

I don't know which of us spoke those words. Maybe we both did. Because in the next instant we spilled apart just as the grenade landed in the gap we'd made.

The L2A2 is an anti-personnel weapon, a tin-plated fragmentation device with a coil of notched wire and packed with one hundred and seventy grams of high-explosive filling. It is designed to kill anyone in a radius of up to eighteen yards. The room we were in was no more than eight or nine yards square. It didn't give either of us very good odds at survival.

There was only seconds until detonation.

I went one way and Rickard the other. To be honest I forgot all about him in that instant, was only vaguely aware that he was nearer the exit door than I was. I threw myself over Jimena's still form and on to the floor, crouched and got my fingers under the edge of her bed and heaved it up so that the bed toppled, spilling its occupant on to the floor. The bed on its side wasn't much of a shield, but it was all I had.

It's hard to describe the explosion. I was so close that I didn't actually hear it, just felt the metal frame of the bed slam me and throw me back against the near wall. For the briefest of moments it seemed the frame was going to cut me to pieces, as though I was being passed through a massive dicing machine. But then the pressure was gone, I went face down on the floor and the bed collapsed on top of me.

That wasn't so bad.

Until I tried to raise my head and found that the commands of my brain were being ignored by my body. Then I heard noise: the slamming beat of blood pounding through my inner ears, someone roaring in deep-throated agony.

Pain assaulted me in every fibre.

My fingertips were twitching and I was oddly aware of the movement as though watching from outside myself. I wondered who was groaning in agony. A black wave passed through my mind and I felt like I was falling into a deep hole. I clawed at a dull spark of lucidity, refusing to succumb to the darkness, except it was a losing battle.

It was as though a black drape dropped over my head. In panic I imagined that I was being zipped into a body bag and I fought against the enfolding material. I'm still alive, I wanted to scream, but nothing came out. I kicked, bucked and came to my knees. Or that's how it seemed. When I opened my eyes again I was still face down. A troop of Nazis marched over my spine stamping down with their jackboots.

And someone was still groaning.

Me.

I shoved over on to my side. It was an Olympic-scale effort just to do that. My hearing was compressed by the pressure of the detonation, so that all I could hear were screeches and clicks and the beating of my own heart. The latter at least was a good thing. Didn't mean I was going to survive but it was a start.

Coming to some semblance of lucidity, I unfolded my arms; only then realising that I'd wrapped them round my skull at the last moment. It meant that my earlier image of watching my twitching fingers couldn't have been true, but everything about the entire situation felt more than surreal. Pressing an elbow to the bed frame, I pushed against it. The bed wouldn't move. Blinking through dust, I saw that one of the legs had been thrust into the wall, skewering deep into the plaster covering. It had missed my body by inches.

It was a Herculean task to get a knee under me and press my shoulder against the bed and move it away. As the bed frame scraped across the floor, I slipped and went down hard on my damaged hand. I cringed, but pushed up again. Part of me wanted to give in, to lie down and succumb to the bliss of unconsciousness. Another part screamed at me to get my arse in gear. The screamer was the most adamant. Even if Rickard was dead, the one who'd thrown the grenade at us wasn't. Any second now, he'd be coming back to make sure the explosion had done its work.

The room was full of smoke and dust, and dripping stuff. I didn't like to think about what was smeared on the ceiling and walls, or what the crimson chunks were that had been scattered to the four corners of the room. No way possible to count if those steaming entrails belonged to three corpses or four.

Staggering, I made it round the edge of the bed. First I looked to the door but I could detect no movement through the acrid smoke so I looked at the bed instead. The mattress had been shredded. Clumps of foam erupted from ragged holes where shrapnel had torn into it. The metal headboard had been ripped loose and was a mangled wreck a few feet away. A dark banner floated on the unnatural breeze as displaced air began forcing its way back into the room. It took a moment or so to realise that it was a lock of Jimena Grajales' hair. I closed my eyes against the sight and turned away.

My ears were pulsating.

Gunfire crackled from somewhere, but my senses were so rattled that I couldn't get a fix on the direction. I placed my palms on my ears, pressing and releasing, attempting to pop my eardrums into a more natural configuration. When I withdrew, the palm of my left hand was spotted with blood. I didn't think that my eardrum was ruptured; the blood was more likely from a superficial wound on my face. Who knew?

I'd more important things to worry about.

I gave myself a once-over. I hurt everywhere but, apart from my throbbing hand, nothing seemed to have been broken or torn loose. So I bent in search of a weapon.

First thing I found was my SIG Sauer. There was an indentation on the slide where Rickard's lucky shot had struck it. I doubted it would function properly, but still jammed it into my waistband. Call me sentimental but the gun had been with me through too many trials to leave it lying there.

I kicked through drifts of collapsed ceiling and

293

shattered bodies and saw my assault rifle. I shook off the dust, ejected the magazine, slapped it back in place. Sliding the bolt, I ejected a shell, then racked a new one in the chamber. Round about then I felt blood spatter on my chin. It wasn't the red rain falling from the ceiling, but my nose in full flow. I wiped the blood from my face with a sleeve, starting walking cradling the gun.

My coordination was still shot to pieces, but movement helped. I only staggered twice before reaching the door. Leaning against the frame, I checked the short passageway ahead. Placing my finger on the trigger, I was acutely aware of the pain in my hand. Broken or not, it would just have to work.

Fifteen feet away a man lay face down.

Hoping it was Rickard, I moved forwards. At the body I paused long enough to kick it over on to its back. The round-faced soldier grinned up at me. Except this grin was a rictus smile. Beneath his chin a wound stretched equally wide. His throat had been opened from ear to ear and I guessed that Rickard had made it out of the room after all. Guarapo – the grenade thrower – had felt his wrath.

And now it was Rickard's turn to feel mine.

The only thing stopping me was the man at the head of the stairs pointing a machine gun at me.

CHAPTER 37

Rickard was both exhilarated and furious. Exhilarated because he was still alive. Intensely angered by more than one thing. Foremost in his rage was that the cowardly son of a bitch, Guarapo, had tried to kill him by lobbing a hand grenade at him. Well, he'd shown that asshole the error of his ways soon enough. When the L2A2 had clattered to the floor between him and Joe Hunter, Rickard had known he had seconds to live. It's surprising how much ground a man can cover when trying to save his ass. He made it out of the door just as the grenade blasted the room. The percussion knocked him sprawling, but he avoided the flying shrapnel and came immediately to his feet again. As he did he whipped out his ceramic knife, the same moment as Guarapo popped up from where he'd been crouching and blinked at him in dismay.

Guarapo didn't expect anyone to survive the bomb.

He certainly wasn't prepared for when Rickard grabbed him, spun him and wrapped a hand round his jaw. A quick jerk back on the man's head and a swipe of the blade and that was all it took.

Next on his checklist was that Guarapo's indiscreet betrayal had killed Joe Hunter when the honour should have been his. Rickard might have come here to murder his employer, but it didn't mean that he wouldn't have seen the job through. A deal was a deal, the way he viewed things: only Jimena Grajales broke contracts.

Alvaro Silva was another point of anger. Had he ordered Rickard murdered or was that solely Guarapo's plan? Maybe he'd been harbouring a plan for revenge since they first met and Rickard had tickled his balls with the tip of his knife. That was something to think on later. There was something far more pressing on his mind.

Alisha.

The way Jimena made it sound, his wife hadn't betrayed him at all. She hadn't led men to his apartment. Not killers sent by Jimena. But the fact remained, Alisha had conspired against him with the men he'd killed in Miami. Any way that he looked at it, the bitch needed punishing. Maybe it was as simple as that Alisha had been having an affair with the man he'd surprised in the elevator and the man had come back with some friends to do away with the competition. In retrospect Rickard recalled thinking that they weren't very good when he'd killed them, not professionals. Proof of his theory of Alisha's infidelity was the way in which she'd run off, seeking solace

296

and protection in the arms of another man. Rickard had never learned the name of the cocaine dealer in Liberty City, but he didn't doubt that he'd been screwing Alisha when Rickard was out of town.

Bitch!

The thing that angered him most was that Alisha hadn't died. He believed Jimena's words. There was no reason for her to lie. She knew she was going to die, so why mention that his wife had survived? Unless it was to anger him, to throw him off while she positioned the gun she had hidden in her bed. Perhaps she thought he'd be so stunned that he wouldn't notice what she was doing and would not react in time. But he didn't think so. Jimena wasn't afraid to die; in fact it looked like she had fully embraced the idea. She'd only intended taking him with her. She'd told him that Alisha was still alive to score some points on him before she died. One up for the girls!

Yeah, we'll see about that.

And after he finished with Alisha he had a date with that other cow, Imogen Ballard. He'd promised her that things weren't finished.

No woman would ever fuck him over again.

First things first, though. He had to get away from this battleground, avoid the opposing armies and get himself back to the States.

Armed with the gun he'd taken from Guarapo's dead body and the knife sheathed once again at his belt, he felt he was up to it. He wouldn't let the wounds he'd picked up stop him. They required medical attention, primarily the gunshot in his shoulder and the one that had creased his ribs, but they could wait until he was safely away from here.

He used the window he'd shattered to climb outside, where he crouched next to some flowering shrubs as a tall black man raced towards the front of the house. He was followed a moment later by a muscular Asian-American. Rickard blinked in confusion, but when he thought about it he wasn't that surprised. They were the two men that had been with Hunter when Jimena's hit team had failed to take Hunter out at the Miami diner. The Japanese dude, he recalled, had also been there when he had riddled Alisha full of bullets.

Maybe these two men would be as relentless as adversaries as their friend had proved. Or maybe when they found his eviscerated body down in the bombed chamber, they'd just give up.

He thought about following them back inside the house, killing them, but then decided, what the hell. Why tempt fate? Once Alisha and Imogen Ballard were dead, he could always track them down later.

Romeo, his one-eyed pilot, had mentioned staying on a couple of nights at the village where he'd delivered him. Couple of young señoritas he was going to hook up with. Apparently he wasn't known as Romeo for nothing.

Gunfire still echoed through the valley, but it

was sporadic now, Silva's troops mopping up the last resistance. The shots were single cracks: more executions than they were all-out gunfights. Silva would be pleased. Calle's home was now Silva's, and so was his niche in the drug market.

You're welcome to it, Rickard thought. He headed for the jeep in which he'd originally arrived. The windscreen was shattered and the driver dead inside, but otherwise it was still drive-able. He tugged the dead man out, allowed him to crumple to the ground, then climbed inside. The keys were still in the ignition. He spun the jeep round and away, heading off in search of Romeo.

In his mirrors he saw Metzger running towards the front of the house, a machine gun in his arms, like the indestructible lead in a Schwarzenegger movie.

He looked the part.

Perhaps the big German would kill Hunter's friends and save him the trouble.

CHAPTER 38

Lifting my Heckler and Koch, I was intent on firing. My damaged hand rebelled against me though and my twitching finger couldn't exert the required pressure. It was well that it failed to do so.

The silhouetted figure at the head of the stairs materialised into my friend, Harvey Lucas.

He came down the stairs, the sheen of perspiration on his bald head reflecting the light behind him as if he wore a halo.

'Jesus, Hunter, you look like crap.'

Harvey grabbed hold of me, supporting me under an elbow. I didn't realise that I'd almost gone to my knees until he hauled me upright and held me against the passage wall.

'Believe me,' I croaked. 'I feel much worse than I look.'

'Damn.'

Swaying, I took a quick glance down at myself. My clothing was shredded in places, covered in dust, and I was plastered with blood. Not all of it belonged to me, thankfully. There was even a chunk of shrapnel embedded in the toe of my right boot. Another half-inch higher and it would have taken off my toes. I reached down to tug it loose and almost fell on my face, but Harvey took control of me and pulled me towards the stairs.

'Gotta get outa here, Hunter, this place is a goddamn hell-hole.'

I wasn't arguing. Harvey hauled me up the stairs and I don't think that I got a steady foot on one of them. At the top he propped me against a wall while he checked the way was clear. Then I was being hustled along again.

My friend questioned me as we went. But I was concussed and not a little out of it. His questions were rapid-fire, but I had only one answer for him.

'Rickard got away.'

Harvey stopped and looked at me.

'He was here?'

'Got away.'

We both glanced around, expecting the killer to jump out from hiding. Then I shook my head. 'He thinks I'm dead. Thinks the grenade got me.'

'He's damn right it got you.'

I laughed. It sounded a little insane.

Harvey cursed under his breath and then pulled me on.

Rink materialised out of a doorway beside us. When he saw me his face said it all.

'I'm OK, buddy,' I reassured him.

'Hunter, my great-uncle Jim looks better than you an' he's been buried for fifteen years.'

Transferring his H&K to his left arm, he grabbed

me under my other elbow. Now I had the support of my two best friends and it was a good feeling. Made me want to sing that old brotherly song by the Hollies, but I guessed that I'd probably get a slap from Rink. So I kept the words to myself.

Distantly there came the crack of a rifle followed by silence. Sounded like the battle was over with, but whoever turned out the victors here they were still our enemies.

My friends continued hauling me towards the front of the house.

'Goin' to be difficult gettin' out without being seen,' Rink said.

'Nunez and Charles are still out there. They'll cover for us.' Harvey took a quick glance out the door. 'But we're going to have to get around the back before they'll know we're coming.'

'Window at the side,' I said. 'Where I came in. We can get out that way.'

In silent agreement my friends turned along the passage past the living rooms. I lifted my chin, indicating the room I'd entered the house by. Both Rink and Harvey looked where I was nodding at the same time. It was a mistake, and I cursed myself for compromising us. The crunch of a boot was followed immediately by a barked command.

'Drop your weapons.'

We came to a halt, but none of us complied.

'Drop your weapons and turn around. Slowly. No sudden moves or you all die.'

The accent was guttural, nothing Spanish about

it. Sounded German. When we turned I wasn't surprised to see the muscular fair-haired man I'd noted earlier. He was holding an assault rifle wedged to his shoulder, threatening us with the barrel. He looked the business, standing there as solid as a rock with the cold light of intensity in his eyes.

'I will not say it again.' The mercenary's finger was white on the trigger, and I could swear I could hear the tendons creaking like rigging on a sailboat. He wasn't fucking around with us.

We allowed our H&Ks to drop to the floor.

He jerked the barrel of his gun between us. Choosing his targets. 'Now your sidearms.'

To give up our guns was giving in to the inevitable. I was under no illusions: this man was only stripping us of our weapons so that there was no chance of resistance when he finally gunned us down. He was a stone-hearted killer by trade, but I recognised something in him that maybe even he wasn't aware of. To kill you must be prepared to die. Concern yourself with covering the eventuality of your own demise and you start making mistakes.

'Give them up, guys.'

Rink and Harvey didn't argue with me. They just unsnapped their handguns and dropped them on the floor.

The mercenary jabbed his rifle directly at me. 'You as well, asshole. Do it.'

I was hanging on to my friends' shoulders. 'Back pocket.'

'You do it then.' The mercenary indicated Rink. 'Fingertips only.'

Rink reached a hand behind me, pulled my damaged SIG from my waistband and tossed it on the floor. The merc nodded, a smile creeping on to his lips. Rink allowed his arm to loop round my back again, and I felt his fingers dig into my hip pocket.

'I don't know who the fuck you are, but you should not be here.' The merc's words were a final indication of our fate.

'We came here to kill you,' I snapped. My words covered the faint click from behind my back.

They also served to focus the mercenary's attention fully on me. He sneered, aimed the gun directly at my head. 'You are in no shape for killing anyone.'

Rink is right-handed. But he has trained to use his left when in a pinch. As I dipped away from him, shoving against Harvey with my shoulder, the mercenary's gun followed. Rink's left arm had clearance and it came up in a blur. He launched the switchblade like some sort of Ninja move, a weird underhand flick that sent it unerringly at the mercenary's gut.

The man reacted, trying to avoid the missile. His bullets churned a line through the ceiling even as Harvey and I ducked low. The knife jabbed into him just below his left ribs. Not a fatal wound by any stretch of the imagination, but Rink was already moving.

Ten feet had separated us, and Rink covered it in less than a second. He got an arm under the machine gun, ramming it higher in the air. Wasted bullets blasted plaster from the ceiling a second time. He got his other hand on the hilt of the knife and he ripped sideways. The man's gut was laid open, but Rink wasn't finished. He tugged the blade loose, then jammed it into the meat of the man's neck just below the lobe of his left ear.

Now that wound *was* fatal.

The German dropped face down. Rink stood over him, then reached down to pluck the knife free and wiped it clean on the man's shirt. He turned to me with a cold smile, waggling the knife. 'Bet you're pleased I gave you this now?'

I'd almost forgotten about the knife that Rink took off Wetherby's henchman back in Miami. It had just been one of those things that I'd transferred from my pockets with each change of clothing, along with cash and wallet and a couple of other oddments.

Harvey ran a palm over his slick forehead. 'Jesus, you guys, I wish you'd warn me when you're going to go all *Shogun Assassin* on me.'

We laughed. Sometimes I forget that Harvey didn't spend all those years fighting alongside the two of us. Together Rink and me are finely tuned and can work as though symbiotically. But Harvey was getting there. Couple more situations like this and he would be part of the hive mentality we shared.

'Wasn't no samurai move.' Rink grinned at Harvey as he joined us. 'Got that one from *West Side Story.*'

We gathered up our weapons. Harvey was muttering at Rink in good nature, eliciting an even wider grin.

'You want this?' Rink showed me my damaged SIG.

I took it from him. It was an old friend, and you never left a friend behind. 'I'll fix it.'

Rink went out the window first and covered while I negotiated the space. I didn't want to feel like a hindrance, and when he offered me his elbow, I showed him I was OK by lifting my H&K to cover the opposite direction. Life in the old dog yet.

Harvey clambered out and we pepper-potted back towards the cleft in the cliff. Nunez scrambled down the rocks and then dropped to a knee, covering our retreat. Above him, Charles also covered us, his adrenalin-pale face looking as solid as the boulders surrounding him.

It was tough scaling the rocks up to the cleft. My right hand was alternating between numb and screaming in pain. I couldn't decide which I preferred. When it was hurting I could at least use it. In the end, Rink swarmed past me, grabbed hold of the back of my jacket and dragged me up and past Charles. Harvey followed, and then Nunez came up as fleet as a cat.

The cleft was no place to linger. Not because there were sentries up on the cliffs any more: Rink and Harvey wouldn't have joined me without finishing them first. Anyone – with the exception of Luke Rickard – who'd seen any of us was now dead. However no one down at Cesar Calle's house was aware of our presence and it was better to keep things that way.

We hurried through the cleft, climbed down at the far end and got back on the trail where we followed the river upstream. We didn't slow down for a mile. Then Rink called a halt. He was concerned about me.

'Keep going, guys. I'm not so bad now that I've shaken off the effects of the explosion.' I caught glances from the Jungla troopers. Neither one of them were party to how close I'd come to being shredded by the frag grenade. Now they were studying me like I was a walking miracle. Maybe I was.

Nunez handed me a flask. 'Drink.'

It wasn't in me to say no. I swallowed noisily. The bottle contained distilled water, glucose, electrolytes. I needed them all.

No one followed us from the valley.

We were pretty sure, but Charles fell back to keep rear guard while Nunez went ahead. As we moved along the trail,

I brought Rink and Harvey up to speed with all that had gone down and what I'd overheard.

'The woman was behind all this? She ordered the hits on Bryce's team?' Rink shook his head. 'Goddamn . . .'

'I couldn't save her.'

'Why would you want to?' Harvey had the same hatred for men who hurt women as I did, but he wasn't thinking of Jimena Grajales in the same way as me. 'She's responsible for more murders than Hannibal freakin' Lecter.'

'She was hurting . . .'

'She was insane.'

'Yeah,' I nodded. 'But maybe we would've been the same if we'd seen our child murdered.'

The silence that followed my words was interrupted only by the flap of a bird's wings as it broke cover. We had already paused in our march, but the bird's frantic flight now made us crouch and scan the forest for whatever had disturbed it. In the end I decided that it was most likely only the weight of our words and I gave the all-clear sign. We moved on.

'So what do you make of Rickard turning up here?'

Glancing at Rink, I lifted my shoulders in a shrug. 'Revenge? From what I heard, he blamed Jimena for sending a team to kill him. He was talking about Del Chisholm and his men.'

'He didn't know that they were only there to take Alisha to safety?'

'Jimena told him she'd nothing to do with that, but it made no difference. Rickard came here to kill her, and nothing she said was going to change his mind.'

'The guys that were with Rickard,' Harvey said. 'Who were they?'

Harvey, I recalled, hadn't been party to the conversation I'd had earlier with Nunez when he'd recognised those attacking Cesar Calle's stronghold. I kept it simple.

'A rival outfit. Jimena mentioned someone called Silva. It looks like Rickard changed sides but my guess is he was only using Silva's resources so he could get at Jimena.'

'Looks that way,' Rink said. 'You think Rickard has run back to this Silva dude now?'

'No. I think he's done what he came here for. If he was going to stick around, he'd just have waited at Calle's place for Silva to arrive.'

'So what's your best guess?'

'He's on his way back to Miami.'

'You sound pretty sure about that.'

'I am. Jimena told him that Alisha survived.' Scrubbing a palm through my dusty hair, I could feel gobbets of blood sticking to my scalp. 'And knowing what he is now, I think he'll want to put that right.'

'First chance we get, we should warn Walter.'

'We'll do that once we're back at the staging post. The Junglas have satcom: I want Walter to pull a few strings and organise us a fast pick-up and get back there before Rickard does.'

'You're planning on using Alisha as bait?' Harvey rolled his head.

'Rickard's going after her. It's best that it's under controlled circumstances when he makes his play.'

'She's in a hospital, Hunter,' Harvey said. Not

that I required reminding. I just nodded. The logistics were troubling, but there was one good thing going for a showdown at the hospital. Rickard wouldn't have far to travel if we met again: the hospital also had a morgue.

CHAPTER 39

Walter met the news that Rickard had given us the slip with less hostility than I expected. He was sticking his neck over the headsman's block on our behalf and he'd have preferred it if we'd buried the son of a bitch in a nameless grave out in the Colombian jungle. His decades of experience in black ops had somewhat tempered his reaction to the possibility of failure, though, and he simply asked the question, what did I need?

First on the list was establishing a pick-up point and a rapid evacuation. Next I needed him to influence the turn out of events here in Colombia. I then told him what I wanted to do with Alisha. Everything else could wait for our return to Florida.

Nunez and Charles delivered us to a hilltop designated only by coordinates punched into a GPS system. Undulating foothills spread out beneath us. The sky was pale blue with a bank of grey thunderheads building on the Andes to the west. The sun was hidden by the clouds but made a last-gasp attempt at holding back the night, making a fiery display of gold and lapis lazuli over the tallest peaks. It was a pretty way to end this trip to Colombia.

From the north a black speck grew steadily larger and more defined. We'd come in at high altitude but we'd be leaving below radar. As we waited for the arrival of the helicopter, I shook the hands of the Jungla troopers.

'It was a pleasure working with you both.' My words sounded standard, but I meant every one of them.

As usual it was Nunez who did most of the talking. 'The pleasure was all ours. Thank you for what you did here, Hunter. You have been of great service to this country.'

I nodded at his words. Anything I'd done for his country was a mere consequence of my attempt at finding Rickard, but both Nunez and Charles seemed pleased by the result. We'd already discussed what had befallen Cesar Calle, and how Alvaro Silva had now doubled the size of his empire. But the Junglas seemed unconcerned by that. The way they saw it was that one enemy of the country would be easier to bring down than two, and they had enough evidence to destroy him through what they'd witnessed. We wouldn't enter the equation: Nunez and Charles were to receive backdated orders to conduct CTR – close target reconnaissance – of Calle's activities. The order was arranged between Walter and a local contact with DET,

Colombia's own intelligence-gathering community, and the Junglas would report their findings. The fact that they witnessed the massacre of Cesar Calle and all his people was enough that a strike force was already being assembled to take down *Organizacion Halcón de Roja*.

Charles placed his fists on his hips as he turned to watch the approaching chopper. He had a distant look in his eye, as though perhaps he wanted to jump on board and leave the troubles of Colombia behind him to go back to the home of his father. Even with Calle and Silva out of the picture, there were still many problems plaguing this country, but there was nothing to say that anywhere else was any less troubled. The USA and Florida in particular, I thought, could be witnessing terrible happenings before long.

The speck had grown into a UH-72A Lakota helicopter. The chopper swept in, bending the tops of trees below us and sending up a vortex of dust and loose foliage. Shielding our eyes, we moved forwards, leaving the Junglas standing next to their jeep. I wondered if I'd see either of them again, but decided not in this lifetime. The helicopter was a light utility transporter with room for two crew and six passengers. It didn't feel very spacious when I followed Rink and Harvey inside, but that's what comes of travelling with two large friends.

The crewmen were locals with no capacity for the English language. They didn't try to communicate anyway, they had their instructions and that was all. They flew us almost due north to a strip of land in a valley of the Santa Marta Mountains, where we found a transport plane of the 920th Rescue Wing waiting for us. A few hours after that and we descended towards Patrick Air Force Base, Cocoa Beach a luminescent silver strip against the dark of the Atlantic Ocean on our right. A limousine – a government battlewagon – waited for us in the tepid evening warmth. Walter, Bryce Lang and SAC Ron Hubbard stood next to the limo, and I noted at least four armed guards covering their asses: Luke Rickard was the type for direct attack and not even an air force base overflowing with security and crawling with Homeland Security personnel would put him off.

On the flight there I'd cleaned myself up as best I could, but I still looked like a herd of wild bulls had stampeded over me. I felt a little like that too. As I walked across the tarmac it was with the robotic steps of an alien from a 1950s B-movie. Shaking loose the kinks in my muscles was on the agenda if I ever hoped to be ready for when I caught up with Rickard.

Walter gave me a fatherly clap on the shoulder. 'Things were pretty rough down there, huh?'

'It got a little out of hand, if that's what you mean.'

'Looks like it.' He wrinkled his nose. I probably smelled like a herd of bulls had run over me.

'I know. I need a shower.'

'And food, drink and rest,' Walter said. He scrutinised Rink and Harvey. 'All of you.'

'Jeez, we didn't get this type of treatment in the old days,' Rink said. He eyed the limousine with unabashed admiration. Rink likes expensive vehicles, but his are usually sportier. He was possibly wondering if his Porsche had been delivered back to his place yet.

Bryce exchanged greetings with us. Then, eyes downcast, he said, 'Jimena Grajales. I can't believe it.'

'Like you told me, Bryce, I should've taken the shot. None of this would've happened if I'd done Abadia when I had the chance.'

Now it was he who laid a hand on my shoulder. 'A man like Luke Rickard would commit murder whoever was behind him. It doesn't matter now.' When he stepped away from me to shake hands with Rink and then Harvey I could see tears in his eyes. I couldn't decide if it was with relief or with regret that he had led our old team-mates to a horrible ending.

SAC Hubbard was an unexpected guest at this reunion. When I looked at him he returned my gaze and it was as if he read my mind.

'I've done everything I could in Maine, so I pulled a few strings and have come here to help coordinate the capture of Luke Rickard.'

Recalling his sour, raisin eyes from the first time we met, I noticed that he was less pinched now. In fact he looked genuinely pleased to see me back safe and sound. But there was still something about him I didn't like. I shook his hand and kept hold.

'How's Imogen?'

'She's under guard at a safe house. You needn't worry about her.'

'That's not what I asked.'

'She's fine. A little shook up by her ordeal, but physically she's OK.'

'Thanks,' I said. 'For looking after her while I was gone.'

Finally I let his hand go and he put it in his trouser pocket like he didn't know what to do with it. Maybe I'd been squeezing a little too tightly and he was discreetly checking for broken fingers.

Walter waved us into the limousine. Creaking horribly in my knees, I climbed inside. The leather upholstery was plush. It was a shame that my clothing was going to make a mess of it. I had to bunch over to allow Rink and Harvey in alongside me, but the car was big enough to accommodate even them – it was roomier than the Lakota helicopter, or maybe it just felt more comfortable. Walter, Bryce and Hubbard all sat in the seats in front. Walter hung an arm over the back of his chair so that he could look at us.

Walter's famous for obfuscating – his word not mine – but this time everything was in his favour to come clean and say it as it was. For a certain pair of ears at any rate.

'I want to thank you all for what you did down there, but I'm going to have to ask you to stand down.' His eyes flicked once to Hubbard. 'The FBI is taking over the hunt for Rickard now.'

Hubbard must have felt our eyes boring into the back of his skull because he stirred, twisting round so he could stare back at us. 'People are still dying here, and that's my first concern.

People? I didn't know who he was referring to.

'The man you captured during the gunfight at the diner was stabbed to death last night,' he explained. 'I've no doubt that his death was to cover the trail back to Jimena Grajales.

I sniffed. No great loss.

'Maybe you don't care about that,' Hubbard went on, 'but this thing is not finished yet. Not until Rickard is captured. A threat to *any* citizens of our country is too important for the Bureau to ignore. Primarily, we have to protect Alisha Rickard and the other patients and medical staff from any harm. I've activated HRT and they will be in place to take out Rickard when he shows up.'

It looked like Hubbard was ready for an argument because the raisin eyes had returned. Lying back in my seat, I closed my eyes. I let out a weary sigh and there was nothing faked about it. Then looking at him again I said calmly, 'The HRT are good. Just make sure that they're ready for anything. Rickard's good as well.'

His mouth dropped open, as though he'd prepared his next speech, but nothing came. Instead he licked his lips and tapped the window separating the driver from us. Walter shot me a

317

wink, then shared a glance with Bryce over the back of Hubbard's head.

The limousine headed south for Miami, followed by a car containing Walter's bodyguards. It had been a long day, and the last sleep I'd had in the shack in Colombia hadn't been what you'd call quality. I wanted to nap, just as my friends did beside me, but I couldn't. Rink snored like an idling bulldozer but that wasn't what kept me awake. Thoughts of Jimena Grajales' hatred nipped at me, making me fidget. Funny, but the fact that I *hadn't* shot her lover dead had made me her worst enemy. That animosity had festered for seven years and had finally erupted a continent's length away. The number who'd died was lost to me now; I'd stopped counting after the photographs that Bryce showed me at the beach house a couple of days ago, but the dead now numbered dozens. Senseless dozens. I still couldn't blame the woman though. My ire was centred directly on Luke Rickard and my inability to kill him when I'd had the chance. The small matter of a fragmentation grenade coming between us didn't mean much. Not now.

We still had no idea who Rickard really was. I knew *what* he was: a monster. He was a cold-blooded murderer masquerading as a contract killer. If he wasn't being paid for his services he'd be tagged with a different title: serial killer. He shared traits with Tubal Cain – the Harvestman who'd almost succeeded in murdering my younger

318

brother, and had come close to cutting a hole through my heart – and also the other contract killer I'd fought more recently who went by the name of Dantalion. I had the horrible feeling that Rickard was worse than either of those I'd stopped and that he was nowhere near finished with his murder spree yet.

Walter had organised us rooms at a hotel in downtown Miami, and the limousine dropped us on the third level of a parking garage. We entered the hotel via a connecting walkway and it was now late enough in the evening that we didn't attract too much attention. We were still in the clothing we'd worn during the battle in Colombia, and mine in particular was a mess. What glances we did get from the patrons and staff were of the raised-eyebrow variety, but there was no fear. Maybe they thought we were business executives returning from a team-building exercise and the dried blood on my clothing was paint-ball splatter. Walter and Bryce in their suits added to the look: the older chief execs pardoned the physical stuff and turning up later for brandy and cigars. All that was missing were the call girls.

Hubbard stayed with the limo, heading off to coordinate the effort between the Hostage Rescue Team and the corresponding Miami-Dade police commander. I was glad that he had gone. Now we could make our own plans without watching our words. We headed for the elevator and up to the uppermost level fifteen floors above. Two of

Walter's bodyguards trailed behind, and judging by their cool glances they were a little miffed that their mark felt more comfortable when flanked by me or Rink. They were professional enough not to complain, even when Walter made them wait outside in the hall.

The CIA expenses bill would shoot up by thousands of dollars, judging by the opulence of the rooms. Walter had secured the entire floor and we had our pick of four different rich men's apartments. We went off to separate en-suite bathrooms to clean up while Walter and Bryce settled in the fourth room, organising to meet there when I'd scrubbed the blood and stink from my body. When I came out of the shower, I found new jeans, T-shirt and underwear, a pair of boots and a leather jacket lying on the bed. There was even a clinical waste sack to dump my old clothes in, the sack destined for an incinerator someplace. Putting on the fresh clothes made me feel ten times better.

My hair damp, I went back across the hall, shared a joke with the two bodyguards which helped relax them a little, then went inside Walt's room.

'You fall asleep in the bath, Hunter?'

The stench of death had taken some expunging and shampoo and soap had struggled to shift it, but maybe I had lingered under the shower longer than usual. I'd been trying to wash away the sight of Jimena Grajales screaming in sheer hatred as she'd tried to shoot me. I smiled at Rink's jibe, though.

Rink looked as fresh as the proverbial daisy, his hair almost blue under the overhead lighting. Harvey always looks snappy. They both had a new set of clothing like mine. In comparison it was Walter and Bryce who came across as a little rumpled.

'Food's coming,' Bryce announced. But none of us was interested yet.

I looked at Walter. 'Hubbard's running the show now? I didn't expect him to show up.'

Walter had claimed a huge easy chair but it struggled to contain his bulky body. With his bald pate and fringe of grey hair round his ears, he looked a lot like my grandfather. All that was lacking from the picture was the smouldering pipe, but Walter helped by taking out his cigar that he wedged between his teeth. He didn't light it: he never did. He chewed it as he spoke. 'Nothing I could do about that. My power isn't infinite, you should know that.'

'You normally have more say than a feebie SAC does,' I said.

He sniffed as though my comment came with a nasty smell. 'Orders came direct from the J. Edgar Hoover building this time. All the way from the top, and even I don't tramp those corridors. It's enough that I'm still being given the courtesy of being kept in the loop.'

'How does this affect our *arrangement*?'

'Things stay the same as far as I'm concerned,

son.' He indicated my friends. 'All of you. But I can't promise that anyone else will see things my way.'

I shrugged. 'Doesn't matter.'

Walter laughed, tugging out the cigar to emphasise his point. 'You'll probably do things your way as usual. It doesn't matter if I give you official sanction or not.'

'I've a man looking to kill me. The way I see it is I've a right to protect myself.'

'Self-defence won't be any defence if you go looking for trouble, Hunter,' Bryce chipped in.

'That's why I'm going to let Rickard come to me this time.'

The food arrived but the bodyguards took it from the hotel staff and wheeled it into the room on a trolley. They eyed the coffee pots wistfully, but Walter ushered them out the room again. At my frown, Walter told one of them to order themselves a pot brought up, which elicited me a grateful nod from one of the men. I'd just scored myself some points, which was good: I'd been at the other end of this scenario on so many occasions that sometimes I thought that the mark saw me as an invaluable piece of furniture to be ignored. The occasional small kindness reminded a BG that you were worth taking a bullet for.

The first coffee I gulped barely caressed the sides of my throat and I moved on to my second. I didn't have much of an appetite for the sandwiches Bryce had ordered, but the coffee was damn good, and well received. I felt a spark ignite inside me as the caffeine kicked in. I reached for a third mug. Then I got down to what was important. Luke Rickard would be coming soon – there was no doubt in my mind – and I wanted to be ready for him. My SIG Sauer demanded attention.

CHAPTER 40

Nineteen eighty-two.

That was the year the serpent first wormed its way up from his bowel and coiled a nest in his gut. He remembered it well.

He was hiding in the woodshed, safe among the cobwebs and spiders and the smell of pine resin, listening to the shrieking of his mother and the man he'd been ordered to call Father as they fought drunkenly inside the cabin. The screaming was nothing new. It had gone on almost since the first day that Etienne Pagnon had moved in. Usually eight-year-old Luke would lie low until the arguing stopped and Mother and Etienne disappeared inside her room. Then the other noises would start. But this time it was different. This time the yelling had gone on for much longer.

He heard a crash as though furniture had been thrown over and splintered on the hardwood floor. Then there was no more screaming.

He waited.

At Etienne's drunken stumbling, Mother would usually rant at him for his clumsiness. But Mother was silent.

From his hiding place, Luke crept forwards and placed an eye to a knothole in the shed wall. He blinked slowly, peering through the evening gloom towards the only home he'd known in all of his life. Dull light from the overhead bulb in the living room was blocked by a ragged blanket nailed over the window, but the blanket was threadbare and he could see a swelling shadow moving slowly for the front door. Luke ducked back, fearful of being seen.

He held his breath, listening. He heard the latch lift and the door creak open on rusty hinges and heavy footfall down the steps. There was a thud. Then followed a sound the like of which he'd never heard before, like a wild beast howling at the sky in open-throated fury. Luke huddled back, as though the noise itself was alive and would find him in his hiding place. The howl petered out, became a bark that turned to a series of grunts; Luke realised he was listening to laughter.

As silently as he could, he crept back to the knothole and peered out.

Etienne was on his knees in the yard and he was hauling down on the front of his shirt as he laughed like a madman. There were streaks on his shirt and on his hands. In the evening shadow they looked like dirt, but even the boy's young mind understood what they were.

'Mother?'

He hadn't meant to speak out loud, but he must have, because Etienne's laughter stopped. His head lowered and he looked directly at the wood-shed. Luke moved quickly from the hole and hid under a stack of pilings leaning against the opposite wall. At any second he thought that the door would burst open and Etienne would come inside, pulling off the wide leather belt he'd used in the past. But Etienne didn't come.

Luke couldn't tell how long he hid there. His only measure of time was how the knothole in the wall darkened and finally became invisible against the night. He heard occasional noises: thuds and clatters, thumps on the back porch. He caught the grumble of Etienne's pick-up truck starting and the crunch of tyres on the dirt road. But still he was too afraid to come out of hiding. For some time the only sound he heard was the soft creaking of the shed walls as the breeze picked up and tugged and pressed at the shingles as if trying to get inside.

Maybe he fell asleep. He couldn't tell. All he knew was that he started violently, almost dislodging the pilings around him as he fought against the shadows. He held his breath again. A door slammed. He'd missed Etienne returning, because it was undoubtedly his truck door. That noise had become recognisable as his cue to lie low for a while but this time it drew him out of the shed.

He crossed the hard-packed yard, feeling the stones in the earth through the thin soles of his sneakers. It made him walk funny, like he was afraid that the earth would crack open beneath his tread and swallow him whole. It felt like an age passed before he made it to the low steps that led up to the cabin. He stood on the bottom step, thankful to be off the yard but afraid to go any further.

The door opened and he flinched.

Etienne was silhouetted against the light from within, looking even larger than usual. Luke's eyes went to his hands, searching for the belt, but it wasn't there. The man just watched him, the rank smell of liquor wafting off him in waves. There was another smell coming off the man that Luke was unfamiliar with. Soap.

'Luc, where 'ave you bin?'

Etienne's voice was thick with alcohol. His accent was more prominent than when he was sober, which wasn't that often. Whatever state of intoxication he was in he always called the boy Luc. Luke hated it, but he answered this time. 'I was playing in the woods.'

Etienne's gaze went over the boy's head towards the woodshed. He looked down slowly. 'Come in, boy.'

Luke paused, expecting the man's voice to rise at any second. For his hands to start pulling at the belt.

'Come inside.' Etienne's voice remained soft and his hands by his sides.

'Where is my mother?'

'Come inside. I 'ave somethin to tell you.'

Luke began to shiver. He could barely support his own weight as he went up the steps and into the cabin. Etienne stood aside to let him in. Luke stood on the threshold and he could feel the man's presence looming over him. Etienne placed a hand on Luke's shoulder. It was a surprisingly tender touch that the boy had never known before. Etienne gently pressed him into the room. Luke went with faltering steps. The room looked different. The scratched and sinking old furniture was still the same, but the rug was missing from the centre of the floor. Luke could see where the boards were less faded: the rug had been a feature of the room for as long as he could remember. There was another pale patch on the floor. It looked like it had been scrubbed with a wire brush and the smell of detergent hung heavy in the air.

'Where's my mother?' Luke felt that he was stuck in a loop and those were the only words he could find.

'Come sit with me.' Etienne picked up the boy and took him to a chair in front of the stove. The door of the stove stood open and Luke could see rags smouldering inside. The rags looked wet and darker red than the flames. Luke wanted to pull out of Etienne's grasp, but he was both repelled and comforted by the man's arms. Etienne ran a callused palm over the boy's head, ruffling his unkempt hair. 'Your mother was never very good to you, Luc. She cared only for herself and for her next drink. You know that, *oui?*'

Luke nodded dumbly.

'Your mother, she is gone. She has run away. She has left us both, young Luc. But do not be afraid. I will be your daddee from now on.'

Etienne turned Luke on his knee, so that they were staring into each other's eyes. 'We do not need your mother. We do not need *any* woman. They think they are better than us, Luc, but we will show them. Together, we will show them that no woman is better than a man. I will teach you how.'

Twenty-eight years on, the adult Luke Rickard remembered the coldness in his gut at Etienne's words. He could see the pale boards on the floor, the freshly scrubbed floor, a couple of darker spatters that Etienne had missed. He had looked up at the big unshaven face that filled his vision and he had spoken a single word. 'Yes.'

He was a child back then, but he wasn't a fool. He knew that his mother hadn't run away, but she had abandoned him. Her drunken rages had pushed away Luke's real father and a succession of other surrogates before Etienne arrived on the scene. Luke hated her. She was cruel and unloving. She thought her needs came before all others, and she had been ready to show Luke how he got in her way with the flat of her hand or with the green stick switch she kept by the front door. Well, Etienne had stood up to her, and now he was showing his true side, a kindness to a boy who'd never known its like.

The cold feeling in Luke's belly had roiled and squirmed. It felt like he would be sick, but he wasn't. Saliva had invaded his mouth, as though something pushed up from inside seeking release, but that was as far as it went. He'd swallowed down, then leaned into the embrace that Etienne offered.

And there the serpent was born and his education began.

They moved from Oregon to North Carolina, exchanging one remote home for another that was even further removed from prying eyes. Luke loved the woods and the mountains, but he always held on to a yearning for the sea which he'd only ever seen on TV. Someday, he'd told Etienne, he would be rich and he would own a house over-looking the ocean. Etienne had laughed at him, told him that he'd better find a way of making good money. And then he'd shown him how.

Etienne Pagnon had been a warrior before he was a drunkard. Being Canadian and around before the events that formed JTF-2, the modern Canadian Special Forces, he had first been recruited into the Royal Canadian Mounted Police Special Emergency Response Team. Etienne had been a sniper and that was not good for a man who had begun imbibing strong liquor. Released from duty, he'd spelled for a tour with the *Légion étrangére*, but had found his tastes more suited to that of a freelance mercenary. He had been in demand as a sniper but his desire for alcohol let him and his sponsors down. Having nowhere to turn but to crime, he'd embraced his new profession, working for a succession of low-life gangsters, first in Canada, then Seattle. Burned out and feeling the daily shakes, he drifted south to Oregon where he'd hooked up with Luke's mother. He was a shadow of his former self, but he had much to share with his willing student.

From Etienne, Luke learned everything about stalking and killing men. He also earned a secondary education: Etienne showed him that women were below them and were things to be used and abused. At thirteen Luke took his first woman, paid for by Etienne, and Etienne had made sure that the woman earned every cent. She was the first person Luke killed.

Luke was a good apprentice. His surrogate father wasn't always the best teacher, his way of ensuring that the growing boy learned his lessons well was to beat the idea into him. Always afterwards he would hug the boy and tell him he was proud of him. The beatings were a necessary evil he said; they would make the boy into a strong man. Luke took the licks until he was eighteen years old. Then Etienne wasn't capable of hurting him any more. When he was drunk and Luke sober, he'd struck at the younger man's face. Luke caught the man's chin in the crook of his elbow, gripped his opposite bicep and placed a hand to the back of Etienne's head. He constricted the life from the man, while remembering that patch of pale wooden floor in the cabin ten years earlier. Luke hated women, he'd hated the bitch that had birthed him, but when it came down to it, Etienne had it coming.

Luke struck out on his own. Taking his original father's surname, he'd offered his services to the highest bidders. For eighteen years he'd been in the trade. He'd earned his house overlooking the ocean, riches that a mountain boy could never have imagined, and a wife who was his very own slave. Until that bitch had betrayed him and he'd been forced to leave his dream behind.

Jimena Grajales, just like his mother, was another bitch who'd cared only for her selfish needs and thought that he could be slapped aside, but he'd shown her who she was messing with. No stinking whore used and then abandoned him.

Especially not his wife.

CHAPTER 41

'Sleep well?'

'Yes.'

Rink eyed me with his mouth down-turned. 'Sure doesn't look like it.'

In truth, my sleep had been disturbed by dreams of Jimena Grajales and her boy dying in the street. When I tried to help them, Jimena sat up and riddled me full of bullets. I'd woken lathered in sweat with the sheets twisted between my fists.

'I only got my head down for a couple hours,' I admitted.

'Here.' He passed me a waxed-paper cup the size of a bucket. 'Just the way you like it: sump oil with an extra shot of espresso.'

I accepted the take-out coffee gratefully, taking a sip. It was scalding hot and tasted as bad as it looked, but it was just what I needed.

'That stuff's gonna kill you.'

'Beats a bullet in the skull,' I told him, thinking again of my nightmare.

We were in a nondescript government car. It wouldn't fool any criminal worth his salt, or Luke Rickard, but it didn't matter. The car was only a means to an end. Rink drove to allow me both hands to control my super-sized caffeine fix.

The Cedars Medical Center, part of the University of Miami Hospital, is situated in the heart of the city, a full service facility providing acute care to over five hundred patients. Alisha had been rushed there after Rickard shot her, but she'd been moved since. There was no way on earth that the FBI Hostage Rescue Team could protect the building or its occupants from an attack by a determined and resourceful killer like Rickard. There were far too many variables to contend with. Many people would die, thousands of dollars' worth of damage would ensue, and possibly millions in lawsuits would follow. Instead, the seriously injured woman had been taken to a private medical centre on the outskirts of Florida City, and a stone's throw away from the Everglades National Park. Smaller location, smaller numbers, easier to defend, that was the thinking behind it all.

We took the South Dixie highway out of the city all the way down past Homestead to Florida City and on to Palm Drive. I missed the twists and turns after that as I concentrated on the last dregs of coffee. Once one base need was seen to, I attended to another. While cooped up in the gilded prison of my hotel room I'd been busy rebuilding my SIG from parts gleaned from other weapons. It would probably have made sense to ditch my old gun and familiarise myself with a new one, but I'd used the modified P226 for so long that it had become an extension of my hand. My palm was familiar with the contours of the grip and anything else would have felt a little alien. While Rink negotiated the roads leading out into the wilderness, I dismantled the gun and put it back together again, checked the slide and the progression of the trigger. I unloaded and then reloaded the magazine, chambered a round. The gun had survived being shot and blown up by a grenade: we had a lot in common. It seemed the injury to my hand had been superficial and I'd held the swelling under control by way of an ice pack. There was some residual pain, but I could live with it.

We followed a road that wound through groves of live oak and bald cypress trees, Spanish moss hanging like old men's beards from the branches. It was daytime, but even then the spidery growths lent a Gothic air to the scene. It reminded me of stories I'd read of haunted swamps and witch-women mumbling curses over animal bones. Myth says that a beautiful bride-to-be was killed by Cherokee warriors, and as a warning to other interlopers on their land her hair was hacked off and thrown in a tree. As time passed, her hair grew grey and withered and spread from tree to tree. The story said that if you tried to remove the hair it would leap away and defend itself with hordes of beetles. Fanciful stuff, but like a lot of soldiers I'm superstitious and felt a trickle of unease at the thought of being eaten alive by a swarm of insects. Of course, there was only one roach I was concerned about.

'You're sure he's coming, huh?'

'No doubt about it, Rink. When Jimena told him that Alisha survived . . . I don't know . . . it was like I could feel the anger radiating from him.'

'What's his goddamn problem, anyway? I'd've thought he'd lie low for a while, maybe set himself up a new identity. Who's gonna hire an asshole like him when he can't be trusted any more?'

'The way I see things, he's a complete maniac. He isn't acting rationally; he's being led by more than the lure of money. Always has been, probably.'

'Imogen said the punk would've raped her given the chance. You think he's a sex beast?'

'Yeah, and the contract killing is just a sideline. My guess is that the money has never been that important, it's always been about him fulfilling his sick fantasies.'

'Dirty motherfucker.'

'I'm with you there, buddy.'

'Doesn't explain why he's so proficient with weapons.'

'Never did get to the bottom of that,' I agreed. 'But it doesn't mean a thing now. I know Harvey, though: he won't stop looking until he finds out. Personally, I don't think we'll ever know.'

'Not unless we make him tell us.'

'He won't have the opportunity. First chance I get, I'm putting him down.'

'Not if I beat you to him.' Rink grinned at me. Then he nodded ahead and I saw the outlines of a white building through the trees.

'That the hospital?'

Rink looked at a printed page folded on the dashboard of the car. It was a map of the area that Harvey had supplied us with. 'Outer administration buildings, the hospital's a bit further back. Maybe a little over a mile into the swamp.'

'OK. This is as far as we go.'

Rink pulled the vehicle off the road and down a beaten track. The Spanish moss scraped along the roof of the car. No beetles attacked, but there were plenty of tiny gnats knocked from the branches scuttling down the windscreen. Rink hit the wipers and tiny streaks of blood made rainbows on the glass. 'Hope you fetched plenty of Deet,' I said.

'I don't think you need to worry about that, Hunter. The mosquitoes drink your blood, they'll probably be struck dead by all the caffeine.'

'Either that or they'll be hooked and head off to a Starbucks for their next hit. Both are OK by me.'

'Amen to that,' Rink laughed.

We were engaged in nonsense. It was usually the way we prepared for impending violence. Pretty soon, it would be time for silence. Rink would grow fidgety, I'd go sullen, and then we'd both slide into the calmness more befitting the task ahead.

Anhinga Key Medical Center was a heavy slog through the swamp away from us. Would have been easier by the road, but Hubbard's men would be watching the main approach, and probably many of the lesser trails. We would have to move in via a route unlikely even for someone intent on murder. The plan was to go in, set up a lying-up point and then wait for the inevitable arrival of Luke Rickard. Then we'd kill him. Or at least try to.

His arrival at the remote AKMC was inevitable for two reasons: he wouldn't stop coming until he'd killed Alisha and we had Harvey on the case ensuring that he'd be sent directly to her. I'm not known for placing women in the way of harm, but this was different. Rickard was hell-bent on killing his wife, so it made sense to use her as bait. Harvey was currently hacking into the records at The Cedars so that a simple check would send the killer our way.

Rickard believed that I'd been eviscerated by a fragmentation grenade; he wouldn't expect me to be waiting for him to arrive. However, the proliferation of feebies and cops at the scene would put him on high alert. Wouldn't stop him coming, but he'd be prepared for war. That was all supposing that he'd survived the events in Colombia and was now headed here. If not, we could have a few uncomfortable days squatting in a swamp to look forward to. But Rink and I were up to it: we'd spent many days and nights waiting in even less appealing locations throughout our careers.

Coming to the end of the trail, Rink parked the car under a stand of live oak. We made sure that the windows were all shut tight before climbing out. We didn't want to return to a vehicle infested with swamp life. Rink popped the trunk and I joined him to haul out our equipment. We'd travelled here in the clothing that Walter had supplied to us the night before, but now we stripped down to our boxers and then slipped into the lightweight DPMs we'd brought. The *disruptive pattern material* was good camouflage against the swamp. There was netting that we pulled around our faces and peaked caps to cover our hair, but Rink still pulled out a canister of insecticide that we sprayed ourselves with. I was conscious of the chemical smell, but five minutes into the swamp and even a bloodhound would struggle to sniff us out.

Rink dished out the weapons. Courtesy of Walter, we each had a Colt M4 carbine – basically the shorter version of the US Army M16A2 assault rifle – with its capacity for firing one or three bullets with each pull of the trigger. The guns were favoured by special forces teams engaged in urban warfare as they provided more control over where bullets were placed when fired in shorter bursts. If we ended up entering the hospital buildings that feature would become very important.

Next Rink handed me a Ka-Bar knife in black epoxy and I clipped it to my belt. I had the switch-blade as a back-up knife in its obligatory place in my hip pocket. Then there was the SIG Sauer P226, my weapon of choice.

If all these weapons failed, I still had my fists to fall back on – part of me even relished the opportunity to take up with Rickard where we'd left off before the interruption of the L2A2 hand grenade.

'Ready, bud?'

I nodded. 'More than.'

Throwing our discarded clothing inside the trunk, we lifted out backpacks nowhere near as large as the bergens we once carried on military operations but roomy enough to carry field rations, water, a small medical kit and extra ammunition. Rink also brought extras in the way of a nylon DPM sheet and more netting. Then we slipped down an animal trail and under the trees.

'You'd think we were a thousand miles from nowhere,' Rink drawled.

He was right but that of course wasn't the case. Nearby were the hospital buildings and not too distantly the historical Anhinga Trail. There could be any number of civilians wandering around out there, so we'd have to be extra careful.

The last thing either of us wanted was to come across a group of trigger-happy hunters who might mistake us for a couple of deer. It would be a grossly unjust way to end our days.

For such a big man Rink moved with the casual grace normally associated with dancers. He had the build and size of his Scottish-Canadian father, but the fluidity of movement was reminiscent of

340

his mother, Yukiko, as were his hooded eyes. He loped along the barely discernible trail without stirring any of the branches that tried their damndest to snag on his clothing. I followed three paces behind, conscious of my footfall and the thud of my heart.

The stench of rotting vegetation clogged my senses. Nearby something large splashed though water. Alligator, I thought, or maybe just a bird diving for fish. Worst-case scenario was that it was Luke Rickard already on his way to assault the hospital. I came to a halt, listening intently, but the sound didn't repeat itself. Alligator, I thought a second time. Then I moved on, trying to cut down on the lead that Rink had set in those few seconds.

Coming to a sluggish inlet of water, we paused.

'We're gonna have to cross it,' Rink said. 'Else we'll be too close to Hubbard's crew.'

The water looked murky and deep, almost black with silt and decomposing plant life. On the far side the bank was choked with mangrove roots. I studied the still water. Anything could lurk beneath the surface and the first we'd know about it was when jaws clamped on to our limbs. Maybe I studied it for just a little too long, because Rink turned to me with a smile. 'Don't worry about the 'gators; it's the turtles you have to watch out for.'

He was making light of things, but I'd seen a TV programme where a snapping turtle bit through the boot of a naturalist. It had done so as easily as had the shrapnel that shredded mine back in Cesar Calle's house. 'More concerned about getting our weapons wet.'

Rink chuckled at me and I nudged him in the gut with my elbow. To show him I wasn't afraid of critters I went down the slick bank and into the water. My boots sank deep in the muddy bottom and the water crept up towards my waist. I transferred my SIG to my left hand, the rifle to my right and waded out, holding the guns above my head. When I pushed among the mangroves at the far side Rink followed. If we'd just been on a hiking trip he'd most likely have pretended that some huge reptile had grabbed him, but he was totally serious this time, coming through the water with his face set and his weapons held high. The time for fooling was over: now it was all business. The calm came on us.

The mangrove roots were like the gnarled bars of a huge cage, some poked from the surface like the teasing fingers of a water nymph inviting us down to her deathly realms. The going wasn't easy and judging by how far the tangled branches stretched out before us it wasn't going to get any better.

We slogged through the swamp, using our uncanny knack for directions to steer us. The mangroves were tortuous to push through, but we made it, using some of the more exposed roots as stepping stones. Then we came out on to a wide sandbank where saw-tooth grass proliferated. The grass hid us well as we moved towards the hospital. The only problem was it concealed other things too. At one point a bird broke from cover, its wings clattering through the branches of an overhead tree as it sought to flee us. We halted, waited, but apparently no one was alerted by the bird's frantic escape, so we moved on again.

There was another channel of water and a stand of trees to contend with before we reached the outer perimeter of the hospital grounds. A fence of interwoven branches made a windbreak to keep some of the smells of the swamp at bay, but as a security measure it was hopeless. The wood was so dry and brittle that anyone could push it over or dive directly through it. We weren't intending to go to such extremes; we just followed the fence to a point where a gate had been erected. Here a track led from the hospital grounds and into the woods. There was a small cluster of sheds, one of which was a parking garage for the sit-on lawn mowers that the groundskeepers used. A small compound formed from tin sheets held a variety of unused office furniture, and also the remains of a bonfire from where combustible waste was burned. It was mad to bypass the workspace without checking it out first. Could be a gardener lurking around who might spot us.

The area was clear of people, so we moved to the gate and scanned the lawns and the huddle of buildings that formed the hospital. Clinic might

343

have been a better description, or maybe holiday retreat. From the map Harvey supplied I'd been expecting a modern structure of preformed concrete and glass, but the hospital looked more like it had once been at the centre of a wealthy estate or plantation. It brought to my mind the glossy magazine adverts for Southern Comfort. It was obvious from the plushness of the building and its surroundings that the AKMC was a strictly fee-paying and very private facility. What surprised me most was that this beautiful old building had been selected: it made me wonder who the actual owners of the hospital were. CIA, I decided, seeing as Walter had given his blessing for us to stage our war with Luke Rickard here.

CHAPTER 42

Astack of twenty-dollar bills on the counter were all that stood between Rickard's anonymity and the doctor's hopes for a long life. It would be a shame if he had to kill the doc; he was one of the few people that Rickard actually liked.

'Two thousand,' Rickard said. 'It's the fee you always asked for before.'

Adam Rothman, the disgraced surgeon who had once numbered the social elite of Florida among his clients, picked up the thick wad of notes and riffled them between his long, almost feminine fingers. 'Times change, Luke, and so does my expense bill.'

'It's more than you make performing illegal abortions and cutting gangrenous limbs from junkies poisoned by dirty needles.'

Rothman was a big man, flabby and ungainly. He looked nothing like the man who'd served his internship at Johns Hopkins before moving into private practice in downtown Miami. But his looks suited him now that he'd relocated to this dingy apartment on the fringe of South Beach. His face was florid, with broken veins across his bulbous nose, testament to his secret drinking problem. With his grey watery eyes and thin lips; he did not look like someone you'd trust to guide a scalpel. He waved the notes towards Rickard, who was sitting on the gurney checking out the dressings on his wounded ribs. 'As ever, you are not buying my expertise, you are buying my silence.'

Rickard looked up at Rothman, the contact lenses removed so he caught the man under a baleful, icy stare. 'Silence works both ways, Doctor.'

Rothman smiled. 'That it does.'

He stuffed the two grand in the pocket of his white overcoat. Then he reached into a cardboard box and pulled out a couple of packets. He tossed them on the gurney beside Rickard. 'Take those three times a day; they'll keep any infection at bay. Take the NAIDs as and when required.'

Rickard studied the packets. The first contained brandnamed antibiotics, but the second was an anonymous white box. 'NAIDs?'

'Non-steroidal anti-inflammatory drugs. They'll keep the fever down without impairing consciousness. You want to remain alert, don't you?'

'For two thousand dollars I get cheap drugs you've purchased off the internet?'

Rothman flicked him a smile. 'If you're not up to paying my going rate I have to make a profit elsewhere. Any way, what are you complaining about? I've thrown the bandages in for free.'

'You're all heart, Doc.'

'Yeah, right.' Rothman bustled over to a trash can overflowing with blood-speckled tissue and used syringes. He peeled off his latex gloves and dropped them in the can. He pointed a skinny digit at Rickard. 'The bullet barely grazed your ribs, Luke. It's your shoulder wound you'll have to be most careful of. Luckily the wound was a through and through, superficial, but there is the threat of infection if you don't keep it clean.'

Rickard touched the wad of dressing on his left trapezius muscle, just below his collar-line. 'Feels OK to me.'

'It'll stay that way if you dress it regularly. Here.' He passed over a tube of antiseptic cream. 'No charge.'

'Thanks,' Rickard said with no real enthusiasm.

'The sutures will dissolve themselves, no need to come back to have them removed.'

'You don't want to see me again?'

Rothman pulled a hurt face that was as much a sham as Rickard's pout. 'Luke, I'm quite willing to take your money any time you please. Just more of it next time, eh?'

Rickard stood up off the gurney and studied himself in a full-length mirror riveted to the wall of the consulting room. Apart from the criss-crossed bandages, he still struck quite an imposing figure. He'd changed his looks, but this time without the need of Rothman's expertise. His latest disguise was purely cosmetic. He thought that his newly shaved head gave him a tough look that the bruising on his face actually helped. Turning from his reflection, he pulled on a black T-shirt emblazoned with a Gothic image for a rock band he'd never heard of. He let the shirt hang outside his jeans to cover the blade clipped on his belt. Then he shrugged into a black leather motorcycle jacket that had a contrasting red collar and stripes down the sleeves. Lastly he thumbed a pair of wraparound shades on.

'What do you think?'

'If I was a woman I'd have you back on that gurney in a flash.'

Rickard grinned. 'No wonder you got yourself struck off, Doc!'

Rothman seemed pleased with that. He fed a hand into his coat pocket and pulled out a slip of paper. He held it out to Rickard. 'Here.'

'You got it for me.' Rickard eyed the handwritten address, a smile playing over his lips. He folded it over and placed the note in his hip pocket.

'Cost you.'

Rickard dug another stack of bills from his jacket pocket and handed them over. 'I didn't think you'd be able to get this for me. Not now you're the pariah of the medical world.'

Rothman nipped his bottom lip between his nicotine-stained teeth. Then he nodded at the out-of-date certificate displayed on his wall. 'I called The Cedars. Asked. Simple as that, when you have letters after your name. No one checks credentials these days, especially not a first-year intern who's already done a twenty-three-hour shift with God knows how many more before he gets to go home.'

'Letters after your name.' Rickard read Rothman's glowing endorsements as he shoved his handgun into his waistband. 'Just make sure RIP doesn't join them, Doc. I might need you again before long.'

'I'm pretty fond of the green stuff,' Rothman reassured him, 'and I don't intend dying any time soon.'

'Both things we have in common,' Rickard said. He clapped a hand on the doctor's shoulder as he passed him by. 'Take it easy, Doc.'

'You too, Luke. You know how badly the cops are searching for you, right?'

'Keeps life interesting.'

'Hey, when you find her give your wife a kiss for me, will ya?'

Rickard lifted his sunglasses and peered back at the doctor from the doorway. 'That I will do, Doc.'

He left Rothman chuckling to himself, letting himself out into a corridor in the apartment block where the quack had set up practice. The hallway stank of urine. A little way up the hall a kid no older than sixteen was huddled in a doorway. Rickard walked past him and the boy stuck out a grimy hand. 'Any change, sir?'

'Yes,' Rickard said, 'the doctor's a miracle worker: I'm feeling quite good now.'

The boy blinked at him in a confusion hindered

by his latest fix. He slowly withdrew his hand as Rickard walked away, laughing at his own joke.

He was three floors up but there was no way he would use the elevator. He suspected it was the source of the smell. Instead he went down the stairs, negotiating the trash and puddles while he made a call on his mobile phone. He'd finished the call by the time he pushed through an exit door on to the sidewalk. It was a fine morning in SoBe. The shadows of the buildings across the way blocked much of the sunlight, but it was already growing warm. By midday these streets would be bleached out, so the sunglasses were a good idea.

He walked across the street, flagrantly ignoring the jaywalking laws, and approached his newly acquired Honda Fireblade. The bike was a beauty, voted top for its looks and performance by many aficionados, but it was just a tool to Rickard. And part of his new disguise. Two young gangbangers were leaning on the hood of a muscle car, the bumper of their Chevrolet Camaro almost nudging the Fireblade. They stirred as he approached.

'Thanks for watching my ride, guys.' Rickard peeled a couple of twenty notes out, thinking that he might have to withdraw some more pocket money from his emergency stash. He'd already given the young toughs a hundred bucks each, but the extra cash would sweeten them even more. He wasn't afraid of them, but at least this way he wouldn't be troubled by having them follow him with the idea of taking everything from him. On any other occasion he'd lead them somewhere remote and then show them who the fuck they were trying to roll, but he had a more pressing date with Alisha.

The gangbangers accepted the money with their chins lifted. They looked like they were sniffing the air, trying to decide if he was friend or foe.

'Call it a bonus,' Rickard said.

He straddled the Fireblade, flicked them a quick salute then started the bike. He shot off along the road and took the next corner almost leaning into the asphalt. Let them try to follow me now, he thought.

He took the McArthur Causeway across Biscayne Bay and on to the I-95 south, breezing by traffic at seventy miles an hour all the way down through the city to where the interstate merged with Route 1 and became the South Dixie Highway. There he opened up the bike, shooting along past Pine Crest and Perrine and heading for Florida City at the southernmost tip of the sprawling city. At a strip mall complete with a Denny's, a Comfort Inn and a Texaco petrol station, he pulled the Fireblade to a halt under a stand of palm. Searching for the golden arches, he pulled out into the highway and drove into the fast food take-out lot a little further on.

There he waited, resting with his butt on the bike seat, arms crossed over his chest. He could feel the heat on his forehead as he stared back at the road, searching for the arrival of the man he'd called on his phone. Quite a large number of vehicles passed through the drive-thru before he saw the silver Land Rover he was expecting.

He stood still, waiting for the large vehicle to come to him. He could see three men inside, indistinct shadows, two in the front and one in the back. The Land Rover drew alongside the bike and he exchanged a nod with the passenger. Guy had a nasty bruise under his eyes. Like Rickard's, the swelling on this man's face was courtesy of Joe Hunter. Rickard hopped back on the Fireblade and peeled out of the lot, the Land Rover following to somewhere less public.

Next stop the Florida Keys. Rickard read signs on the road, but he'd no intention of travelling so far. He found an agricultural trail just outside of town and pulled on to the track. His wheels kicked up dust as he sped down it with the Land Rover following close behind.

He found a place where the track widened out, a grass verge on one side next to an irrigation channel. A wide field of tall grass spread away to the distant horizon on his right, but the other side of the trail was bordered by spindly trees choked with Spanish moss. There were also gumbo limbo trees, with weird twisted trunks and bark like leather.

Putting the bike on its stand, he walked out as the Land Rover passed by. He watched the driver throw the big vehicle into reverse and then pull in near to the bike. Rickard stood with his arms folded across his chest, watching closely as all three men got out, dust settling round them.

The driver leaned against the tailgate of the Land Rover, folding his arms on his chest in a copy of Rickard's stance. The man from the back stood with a thumb tucked into his belt. Rickard saw a cast on the man's forearm, poking out from under the cuff of his sleeve. The third man walked towards him, extending a hand in greeting. Rickard didn't take it, just observed the man from behind his sunglasses. Finally he unfolded his arms, but only to reach up and push the shades back on his head.

Kenneth Wetherby didn't know what to do with his hand and it took him a second or two to withdraw it. He rubbed his palm down the thigh of his trousers, leaving a damp smear on the material.

'You brought what I wanted?' Rickard stared at the livid bruise on the man's face.

Wetherby nodded at the man standing by the Land Rover and he unlocked and dropped the tailgate. He leaned inside and pulled a large plastic trunk towards him, flipped open the lid. He stepped away as Rickard approached, crossing his arms again. Rickard knew the man's pose wasn't as nonchalant as it looked: there was a gun in a shoulder rig inside his jacket.

Rickard took a quick glance in the box. 'How current is this?'

Behind him, Wetherby said, 'Brand new issue.

Have a contact at SWAT who moonlights for me off and on.'

Rickard nodded, satisfied. When he turned round, Wetherby took a step backwards, he'd been so close. 'Quite a mess Hunter made of your face, Ken.'

Wetherby touched the swelling under his eye. 'Asshole sucker-punched me.'

Rickard grunted, taking in the scrapes on the face of the man with his arms folded, the broken arm of the other. 'He sucker-punched the three of you?'

'He had help.' Wetherby scowled, touched the swelling again. 'I took this for you, Rickard. He wanted me to tell him who you were.'

'So you told him?'

All three men stirred uncomfortably, a sign of the lies to follow.

'No way,' Wetherby said. 'Why'd you think he hit me?'

'Just wondering how he happened to turn up in Colombia. Bit of a coincidence, huh?'

'Don't know how he did it, but does it really matter now? He's dead, right?'

'Blown to hell,' Rickard said.

'Good fuckin' riddance, I say.'

'You said that he had help?'

'Jared Rington.'

'A tall black guy?'

'No. A Jap.'

'Odd name for an Oriental.'

'Goes by Rink. He's a PI outa Tampa. Hunter works with him, does the dirty work when required.'

'So who's the black guy?'

'Don't know any black guy,' Wetherby said.

Rickard shrugged. It paid to know who he might be going up against, but maybe the point was immaterial. He fully expected that Rink and the black guy hadn't made it out of Cesar Calle's house alive. The German mercenary, Metzger, looked like he was their equal, plus he had more than a dozen others to back him up.

Out of nowhere, Rickard said, 'I killed Gutierrez.'

Wetherby exhaled loudly, shaking his head. 'He was your ticket, man. Why'd you do that?'

'He was playing both sides: sooner or later he'd have betrayed me. I don't tolerate betrayal.'

His words were loaded and Wetherby wasn't too slow to pick up on that.

'I didn't tell Hunter where to find you.'

Rickard ignored him. He looked inside the plastic box again. 'The SWAT guy: he didn't ask why you wanted these?'

'I pay him enough that he doesn't ask.'

'Even if I'm going up against his own people?'

'Like I said, he takes the money and he doesn't ask.'

'Good enough,' Rickard nodded. 'Weapons?'

This time the man with the cast on his arm opened the rear door of the Land Rover. Pulling out a long black lacquered case from the back seat, he unsnapped clips and swung open the lid, holding it like an emissary bearing gifts to a foreign court.

'Same rifle I used in Tampa,' Rickard noted. 'I thought you were going to get rid of it, Ken.'

'There was no chance that the cops would find it. They were looking for Hunter. No way that they would come to my office.'

'Hunter did.'

'He had no idea I'd hired you on behalf of the Colombians. He was just clutching at straws when he turned up.'

'But you didn't tell him anything.' Lifting out the M-40A3 bolt-action rifle, Rickard studied it. The gun was an original Remington 700, extensively remodelled by United States Marine Corps armourers. It had a five-round detachable box magazine and telescopic sights. Spare 7.62 x 51 mm NATO rounds were arranged in the lining of the case, alongside a long suppressor. The cartridges he'd used when killing the two cops, Castle and Soames, had been replaced. He put the rifle back into the box and closed the lid. Placed it on the ground.

He turned slowly to look at Wetherby.

'It's going to be difficult carrying the rifle while driving a motorcycle.' Rickard scratched idly at his lower back while thinking the problem over. 'I'm going to have to take the Land Rover.'

'What? Leave us out here? No way.'

356

Rickard pulled out his gun. Back in Dr Rothman's office he'd primed the weapon, screwing a suppressor in place. 'I'm taking it.'

This wasn't about the Land Rover. Rickard had planned to kill Wetherby and his goons the instant he'd called the man. After he killed Alisha, he was going to disappear, and Wetherby was the only living person who could lead the cops to him. He couldn't leave behind any loose threads if he was to set himself up in another part of the country.

He shot the first man in the heart, just beneath his folded arms, and in the same movement swung on the man with the broken arm. The guy shrieked in panic, trying to get at the gun in his jacket but impeded by the cast. Rickard fired once and the bullet struck the man's left cheek. Blood and brain matter puffed in the dusty air behind him. Both men collapsed at the same time, one to each side of Rickard's extended arm. A little over two seconds was all that had elapsed between Rickard drawing the handgun and both men lying dead in the road.

In those couple of seconds Wetherby knew the truth, but his reaction wasn't to fight back. Fear struck him and gave him the false sense of capability that said he could outrace a bullet. He set off running along the road, kicking up dirt.

Rickard shook his head at the man's cowardice. He lifted the gun and aimed, firing a single round.

Wetherby slapped a hand down hard on his right

buttock. It did nothing to stop the damage caused by the bullet. His leg gave under him and he spun to the ground, screaming in pain. He rolled over on his back, eyes wide as he watched Rickard walk calmly towards him. Finally he went for the gun clipped in a snap-holster on his hip.

Rickard stamped on his elbow, pinning his arm to the ground. He pulled loose Wetherby's gun. It was a stainless steel revolver, six-shot, an old-timer's weapon.

'Please.' The word came out as a long whine.

'The truth now, Ken.' Rickard stepped off his elbow. 'You told Hunter how to find me.'

'I didn't . . .'

'The truth, I said.'

'He must have figured it out himself.'

Rickard shook his head slowly. He leaned down so he was staring deeply into Wetherby's face. 'You were at the centre of this, Ken. It was you who fed Jimena Grajales the information on Hunter and his team and who directed my movements on her behalf. You're the only person who knew the connection between me and Gutierrez, and with Jimena. Hunter didn't just turn up at Cesar Calle's place by chance: someone gave him the tip-off.'

'Why would I do that? I wanted him dead as much as Jimena did.'

'Because you're a coward, Ken, and you're afraid of Hunter. You were the only person who knew I was going to Colombia. You hoped that by sending him after me we'd end up killing each other. You didn't expect either of us to come back.' Wetherby tried to sit up, his hands coming up imploringly. Rickard placed the toe of his boot to the man's chest and pressed him down again. 'You must have hated Joe Hunter a great deal to decide you'd set me up as well. Did you not consider what that would mean if I survived?'

'I did hate him, Rickard. He threatened to close my business down, I couldn't let that happen. So, yeah, I jumped at the chance to have him murdered. When Gutierrez contacted me looking for someone to do the job, you were the first name that came to my mind. I knew you were better than him. I knew that you could take him wherever you met.'

'I thought you said you had nothing to do with sending him after me?'

'Jesus, Rickard, you're putting words in my mouth.'

'No, Ken, I'm putting *this* in your mouth.' He jammed the end of the suppressor against Wetherby's teeth. 'Say aah!'

Wetherby cried now. Rickard thought it strange that someone could screw their eyes so tight and still produce tears. His lips were equally puckered.

Rickard pulled the gun away.

'Open your eyes, Ken.'

Wetherby couldn't. The prospect of a horrible death had such a powerful hold on him that his brain function temporarily rebelled. He just lay there mewling like a broken-backed cat.

'Open your freakin' eyes. Look at me like a man, not crying like a little girl.'

Rickard kicked Wetherby in the backside, toe digging painfully into the bullet wound. The pain did the trick and Wetherby's eyelids shot open. His pupils remained unfocused for a few seconds afterwards, but he finally looked up at Rickard.

'Jesus . . . God . . .'

'Shut up, Ken. You're embarrassing yourself. You're beginning to sound like my goddamn wife.'

'Don't hurt me . . . please!'

'Well,' Rickard said, 'I've nothing else I can come up with. I was going to let you take the Fireblade back, but I can't have you bleeding over such a beautiful piece of machinery.'

Rickard smiled, making the ill-concealed lie even more obvious.

'Please . . .'

'Can't allow it. You betrayed me. Goodbye, Ken.'

He shot Wetherby in the chest.

The life went out of Wetherby like a tyre with a slow puncture, his arms flopping in slow-motion by his sides, mouth drooping open.

Rickard ejected the magazine from his gun, checked how many rounds he'd used. Still plenty left, so he pushed it back in place. While unscrewing the suppressor, he looked down at Wetherby dispassionately.

He thought that killing the man might cause more of a reaction. Wetherby had been his major source of income over the last few years and for most of them they'd been friends. It was a shame that Wetherby had allowed his hatred of Joe Hunter to come between them.

'You should have just hired me to kill him straight off, Ken, kept things simple, instead of allowing a woman to call the shots. Do you see where a scheming bitch has got us now?'

CHAPTER 43

I'd been meaning to take an air-boat ride for the last couple of years, ever since I'd taken up residence here in Florida. Riding the air-boats with their huge rotating fan on the back has always summed up my idea of seeing the beauty of the Everglades in style, but I hadn't got round to it yet. In the time I'd been here, other things just seemed to get in the way. Too often those things had meant violent death to too many people. A lot of those people should have still been around, but some of them deserved exactly what they got.

'We get out of this alive,' I had told Rink earlier, 'I'm gonna hire an air-boat and go and look at the 'gators.'

'Keep your eyes peeled, buddy, or you might see 'em sooner than you think.'

He wasn't kidding.

Rink then slipped away through tall grass, heading in a circuitous route round the back end of the hospital grounds. We had our mobile phones to communicate by, but that was the last I'd heard from the big guy in the last few hours.

Instead of careening through the swamp on a flat-bottomed boat, the huge propeller whirring behind me, my view of the swamp was from a raised hummock of limestone. I'd built an observation post there, scraping a narrow furrow in the earth to make lying down a little more comfortable. I had my carbine propped in a natural V between two rocks, the DPM sheet spread over me with tufts of grass strewn over it to aid the camouflage.

Oddly enough, I wasn't hiding from Luke Rickard. My reason for remaining so still and silent was so that the men in the grounds of the hospital were unaware of my presence. The men – Hubbard's HRT troopers – would see my being there as a interference in lawful process worthy of my being arrested and thrown in chains. We were on the same side; it was just a pity they couldn't see things that way. They wanted to arrest Luke Rickard, hurl the weight of the Federal Court system at him and lock him away for life, while I just wanted to bury the asshole.

Hubbard's men were highly trained – probably the cream of all SWAT teams in the country – but they weren't the right men for this job. They were specialists in hostage rescue, not standing guard against a determined assassin. I'd counted half a dozen storm troopers up until now, intimidating in their black Kevlar armour and helmets but no deterrent to someone like Luke Rickard. Maybe Hubbard thought he could frighten off the killer with this show of force, when instead all he was doing was showing his hand and allowing the planning of countermeasures. He should have brought only a small handpicked team of under-cover agents, men and women who could blend with the hospital staff. That way Rickard wouldn't find it so easy to determine the strength of his enemy. That would give him more pause, make him worry that everyone inside the hospital was a potential threat and that this was neither the correct time nor place for a hit. That would slow him down more than any skirmish line of heavy artillery would. To stop an assassin you had to think like one.

It had been a long day.

Rink can sit for days without moving, but I felt the need for action like a case of hives all over my body. There was the possibility that Rickard had seen sense and had made off to some remote corner of the world where he could concentrate on rebuilding his trade as a contract killer. Lying here, watching the grounds of the hospital over the top of the fence could be a supreme waste of my time, but I didn't think so. I'd told the others as much: Rickard was coming, and I still stood by my words. More than anything, he had to be stopped. Everything about him was exactly what I hated – especially the face he'd stolen from me: it reminded me too much of the dark things I'd had to do in the past.

As I've said, Rapid Intuitive Experience is the

designated military term for that sixth sense you get when you feel you are being watched. I've felt the cold prod between my shoulder blades on too many occasions to ignore it. Going very still, I listened, used my peripheral vision to pick out any subtle movement a direct stare would miss. But I found nothing out of the ordinary.

Not until my mobile phone vibrated against my chest.

The old *spider sense* had picked up on the urgency of the incoming call.

'You got your face on, Hunter?'

Rink says that I have some sort of stone-cold expression that I wear on missions. I've tried to catch my reflection to see what he sees, but I've just looked the same to me. Nonetheless, Rink is adamant and he calls it my *face*. Maybe that's what I'd recognised in Rickard's features and was why I hated him so much.

'What's up?'

'Unless the feebie on this side has just had a major cardiac arrest, someone just shot him with a silenced gun.'

'He's dead?'

'Hasn't got up again.'

'Someone with a high-powered rifle,' I said. 'Has to be to go through his armour.'

'Wait up . . .'

There was a few seconds of silence. When Rink came back on he was whispering lower than before. 'There's another feebie who came out of the trees and is checking on his buddy. Now . . . hmm, that's strange.'

'It's him.'

'Think you're right, Hunter. He's dragging the dead man into some bushes.'

'Think you can take him, Rink?'

'Not from here. Gotta move in.'

'Hold tight. I'm coming, OK.'

'He gets inside, we'll be hard put to differentiate him from the other HRT guys.'

'He gets inside, he'll be going for Alisha. We'll catch him there if needs be.'

Ending the call, I came up to a crouch, pulled back the DPM sheet and then jumped down from the limestone outcrop. Angling left, the fence gave me cover as I moved in, but then I headed for the gate. As soon as I was through it I had to cross open lawn that offered only sporadic cover by way of shrubs and flower beds. I zigzagged between the bushes, stopping at each while I scanned for the FBI troopers. One of the HRT men was about fifty yards away, but he had his back turned. Silently I ran to the next cover, going down on my belly in a flower display. Through the leaves and blooms I searched for the trooper. He still stood cradling his gun and staring off into the distance. His shoulders were slumped, disillusioned by many hours of standing eventless guard duty. Coming to my feet I hurried on. I reached the side of the hospital building without raising the alarm.

My phone vibrated again.

The building came with a crawl space. A lattice frame stopped animals larger than snakes or rodents from getting under the building, but it was brittle, dried out by the Floridian heat. I grabbed and tugged loose a five-foot-long section and then swung under the crawl space. I pulled the frame back up, just in case anyone came along while I spoke to Rink.

'He's just standing there, Hunter. Like he's taken the place of the dead man.'

I told Rink where I was. Then I said, 'Maybe I can get him as he makes his move for the hospital.'

'Too late, he's on the move now. Taking it easy, heading for the front door.'

'You still in a bad position?'

'Don't trust the carbine to hit him from here. I can fire on him, but all hell will break loose. He might run. You want to take that chance?'

'No. Looks like we're going to have to take him inside.'

'Feebies might fire on us.'

'Yeah, that's a problem.'

'The *problem* is we can't shoot back at them.'

'Going to be difficult,' I agreed. 'But we can't let them stop us. Rickard's not getting away this time.'

'OK. Hunter, he's at the steps now. He's going in. Better hustle, buddy.'

I hustled.

But I still had to be careful. Pushing over the

lattice frame again I peeked outside. The trooper was oblivious to what was going on, which meant that his team-mates were equally ignorant that Rickard had launched his attack. Rolling from under the building, I came to my feet and ran towards the front corner. Snatching a quick glance around the wall, I just caught the blur of movement as someone went in through the front door. Looking past the façade of the building I saw Rink moving in. We acknowledged each other with a nod, and then I ran towards the door through which Rickard had entered a moment ago. Rink covered me, dipping to a knee as he searched the grounds through his sights.

Steps led up to the front door, a large expanse of white oak. I went up them and pressed myself to the wall, hips against the discreet sign bearing the acronym AKMC. From there I covered while Rink moved up to the steps. No one was aware of us and I again concluded that Hubbard had the wrong team on this case: Walter's people would have taken us prisoner out there in the swamp. There was a large brass push-button bell but I'd no intention of advertising my arrival. I pushed down on the handle and the door swung inward silently.

Rink moved up the steps and I went inside.

A short vestibule with double glass doors – a recent addition – separated the entrance from a reception area. The doors were on a sensor and hissed open as I stepped forwards. A woman dressed in a pale blue tunic was bent over the desk and didn't even look up. Maybe she'd grown used to armed men coming in and out. The second that she saw my camouflage get-up could have been a crucial turning point, but she only glanced my way nonplussed. Funny how people can be desensitised to danger so quickly. I was in a different uniform but she must have taken me, as well as Rink coming in behind me, as FBI agents. No way I'd make her any the wiser.

The receptionist went back to whatever she was doing on her computer and I walked by her, allowing my gun to drop so I didn't represent a threat. I passed through the next set of doors without challenge and waited there for Rink to catch up. We were inside so easily it made my guts squirm because dressed in the anonymous garb of an HRT trooper Rickard would probably have free range throughout the hospital. He would head directly for Alisha's room.

A flight of stairs gave access to the upper floors and I went up them with Rink close behind. At the top was a narrow corridor. Checking out the signs hanging from the ceiling, I tried to figure out where Alisha's room would be. At times like this I wished that Rapid Intuitive Experience went beyond a warning of danger, but that was about as psychic as I got. The signs were for different wards, all named after nearby islands in the Florida Keys, and none of them was distinguished from the next. Going for us was the fact that there were only four of them, two on the left and two on the right. They'd take no checking at all if it weren't for the HRT commando striding along the hall towards us.

My first instinct was that this was Luke Rickard and I almost brought up my gun. I didn't, though. This man was shorter and stockier built than the man I'd fought in Jimena Grajales' sickroom.

I expected the feebie to challenge us, to try to disarm us, but all he did was speak into his throat mike. 'They're here, sir.'

I shared a glance with Rink. 'Sounds like Hubbard's expecting us.'

Rink scowled.

'Come with me,' the trooper said. Without waiting for us to comply, he turned and strode away down the hall.

'What the hell's going on?'

'Don't know, Rink, but we have to find out. We can refuse to follow this guy but you can bet his buddies will show up in a few seconds.'

'Don't want to make an enemy of the feds.'

We followed the trooper past the wards. Glancing inside, I saw only empty beds. Made sense; the patients having all been moved in anticipation of what was coming. I couldn't stop the smile that crept on to my lips.

'You realise what's going on here?'

Rink nodded. 'We're not the only ones setting Rickard up.'

The trooper took us to another flight of stairs, this

time leading down to a kitchen area full of stainless steel counters and ultra-modern ovens and ranges. It was empty of domestic staff. We headed directly through and into a short corridor. Two suited men stood guard at a door. Seeing us coming, one of them knocked on the door then opened it. He stood aside and allowed me and Rink to enter. The FBI trooper waited outside with the guards.

Part of me wasn't surprised to see Walter sitting in an office chair next to a bank of CCTV monitors, not when I recognised the two men outside as being the bodyguards who'd been at the hotel with us. Opposite Walter, SAC Hubbard leaned against a wall with his arms crossed. His beady eyes gave us the once-over before he turned his attention back to the screens.

'Relax, boys,' Walter said, 'you're amongst friends.'

'I take it that you're back in charge, Walt?'

He gave me a grin that caused Hubbard to shake his head. 'Orders from the White House supersede those coming from the Hoover building.'

Hubbard said, 'I'm not happy with this situation. Neither are my superiors. We'll make our feelings known after this, but for now we've handed over command and control to Mr Conrad. You have our full cooperation.' His last words were delivered with plenty of vinegar.

'How long have you been here, Walter?'

'Must have arrived before you set up out in the swamp.'

'Could have saved us the trouble if you'd thought to get in touch.'

'I was busy organising things.' He gave us a sickly smile. 'And anyway, I wanted someone out there who'd spot Rickard coming.'

'My men had that under control,' Hubbard said.

'They didn't see us,' Rink pointed out.

Hubbard shrugged, dug his hands into his trouser pockets. 'We weren't watching for you, Rington. We're here to catch a murderer. We can't do that if we're traipsing all over the Everglades playing hide and seek.'

'If you'd set up in the swamp you might have caught him coming in. Now you've lost a guy who didn't have to die.' Hubbard closed his eyes at my words. I'd already noticed that the nearest CCTV screen showed a view of the front lawn. It was zoomed in on a body partly concealed by shrubbery. 'You sacrificed that man to ensure that Rickard entered this building.'

'I sacrificed *no one*' Hubbard glared not at me but directly at Walter.

'It was necessary to contain the problem,' Walter said. 'It also allowed Rickard a way inside without raising suspicion.'

'This a killing house, Walt?'

'Soon as you were inside, I had it locked down. I'm having the FBI people moved out. Then it's down to you boys.'

'What about Alisha?'

Walter tapped a TV screen. On it a helmeted

black-clad figure crept along a corridor. Alert and armed, he looked like he had a firm destination in mind.

'Rickard should be with her in the next few seconds.' Walter sat back in his chair, almost as though relaxing in front of a TV to watch an afternoon matinee. 'There's no rush, Hunter. Wait and catch the show, you can always get him on his way back out.'

CHAPTER 44

'When attacking', you must be determined and forthright. Worry about the consequences and that worry will kill you. Be bold, Luc, cut down your enemies while fear for their lives gives them pause.'

Etienne Pagnon, the man who had murdered his mother, but had also taken him under his wing and made from him a warrior without equal, was more than just a burnt-out soldier living for his next gulp of strong liquor. He was also a man of books and study, with an enquiring mind and a will to pass on his knowledge to his worthy pupil. He was a master when it came to the methods of killing men and when he was sober – or only mildly inebriated – he sought to expand his knowledge further. Rickard had often found him with his nose in a book, normally ancient treatises on warfare; Sun Tzu's *The Art of War*; Chanakya's *Arthashastra* or Miyamoto Musashi's *Go Rin No Sho*. If he hadn't succumbed to his base weaknesses, he'd quite probably have become a great military strategist.

Of all the books that he studied, Etienne

advocated Musashi's *Book of Five Rings,* a seventeenth-century manual on sword-fighting that was as applicable in modern warfare as it had been back in the days of the samurai warrior. Musashi said that technical flourishes were excessive and what was most important was simply the cutting down of one's opponent without fearing for one's own life. Etienne liked Musashi's no-nonsense approach to killing and impressed this ethos on his young pupil. The great sword master also advocated practice in combat: you must experience much killing to achieve mastery over it. Etienne's enthusiasm – put across in his accented psychobabble – had resonated within Rickard and he'd learned his trade well, following Musashi's wisdom, basically learning to kill by killing.

He remembered his lessons clearly and would follow them to the letter. Etienne advocated crashing through the enemy's defences and cutting them down. So that, Rickard decided, was how he would approach his attack on the hospital. First, though, he had to get inside.

He travelled to within a mile of the Anhinga Key hospital in Wetherby's Land Rover, leaving his betrayer and his two henchmen where they lay alongside the discarded Fireblade. There, after concealing the 4x4 from view, he dressed in the clothing supplied to him by Wetherby's SWAT contact, the full tactical kit including body armour, gauntlets and helmet. There he also loaded the M-40A3 bolt-action rifle, and shoved more rounds in a pouch on his utility belt. Lastly he screwed on the suppressor that was lodged in the Styrofoam interior of the black case.

Musashi favoured the two-sword style, but he'd always taught that weapons should be interchangeable to suit the battlefield. Instead of the *katana* and *wakazashi* that the legendary sword master wielded in battle, Rickard had his gun and his ceramic knife. He felt ready for anything.

He jogged through the swampy terrain, eager to get started. The coldness in his gut demanded immediate release. Crash through their defences, cut them down, he repeated the mantra in his mind.

Coming to the entrance to the hospital, he saw a group of buildings. These he could tell were the administration offices. They looked like they had been closed down and there was no sign of life except for two men sitting in a black SUV. The men were obviously FBI agents. The shades and conservative suits were a cliché but evident nonetheless. He wasn't surprised to find the feebies on site: it was for that reason he'd arranged his disguise, expecting that Alisha would be placed in protective custody until he was caught.

Rickard slipped by the FBI guards like he was invisible and continued in towards the hospital. It was a fair jog through the forest, but he didn't see it as a task. It only warmed him up and prepped him for action.

A windbreak encircled the hospital grounds. It

gave great cover for him while he surveyed the layout and position of anyone standing guard. He merely pulled free a handful of the interwoven branches, and was able to get a good view through the fence without exposing himself.

In the distance armoured FBI troopers patrolled the grounds, but they were more concerned with watching the points leading in from the swamp than they were the front approach. They probably didn't believe he'd have the nerve for a full-frontal assault. That had been Cesar Calle's mistake and Rickard recalled where that lapse of judgement had got him.

Rickard brought the sniper rifle to his shoulder and extended the silenced barrel through the hole in the fence. Through the scopes the solitary trooper standing guard at the front of the property looked as close as could be without becoming intimate. Rickard studied him through the scope. The man was fully armoured, but his chin and a notch of skin at his throat were exposed when viewed through ten times the magnification. He was only fifty yards away. Shit, Rickard thought, I could drop him without the sights.

The shot was an easy one for him.

So why was he waiting?

Crash through their defences, cut them down.

He touched the trigger, but again he paused.

Thinking rationally, he knew that this was a fool's errand he'd set himself. What would he gain from murdering Alisha that he hadn't already achieved? This was an insane plan he'd embarked on, whatever way he looked at it. He was chancing death when he could simply walk away. He was wealthy; he could turn his back on his apartment in Miami, move anywhere in the world he chose and live a good life on the proceeds of his trade he'd tucked away in offshore accounts.

'You can't let a woman see any weakness in you, Luc. None at all. Do that and she'll despise you. You will become nothing in her eyes. You understand, *oui?*'

Nothing.

'You must make women fear you. It is the only way you will gain their respect.'

The serpent, the manifestation of his rage, pulled the trigger.

The trooper dropped in a boneless heap on the lawn.

Rickard waited for the alarm to be raised, but except for the distant call of a bird nothing else could be heard.

He propped the rifle against the fence, then scrambled over the top of it and into the hospital grounds.

He went directly to the dead man. He caught him under his armpits and dragged him into some nearby shrubs. There he peeled the Velcro patches from the man's uniform, discarded the redundant SWAT insignia from his own and replaced them with the FBI ones. The uniforms weren't exactly the same, but they were close enough. By the time anyone noticed the differences they'd only be a split second from death.

He took the guard's place, standing with his back to the hospital while surreptitiously searching for danger. Then slowly he ambled towards the front of the building like a man bored by routine and killing time by patrolling the grounds. No one watched him from any of the windows. He noted CCTV cameras, but doubted that he'd been observed due to the lack of troopers charging in his direction. He went up the steps and through the front door as if he had the right to do so.

Immediately inside was an automatic door. Beyond it an auxiliary nurse was busy at a desk. Rickard moved through the doors as they whisked open. The faint purr of the motor caused the woman to glance up at him.

'Toilet break,' Rickard told her.

'You know where they are.' The nurse gave him no more attention, turning back to her work. A spurt of anger went through him. Teaching her a lesson wasn't a good idea, not at this moment, but maybe on his way out he'd show her he wasn't to be ignored. He marched by her, looking like he knew exactly where he was going.

Signs pointed him upwards.

He went that way.

At the top he found a hallway bordered by wards. This being a private facility, he expected each ward to be separated into more individual rooms, but to his surprise found them to be open spaces lined

379

with beds. The fact that the beds contained no patients gave him a trickle of unease.

He recalled the administration buildings and how deserted they'd looked.

Something else: where were all the staff? A hospital like this should be bustling with doctors, nurses and support personnel. That solitary woman at the front desk? She was a plant. Probably FBI. Everyone else had been moved because they were expecting him.

He'd just walked into a trap.

Panic clutched fleetingly at him. In the next second he pushed it aside, feeling instead the rage roiling in his innards.

He turned back, ready to return to the reception area and show this latest bitch what became of those who schemed against him. He pulled out his ceramic blade and thumbed it open.

Another thought struck him.

Maybe it made sense that Alisha had been brought here.

Perhaps it was a logistical – and logical – decision to take Alisha out of the Cedars and bring her somewhere more remote. Less chance of collateral damage if Rickard did come calling. Perhaps this facility had only recently closed down, and had been commandeered as a temporary safe house for the critically ill woman. That would explain the lack of patients and medical staff.

Feasible?

Not very, but Rickard wasn't going to run away without first checking out his theory.

He gave the wards only a cursory inspection, then moved further along the hall. A door led into a descending stairwell. He could detect the faint residue of cooking smells left over from a once-bustling kitchen area. She wouldn't be down there. Instead he went a little further along the corridor and found another staircase, this one leading up to the third level. It would be unusual for a patient to be closeted away up there when there were so many rooms on the lower levels, which was exactly why he thought that was where Alisha was roomed. He went up the stairs, passing his knife to his left hand and drawing his gun in his right – the two-weapon style of Musashi.

The upper hall was dull under muted lighting. But at the far end he could see a door and around the jamb leaked brighter light. The obligatory armed guards were nowhere to be seen, which was peculiar. Perhaps they were inside.

He moved forwards stealthily, ears straining to hear voices from within the room. He could make out the electronic blip . . . blip . . . blip of monitors and something else like a distant chorus of voices. As he progressed he heard music and realised that a radio or TV was playing in the room, the volume low.

He was walking into a bottleneck. The hall behind him had only one exit and that was the way he'd come up. A couple of doors on each side led into cupboards or maintenance rooms with blind walls formed from the sloping roof. Should anyone come up the stairs, his only recourse would be to go directly into the room and damn the consequences.

But that was OK by him.

His mantra still played in his head.

Moving right up to the door, he placed an ear to the wood. He thought he heard the shifting of a body on a bed but couldn't be sure, as it could easily have been noise from the radio or TV programme. He glanced behind him, checking that the hall was still empty. It was.

Having no idea of the dimensions or layout of the room behind the door, he only had one plan of attack. Go in hard and fast, shoot anyone standing.

This was wrong.

Not his intention but the scenario.

His mind was screaming at him that he was walking into a trap.

He felt that the second he burst through that door he'd be confronted by a dozen armed troopers who would open up on him like a firing squad.

Let them try. He'd kill them all anyway.

He took in a deep breath, settling himself.

Used his left hand, the knife palmed in it, to twist the doorknob.

Then he threw the door open and followed it inside with a lunge. He was wearing Kevlar and could trust the armour to stop any return fire while he chose his targets.

Except there were none.

The room was empty of FBI commandos.

He checked a second time.

No one.

At the far end of the long, narrow room was a bed. Someone was swaddled in blankets, tucked up high under the armpits. Arms lay flat to each side, intravenous tubes hooked up to bags and electronic monitors. Bandages covered much of the head – funny, because he hadn't shot her in the head. Maybe Alisha had banged her skull on the floor as she'd fallen down and had required surgery. He could just see a couple of locks of corn-coloured hair peeking from under the bandages. An oxygen mask covered the mouth and chin. A table had been wheeled alongside the bed, and a tray with a water jug and an empty glass tumbler had been twisted so it extended across the person's middle. A small wall-mounted TV screen had been positioned so that the patient could watch without having to sit up.

He couldn't clearly see the figure in the bed, but the hair was the correct colour.

He slowly closed the door behind him.

Walked forwards.

With each step he took, that trickle of unease he'd experienced earlier intensified.

He looked at his gun. Redundant for the time being. He tucked it into the holster on his utility belt. Transferred the knife to his right hand.

He was twenty feet away from the patient and closing.

Her face was hidden by the mask and by the bandages but even so she looked different than he remembered. Maybe it was the lack of make-up that made her skin look so pale and waxy.

Ten feet from the bed he paused.

'Alisha . . . it's me, babe.'

The woman in the bed didn't stir.

Had her unconscious mind grown accustomed to the droning voices on the TV?

'Alisha.'

He moved the final few feet and stood at the foot of the bed.

'Honey, it's me.'

Then he ripped back the blankets.

The knife was forgotten as his mind tried to make sense of what he found.

'What the hell is *this*?'

The woman in the bed was already a corpse.

CHAPTER 45

'**W**ait here, Rink. Anyone but me walks out of that room, just kill them.'

'Rather be coming in with you, brother.'

'Don't know what we're walking into. I'd rather one of us gets a second chance at him.'

'What about Hubbard's men? They come up, you want me to stall them?'

I gave my friend a wink and he shook his head, laughing deeply in his throat. 'Second chance, my ass; you just want Rickard to yourself.'

'If he gets by me he's all yours.'

Rink shrugged. After all, it was me that Rickard had originally targeted, so there was personal investment in it for me.

'Just be careful, OK?'

'I will.'

I left Rink at the head of the stairs and moved along the hall. My carbine was with Rink, as I'd chosen to go with the SIG that was such an integral part of me. The gun was held alongside my ribs, my elbow bent, finger on the trigger, ready for anything.

The intense feeling of déjà vu struck me. The astringent smell of disinfectant was heavy in the air, just like when I approached Jimena Grajales' sickroom. Inside I would find Luke Rickard poised to strike. The only difference this time would be that Rink was watching my back so there'd be no one lobbing hand grenades at us.

Didn't mean that I'd walk away from this encounter alive, but I was more determined than ever that Rickard wouldn't either.

The irony wasn't lost on me that here again we were about to fight to the death alongside a woman's hospital bed, but at least the patient wouldn't attempt to shoot me this time. This poor soul, a Jane Doe with a passing resemblance to Alisha Rickard, had died from a drug overdose and had been brought here to pose as the killer's wife. Maybe the trap Walter laid was a little unethical but when it was weighed against the alternative I couldn't really argue. Alisha was out of danger, tucked up nice and safe at another medical facility to the north of the city.

The ruse would only last seconds after Rickard entered the room, which was why I now hurried along the hall. I expected the door to fly open, for Rickard to come out in a rage. The hall didn't offer much in the way of cover, just a couple of utility closets, and he'd cut me down in the enclosed space. I had to make it inside the room before he recovered from the shock of finding a corpse.

Running, I felt as if I did so through a nightmare. Each yard felt like a mile and the door seemed to recede away from me. But it was all a lie of my strung nerves, a result of adrenalin overdrive, and I almost careened through the door without stopping. At the final moment I did manage to slide to a halt and ducked low to the left of the door jamb. Briefly I glanced back, and I could just make out Rink's tawny features as he watched me from along the hall. I pumped my clenched fist in the air counting down from three, then grabbed for the doorknob and opened the door. At the same time, I went to my belly on the floor, training my SIG on the far end of the room, expecting a swarm of bullets to cut through the space above me.

The bullets didn't come.

Pushing with my feet I cleared the door frame and checked left and right.

No sign of Rickard.

With my worm's-eye view I could see under the bed. Rickard wasn't hiding there. The blankets had been pulled off the corpse and hung over one side of the bed, and I could tell that the only person on the mattress was the dead woman.

'Where are you, you bas . . . ?'

I saw the black rectangle in the ceiling and knew.

The tricky son of a bitch.

Coming quickly to my feet, I moved into the room, gun now aiming high as I approached the bed. Now that I was much closer, the rectangle didn't look so black, just an empty space in the hung ceiling. Dust filtered down from above and I heard the subtle movement of a shifting weight. Glancing once at the woman was enough to cause an involuntary cringe. A dusty boot print was centred on the white slip she'd been clothed in. Rickard had used her as a step up while he clambered into the roof space above.

Clever. I'd used a similar escape once when cornered by sheriff's deputies who'd been misled into thinking I was a dangerous fugitive. The difference here was that I'd used a credenza as a stepping stone to an attic; using the woman like this was sacrilegious.

Then again, just about everything that Rickard did went against what was good or holy, so I shouldn't have been surprised.

A low noise from behind alerted me to Rink's presence. The lack of gunfire had brought him to the room to see what was going on. We shared a glance and I nodded up at the ceiling. 'He's getting away.'

'You going after him?'

'There's nothing else for it.'

'Of course there is. We could go outside and pick the punk off with rifles when he shows.'

'Where's the satisfaction in that?'

I waved him back out into the hall. Rickard had to come out somewhere and I didn't want it to be behind us.

Sweeping a jug of water and a glass off a wheeled

388

table, I stepped up on to the bed, careful not to touch the woman, using the table to steady myself as I reached into the dark space. Hooking my left forearm over a roof beam, I hauled myself up with the power of that one arm. I needed the other free for my gun. It was like doing a one-handed chin-up at the gym, and I could feel the strain throughout my entire body, but I ignored it as I searched the crawl space for any sign of Rickard. It was too dark to see anything clearly, but I caught an impression of movement a good distance away. Animal, spook or contract killer, I shot at it.

My bullet didn't kill Rickard. That was instantly evident from the bullets that splattered against the beams next to me. The flash of his pistol marked his position more easily than did the dull cracks emitted from the suppressor. Vectoring in on the flashes, I held my nerve and took aim. I fired three rounds in quick succession. My reward was a throaty yell and the sound of something crashing down into the room below me. Quickly I lowered myself beneath the hung ceiling, but all that was scattered on the floor was more of the tiles and bits of aluminium framework. A boot was hanging from the new hole in the ceiling, but even as I looked Rickard tugged it back up inside the roof space. There then followed a dull rumble as he scrambled away.

I powered up into the attic, squirming so that I bent forwards over the joist beam, then swung my legs up and balanced there for a second. My night vision was beginning to kick in and the space didn't look as impenetrable now. I could make out arched beams above me and a sequence of horizontal joists that had formed the original support structure for an earlier ceiling. It was like being in the upturned hull of a ship.

Coming to my feet, I reached with a toe for the next horizontal. Couldn't quite reach it without jumping, but there was nothing else for it. Rickard was already a good way off and I couldn't see him, only hear the thuds as he hopped from beam to beam. I followed. Reaching the spot where he'd almost fallen through into the room below, I saw that a support wall actually extended into the attic here, making a tombstone-shaped bulwark between me and Rickard. He had to have gone up and over it and into the attic above the hallway where Rink was stationed. I went along a beam like a tightrope walker, found where the wall and the roof were conjoined. Large metal bolts strapped the roof beams to the brick structure but there was enough room between them to squirm through. First I listened to try to get an idea of how close Rickard was. I didn't want him to catch me halfway through the gap. Thuds resounded from a distance, then the unmistakable sound of someone kicking loose roof tiles.

Didn't matter how much sound I made now, I shouted at the top of my lungs. 'Rink, he's getting away. He's trying to smash his way on to the roof.'

I was rewarded by a couple of bullets fired at

me, but Rickard was more intent on making an escape route than he was on hitting me. The bullets struck the wall, spitting shards of brick-dust at my face. I screwed my eyes tightly to avoid being blinded, and when I looked again I could see a spill of light cutting an oblique slash through the darkness about twenty yards ahead of me. Judging by the lack of movement within the light-spill, Rickard had already forced his way outside.

Mindless of the grazes I picked up, I eased my way through the gap and clambered upright on another beam. Then I loped through the attic, jumping from one beam to the next as I tried to recall what the building looked like from outside. I'd watched it for long enough from my limestone perch in the swamp, but now when my mind was working on overtime I could only dredge up an impression of a large mainly wooden structure of three floors with a crenellated balustrade around a peaked roof. As I hurried after Rickard, more details came to me. Chimney stacks stretched into the sky in at least four different locations along the length of the rooftop. I also recalled that at the back of the building more recent extensions had been added, with two annexe wings erected at right angles to the main structure. These wings stood two storeys tall, with sloping roofs abutting the back wall. It was a feasible escape route for Rickard to drop on to one of those roofs, then from there to the ground below. Maybe there was even a fire escape, but I couldn't remember.

Arriving at the exit hole, I found that Rickard had smashed loose the tiles and wooden lats and had slashed a hole through an asphalt inner lining. The hole was barely large enough for my head and shoulders. I was risking things by looking outside. I couldn't hear where Rickard was; he could be standing a couple of feet away for all I knew, waiting for my head to pop out like a target in a shooting gallery.

I had to go after him, nothing else for it.

Positioning myself next to the hole, I quickly lunged out, looking one way then the other. He could be above me, up towards the peak of the roof, and I twisted to get a look. No sign of him. The fact that my head didn't explode was a good thing too, meaning he was more concerned with escaping than finishing things between us. I clattered through the hole, dislodging more tiles that slid to the edge of the balustrade. I followed them, sliding on my backside, using my boot heels as brakes to halt me from pitching over the low wall and to the ground. From up here it looked a lot more than three storeys high.

We had come out on the roof towards the back left corner of the hospital and there was a chimney stack thirty feet to my left, another twenty feet to my right. Rickard had to be hiding behind one of them; I just wasn't sure which one. I chose to go right because the one on the left was too near to the side of the building. From below Rickard would be exposed to fire from the FBI men in the grounds.

There was a narrow catwalk on the inner side of the balustrade, a thin strip of lead flashing that acted as a drainage channel for the infrequent but tumultuous rain showers that hit the area. I could fit one boot in at a time which made me keep moving to avoid losing my balance. I jogged along, left arm extended from my side, my right busy with my SIG. Occasionally I had to steady myself with the butt of my gun striking the roof tiles. The sound was a giveaway, but then again so was the hollow thud of my boots. As I approached the chimney stack I raised my gun, expecting Rickard to pop out and take a shot at me. Thankfully I made it to the brick stack without being shot, and I jammed my back to the wall. I waited, steadying my breathing, then swung round the stack.

The son of a bitch wasn't there.

I'd picked the wrong hiding place.

Looking back the way I'd come I couldn't see him either.

Further on – a good fifty feet at least – was the next chimney stack, but there was no way he could have got that far without me seeing him.

I even looked over the edge of the roof. The two annexes were below but too far away for him to have jumped to the rooftops unless he was as agile as a spider monkey. The fire escape I expected wasn't there; it must have been on the side of the building. Rickard wasn't flattened in the earth below me so he hadn't fallen. That left only one place he could have gone: up and over.

Studying the roof tiles, I saw that there were indeed a number of scuff marks, a smear where a boot had slipped and dislodged a growth of algae. The peaked roofline was about twelve feet above me, on an angle of about thirty-five degrees. He must have scaled it, using the bricks of the chimney as handholds.

I was just about to start up when I heard shouts from down on the ground. Three troopers were down there, guns raised. In silhouette against the sky my clothing would be indistinguishable from any other and Rickard had a similar body type to mine so I suppose their mistake could be forgiven. They began firing at me. I plastered myself flat to the roof as bullets cut chunks from the brickwork and balustrade.

Pinned down, I had nowhere to go.

I shouted something, but my words were lost amid the racket of bullets and challenges from below.

Next second I heard a bellow like an enraged bull and the FBI guns fell silent. Chancing a bullet in the face, I leaned forwards and saw Rink stalking among the men, yelling at them and generally threatening to tear their heads off if any of them had hurt me. He looked up and I waved. He nodded back at me, but then turned on the men, shouting again. HRT troopers are very tough guys, but Rink's tougher. They acquiesced to his command, moving back to offer covering fire for me instead.

I'd been distracted for the last few seconds.

Those seconds had almost proven fatal, but the next few weren't that much different.

As I turned I caught a blur of movement from above me.

Instinct caused me to dodge and to bring up my SIG in response.

I fired at the exact same moment that Rickard did. Déjá vu all over again.

This time there was no striking of my gun to put off my aim. My bullet hit Rickard in the chest and he slid back down beyond the peak of the roof. It was gratifying, but it didn't stop Rickard's bullet from striking me in my right thigh. My leg was knocked from under me and I crashed face first against the tiles, rebounded off and pitched backwards.

Three floors up, it looked a long way to the ground.

It looked a whole lot further when spilling head first over a crumbling balustrade.

CHAPTER 46

Being shot in the chest was just the latest in a series of shocks to his system that Rickard had to contend with. Surprisingly enough, it wasn't the worst.

Finding the corpse in lieu of his wife was the first. That had thrown him more than he liked to admit. It had made him realise how stupid he'd been. Walking directly into a trap that was simple to avoid had been an amateur's mistake. It slowed him momentarily as he considered his next move. He'd been led to the chamber with the intention of blocking him in. Any minute the FBI would come boiling into the room and he didn't expect to be taken alive. He decided that the hall was no way out; the room had no other exits, not even a window he could smash his way through, so that left him only one escape route. Decision made, he had no qualms about standing on the corpse while he dislodged a ceiling tile and swarmed up and on to a joist.

Discovering that Joe Hunter had survived the explosion and had tracked him back here was next. He had really believed that Guarapo's grenade had torn Hunter to pieces and he couldn't imagine how he'd got out of that room alive. He supposed that how wasn't an issue now, only that Hunter was there and firing at him in the attic space. Hunter had hit him, but the armour had kept him safe.

Breaking through on to the roof of the hospital maybe hadn't been his greatest plan, but it was all he had left to him. Hunter had shouted to someone down below, cutting off his escape that way. On the roof he was forced to run like a coward to avoid being pinned down by the HRT troopers at ground level. He'd gone up and over the peak, had only made it there before he heard machine gun fire. When he looked back over the roof, there was Hunter in all his glory, wide open for a killing shot. Hunter, unlike him, didn't have the comfort of a bullet-proof vest.

Hunter's return shot struck him in the chest, knocking him backwards, but not before he saw his nemesis hit in the leg and tumbling towards the roof's edge. Nowhere for Hunter to go but down.

Biggest shock of all was that Hunter had died after all this by falling off a roof.

Rickard touched the spot where Hunter's bullet had hit him in the chest. The vest was punctured, singed stuffing poking out the hole, but the flattened slug must have fallen out as he slid down the roof. If he hadn't been wearing the vest he'd be a corpse, no doubt about it. Hunter's bullet had struck him dead centre. That was some shooting. Admirable in a way.

He wasn't going to dwell on it.

Hunter was dead but there were others out there who were equally dangerous. Jared Rington, for example; and who knew who else had been drafted in to bring him down?

He was at the front of the building now. Here the balustrade was taller and more ornamental, providing better cover from the troopers running round the front and taking up positions. If he'd had the sniper rifle with him he was confident that he could take them all out one by one. But the reality was it was now him who'd have to be careful not to fall into the sights of a sharpshooter.

He checked his weapons. He unscrewed the suppressor from his gun, then fed a fresh magazine into it. He touched his knife in its pouch.

Staying under cover of the balustrade, he began crawling towards the left front corner of the hospital. He couldn't stay up here forever because it was only a matter of time before gunmen made their way on to the roof, or the FBI called in air support. His best chance at getting away and re-establishing his plan for killing Alisha was making his way to the ground. If he made it into the swamp he was confident that no one would find him there.

Coming to the corner of the hospital, he found that a fancy embellishment of the balustrade allowed him to come to his feet, while still being blocked from two angles from those searching for him from below. He looked for a fire escape on the side of the building and found it, the problem being it was a floor lower than his current position and could only be accessed via doors from the building. An awning with latticed sides had been erected above the stairs to stop birds from nesting on the steps, but it looked a little flimsy and he doubted it would bear his weight as he climbed down. He could possibly grip the awning and use it to swing on to the stairs but as he did so he'd be open to a sniper on the ground. He didn't fancy his chances.

At the back of the building there were a couple of structures jutting out from the main building. If he could get down to the roof of either of those he could smash his way back inside the building and reach the fire escape. Or he could take his chances by going back down through the building, finding himself a hostage to use as a shield while he made his escape. Preferably that bogus nurse at the front counter: he'd come here to kill a woman and she would do.

Decision made, he went to his hands and knees and set off for the next corner. He heard the pounding of feet below him. He glanced between the crenellations and saw two troopers running to add extra firepower to those at the front of the building. Good, less for him to worry about at the back.

A chimney stack loomed on his right, but he

went past it, determined now that he knew his way down.

He was on all fours, gun pressed against the duct work, a compromising position in the purest sense. Not the best of places to find yourself when a man with a huge knife attacks you from above.

CHAPTER 47

Having four hands would have been useful. One to hold my gun, one to slap on the wound in my thigh to stop the bleeding, another two to hold on to the edge of the roof to stop me from plunging three floors to a nasty landing.

As it was I only had one free hand, which didn't say much for my chances of survival.

Rickard's bullet had struck me in the meat of my thigh. It felt like Thor had smacked me with his hammer, the pain a white hot flame followed by the numb sensation of traumatised nerve-endings. My leg had lost its ability to support me and I'd nowhere to go but down. The balustrade would have halted my fall, if not for the fact the bullets fired by the HRT troopers had cut it to pieces. It crumbled and I fell.

Experiencing slow motion is an aspect of endor-phine overload. My mind was working faster than the ability of the real world to keep up. My eyes saw and pigeon-holed the various images that flashed before me.

Bits of the railing drifting towards the ground

401

like feathers caught on a breeze, intermingling with droplets of my blood.

The sky pitching slowly, becoming the green of the lawns and then the grey of the gravel path at the base of the wall.

Rink running, arms outstretched, intending snatching me out of the air like he was Superman coming to the rescue.

My left hand shooting out and grabbing at the edge of the roofline. Fingertips digging in, thumb curling under the stone ridge.

The wall coming at me.

Then things returned to normal as I slammed against the wall, my nose and left eyebrow taking the brunt of the force. It was almost sickening enough to make me loosen my grip and give in to the inevitable.

But I didn't.

I clung on for dear life.

I'm a fatalist. I know I'm not going to live forever, but I wasn't ready to cash in my chips just yet. When it's my time to go then so be it, but I wanted it to be after Luke Rickard wasn't a threat to anyone else.

I kicked and scrabbled at the wall with the toes of my boots. My right leg was numb, couldn't rely on it to support my weight, so I concentrated on finding a foothold with my left. My arm felt stretched beyond belief, like it was coming undone at all the joints. I had seconds before it gave out. Glancing down, I knew that Rink wouldn't make it to stop my fall, and even if he did I'd probably kill the two of us.

I needed my right hand.

It was holding my SIG and I loathed giving it up.

With not even enough time to slip it into my waistband, I had no option.

I let it drop, arching it out towards Rink.

Let him save my gun instead. I'd collect it from him later if I managed to stay alive.

Unencumbered by my gun, I now had two hands free. My right was still weakened from the injury I'd taken in Colombia, but it was better than nothing. I got a hold on the roofline, then grabbed up at the balustrade with my other. Kicking and digging with my toes, I finally found a seam in the wall and I pushed and pulled myself up and got my forearm over the edge of the catwalk. It was an effort to drag myself up on to the roof, and when I finally looked there was a broad smear of blood advertising my exertions. I lay there a moment, my view full of blue sky as I sucked in air.

Finally, I craned my head over the edge and peered down at Rink.

He grinned back at me, teeth just a shade whiter than his drained features. Rink worries about me, even though I tell him not to.

He was holding my SIG.

For a second I expected that he'd try to throw it back up to me. I pulled out my Ka-Bar and

403

showed him I was armed, so he jammed the SIG into his belt.

'Where is he?'

It was strange hearing my own voice. It came to me like an echo in a tunnel, another effect of adrenalin.

'Must have gone to the front. Forget him, Hunter. Come down, we can take him when he tries to make a break for it.'

I held up the knife. 'Got to finish this, Rink. You know me, right?'

'Right. Except you're bleeding like a stuck pig and he's still got a gun.'

'What's new?'

He shrugged, seeing the point. I'd been injured and outgunned before and when had that deterred me? Sometimes when the thrill of battle takes me I'm just too pig-headed for my own good, and it takes Rink to remind me. This time, he just held his peace. He knew this was our best chance of stopping the murderer.

Two troopers ran past, heading for the front of the hospital.

Taking it that they'd been summoned by their colleagues, I had a good idea where Rickard had got to. Didn't fancy my chances of making it up and over the roof with my lame leg, so I set off along the catwalk, heading for the corner. Blood pulsed from my wound with every step.

Ideally I needed to staunch the blood loss and lower my racing heartbeat or I'd bleed out in minutes, but I guessed that reacquainting myself with Rickard was more imminent than that. I could hear the thuds of someone making their way along the roofline just round the corner.

My first thought was: *Maybe I shouldn't have given up the gun after all.*

Rickard had one and I didn't.

That put me at a distinct disadvantage.

But then again, I had the fact that he wasn't expecting me working in my favour. I had a knife too, and it would prove more effective against his anti-ballistics armour than a nine mm Parabellum would.

The chimney stack I'd earlier discounted as his hiding place was now only feet away from me. I grabbed at it and pulled myself up, pressing myself against the brickwork. From this vantage I could see over the slope of the roof going down to the side of the building. Rickard was on his hands and knees.

Perfect.

Without fear of the consequences I pushed out from the chimney, as if I was taking that HALO jump from the airplane over Colombia all over again.

CHAPTER 48

Joe Hunter?

How many lives does this son of a bitch have?

That was all the thinking that Rickard managed.

Then Hunter was on top of him and he had to forget about thinking and go on instinct.

He spun on his side, lifting and discharging his gun in the same instant. Would have got him in the guts, but Hunter's knee came down on his wrist and plastered it to the roof tiles. The bullets careened off the slick surface, ricocheting off into the heavens. Hunter's hand plunged and only a twist of Rickard's body saved his life. The military knife jammed through the material of his bulletproof vest but was halted before it found flesh by Rickard's catlike movement that twisted the blade off-line. Undeterred Hunter ripped out the knife and stabbed again.

Rickard pulled loose from under Hunter's knee, swinging his elbow up and back and catching the crook of Hunter's arm. The blade missed his throat by less than a thumb's width. Rickard twisted again, getting himself under Hunter's chest, and thrust with all his power, throwing them both back against the roof. He tried to turn, to bring round the gun, but Hunter wasn't having any of it. He grabbed a fistful of collar and dragged Rickard backwards, driving into his ribs with the knife. Kevlar vests often had exposed areas under the arms where the straps were fixed round the body, but this was full tactical armour and the opening wasn't there. It didn't deter Hunter, he just kept on digging with the razor tip, drilling his way through the material. The armour was designed to stop the blunt trauma of a bullet, not sharp pointy things. It was only a matter of time before the knife would penetrate and start to saw its way through his ribs.

Rickard reared back again, using the edge of his helmet as a weapon against Hunter's jaw. He struck twice, felt the pressure go from his ribs. Then he dropped his gun and snatched at the ceramic knife on his belt. Thumbed it open.

He jabbed down, slashing open another wound in Hunter's injured leg. Then he swung from the hips, using his elbow to drive Hunter away from him. He reversed, swinging now with the knife at Hunter's throat.

Hunter got his own arm in the way and their forearms clashed.

Hunter kicked at his groin, but there was no power in his leg. Rickard took the kick, allowing the steel cup in his jockstrap to take the brunt, and cut again at Hunter's throat.

Hunter ducked, but Rickard felt the knife graze the top of his skull and saw a lock of hair spinning in the breeze of their making.

Hunter came back at him with the big knife and Rickard twisted so that it missed. The only problem was it left him teetering over the balustrade and he had to make a quick adjustment to avoid crashing through it. He threw a back kick into Hunter's legs. But now it was his kick that held little power.

Hunter slammed him from behind, an elbow across the nape of his neck. The armour didn't help cushion this blow, and Rickard staggered away, almost going over the balustrade again. Below him he saw the Japanese dude – Jared Rington, Wetherby had called him – lift up an assault rifle. He saw the flash before he heard the rattle, and he felt the impact of bullets hit his body before he felt the pain. He stumbled away, feeling like he was being pummelled by a crowd of determined pugilists.

Then he was out of the line of fire.

The cessation of bullets left him as dazed as the incoming fire had. He wondered for the briefest fraction of a second if he was still alive.

Of course he was.

Testament to that was the intensity with which Joe Hunter lurched after him to finish the job.

How none of Rington's bullets had found flesh he had no idea, but he didn't want to chance them again. He was at the corner of the building now and he dodged round it, causing Hunter to follow.

'Come on.'

He beckoned Hunter after him. He was confident that the armour would halt Hunter's knife whereas there was nothing to stop him from slicing the man to ribbons.

'Come on, Hunter.'

'Don't worry, I'm coming.'

Hunter was pale, weakened by blood loss and favouring his right leg. The material of his trousers was slick with blood and he was limping on the ball of his foot. His balance was off. No way could he avoid Rickard's lunge.

Rickard leaped at him, slashing upwards at Hunter's belly.

Hunter didn't dodge back.

He came forwards, swerving his hips to one side even as he leaned down and slammed the butt of his knife against Rickard's extended arm. The armour did nothing to protect his forearm from the power of the blow. His knife jumped from his fingers as they opened in reflex. It was a move worthy of Musashi himself.

Crash through their defences, cut them down.

Hunter palmed him under the chin. The hand felt like a wedge of wood as it drove his jaw up and back. Rickard felt the bone snap up near his left ear. The pain was excruciating. Rickard almost blacked out.

He wove on his feet.

Hunter actually stopped him from slipping off the roof. He clamped a hand on the neckline of his vest, while he readied the knife in the other. Then Hunter tugged down and Rickard realised what he was doing. The vest was fastened down the front by a flap of Kevlar that concealed a zip. The zip itself was the weak point of his armour. Hunter jabbed through the plastic zipper like it wasn't even there. There was more Kevlar behind it, but only a narrow strip. Hunter merely angled the point of the blade so that it slid round the armour and into his chest.

Rickard could feel the steel pushing into his body.

How was this even possible?

He was better than this . . . better than Hunter.

He grabbed Hunter's wrists. Tried to stop the pressure. Hunter was weakened by the loss of pints of blood – how did he still have the strength? Hunter's face contorted with effort, beads of sweat breaking along his hairline, and Rickard felt the knife slide in another half-inch.

He thought that having his jaw broken was bad.

That was nothing.

'Noooo . . .'

'Yes,' Hunter told him.

Rickard reached for Hunter's face, trying to gouge his eyes with his thumbs. Hunter twisted out of his grip, pushing even harder on the knife.

'You won't hurt Alisha now, you bastard.' Hunter pushed again and Rickard felt something pop

410

inside him. 'You won't hurt Imogen Ballard. You won't hurt *any woman* ever again.'

'No . . . I won't.'

His answer wasn't agreement, just resignation. Hunter it seemed didn't like the tone of voice he delivered it in. He pushed on the knife again. Blood frothed between Rickard's lips. Sign of a punctured lung, maybe something even worse. Whatever, he knew that he wasn't getting out of this alive. He spat the mouthful of oxygen-rich blood in Hunter's face.

He could feel the serpent inside him.

But it was shuddering now.

Not with rage but fear.

And ignominy.

The serpent was dying.

'At least I'm not going to die alone.'

With his failing breath he grabbed tightly at Hunter, clutching the hand holding the knife around the wrist so that Hunter could not release him. Then he kicked at Hunter's good leg, even as he swung out and over the edge of the roof.

'Shit!'

He heard Hunter's expletive and it made him smile. He kept that expression with him all the way down until the crushing impact on the ground knocked it loose.

CHAPTER 49

My leg was threatening to collapse under me, my head full of fog from the pain and the loss of blood, and Luke Rickard was fully armoured. It was a fight I should never have won. But I was driven by a rage that was almost overwhelming. No way was I going to let Rickard walk away from this alive.

Even though he was wearing a helmet, it was the first good look at his face I'd had since our fight in Colombia. He'd changed, but there were still enough of my features in his to give me the uncanny feeling that I was fighting my own personal demon. It sent me a little insane, I guess.

I went at him like something demented, and though our fight was short and brutal it was one of the most desperate I'd ever been involved in.

In my early days as a soldier in the British Army I was shot by a player in the Provisional IRA. I still bear the scar where his bullet cut through my chest and exited from my back. It's the closest I've ever come to dying, but this was a close second.

Tubal Cain, the Harvestman, tried to cut out

my heart, and a monstrous killer called Larry Bolan tried to carry me into an inferno, but I'd stopped both of them. Despite how good they were, it was Luke Rickard who almost ended my life. In his last moment on earth he tried to take me with him by pulling me off the roof.

Weak with the loss of blood, faint from my exertions, I couldn't stop the tug of his weight pulling me over the balustrade. And the only epitaph I could come up with to sum up my eventful life was *shit*.

It was how I felt, I suppose.

I fell with Rickard beneath me, then we somehow turned in mid-air and I was under him. Lucky in a way. It meant that I crashed down on the roof of the annexe wing, while he bounced off, somersaulted away and struck the ground headfirst another thirty or so feet below. His helmet didn't help save him. Where I hit, the roof collapsed under me and I ended up lying on the floor of a ward that had fortunately been stripped of furniture.

Surprisingly – to me – I retained consciousness. I stared up through the shattered remains of the roof at the blue sky, thinking how beautiful a day it was. But that could only go on for so long.

Shadows began forming at the edges of my vision, and these twisted into faces that began swarming around me: they were the faces of all those who had died because I'd failed to shoot Jesus Abadia when I'd had the chance. It was a large crowd. They were all screaming wordlessly at me like all the other echoes of my past did. I closed my eyes to block them out of my mind, but they stayed with me as I drifted away into blackness.

My next conscious memory was of Rink leaning over me and shaking my shoulder.

'You alive, Hunter?'

'Wish I wasn't.'

'You hurting?'

'Nah!'

Rink laughed at my bravado, but I meant it. I was so seriously injured I was beyond pain. Rink immediately jammed his fist against the pulsing wound in my upper thigh and started to shout for a medic, but then I was gone again, surrounded by those angry victims of Luke Rickard. At least he wasn't there, or maybe we'd have taken up where we'd left off and fought our way through all the sub-levels of hell. Thinking of Rickard finally stilled the voices of the dead: when next their faces swam in my vision they were nodding in gratitude. They'd died horribly, but at least I'd avenged them.

The peace that came with that realisation allowed me to sink into oblivion. But that only lasted until Jimena and her boy decided to scream at me instead. I knew their deaths would never be resolved in my heart.

My next bout of wakefulness was when I was loaded into a chopper and strangers began fussing over me. Rink was still with me, hovering over my shoulder like my personal guardian angel. Walter was there too, and he was frowning at me.

'I'll try not to bleed all over the place.' There wasn't that much blood left in me, so I was confident I could keep my promise. Walter leaned in and squeezed my shoulder. For a second there he looked remorseful. I winked up at him. 'Don't worry, I'll pull through.'

'You do that, son.'

'Can't let you take all the shit for this, can I?'

An oxygen mask was placed on me. There was a sting of catheters administered to my arms. Medics crowded me. I blinked and the blackness came back. Then Walter was gone and I was up in the air. Scraping the underbelly of heaven: quite literally. I was later told by Rink that the medics almost lost me. My blood pressure was so low that it was off the charts. They had to do an immediate transfusion while we were still up in the air, and Rink had donated a few pints of his own to keep me going. Afterwards he joked about it, of course, telling me I was now part Japanese. Then he got more maudlin, hugged me and said that now we really were brothers. Blood brothers. I liked that.

I was transported to the trauma centre at the University of Miami Hospital, but have no recollection whatsoever of my time there. When next I drifted up out of delirium I was at the same hospital where Walter had secreted Alisha Rickard.

She was my first visitor. She hobbled in, one leg in plaster and her body swathed in dressings under her shift, toting an intravenous drip on wheels along with her.

I didn't know what to say.

I was responsible for murdering her husband and even though he'd abused her, tried to kill her, that might still mean something.

Maybe like Jimena Grajales she'd pull out a gun and start shooting at me.

But that didn't happen.

Instead Alisha just came up and kissed me on the forehead. We didn't need words. We understood each other. Alisha walked out again and that's the last I saw of her.

Rink arrived next.

'When are you gonna get your ass outa bed? We've got work piling up.'

He was back to his old self now that my imminent death was out of the picture.

'It could be a while before I'm back to my best, Rink.'

'I know. Maybe it would be a good idea if you took some time off,' he offered. 'You've some vacation time coming, I guess.'

Not a bad idea. 'I'm thinking of heading back home for a while. It's been a while and I want to check my dogs are OK.'

I'd no doubt that my German shepherds, Hector and Paris, were fine. It was Diane I wanted to see most. For a start, she deserved an explanation for why a friend of mine had been stationed outside her house for the best part of a week. And then there was the other fact . . . I just wanted to see her.

'That'd be great,' Rink said, but there wasn't as much enthusiasm as I expected. 'Just don't forget you've people here who love you, OK?'

He glanced away. He needn't have: a big tough guy admitting their feelings was OK by me. But maybe embarrassment wasn't his reason.

'Just hurry up an' get better, huh?' he said.

'I will.' Now I was the one who didn't sound so enthusiastic.

The bullet wound was bad enough, but it was all tissue damage. That would heal soon enough, leaving nothing behind but another scar to match all the others. What had almost finished me was the jab of Rickard's knife. He had nicked the femoral artery. Fortunately for me, the trauma caused by the bullet wound had already caused many of the blood vessels to contract so I hadn't bled as profusely as I should have. Any other time I'd have died within minutes. Who'd ever guess I was happy to have been shot? My fall on to the roof had broken ribs, and also finished the job started in Colombia on my right hand. The ribs would heal by themselves, but my hand, broken in three places, might require some physiotherapy.

Harvey had gone home to Arkansas. I was sorry to have missed him, but he promised to come and visit soon.

'He'd better,' Rink said. 'I think we owe him a drink after all this.'

'Maybe more than one.'

Rink brought me up to date on the entire Luke Rickard thing.

'Wetherby was behind it.'

'Should have known,' I said. 'I never trusted that bastard.'

'Neither did Rickard. He killed him and two of his guys before going to the hospital.'

I frowned. 'Saves us the trouble, I suppose.'

Rink was silent for a short time as though weighing my words. Finally he just nodded. 'Wetherby hated you. When he heard that someone down in Colombia was trying to locate the members of a CIA hit team he jumped at the chance to set you up. Apparently after your original falling out he'd dug into your background and discovered that you worked on the team with Bryce Lang. Guess he thought all his Christmases had come at once. He contacted this Gutierrez and promised him the best man for the job. Enter Luke Rickard. Pity Rickard was a woman-hating asshole, or maybe he'd have won. He let his personal agenda direct him.'

'We both made a mistake in not taking the shot when we had the chance. Me when I failed to shoot Jesus Abadia, Rickard when he killed the two cops and let me live.'

Rink sighed. 'You know, Rickard thought that Alisha was working with Jimena and Wetherby. He thought she set him up to die. How fucked up is that?'

I remembered Alisha's kiss on my forehead. Maybe she did want him dead, but she'd had nothing to do with any of that. 'She's safe from him now.'

'Good job, Hunter.'

'Yeah. Good job.'

We just sat there in companionable silence for a minute or two. Finally Rink stood up, stretching his tall frame. 'Anyway, gotta be going. I'm keeping your next visitor back.'

'Before you go,' I said. 'What's the fallout?'

'None whatsoever. Walter works wonders. You know that. As far as anyone's concerned the FBI took out a very dangerous felon. End of.'

'The cops?'

'Going along with it. Our names have been struck from their files all the way back to before Castle and Soames.'

'What about Linden Case and his daughter?'

'Like I said: way back before the cops. They know now that Rickard disguised himself. They even caught the doctor who carried out the surgery on him: some asshole called Rothman. The doc squealed like a stuck pig, told them that Rickard brought photos of you and asked to be made to look like you. The doc swears he'd no idea why that was so, but the cops know he's lying. It'll be a long time before he does any kind of surgery again. You're in the clear, Hunter.'

'Good enough.' My tone didn't match the sentiment.

Rink knew what I meant. Jessica Case was a total innocent in all of this and it hurt to think my name had been tied to her senseless murder. It was good that that was cleared up, just sad that she'd died in the first place.

Rink patted me on the shoulder. 'You can put the details straight but you can't change the past, brother. Don't dwell on the bad things. Give the good a chance.' He winked at me and went outside.

I wondered what the hell that meant. Then the door opened and in walked Imogen Ballard.

She looked so much like her sister Kate that it hurt to look at her.

I think she knew that. She had the same look in her eyes as when I'd last seen her. And now I better understood Rink's words about there being people here who loved me too.

Like Alisha before her, she just came and planted a kiss on me. Except hers was on my mouth and it lingered a lot longer.

Not all the echoes from my past were a bad thing.

CURRICULUM VITAE –
JOE HUNTER

NAME: Joe Hunter.

DATE OF BIRTH: 8th August 1969.

PLACE OF BIRTH: Manchester, England.

HOME: Manchester, England but in process of relocating to Florida, USA.

MARITAL STATUS: Divorced from Diane, who has now remarried.

CHILDREN: None.

OTHER DEPENDENTS: Two German shepherd dogs, Hector and Paris (currently residing with Diane).

PARENTS: Joe's father died when he was a child and his mother remarried. Both his mother and stepfather reside in Manchester.

SIBLINGS: Half-brother, John Telfer.

KNOWN ASSOCIATES: Jared 'Rink' Rington, Walter Hayes Conrad, Harvey Lucas.

EDUCATION: Secondary school education to 'O' level standard. Joe received further education and underwent self-teaching while in the British Army and Special Forces.

EMPLOYMENT HISTORY: Joined British Army at age 16. Transferred to the Parachute Regiment at age 19 and was drafted into an experimental coalition counterterrorism team code named 'ARROWSAKE' at age 20. As a sergeant, Joe headed his own unit comprising members from various Special Forces teams. Joe retired from 'ARROWSAKE' in 2004 when the unit was disbanded and has since then supported himself by working as a freelance security consultant.

HEIGHT: 5′ 11″.

WEIGHT: 13 stone.

BUILD: Athletic.

HAIR COLOUR/STYLE: Short brown hair with slight greying.

EYE COLOUR: Blue/brown.

APPEARANCE: Muscular but more lean than bulky, he has the appearance of a competitive athlete. His demeanour is generally calm and unhurried. Due to his background, Joe has the ability to blend with the general public when necessary, but when relaxed he tends to dress casually. He doesn't consider himself handsome, but women find him attractive.

His eyes are his most striking feature and the colour appears to change dependent on his mood.

BLOOD TYPE: AB

MEDICAL HISTORY: Childhood complaints include measles and chicken pox. As an adult Joe has had no major medical conditions, but has been wounded on several occasions. Joe carries numerous scars including a bullet wound in his chest and various scars from knife and shrapnel wounds on his arms and legs. He has had various bone breakages, but none that have proven a continued disability.

RELIGION: Joe was raised in a Church of England environment, but is currently non-practising.

POLITICS: Joe has no political preferences and prefers morals and ethics.

CHARACTER: Joe can come over as a little aloof at times. He is a deep thinker who prefers only to speak when he has something important to say. He is very loyal to his family and friends. He dislikes injustice, hates bullies and will stand up to defend others in need of help.

MUSIC: Wide choice of music, but particularly enjoys vintage rhythm and blues.

MOVIES: Joe's favourite movie is 'It's a Wonderful Life'. It is a morality tale that resonates with his belief that a person's actions – good or bad – continually affect those around them.

BOOKS: When he was younger he enjoyed classic fiction by HP Lovecraft, RE Howard and Edgar Allan Poe, but currently reads a wide range of crime and suspense novels.

CIGARETTES: Smoked various brands but gave up.

ALCOHOL: Drinks only moderately and infrequently. Prefers beer to liquor.

DRUGS: Has been subjected to drugs during his military career, but has never personally taken any illegal drugs. Joe hates the influence that drugs have on the world and stands against those producing and supplying them.

HOBBIES: Fitness. Joe works out whenever he can with a combination of running, circuit training and martial arts.

SPECIAL SKILLS: As a soldier Joe gained many skills pertinent to his job, but also specialised in CQB (Close Quarter Battle), Point Shooting, Defensive Driving and in Urban Warfare Tactics. He is particularly adept with the handgun (usually a SIG Sauer P226) and with the knife (usually a military issue Ka-Bar).

CURRENT OCCUPATION: Joe describes himself as a security consultant and sometimes PI, but some people call him a vigilante.

CURRENT WHEREABOUTS: USA.